The Hourim of innocence

MUSTAPHA BOUKTAB

THE HOURIM OF INNOCENCE

NOVEMBER 2024
BOOK-KITAB

The Hourim of innocence

The Hourim of innocence

Warning

This novel is a work of fiction, a blend of the imaginary and the real, where the boundaries are deliberately blurred. Although certain events or figures may evoke familiar situations, all the characters, groups and entities described are entirely fictitious and the fruit of my imagination. Any resemblance to real people or organisations is purely coincidental.

The thoughts, emotions and actions expressed in these pages are those of the characters, shaped by their own fictional experiences. They in no way reflect personal, institutional or real positions.

Through Abigael and Moussa, young heroes caught up in the turmoil of a fractured world, this novel explores hope, revolt and the price of innocence in the face of the forces of evil. Their poignant and sometimes harrowing story reminds us that even in the face of horror, humanity can still find the strength to fight for peace and truth.

* Warning : This book deals with powerful and sometimes disturbing themes. It is for those prepared to delve into the psychological depths of the characters and confront disturbing realities. Some passages may arouse strong emotions. Readers are advised to approach this book with discernment.

Mustapha Bouktab

The Hourim of innocence

The Two Prunes of My Soul

"I am an author whose gaze embraces two horizons, Algeria and France, my two homelands, my two eyes. Each illuminates an eye, each carries a part of my soul. I love these lands with equal fervour, as I cherish the very breath of life. Yet the absurd idea that one day I might be asked to sacrifice one for the other, to close one eye and keep only one, would be unbearable. How can I choose between two lights, two heartbeats ? To become one-eyed would be to mutilate love, to give up seeing the world in all its richness. I refuse this fate, because my two eyes, carried by this inseparable love, will continue to contemplate these two countries that make me a whole being."

Mustapha Bouktab

The Hourim of innocence

Dedication

To you, children of ashes, children of silence, stars extinguished before dawn. You, whom war has targeted without ever giving you time to dream. Your laughter, barely hatched, was extinguished by the crash of bombs, and your hopes dissipated in the tumult of weapons. You have known neither the gentle rocking of carefree days, nor the warmth of peaceful days. You were torn from life too soon, victims of a world blinded by hatred and senseless ambition.

Your brief lives, shattered like trampled flowers, held the promise of a radiant tomorrow. This book is an offering to your memory, a tribute to that shattered innocence. You are not mere collateral damage, but the real targets of an evil that is attacking the very roots of the future. For the destruction of a people begins with the enslavement of its children, with the smothering of their light.

You, who were thought to be silent, carried a strength that even weapons could not extinguish: that of innocence. Your laughter, bursts of life defying chaos, still resonate in eternity. Every bullet fired, every bomb dropped, takes away a fragment of your light, but never manages to erase the truth of your existence.

Your stolen lives, your dreams snatched from you before they've even taken flight, will not be forgotten. This book is your refuge, a casket for your faded smiles, a flame to illuminate the collective memory. Let the world no longer look away. May it remember that behind every figure, every balance sheet, there was a name, a face, a child's soul.

The Hourim of innocence

To you, who in your final moments knew only fiery skies and heart-rending cries, this book is a promise : that your fleeting passage will never be erased from our hearts. Your eyes, filled with silent pain, deserved tenderness, not indifference; peace, not horror.

You are the heirs to a future that the world has betrayed, the flickering flames of a humanity that violence seeks to extinguish. But even in the dust and rubble, your voices rise up, piercing the silence and demanding that you not be forgotten.

To you, children of ruins, starless nights and tormented horizons, this book is your voice. May they resonate, may they shatter sleeping consciences. May this novel be a star, an eternal flame to remind the world that you were there, that your lives, short as they were, illuminated our hearts far more than all the empty promises of the powerful.

You are the forgotten heroes, the promises of a future that hatred has tried to erase. But as long as there are words, memories and beating hearts, you will never be lost. This book is your silent song, a fervent prayer, a cry that the world will never, ever forget you.

Mustapha Bouktab

The Hourim of innocence

Introduction

"When the hands of men unleash war, it is the hearts of children that bear the scars, burnt by flames they never lit."

I'm about to tell you a story. The story of our children, of all children, because every child who breathes on this earth is also my child. Whatever their language, faith or country, a child is a flash of innocence, a fragile flame that lights up the future. Every birth is a new light, a hope that tomorrow will be kinder, fairer and more loving. But all too often, it is the adults, the guardians of that light, who are the first to betray that hope.

Children do not choose to be born under dark skies, in a world torn apart by violence. They deserve to run free under clear skies, to laugh without fear, to dream without hindrance. Yet in so many corners of the world, this fundamental right is snatched away from them. Their laughter is lost in the roar of bombs, their play is cut short by the wail of sirens, and their bright, colourful dreams are buried under the rubble of wars they never started.

These children become shadows, reduced to cold figures in war assessments. Their destinies are sacrificed on the altar of the interests of the powerful, of blind ambitions that turn their innocence into ashes. They are nothing more than "collateral damage", anonymous victims of a relentless war machine fuelled by greed and indifference. Each missile, each detonation, wipes out slivers of life that have not had time to blossom.

But the wounds of childhood do not stop at the battlefield. Even in our so-called "civilised" societies, children are

The Hourim of innocence

imprisoned in invisible shackles. They are drowned in a flood of futile information, trapped in a frenzied consumerism that distances them from essential values : love, simplicity, connection to others and to nature. They grow up with heavy hearts, deprived of the freedom to marvel that should be their most sacred right.

And then there are the guilty silences, the grey areas where an even more insidious evil thrives: paedo-crime. Where children should be protected, they fall prey to monsters lurking in the shadows, encouraged by our inaction and complicit silences. This evil, even more despicable than war, destroys forever what is purest in them. But there is still time to stand up, to refuse to remain a spectator. This book is a cry, a call to action, compassion and love. It is a reminder that every lost child's smile is a star extinguished in the sky of humanity. We have an immense responsibility: to protect innocence, to restore childhood, to offer a future to those who carry within them the light of days to come.

In the following pages, I invite you to follow Abigael and Moussa, two children whose destinies, separated by walls of hatred, are intertwined despite everything. They mirror the millions of children caught in the web of a world at war, a world where love and peace always seem out of reach. See through their eyes, feel their fear, their hope, their strength. For it is by connecting with them, by sharing their humanity, that we may find the courage to change, to rebuild a world where every child has the right to dream, to grow and to love.

"Where war robs innocence, it is our duty to rebuild childhood, because every smile lost is a light that the world will never find again."

The Hourim of innocence

CHAPTER I
AT THE VERY BEGINNING

« AMID THE CLAMOUR OF BOMBS AND THE TEARS OF MOURNING, ONLY THE PURE OF HEART CAN TURN PAIN INTO LIGHT AND LOVE INTO A WEAPON AGAINST HATRED. »

February 2020. The world, like a giant in suspense, held its breath, unaware of the insidious storm that was about to break and redefine the fabric of humanity.

The Hourim of innocence

At the time, the virus was no more than an imperceptible murmur, a whisper in the distance, a still diffuse threat. In Jerusalem, a city where every stone whispered secrets thousands of years old, concerns remained rooted in older quarrels, with roots as deep as the unhealed wounds of the three great religions.

Here, every breath of wind seemed to carry the burden of generations, interweaving faint hopes with memories of endless struggles. Yet on this very day, a fragile, almost miraculous harmony floated in the air, ready to be discovered by two innocent souls.

The winter sun, soft and crystalline, rose like a heavenly balm over this land exhausted by conflict. Its rays, scattered like splinters of gold, caressed the stones of the old city, lingering on the Dome of the Rock, where the light curled around the golden dome, before slipping between the gnarled branches of a hundred-year-old olive tree. This sacred tree, rooted not far from Golgotha, carried within it the memory of the centuries, a silent guardian of the prayers and tears that had permeated the earth. And under this same sky dotted with light clouds, two children were about to cross paths for the first time, at that precise moment when the course of history seemed to be suspended, barely a breath away, just before the world plunged into an unprecedented crisis.

Eleven-year-old Moussa walked at a measured pace through the dusty alleys of a Palestinian neighbourhood, not far from the Dome of the Rock, where the echoes of prayers wrapped themselves around the sacred stones. The tumult of voices, the shouts of merchants and the laughter of children, faded as they moved away, evaporating in the wind, which was full of dust and mystery. The boy, his features marked by premature

The Hourim of innocence

maturity, sought refuge in an olive grove, close to the thousand-year-old tree that seemed to have watched over Jerusalem since the dawn of time. This place was his sanctuary, a haven of peace where he would take shelter when the weight of existence became too heavy to bear. The war had etched an unusual gravity on his face, a painful wisdom, but despite the shadows that inhabited him, Moussa remained a dreamer. He was one of those people who still found beauty in the dance of the leaves, the rustle of a bird taking flight, or the secret melody of the wind seeping through the branches.

Several metres away, on the other side of the walls of Jerusalem, Abigael walked slowly, her steps gliding with an almost ethereal elegance over the ancient cobblestones, where history had left its indelible mark. Her world, though protected by stone walls, was no less charged with invisible tensions. Abigael, whose eyes were as deep green as twilight, felt the weight of past generations like a dull echo resonating within her, a burden she carried without understanding. Sensitive, almost clairvoyant, she picked up the subtle vibrations of the old town, where every stone seemed to whisper the secrets of a painful past.

But on that February day, her thoughts were only light. Abigael dreamt of nothing more than flying her red and blue kite, a precious gift from her grandfather that she held like a talisman. For her, this kite, light and free, was a promise of escape, a symbol of hope that soared into the sky, carrying her silent prayers above the Dome of the Rock, where the sacred and the ineffable seemed to meet. With her kite, she felt connected to the heavens, to the divine mystery that encased Jerusalem in a jewel case of light and pain.

The Hourim of innocence

They should never have met. Their respective worlds were separated by impassable borders, visible and invisible ramparts, erected long before they were born. These walls of stone and silence, of accumulated resentment and hereditary hatred, had woven subtle prisons around their young souls, where the very breath of hope seemed rare and precious. And yet, under this winter sky, a blue so clear that it seemed unreal, something unspeakable was about to happen, an event that not even the millennia-old course of this sacred land could have predicted.

Moussa moved forward, his steps marking a regular rhythm on the cracked ground of the Old City of Jerusalem, as if he were walking not only on the earth but also on the remains of so many shattered dreams. A gravity weighed on his frail shoulders, a heaviness shaped by the violence and pain of a life too soon confronted by war. Yet there was a hidden light within him, a radiance that not even the storms had been able to extinguish. He followed the winding path that led him, almost instinctively, towards the hundred-year-old olive tree, the immovable guardian of Golgotha, where eternity seemed to whisper its secrets to those who knew how to listen.

But that day, something different, something unexpected, attracted him. Another invisible force, gentler, more delicate. He walked along the city walls, and his dark eyes, imbued with a painful wisdom, widened as he caught sight of a figure. A little girl stood there among the olive trees, surrounded by an almost supernatural glow. She was moving, running, playing with the wind like a child who, despite everything, still believed in the beauty of this broken world.

Abigael was this figure, frail and vivacious, a child with bright hair that seemed to capture the sun's rays. Her white dress

The Hourim of innocence

swirled around her, and her feet, so light, barely caressed the earth, as if she feared awakening the memories buried beneath these thousand-year-old stones. In her hands, she held the string of a red and blue kite, a gift from her grandfather, such a simple toy but one that held so many memories. The kite, fragile though it was, withstood the gusts of wind, rising, struggling and twirling in the azure sky, like a challenge to the laws of gravity and war.

And Abigael understood this kite. She had learnt to run with it, to give it all the freedom it needed, never to try to force it. The wind played in her hair and crept under her dress, but she ran, tirelessly, with feline grace, her crystalline laughter mingling with the rustling of the leaves. She knew this secret : freedom could not be possessed, it had to be offered, like a gift, lovingly and unconditionally.

It was this laughter, this lightness, that captivated Moussa, and in an instant, everything changed in him. It was as if the weight of his years, his fears, his anger, had suddenly been lifted. He watched Abigael, fascinated, feeling his heart beat at a rhythm he had never known before. And this kite, this symbol of freedom, twirled above their heads, defying the forces of the earth, indifferent to the scars of men. He moved closer to her, shyly at first, then with curiosity mixed with hope.

Their eyes met at last, and it was a collision of worlds, a meeting of two lost stars who, in the space of a breath, recognised each other. Abigael's crystalline green eyes looked deep into Moussa's dark ones, as if to discover the secrets they were hiding. There was no mistrust, no enmity. Just a silent exchange, a language that only young, sincere hearts can speak. A language made up of silences, smiles and delicate gestures.

The Hourim of innocence

Abigael broke the suspended magic, her voice clear and vibrant with life :

"What's your name?" Such a simple question, but at that moment it seemed to upset the order of things, to break an invisible ban.

"Moussa", he replied, his voice low but filled with a gentleness he hadn't heard in him for years.

"I'm Abigael," she said with a smile that held all the light of that winter's day. She held out the kite string to him, a silent invitation, an offering. As if to say to him: Take it, feel what it's like to soar, to escape the walls that enclose us.

Moussa hesitantly reached out his hand, and when his fingers touched the string, an almost sacred shiver ran down his arm. Instinctively, he withdrew it, as if he had just touched a fragile star. This simple contact, ephemeral but full of promise, had already linked their destinies. The hundred-year-old olive tree, a silent witness to the ages, shivered gently, as if remembering a forgotten time, when the laughter of children rose freely under a sky without borders.

This was their first meeting, a moment woven of light and silence. The red and blue kite, this fragment of sky, this dream in suspense, continued to float, unaware of the quarrels of mankind. It let itself be carried by the wind, like a fragile but indestructible hope. And the olive tree, ancient witness to the sufferings and miracles of this land, seemed to bless with a discreet breath this beginning of history, a history that already belonged to legend.

It was there, at the very beginning, in that sanctuary where innocence still held the power to silence ancestral resentments,

The Hourim of innocence

that Moussa and Abigael found each other. A discreet miracle under the February sky, a moment suspended like a musical note that defies the silence of the centuries. They didn't know it yet, these children of candid souls, but this meeting would transform their destinies forever, rewriting lines that history had frozen in the cold stone of conflict.

The wind, capricious messenger of the invisible, continued to blow, ruffling Abigael's hair and playing in Moussa's brown curls. He caressed their youthful faces with the tenderness of a mother, but also with the insistence of a stern teacher, as if to remind them that, even in the midst of the worst storms, there is a fragile hope. That hope, fragile as a blade of grass amid the ruins, could trace a path of peace where hatred had erected walls.

Abigael's kite was still dancing in the air, its bright colours tearing through the greyness of a landscape scarred by history. Red and blue, it rose and fell with the whims of the wind, a living metaphor for freedom, for the aspiration to rise, to break free from the visible and invisible chains their ancestors had bequeathed them. Each movement of the kite seemed to embody a dream, an unfulfilled desire to reach for the heavens, to transcend the weight of the centuries.

After they exchanged first names, the silence returned, but this time it was no longer that heavy silence weighed down by memories of blood and tears. It was a gentle, soothing silence, like that which follows a storm, giving way to a strange and unexpected peace. For a brief moment, it seemed as if the war, that voracious old entity, had chosen to close its eyes and look away from these two children, as if it recognised the sacredness of this moment.

The Hourim of innocence

Abigael stood up, holding the string of her kite firmly, but with a childlike grace that gave the gesture an unexpected nobility. Then, with a delicate movement, she handed the string back to Moussa, her pale green eyes shining with a disarming innocence, a light that defied the surrounding darkness. "Do you want to try it?" she asked, her crystalline voice piercing the surrounding melancholy, like a gentle but precise arrow, an invitation to rise.

Moussa froze, a shadow of surprise crossing his face. He was not used to so much gentleness, especially not from someone he had been taught, insidiously and repeatedly, to perceive as 'the other', 'the enemy'. This other who was supposed to be different, threatening, uninviting. Yet Abigael was nothing like an enemy. She was just a little girl, a child like him, with this kite like a dream in her hands. Slowly, almost solemnly, he held out his hand, his fingers trembling with a hesitation that was not fear but respect, and took hold of the string.

The force of the wind, that breath of freedom, gently drew him forward, urging him to move, to open up. And for the first time in a long time, a shy smile appeared on his lips. It was a rare smile, bursting like a shooting star, briefly lighting up his usually serious face.

"It's fun, isn't it?" Abigael laughed lightly, clear as a spring of living water, the kind of laughter that wakes sleeping hearts and chases away shadows. Her laughter echoed around them, breaking through invisible barriers and rising into the air like a hymn to joy. And that laugh touched something in Moussa, a chord in his soul that hadn't vibrated for ages. He nodded slowly, unable to respond in words, but the smile he gave her said it all.

The Hourim of innocence

At that moment, all that existed was that kite floating in the blue, a fragment of freedom and dream. The ruins around them seemed less imposing, and the hundred-year-old olive tree, a silent witness to their exchange, seemed to observe them with a thousand years of tenderness. Their hearts, still young but already marked by hardship, beat in unison, carrying a silent promise that one day, perhaps, children could teach adults the meaning of peace.

And so, at the beginning of this story, a kite linked two destinies, drawing invisible lines of hope in the winter sky. The olive tree remained motionless, but its ancient soul seemed to bless them with a discreet sigh, as if it had always secretly waited for this moment.

All around them, the world continued to spin, heavy with tension, vibrating with invisible but omnipresent scars. Just a few kilometres away, checkpoints stood like deep scars, guarded by soldiers with impenetrable gazes. Walls bristling with barbed wire cut across the sacred land, and convoys of armoured vehicles criss-crossed the roads like ghosts of iron. In the meantime, adults were getting drunk on interminable debates, journalists were shooting out words like arrows, and politicians, pencil in hand, were redrawing maps whose contours escaped the logic of children. But here, in this place blessed and cursed at the same time, at the foot of the old olive trees that had seen so many dreams born and die, all that seemed distant, almost unreal.

"Why are you here on your own?" asked Moussa, breaking the silence with the sincere awkwardness of a child, but his voice betrayed something more, a curiosity charged with a seriousness that no child should have to bear.

The Hourim of innocence

Abigael shrugged gently, her brown locks dancing in the breeze. "I often come here with my grandfather. She paused, as if the very memory of this venerable man, of his frozen wisdom, inspired both respect and nostalgia. "But today he was tired, so I came on my own. What about you?"

Moussa hesitated, his dark eyes dropping to the ground. He didn't like talking about his life. It was a life of ruins and broken dreams, a life that even local children, scarred by premature grief, learned to hide. But Abigael's eyes were so pure, so foreign to judgement, that the words, almost in spite of himself, found their way in. "I like it here," he murmured. "It's quiet. It's... away from everything." Away from the metallic echoes of the tanks, away from the shrill wail of the sirens that cut through the night like a knife, away from the incessant arguments of adults who never stopped tearing at each other over a territory as old as the breath of the wind.

Abigael stared at him with a rare intensity, an intensity that did not seem to belong to a child. Her clear eyes shone with a brilliance that the pain of the world had not yet dulled, but which already bore the mark of the wounds to come. "It's the same for me," she said simply, but in that simplicity there was a truth that no adult could have told. "It's as if the world left us alone here.

Moussa nodded, feeling, without understanding why, that he could trust her. This feeling of calm was unusual, almost forbidden, but he wasn't afraid. With her, in this place where the wind seemed to whisper forgotten secrets, he felt safe. It was as if they had created, without knowing it, a parallel universe where the weight of war could not touch them, where friendship could be born from a simple glance.

The Hourim of innocence

But this dream was fragile. Reality would not let them escape so easily.

In the distance, far behind them, a muffled roar could be heard. It was an indistinct noise, muffled by the distance, but it sent a cold shiver down their spines. They knew this rumbling. They had heard it a thousand times, enough to understand that it was a foretaste of the violence that was about to erupt, a threat that made the air heavier and harder to breathe. Moussa froze, his smile disappearing like a summer's breath blown away by an icy gust of wind. Abigael's kite, deprived of the wind's dance, slowly fell back to earth, as if yielding to the weight of the heavy realities that were calling them to order.

Abigael lowered her eyes, her lips tightening in a sadness she didn't know how to express. She too understood. They were still children, but children from here, where peace was just an empty word, where hope crumbled like the walls of old buildings. Here, even the youngest knew what a noise like that meant.

"I've got to go home," Moussa murmured, his voice imbued with an almost guilty sadness. It was a farewell he didn't want to say, the end of a moment too beautiful to last. He held out the kite string to Abigael, his fingers trembling with a regret he couldn't hide.

Abigael took the string without a word, her eyes clouded with a melancholy she couldn't banish. "Me too," she murmured. The light in her eyes seemed to flicker, like a flame that a cold wind wanted to extinguish.

They stood there, frozen in the dawning twilight, as if time itself were reluctant to separate them. Then Abigael took a

The Hourim of innocence

breath, her heart clenching under the weight of a fear she didn't want to admit. "Maybe we'll see each other here again one day," she said, her voice full of that unshakeable hope that only children can still carry, that hope that shines even in the darkest darkness.

Moussa gave a shy smile, a frail but sincere smile, like a flickering light in the middle of a storm. "Maybe," he said. It was all he could offer, but it was already a lot.

Then, without another word, they parted, each returning to his own world. Two worlds that nothing seemed able to reconcile, but where they had left, at least for a moment, the imprint of a shared dream. As the darkness deepened, the golden light of the Dome of the Rock slowly faded, swallowed up by the night. Abigael followed her grandfather, her thoughts wandering far ahead of her. Her feet trod the worn cobbles, but her heart remained there, close to Moussa, the boy she hardly knew, but who carried a familiar light, like an echo of something ancient and essential.

Abigael's grandfather, a stoic and reassuring figure, was still murmuring prayers in Hebrew. His weathered fingers were peppering the beads of his rosary, a gesture that was automatic but charged with a deep and unshakeable faith. For him, religion was a bulwark, a citadel of certainty in a world in ruins. But Abigael, for all the respect she had for him, sometimes felt alienated from such absolute faith. In her heart, gentler, more indefinable truths whispered to her that maybe, just maybe, love and peace were not always to be found where adults thought they were.

On the other side of the wall, in a modest neighbourhood of East Jerusalem, Moussa was on his way home. The evening air

The Hourim of innocence

was permeated with the smell of freshly baked bread and jasmine, while the narrow streets gradually emptied, giving way to the murmur of prayers rising towards the sky, like an ancestral litany. His mother was waiting for him, her veil carefully adjusted, ready for the evening prayer. His father, grave and dignified, adjusted his djellaba as he prepared to go to the mosque. For this family, the Islamic faith was more than just a tradition : it was a compass, a North Star that guided them through a world constantly shaken by the tumult of history.

Every evening, around the Koran, the suras echoed through their house like songs from time immemorial, prayers that stood like an invisible bulwark against desolation. Yet that evening, as Moussa softly recited the sacred verses, his thoughts floated elsewhere, escaping the ritual. They drifted, as if drawn by a magnetic force, towards her. Abigael. This simple first name, this memory, haunted him in a strange way, like an obsessive melody that you can't get out of your mind.

Try as he might to concentrate, to let the sacred words wash over his heart, another voice was whispering deep inside him. He remembered the light from the Dome of the Rock that day, the way it had seemed to shine more brightly, as if to underline this fleeting but sacred moment. And that strange sensation that never left him... that presence. It wasn't the first time he'd felt it, this feeling of being watched, of being protected by something invisible but benevolent. That evening, as the night shrouded the old town in starry shadows, he dared to talk about it.

As his mother finished the prayer, her veil falling in soft folds around her face, Moussa murmured, his eyes lowered, as if afraid that his words would break something sacred. "Mum,

The Hourim of innocence

do you think... do you think there are things that only children can see?"

His mother looked at him with gentle eyes, a gleam of tenderness shining in her eyes, tired by life but still full of love. She stroked his hair, ruffling his brown locks. "Why do you ask, my son ?" Her voice was gentle, but a shadow of worry floated through it, like a silent prayer that he would never see too much of this complicated world.

Moussa hesitated, searching for words. "I don't know... sometimes I think I see things. Someone. But it's not... it's not scary. It's... like a guardian."

A kind smile softened her mother's features. She gently pressed her hand against his cheek. "Perhaps it's the Creator speaking to you, my son. Only the pure of heart can hear His voice. Keep praying, and He will guide you.

He nodded, but deep down he knew it was different. What he was feeling was much more tangible, much closer than a mere divine whisper.

A few days later, their destinies crossed again, this time near the Dome of the Rock. Abigael, obstinate and curious, had insisted on accompanying her grandfather, a dignified and pious old man who carried his years with the wisdom of a biblical patriarch. Moussa, for his part, had convinced his father to take him to the Al-Aqsa mosque, using all his childish eloquence. It was as if an invisible force, imperious and gentle at the same time, was gently pulling the threads of their lives together so that they could meet again, in the golden shadow of this sacred place.

The Hourim of innocence

Their eyes met, and that strange energy, that mystical current they had felt when they first met, seemed to vibrate in the air again. Abigael felt a chill run down her spine, but it wasn't the cold. It was as if something, or someone, was caressing her soul. A soft voice, like a breath from another world, rose in her mind, like a secret whispered by eternity. It was an ancient melody, at once unfamiliar and deeply familiar.

"Abigael... listen..."

She turned round abruptly, her brown curls fluttering around her face as she searched desperately for the source of the whisper. But there was no one. Nothing but Moussa, whose eyes shone with a strange sparkle. He wasn't looking at her, but at an invisible point behind her, in the imposing shadow of the Dome of the Rock.

"Moussa... can you hear that ?" she whispered, her voice trembling with a mixture of wonder and fear.

Moussa's eyes widened and his breathing became shorter. He froze, as if he was seeing something too big, too bright for a mere boy to understand. "I... I see someone," he whispered, his voice barely louder than a breath. "There, just behind you. A figure... but it's not a man. It's... it's like a light."

Their hearts beat in unison, distraught, while the world around them seemed to fade away, as if carried away by a divine breath. It was as if the whole universe held its breath, enveloping them in a mystical presence, elusive but undeniably real.

Abigael turned round once more, her eyes searching desperately for the shadow of the old ramparts, but there was nothing there but the solidity of the sacred wall, the wall that

The Hourim of innocence

had witnessed centuries of prayers and tears, promises and wounds never healed. Yet the voice continued to vibrate in his mind, soft, almost caressing, like a breath from another world.

"We are together," whispered the voice, resonating in every fibre of her being. "You are two children born in separate worlds, but your hearts beat in harmony. Have no fear. There are forces greater than hate, forces that only the pure hearts of children can understand."

Moussa, for his part, remained captivated by the ethereal figure floating before him, an entity made of light, vibrant and translucent, like a reflection of dawn trapped in the air. His heart pounded in his chest, but he felt no fear. No, it was something else, a kind of immaculate peace, a gentle warmth that chased the darkness from his soul. He realised with sudden clarity that this apparition was not a mirage, but a Guardian. A Guardian destined to protect him and Abigael from a world that was trying to tear them apart.

"She's talking..." breathed Moussa, his lips barely trembling, his eyes still fixed on the light.

"He speaks too..." Abigael replied in a whisper, her heart beating in unison with Moussa's, as if their souls shared the same revelation, the same mystical connection.

The majestic golden Dome of the Rock seemed to sparkle with a new, almost supernatural intensity, as if it too were participating in this sacred moment. The rays of the setting sun shimmered off its gold, illuminating the skies with an almost divine light. This place, steeped in history and faith, seemed to bow in silence before the mystery of this meeting, as if granting them a silent blessing.

The Hourim of innocence

Their respective families, absorbed in ritual prayers, had noticed nothing. Abigael's grandfather, a man of unshakeable faith, was still reciting his psalms, his fingers gliding devoutly over the beads of his rosary. As for Moussa's father, his eyes closed and his forehead resting on the ground, he was murmuring the sacred verses of the Koran with an almost palpable fervour. These adults, prisoners of their certainties and their past, could not understand what was happening at that precise moment, on the frontier of the invisible.

"One day... one day, they will understand," whispered the voice in Abigael's head, its resonance like an echo of eternity. "But for now, it's up to you to see beyond their fears. You are children of two worlds, but you share the same light."

Moussa swallowed, his pupils dilated by an emotion he had never felt before. "Who are you?" he dared to ask, his voice broken by a mixture of hope and fascination.

The figure of light didn't reply with words, but a wave of serenity passed through Moussa, a wave of calm that soothed his mind, as if the answer had never needed to be formulated. Everything became clear: this presence was not a dream or an illusion, but a promise. A promise of protection, hope and guidance.

Then, as suddenly as it had appeared, the light vanished, dissolving into the ether like a shooting star disappearing into the immensity of the heavens. The voice echoing in Abigael's mind fell silent, and the silence fell again, heavy and deep. But it was no longer the same silence. Something had changed. An invisible seed had been planted, and they both knew it instinctively.

The Hourim of innocence

This Guardian, invisible to adults but palpable to them, would remain present, watching over their innocent souls, guiding them through the chaos of a world at war. For although faith, religion and hatred would tirelessly seek to separate them, a much older, much more powerful force would watch over them. An ancestral magic, born of the sacred land on which they stood.

The days wore on, and despite the invisible walls that tried to keep them apart, Moussa and Abigael met up regularly near the Dome of the Rock. The place seemed to be inhabited by a divine breath, a magnetic force that drew them together. Their encounters were brief, often silent, but with every glance they exchanged, every smile they shared, an invisible bond was forged, a bond that nothing, neither time nor violence, could break.

In that in-between time, when hope struggled to survive, a dream was born. A simple, beautiful but indestructible dream, of a future where they could come together without fear, without walls, without hatred. Just two children, in love with the same light, in love with a love that not even the darkness could extinguish.

Abigael, her brown hair waving with natural elegance in the wind, her luminous green eyes imbued with a rare purity, seemed to embody the very essence of innocence. There was a gentleness in her features that is typical of children who, despite the shadows hovering around them, continue to dream and hope, whose hearts beat with infinite compassion. She carried within her a subtle grace, a delicate restraint, as if her every gesture was measured so as not to shatter the fragile harmony of this moment stolen from the surrounding turmoil. Moussa, on the other hand, with his raven-black hair that

The Hourim of innocence

always seemed to be in a battle, his deep, meditative black eyes, was a child whose gaze betrayed a precocious seriousness, like a reflection of the battles he had seen too often, but a seriousness softened by an inner light that had never been extinguished. He was handsome, with a simple, discreet beauty, marked by the trials of life, but illuminated by a dream that he still nurtured, even in silence.

They were two children from opposite worlds, two souls that everything should have kept apart, heirs to ancient pains and trans-generational scars. Yet between them, every encounter, every smile, was a victory over the adult world, a transcendence of the doctrines of hatred and mistrust inculcated by past generations.

It was May 2020. The world seemed to be collapsing under the weight of the pandemic, a global crisis that was imposing its reign of fear and isolation. But in Jerusalem, anxiety was never simple. Here, explosions, screams and incessant reprisals were a daily litany, a macabre melody that never stopped. Abigael and Moussa, despite the tenderness of their age, could not ignore the violence that permeated the streets of the holy city, this land of history and discord.

One day, when they had once again found themselves close to the Dome of the Rock, a dull roar shook the ground beneath their feet, a shockwave vibrating the air around them. An explosion somewhere in the city sounded like a thunderclap of doom. Moussa tensed, his muscles stiffening by reflex, used from a very young age to the cruel vigilance imposed by constant conflict. Abigael crouched down, her face pale and her eyes wide with terror. The sound gradually faded, but the sense of danger remained, suspended and overwhelming. Distant cries rose into the air, mingling with the echo of the

The Hourim of innocence

detonation, while black smoke rose slowly into the sky, like an evil omen, a beacon of despair.

"It was an attack", Moussa murmured, his gaze fixed in the direction of the noise, his voice dulled by the habit of this recurring misfortune. "A suicide bomber, probably..."

Abigael, still in shock, sat up slowly, her breath short and her chest tight with a fear she couldn't control. She had heard of suicide bombings, of acts of desperation and hatred, but this time, the proximity of violence made everything more real, more terrifying. The reasons and justifications that were often put forward around her suddenly seemed very derisory. "Why?" she asked, her voice flayed by emotion. "Why are they doing this?

Moussa remained silent, his face darkened by a sadness too great for his age. He knew the answers the adults gave him, the tales of suffering and injustice, but deep down it remained a mystery to him, a cruel incomprehension. Why choose destruction ? Why take lives? It was a question that burned at the back of his mind like poison.

And it was then, in that moment of shared terror, that a voice rose, gentle and soothing, in Abigael's mind. "They are lost, blinded by their own pain," whispered the guardian's voice, a melody from elsewhere, resonating within her with the force of an ancient truth.

Moussa also felt this presence. This time, it was no longer hiding in the recesses of his imagination. It revealed itself fully, a silhouette of light, floating gently between them, bright and benevolent. The Guardian, that being of purity and mystery, had at last materialised, like a silent answer to their fears. His features were indistinct, almost immaterial, but his

The Hourim of innocence

benevolence radiated around them, enveloping the two children in a protective warmth.

The Dome of the Rock seemed to glow with a supernatural intensity, as if this sacred and tormented place recognised the presence of this being. The aura of light seemed to make the air dance, imbuing the place with a strange and unexpected serenity. The prayers, laments and howls of the world seemed to fade away, caught up in this divine presence.

Abigael shivered, but not from fear. "Moussa..." she murmured, tears welling up in her eyes, but not from sadness. "You see him, don't you ?"

Moussa, his eyes wide with fascination, nodded. He had never felt such sweet peace, a peace that contrasted so brutally with the explosions and hatred. "Yes, I see it," he said, his voice trembling but filled with certainty.

The Guardian, made of light and mystery, gazed at them for a moment before whispering into the children's minds, "Never lose hope. You are the bridge between two worlds, the promise of a love that nothing can break." And with that, the figure slowly disappeared, but its essence, its protection, seemed to permeate the air around them.

Moussa and Abigael looked at each other, shocked. Something ineffable had touched them, something that adults could never understand. But in that moment, even with war roaring on their doorstep, they felt that they carried within them a greater strength. A strength made up of hope, innocence and a love stronger than hate.

Abigael, still in shock from the explosion, felt the voice rise in her mind with a new clarity, as if the words were engraved

The Hourim of innocence

directly into her soul : "Their suffering has twisted their hearts. They think they're defending, but in truth, they're only sowing destruction."

Moussa stared at the silhouette of light, and despite the horror of the chaos around them, a feeling of unshakeable peace enveloped him. He clenched his fists, trying to understand. "Why are you showing us this?" he asked, his voice still quivering with emotion, but underpinned by a nascent determination.

The guardian gazed at them with luminous eyes imbued with ancient wisdom, eyes that seemed to pierce the veils of time and souls. "Because you are children, and only children still have the power to perceive what adults have decided they can no longer see. Your love, your purity, are far more powerful weapons than any hatred. The world is suffocating in darkness, and you are the light it is waiting for."

Abigael felt her heart beat faster. A mixture of fear and determination ran through her young mind. "What should we do ?" she whispered, her voice frail but filled with a strength she didn't know she possessed.

The guardian, surrounded by an aura of iridescent sparkles, stepped forward. His presence almost seemed to touch their skin, like a divine breath. "You must protect what is most sacred: the innocence of children. Children who grow up without ever knowing peace, transformed into instruments of violence before they even understand who they are. You must give them back their stolen childhood, break the chains that enslave them to war. You are the light that will pierce this endless night.

The Hourim of innocence

Moussa and Abigael exchanged an intense gaze, a gaze that echoed the burden the guardian had just entrusted to them. The weight of this mission seemed disproportionate, an almost unbearable responsibility for their young shoulders. And yet, they felt invested with a new strength, an energy born of their bond, of this budding love, fragile but indestructible, that united them. This feeling, pure and luminous, was their greatest weapon, their most precious protection. Neither bombs nor cries of hatred could ever alter what they shared.

The guardian, his voice soft but full of prophetic solemnity, continued: "There will come dark hours, moments when war will seek to separate you. But remember, love overcomes all destructive forces. Even in the deepest darkness, your light will continue to shine. You carry within you the hope of a better world. Protect it, nurture it, even if there is pain along the way.

Abigael felt her eyes grow misty, tears running down her cheeks, tracing furrows of sadness and compassion. She thought of all those children, all those innocent people whose peace and innocence had been stolen from them, all those souls who lived each day under the yoke of fear, never understanding why the world inflicted so much suffering on them. Moussa, seeing his friend in tears, gently took her hand, and in that simple gesture there was a silent promise, a commitment they did not yet fully understand, but which they would honour, come what may.

Suddenly, a distant scream pierced the air, muffled by the dust and the echoes of the surrounding chaos. The sound of explosions intensified, this time coming from the Israeli side. The dull roar of violence echoed in their hearts, a cruel reminder of the fragility of their world. Abigael closed her eyes, shaken by terror and powerlessness, while Moussa sat up,

The Hourim of innocence

his gaze fixed on the horizon, as if looking for a sign, for guidance.

They were still only children, but fate had chosen to place them at the centre of a war they had never asked for. Yet they understood, in that moment of shared pain, that they carried within them a flame stronger than any army, a glow that was only waiting to grow, to illuminate even the darkest night.

The guardian dissipated in a flash, but his message remained engraved in them, incandescent and eternal.

"Both sides are guilty," Abigael murmured, her voice breaking under the weight of a truth that no child should have to bear. Her eyes shone with an unfathomable sadness, a reflection of the grief of an entire generation. "But children... children are innocent."

Moussa, at his side, nodded, his jaws clenched. His dark eyes, imbued with the precocious wisdom that only pain could forge, stared out at the horizon tinged with the redness of spilt blood. He knew better than anyone that his own family bore the scars of Israeli attacks, just as Abigael's family lived under the constant threat of Palestinian attacks. It was a hellish loop of violence, a macabre dance in which everyone was in turn victim and executioner. But he and Abigael... they had to escape this fate.

"We have to protect them", says Moussa, his voice firming despite the trembling of his hands, a sign of his combined determination and vulnerability. "Even if no one understands, even if our families refuse to hear us.... we have to protect the children.

The Hourim of innocence

The guardian, this mysterious, luminous entity, gazed at them for a long moment, his aura radiating ineffable benevolence. Then, in a burst of soft light, he disappeared, leaving behind him an imprint of warmth and hope. Now Moussa and Abigael knew they were no longer alone. Their sacred mission had just begun, and they would have to carry it out, even if the world around them tried to break them.

Summer had taken hold of Jerusalem, spreading its scorching mantle over the city. The ancient stones of the old city seemed to exude a suffocating heat, and the palpable tensions made the air even more stifling. Yet for Moussa and Abigael, time had no real hold. Every moment spent together became an oasis of peace, an enchanted interlude in the midst of the tumult.

They were just eleven-year-olds, but the intensity of their emotions, the depth of their connection, defied all logic. What their families, friends and even their elders didn't understand was that this budding love was nothing ordinary. It was a silent resistance, a secret hope that clung to life despite the crushing weight of hatred.

One evening, after a day marked by incessant bombing, when the whole city seemed to be holding its breath, Abigael slipped out of her house. Her heart was pounding in her frail chest, a symphony of fear and anticipation. She knew that her parents would never accept this escapade, that their anger would be terrible if they found out, but the call was too strong, irrepressible. Seeing Moussa, if only for a few moments, seemed more important than anything else.

She made her way through the dark alleys, where the shadows of the stone houses seemed to stretch out as if to hold her

The Hourim of innocence

back. But she crept along, light and fast, with a determination that nothing could shake. The air, still thick with heat, seemed to vibrate around her, but Abigael didn't slow down. She knew where she was going: where she felt most alive, most herself.

Moussa was already waiting for her in the shadow of the Dome of the Rock, the place that had become a sanctuary for them, a haven of peace in the midst of the storm. When he saw her arrive, a shy smile lit up her face, banishing for a moment the seriousness that marked her youthful features. Abigael, with her brown hair waving in the breeze and her bright green eyes, appeared to him like a vision of purity, a breath of hope in a world suffocated by hatred.

They sat side by side, their knees barely touching, as if they were afraid to break the delicacy of the moment. Their hands remained resting on their knees, but the energy between them was palpable, an invisible thread linking them heart to heart. There was silence, but it wasn't a void. It was a space filled with everything they couldn't say, everything they felt.

"Will it ever stop ?" asked Abigael, her voice barely a whisper, as if she dreaded breaking a spell by saying those words.

Moussa looked away, contemplating the golden light that grazed the Dome. He had no answer. How could he have known that this endless war would one day find its appeasement? But he turned to her, searching her eyes, and found a strength in them that surprised him. "I don't know," he murmured, "but I do know that as long as we're together, it won't really matter."

Abigael felt tears welling up in her eyes, but she didn't cry. She simply clasped her hands a little tighter in her lap, as if to give herself courage. She knew they had nothing, not even the

The Hourim of innocence

promise of a better tomorrow, but in that simple moment, in Moussa's presence, she had everything.

Abigael turned her head slowly towards Moussa. His green eyes, hemmed with unshed tears, gleamed in the emerging darkness with such intensity that his heart stopped for a moment. Those eyes seemed to contain a thousand questions, a thousand torments, and at the same time, a light that refused to be extinguished.

"How do you manage to be so brave, Moussa ?" she murmured, her voice broken but filled with a gentleness she reserved only for him. "How do you manage to keep hope alive, even when everything seems so... hopelessly lost?"

Moussa felt his throat knot up. How could he explain to her that it was she, and only she, who gave him this strength, that every smile of hers was like a flash of light in the deepest darkness? He searched for words, words that often escaped him, he who had never been good at speeches.

"Because I see you," he replied at last, simply, but with a truth that made his lips tremble.

Silence fell over them again, but it was no longer the oppressive silence of the war rumbling around them. It was an inhabited silence, charged with meaning, like a promise sealed by the synchronised beating of their youthful hearts. Slowly, almost timidly, their hands brushed against each other, hesitant to cross the invisible boundary that still separated them. Then Moussa moved his fingers forward, intertwining them with Abigael's. This simple gesture, so natural and yet so forbidden by the adult world, resonated within them like a silent oath: we will never leave each other.

The Hourim of innocence

Their intertwined hands, this fragile but powerful contact, became a sanctuary, a wall that not even bullets or bombs could penetrate.

Over time, the guardian became a constant presence, a benevolent glow that seemed to watch over them at every moment stolen from the surrounding chaos. He always floated close to them, ethereal, his soft light making their eyes shine like the stars in a sky too often darkened. This guardian, born of their pure love, seemed to grow in radiance as their bond grew stronger. And one evening, as the night stretched out in a veil of black velvet sprinkled with flashes of gold, they finally dared to ask him the question that had been burning in their hearts.

"Who are you really?" asked Abigael, her crystalline voice wavering between fear and curiosity.

The guardian remained silent for a moment, as if weighing up the importance of his answer. Then, with a breath that seemed to carry away the breeze itself, he replied: "I am what you make me. I was born of your love, your innocence. I am here to guide you, to protect you from what lurks in the darkness."

Moussa, fascinated, scrutinised the floating light, trying to decipher its mysteries. "Why us ?" he asked, his breath taken away by the intensity of what he was feeling. "Why are you following us ?

The guardian turned to him, his luminous features blending into the surrounding shadows, and replied: "Because you are the light in this dark war. Your love is a torch that not even the storms of violence can extinguish. You carry within you a strength that no one can see, a strength that can change hearts.

The Hourim of innocence

You are the protectors of the most precious thing of all : the innocence of children.

The words resonated in Abigael's heart like a painful echo. Every day, she watched helplessly as the innocence around her was lost. Children in her neighbourhood, too young to understand the hatred being instilled in them, were becoming budding soldiers, indoctrinated by speeches of revenge. On the other side of the wall, Moussa saw the same thing. Boys and girls, almost babies, were becoming human weapons, ready to explode for a cause imposed on them, repeating slogans whose meaning they did not understand.

And yet, they both... they both understood. They knew that these children, like themselves, were innocent. That it wasn't their war. "How can we save them?" asked Moussa, his voice trembling under the weight of this overwhelming mission.

The guardian looked at them, and a gentle, melancholy smile lit up his ethereal face. "You must be strong. You must be an example of purity and courage. Your love is the key, but it will be sorely tested. People will try to separate you, to stifle your light, to make you doubt yourselves. But if you remain united, if you continue to protect the innocence that is within you, then you will also protect that of others."

Abigael felt a tear slide down her cheek. This prophecy, this future that was being drawn for them, terrified her as much as it galvanised her. She squeezed Moussa's hand tighter, feeling his warmth, his energy and his determination.

"We will be strong", she murmured, her voice rising like a prayer.

The Hourim of innocence

Moussa turned to her, his dark eyes shining with a gleam of steel and hope. "Yes," he said, his fingers closing gently but firmly around hers. "We will be."

And so, under the starry sky of Jerusalem, two children joined in a sacred pact, a promise of love and light, ready to face together the darkness of a world that seemed intent on destroying them, but which would perhaps eventually awaken to their light.

The days that followed were marked by an escalation of violence, a crescendo of despair and fury that seemed to consume all hope. Suicide attacks came closer and closer, striking at the very heart of the neighbourhoods, and Israeli reprisals struck with merciless precision. Hatred was taking root everywhere, seeping into people's minds like an insidious poison, and the families of Moussa and Abigael were also sinking deeper into fear and suspicion. Every discussion, every piece of news they heard, only fuelled the conviction that war was the only way out. But for Moussa and Abigael, this reality no longer made sense. Their love transcended the borders and battle lines their parents fought so hard to defend.

Their encounters, which had become rare and perilous, were now priceless treasures. Every moment spent together shone with a painful intensity, as if every second stolen from the surrounding horror was a spark of light in the deepest darkness. They knew that these moments were fleeting, fragile, but their love thrived in this precariousness, fuelled by danger and the desperate hope of something greater than themselves.

One evening, after an attack of unprecedented violence had ravaged the Moussa district, Abigael, her heart pounding with anxiety, ran towards the Dome of the Rock. Fear gnawed at

The Hourim of innocence

her. She didn't know if he would come. Every step she took seemed to echo with the crash of her worries. And yet, just as she was beginning to despair, she saw him, coming with long strides. His face was dark with fatigue and pain, but his eyes still shone with the determination that made Abigael's heart beat faster.

They rushed towards each other, and this time there was no hesitation or modesty. The world around them was crumbling, but their embrace was a bulwark against destruction. They held each other, fused in an embrace that transcended anything adults could imagine. The guardian watched them, his soft light caressing the remnants of their shattered childhood, like a silent angel watching over them.

But this light was powerless in the face of the hatred that grew on both sides. The tension between their families, fuelled by years of suffering and grief, soon reached a climax. Moussa and Abigael had tried to conceal their encounters, to keep their love a secret. But mistrust, that insidious enemy, had contaminated the air they breathed, and their families refused to believe that pure love could be born in such a blood-stained context.

July 2020. The sweltering summer heat only inflamed tempers, exacerbating anger, as if the sun itself were complicit in the violence. Poisonous rumours ran through the Moussa neighbourhood, arousing suspicion and turning every street into a potential trap. The Israeli soldiers were on the alert, and the reprisals came regularly, like hammer blows to an already fractured heart.

And that day, by a tragic quirk of fate, the families of Moussa and Abigael found themselves face to face. Was it cruel chance

The Hourim of innocence

or the invisible hand of fate playing with innocent lives? It was there, at the crossroads of their opposing worlds, that everything changed. Moussa and Abigael, hiding behind a wall, watched with bated breath, hoping that this face-to-face confrontation would pass without any casualties.

But they saw Abigael's father step forward, his eyes blazing with anger, and Moussa's father face him, his features twisted by a hatred that did not really belong to him, but that the years of war had imposed on him. The anxious mothers clung desperately to their husbands' arms, trying to pull them back, but the poison of discord had already spread to their hearts.

"What are you doing here, Palestinian?" spat Abigael's father, his fists clenched, his face flushed with a rage he could no longer control. "I could ask you the same question, invader!" retorted Moussa's father, his voice rumbling like a storm about to erupt.

The words, sharp as blades, flew through the heavy July air, turning into shouts and insults. Moussa knew his father. He had been a pious, dignified man, but the war had left indelible scars on his soul. The losses, the humiliations, the daily fear... all this had given rise to a hatred that he had never wanted. And now that hatred was bursting forth, spilled out before the horrified eyes of his son.

"You don't belong here!" shouted Abigael's father, his voice trembling with gut-wrenching rage. "This land is not yours!"

The mothers were almost crying, their fingers clutching their husbands' arms, but nothing could stop the oil slick. Israeli soldiers patrolling nearby perceived the scene as an imminent threat. They lunged, weapons raised, and in a flash threw Moussa's father to the ground. His fall sounded like a

The Hourim of innocence

thunderclap, and Moussa's heart seemed to shatter into a thousand pieces.

The cries of Moussa's mother mingled with the barking orders of the soldiers. The father's pious fists clenched in pain and despair, and the blows began to rain down. Each impact, each scream, each burst of anger was a dissonant note in the macabre symphony of war.

Moussa clutched Abigael's hand with desperate strength, terror freezing his limbs. "We've got to do something..." he whispered, his voice breaking with helplessness.

But what could they do, two children caught up in the turmoil of adulthood?

"Stop !" shouted Moussa, his voice torn by anguish, as he rushed out of his hiding place. "Stop, please!" But his cry, filled with a distress that transcends age, was swallowed up by the surrounding chaos, a cry lost among the all-too-familiar echoes of violence. The soldiers, indifferent to his call, continued their assault, like machines of oppression, implacable and insensitive, crushing all hope under the merciless sole of war. For them, it was just another scene in the long tragedy of this land.

It was then that a new threat emerged, a youthful shadow that walked with spectral slowness. A boy, barely older than Moussa, advanced, dressed in a much too large jacket that hung over his fragile body. His eyes were dead, as if they no longer contained the slightest spark of life. Abigael saw him and her heart contracted in fear. This was no ordinary child. In a flash of icy lucidity, she understood the terrible truth: the child was a suicide bomber.

The Hourim of innocence

"No..." she whispered, her throat tight with terror as she watched the boy approach her family, hiding a trembling hand under his jacket.

The boy carried a detonator, an instrument of death forged by adults who had stolen his innocence. Time slowed, each second stretching out like an agony, as Abigael saw the child's hand reach out, ready to press the fateful button. The moment was suspended, vibrating with unbearable tension, when a shot rang out, piercing the veil of frozen time.

A sniper's merciless shot mowed down Moussa's father, leaving him frozen forever in a tragic posture, sculpted by fate. His inert body became the silent witness to an injustice that only death could seal. Moussa's cry tore through the air, a heart-rending, visceral clamour that seemed to make the thousand-year-old stones of Jerusalem tremble, as if the city itself, weighed down by centuries of suffering, were shedding a silent tear for a life cut short too soon.

And then the child suicide bomber's detonator went off. A blind, brutal blast, a burst of light and destruction that threw Abigael's mother backwards. Her frail, helpless body hit the ground with unbearable violence, as if the world itself had rejected this tragedy.

Chaos descended with the fury of a storm. Cries of horror, the clash of weapons, the din of destruction... all blended together in a hellish cacophony. Moussa and Abigael, paralysed, witnessed the collapse of their worlds. One of their parents, their pillars, their protectors, had just been swept away by the madness that their childhood hearts had always feared.

And in this abyss of despair, a light burst forth, intense, brilliant. The guardian appeared, but this time his aura was not

The Hourim of innocence

gentle. It was a ferocious light, an almost divine force that enveloped the two children in an impenetrable shield. Bullets and splinters from the blast seemed to collide with this barrier of light, unable to penetrate the sanctuary that the light had erected around them. Time stood still, as if suspended over an unfathomable abyss.

Moussa, his face streaming with tears, turned to the guard, his dark eyes pleading for an answer to the incomprehensible. "Why?" he cried, his voice breaking into a sob. "Why couldn't you save them?"

The guard looked at him with infinite sadness, his luminous face radiating a melancholy sweetness. "I can't prevent everything, Moussa," he murmured, his voice sounding like an echo from another world. "But I'm here for you, to protect you, to guide you. Your light must survive."

Abigael, her throat constricted by pain, looked down at her mother's lifeless body. A solitary tear rolled down her cheek before crashing to the dusty floor. "Mum..." she whispered, her heart in tatters. "Why... ?"

The guardian knelt beside him, placing an intangible but luminous hand on his frail shoulder. "The world is full of darkness," he said, "but you are the light that must continue to shine. You must be strong, for your mission is greater than you realise."

Moussa collapsed to his knees beside Abigael, and in that moment of utter despair, he took her in his arms, seeking comfort in that painfully necessary embrace. Their bodies trembled, shattered by the horror they had just experienced, but together they formed a whole, an indestructible bond, a bastion of love in a world ravaged by hatred.

The Hourim of innocence

The guard's light continued to shine, forming a sanctuary around them. They didn't know how they would survive, how they would face the days ahead. But they knew that their love, though bruised and tested, remained their only strength, their only refuge.

The silence that followed was even more terrible than the explosion. It was an infinite void, an abyss of grief where even the cries of agony seemed to have died away. The dust fell gently, like a shroud, enveloping the ruins of their innocence. Moussa's father lay there, his blood seeping into the sacred earth, and Abigael's mother lay frozen in death. An unbearable absence, an irreparable rupture.

Moussa and Abigael were alone, two children facing the immensity of the tragedy. The war had torn away everything that was dear to them, but it could not break their love. In this desolate landscape, their hearts were still beating, carrying a light that even death could not extinguish.

And in this desperate union, a truth emerged: they were bound for eternity, and nothing, not even the tumult of war, could undo this sacred bond.

Losing a parent is like seeing a part of your soul ripped away, leaving behind a gaping wound that will never fully close. It's a loss that creates an abyss of absence, a deafening silence where memories become ghosts and the future a blurred, uncertain horizon. For Abigael and Moussa, this void was unfathomable, filled with a pain all the more unbearable because it was born of hatred, of war, of that relentless spiral of violence that engulfed everything in its path. They were still children, but their grief had already revealed to them the

The Hourim of innocence

implacable cruelty of life, the brutality of a world where even innocence was no longer a sanctuary.

Faced with this unbearable reality, they found themselves at a crossroads, a crossroads where so many children, in this age-old conflict, had had to make a choice: hate or love.

For many, the loss of a parent became a conflagration. Grief turned to rage, and that rage insidiously turned into a desire for revenge, a consuming fire that sought only to burn everything around it. This was how the war went on, how children became soldiers, how children became human bombs, sacrificing their childhoods on the altar of a justice they didn't even understand.

Abigael and Moussa understood, with chilling lucidity, how easy it would be to give in to this hatred. How simple it would be to allow themselves to be consumed by the poison that surrounded them, to embrace the anger that promised a fleeting relief. Their families, their peoples, everything seemed to be screaming at them to give in, to become instruments of this vengeance, to follow the path traced by generations of anger and suffering.

Abigael's father had often spoken of revenge as a sacred obligation. He believed that war was the only way to protect his family and his people, even if it meant losing oneself. For his part, Moussa's father believed that armed resistance was the only possible response, the only way to survive in a world where their existence was under constant threat. But today, one of their relatives lay dead, swept away by the same implacable logic he had defended. The war had consumed them.

The Hourim of innocence

Yet deep in the hearts of Abigael and Moussa, another truth was pulsating, a truth that their parents had never fully grasped. A fragile, but indestructible truth.

Moussa, his hands still trembling, sought out Abigael's, and their fingers found each other, clinging to each other like shipwrecked men trying to save themselves from the storm. This simple yet infinitely meaningful contact brought them back to what was essential : the love they shared, even in the midst of ruins.

"I don't want to..." Abigael whispered, her voice broken by the sobs that were choking her. "I don't want to become like them... even though it hurts so much." Her tears rolled down her dusty cheeks, tracing furrows of light in the gloom of this tragic moment.

Moussa nodded, too upset to speak, but sharing every word, every emotion. Hatred had never built anything. It had never repaired anything. It would only bring more destruction, more heartache. If they gave in to hatred, they would lose the only thing they had left: their love.

The guardian then appeared, luminous and protective, his benevolent aura enveloping the two children. His soft light illuminated the darkness that threatened them, a soothing balm on their invisible wounds. "Don't let hatred destroy you," her voice whispered, like a caress on the wind. "Your love is stronger than war, more powerful than death. You are the promise of a better world. You are hope."

Moussa squeezed Abigael's hand a little tighter, his dark eyes shining with a new determination. "We will not give in to hatred.

The Hourim of innocence

Abigael closed her eyes, letting the grief overwhelm her, but feeling deep inside her a renewed flame, a strength she had never suspected. "We will be the light," she promised, pure resolve seeping into every fibre of her being.

They remained on their knees, surrounded by the ruins of their lives, but united in this silent promise. Their grief, though devastating, would not bend them to hatred. They had chosen another path, a path where love would be their torch, even in the thickest darkness.

Grief is not just a cry of pain. It's a journey. An ordeal where pain can either become a seed of hatred or a source of compassion. Abigael and Moussa, despite their young age, understood this truth. Their love, fragile but unshakeable, was the only weapon they had to defy this world consumed by violence.

The next few days were a journey through darkness, a time when every moment seemed filled with grief. The funeral of Moussa's father took place under a relentless sun, crushing the cortege with its cruel light. The men walked in silence, reciting prayers in Arabic, verses from the Koran that floated in the burning air like age-old laments. Moussa walked on, his legs heavy, his thoughts lost. The words of the prayers escaped him, dissolved in the echo of his pain. Everything seemed unreal.

His father's body, wrapped in a white shroud, had descended into the earth. An arid earth, indifferent to his grief, which accepted the body of this man whose shadow had always watched over him. The men's hands threw the earth over the grave with respect, but for Moussa, it was as if each shovelful tore away a little more of his heart.

The Hourim of innocence

He stood there among the adults, their faces marked by grief and anger. There were whispers of revenge and promises of reprisals. The cycle of hatred fed on death, and in that moment, Moussa felt the futility of it all. His father was dead, and no revenge would bring him back. No war would heal this gaping wound.

He looked at the earth that now covered his father, and his soul, so young, felt crushed by a wisdom too heavy for his shoulders. He didn't want this war, this hatred. He just wanted peace, to feel his father's reassuring warmth again.

Grief, incomprehension, love... all mixed up inside him, but he knew one thing: he and Abigael held the promise of another path. A path where love would always be more powerful than hate.

And it was on this certainty, flickering but present, that he clung to avoid sinking.

The day of Abigael's mother's funeral arrived with painful clarity. The sun, a cruel witness to this tragedy, bathed the Israeli cemetery in a brilliant, almost blinding light, as if to remind us that life goes on despite the unbearable. The air seemed frozen, saturated with grief and silent pain. Muffled sobs echoed here and there, interspersed with prayers in Hebrew, ancient words whispered with a fervour tinged with despair, as if each syllable could alleviate the suffering.

The rabbi, draped in his sacred vestments, stood upright beside the tomb, the Book of Psalms open in his trembling hands. His voice echoed with gravity, chanting the verses that accompanied the soul of the deceased on her final journey. But for Abigael, it all seemed like a distant echo, a cruel melody that failed to reach the depths of her grief. Abigael's mother,

The Hourim of innocence

that tender, protective woman, now lay in a simple wooden coffin, so humble and yet so heavy with the weight of absence.

Every gesture, every word seemed shrouded in the unreality of a nightmare. How could she understand what death really was? How could she accept that her mother, who had cradled her, who had turned the darkest moments into havens of tenderness, was now imprisoned in this lifeless box, ready to be swallowed up by the earth ? It all seemed so brutal, so meaningless. The world as she knew it seemed to have disintegrated in an instant.

The murmurs of her family rose up around her, vibrating with pain but also with a dull anger. There was talk of revenge, of reprisals, of the need to defend their land and their honour. Voices hardened, fists clenched and eyes filled with a rage that generations of suffering had etched into their flesh. But Abigael heard none of it. The hatred they were trying to plant inside her slid down like rain on a stone. All she felt was an immense emptiness, an abyss that nothing could fill, except perhaps the unfailing love she bore for Moussa, the love that remained her only anchor in a world that seemed to be sinking into madness.

As her mother's coffin was lowered into the earth, Abigael felt her heart break, each fragment scattering in the wind. The sobs around her redoubled, and yet, in the midst of this tide of grief, something new emerged in her soul. It wasn't hatred, no. It was strength, a steely resolve, a silent promise that her mother's death would not be the beginning of a spiral of revenge. With every shovelful of earth that covered the coffin, a desire for peace was born in her, a conviction that violence should no longer have the last word.

The Hourim of innocence

On the other hand, in a modest neighbourhood of East Jerusalem, Moussa was mourning the death of his father. Two funerals, two worlds that seemed irreconcilable, and yet the same grief. Their traditions separated them, as did their families, their beliefs and their customs. But in the depths of their grief, Abigael and Moussa shared a unique bond, a common wound that transcended all divisions. Their loss, though rooted in different realities, brought them together with an overwhelming intensity.

Their hearts knew a truth that adults could not understand. Where other children, poisoned by rage, would have given in to the call of vengeance, Moussa and Abigael had only love to guide them. They understood, despite their youth, that hatred would not repair anything, that it would only add layers of pain to a history that was already too heavy.

The guardian appeared, intangible but present, a benevolent glow that only they could perceive. He stood beside them, protective, wrapping their broken hearts in a warmth that seemed to defy the harshness of this world. "Don't let hatred destroy you," he whispered, his voice echoing in their minds, soft and full of wisdom. "You are stronger than that. You are the bearers of a love that can illuminate the darkness."

Moussa, his tears mingling with the dust, felt the comforting presence of the guardian beside him. Abigael, kneeling beside her mother's grave, felt that gentle voice whispering to her tattered soul. "You are stronger."

They did not yet understand the full significance of this mission, but they knew that their love was their only strength, their only hope in this fractured world. They silently promised

The Hourim of innocence

each other never to give in to hatred, never to let their pain be an instrument of destruction.

And so two wounded souls, separated by a few hundred metres but united by an unshakeable love, rose from their grief. The guardian, invisible to adult eyes, watched over them, aware of the immense weight they carried, but also of the light they brought. Moussa and Abigael were to become much more than children broken by war. They were the promise of a different future, the light that would defy the darkness.

Their love had become their shield, a light in the darkness that would never cease to shine, even in the darkest of times. And it was with this conviction that, despite pain and loss, they walked towards a destiny they would have to face together, but always armed with this eternal truth: love, however fragile, was the most powerful force of all.

The sky over Jerusalem, heavy and dense with clouds, seemed that day to weep with those who were mourning their dead. The sweltering heat suffocated hearts already weighed down by grief, making the air almost unbreathable, as if the city itself were weighed down by the burden of lives cut short by war. Two funerals, two worlds so different yet united in the same tragedy.

Moussa, standing in front of his father's gaping grave, could not contain the pain that was rumbling inside him. Up until that moment, he had tried to maintain the dignity expected of him, to remain stoic despite the horror of his loss. But to see the earth swallow up the father he had loved so much, the father who had been his model, his strength, his refuge, was too much. A raw, ancestral pain, that of thousands of children before him, tore at his soul.

The Hourim of innocence

The cry escaped from his chest with the force of a storm, a cry that transcended the simple lamentations of a child. It was a cry that carried with it all the pain and injustice of war, all the absurdity of lives lost for no reason. The procession came to a halt, petrified by the power of the scream. The suras, which until then had been whispered in a solemn chorus, vanished into the suffocating air.

- Baba !" he shouted, his knees hitting the parched earth hard. "Why? Why?"

This cry, this incandescent despair, shook the atmosphere. It rose, ripping through the sky, echoing like the explosions that had ravaged their daily lives. It left no room for indifference; it was a heart-rending reminder of innocence destroyed, a cry so loud that it seemed capable of waking the dead, of bringing them back to repair what had been broken.

The men around him froze, their own suffering muffled by this cry, so pure and so savage. But this cry, unbearable as it was, was not simply a cry of despair: it was a cry of revolt, a refusal to accept injustice. It was a cry that lifted some of the crushing weight from Moussa's still frail shoulders.

On the other side of Jerusalem, Abigael stared at her mother's coffin. She was paralysed, her legs stiff, her hands trembling, frozen despite the suffocating heat. Her whole world was disintegrating, the contours of reality becoming blurred and elusive. How could she accept the death of the woman who had cradled and protected her, who had been the source of her tenderness and unconditional love ?

And suddenly, like an echo from afar, she heard Moussa's cry. It seemed to strike directly at her heart, awakening a grief so immense it could no longer be contained. Abigael's cry rose in

The Hourim of innocence

its turn, tearing through the silence of the cemetery with an intensity that broke the hearts of all who heard it.

- Imaaaaaaaaan!" she screamed, her call ripping through the air like a dagger, imploring her mother once again to come back and undo this nightmare. This cry, charged with infinite love and distress, shook the stones of the tombs, as if even the dead could be moved by this innocent pain.

And then a strange phenomenon occurred. The sky, which seemed ready to burst with sadness, opened slightly, letting in a ray of soft, golden light. The sweltering heat eased and a gentle breeze caressed the tear-soaked faces. At that moment, though separated by miles, Moussa and Abigael were united by something much stronger than war: a bond that transcended pain, a love that could never be broken.

Their cries were not cries of hatred; they were cries of love, cries of rebellion against the cruelty of war. The guardian, that invisible protector, stood beside them. His light, usually soft, had become bright, an invisible but palpable shield, a bulwark against the spiral of hatred.

The adults around them, blinded by their suffering, talked of reprisals and revenge. But for Moussa and Abigael, there was another way. A difficult, almost impossible path, but the only one that could honour the memory of their parents. A path where love became the answer to war.

Moussa, his hands still trembling, murmured, his voice broken by grief: "I won't let them take me away in their hatred... I won't become like them. And in that same breath, at the other end of town, Abigael, her eyes raised to the sky, thought with a new resolve: "Mum, I promise... I won't become like them."

The Hourim of innocence

In the midst of the ruins of their lives, a promise was born. A silent promise, but stronger than the crash of the bombs. The guardian, who witnessed this oath, knew that these children carried within them a strength capable of changing their world. Their love, though fragile, was their armour, a shield of light in a darkness that seemed infinite.

The pain and grief would never go away, but their love had found a way, a meaning. A promise never to give in to hatred, to become bearers of light, even in the darkest moments. And so, two children, united in their loss, chose love. A love that defied war. A love that would never be defeated.

The prayers and tears of the adults continued to rise to the heavens, but on that day, a greater truth had been born: love, even in the midst of the worst tragedies, remained the only truly invincible weapon.

But this tragedy had not only plunged two families into mourning; it had also taken away a third, that of this young child, turned into a living weapon by unworthy hands. This child, a frail figure wrapped in a belt of explosives, had sacrificed his life for a cause he did not understand, an ideal he could only perceive through the poisoned words of those who had manipulated him. He had been promised a heavenly paradise, a place of honour at the right hand of the Creator. But how could such a young mind, still pure and malleable, grasp the significance of his actions, the weight of the lives he was about to take, including his own ?

How, indeed, could humanity turn against itself with such brutality, annihilating what was most precious to it: the innocence of a child? This little being, barely out of childhood, had been torn from his world to become an instrument of

The Hourim of innocence

death. His executioners, for that is what they must be called, had robbed him of his future by burdening him with false promises, by depriving him of the light he still carried deep inside him.

Can we then judge him ? Can we, in the same breath, condemn him while at the same time absolving him? For while it is undeniable that his act was abominable, unforgivable in its consequences, who can say that this child was truly guilty? The real guilt lies on the shoulders of those who stripped him of his humanity, those who, with insidious cowardice, tied the belt of death around his waist. They are the real architects of this tragedy, the ones who planted the poison of ideology in his mind, clouding his reason to the point where he could no longer distinguish between right and wrong.

And yet this child, despite the monstrosity of his act, also paid the ultimate price. He left this world in an explosion as brutal as it was unjust, a crash of fire and debris that left behind only the deafening silence of absence. An innocent life was snuffed out, torn from what it should have been : a life of hope, laughter and dreams.

In the house he left behind, mourning had set in. Perhaps his parents had mourned his loss, collapsing under the unbearable weight of love and guilt. Or perhaps, on the contrary, they had found in this sacrifice a distorted form of pride, glorifying what they perceived as an act of bravery. But whatever the answer, it doesn't matter whether the family mourned the child or elevated his memory to the status of martyrdom: in the end, all that remains is a child gone, a life shattered, a future swept away.

The Hourim of innocence

Mourning, that merciless shadow, would also cover the roof of the house he lived in. The walls, silent witnesses to his former laughter, would now bear the echo of his absence. Every room would become the shrine of a memory, every familiar object a relic of a stolen life. Grief would permeate the place like a persistent mist, flooding every corner with a dull, unspeakable sadness.

This triple tragedy is a shattered mirror of humanity: on the one hand, the direct victims, reduced to dust by blind violence; on the other, this child, a collateral victim of hatred, sacrificed on the altar of adult folly. And behind him, a family who, whether they wanted to or not, now had to come to terms with the loss, shame or glorification of what he had become.

Perhaps, in a secluded corner of this house, a mother would sit, her hands clutching a worn child's garment, still breathing in the familiar scent of the one she had carried and cherished. Perhaps a father, unable to find the words to soothe his own pain, would walk in silence, his eyes empty, haunted by the spectre of the son he had failed to protect. Or perhaps their nights, filled with nightmares, would be haunted by the face of their child, torn between the innocence of a little boy and the disturbing image of a martyr made by others.

And so, in this house, as in those of Moussa and Abigael, the tragedy would continue to unfold, invisible but omnipresent. Three families, three bereavements, linked by the same cruel thread of war and manipulation. The Guardian, a silent observer, knew that this weight, the weight of lost souls, could never be carried by children alone. Yet he hoped that in them, despite the horror, despite the pain, there would remain a spark capable of illuminating the darkness, a light that even death could never extinguish.

The Hourim of innocence

CHAPTER II
DAWN AFTER THE STORM

« IT IS IN THE HEART OF DARKNESS THAT THE GREATEST LIGHTS ARE BORN, FOR IT IS THE SOULS THAT REFUSE HATRED THAT FIND THE PATH TO THE DAWN. »

Mourning, that elusive and implacable shadow, had stretched its dark cloak around them, extinguishing the light of the world. The days following the funeral became a dense grey mist, enveloping Jerusalem in a melancholy languor.

The Hourim of innocence

For Moussa and Abigael, the universe seemed to have frozen in eternal agony, the sky itself refusing to shine, as if the sun, witnessing their suffering, had turned its gaze away.

Every street corner, every stone, seemed to exude the acrid smell of death and violence. Yet within them, something was awakening, a faint but indomitable flame that persisted despite the brutal winds of war. The pain of their loss was immense, a bottomless pit, but it was also the breeding ground for a new, mysterious strength that germinated in their young hearts.

For the first few weeks after the funeral, Moussa and Abigael were separated by a web of hatred woven by adult hands. Moussa's community, ulcerated by the unjust death of his father at the hands of Israeli bullets, erected invisible but impenetrable walls. His uncles and cousins watched his every move, their gazes heavy with mistrust and anger. For them, to see Abigael again would have been a betrayal, an affront to the memory of the man they mourned.

On the other hand, Abigael's father had closed himself off in a fortress of grief and resentment. The loss of his wife had dug an abyss of bitterness in him, and he couldn't bear to hear the name Moussa. For him, this Palestinian boy had become a symbol of the enemy, a living reminder of all that the war had taken away from him. He spoke incessantly of protection, security, and an absolute distrust of those who did not share their faith and blood.

But despite this imposed separation, despite the barriers erected around them, Moussa and Abigael continued to search for each other in the silence of the night. Every evening, Moussa climbed up onto the roof of his house, his eyes riveted to the stars, hoping that Abigael was doing the same,

The Hourim of innocence

somewhere. And every night, Abigael, wrapped up in her sadness, stood by his window, her heart turned towards him, murmuring prayers of hope that only the wind could carry away.

A month passed, slowly, painfully. The void left by their respective parents had not been filled, but in this emptiness, a fragile hope was beginning to take root. One morning, driven by an impulse she didn't yet understand, Abigael decided to defy her father's ban. She knew where to find Moussa : there, under the ancient olive tree not far from the Dome of the Rock, that sacred place where time seemed to stand still.

At dawn, draped in a shawl that hid her face, Abigael left her house in silence. The streets of Jerusalem were still asleep, with only a few voices murmuring morning prayers, and the air carried the gentle coolness of the fading night. Her footsteps echoed on the cobblestones, and her heart beat so fast that for a moment she thought her secret would be betrayed by that inner drum.

When she reached the olive tree, Moussa was already sitting there, looking lost in thoughts she could only imagine. He saw her before she even noticed him. When she finally looked up, she stood still, surprised by the presence she had so hoped for and feared she would not find. They remained silent for a long time. Words seemed superfluous, their pain linking them in a silent symphony that only their hearts could hear.

- I didn't think you'd come," Moussa murmured, his voice marked by restrained emotion, almost broken.

Abigael approached him, her steps hesitant but determined.

The Hourim of innocence

- I had to see you," she replied, each word carrying an undeniable truth.

They stood face to face, their hands brushing against each other, hesitant to unite, as if this simple contact could anchor them in a reality they no longer understood. And finally, their fingers intertwined, a gesture so simple yet so full of promise, an anchor in the storm that surrounded them.

- I don't understand why all this has happened," says Abigael, her voice fragile but filled with a new determination. "But I do know that we are not like them. We mustn't become like them."

Moussa squeezed his hand a little tighter.

- "My father believed in war," he said, his eyes looking into Abigael's. "But I don't want to follow that path. "But I don't want to go down that road. I don't want hate to consume me, as it has consumed so many lives."

At that moment, their bond became indestructible. They knew they had chosen a different path, a dangerous but necessary path, where their love would be the only light capable of piercing the darkness.

Suddenly, a soft glow lit up the branches of the olive tree, like a breath of hope. The guardian appeared, the mystical presence that had accompanied them from the beginning. This time, he was more tangible, more real, his soft, comforting light illuminating their suffering-scarred faces.

- You have chosen the most difficult path," he says in a voice imbued with infinite tenderness, "but it is also the one that will bring peace. Not just for you, but for all those who follow you.

The Hourim of innocence

Moussa and Abigael stood transfixed, fascinated by this benevolent apparition. The guardian was no longer a mere ethereal presence; he was their guide, their protector, the bearer of a promise greater than themselves.

- You hold within you the key to saving the innocence of the children whom war seeks to destroy," he continued. "Your love is your strength, but be prepared: hatred and vengeance will try to tear you apart.

- How ?" asked Abigael, tears welling up in her eyes. "How can we protect others, when we are so fragile ?"

The guard gave them a gentle smile, full of wisdom.

- You will learn. Every day you will grow, and every day your love will grow stronger. But first, you must heal your own hearts. Your pain can become your greatest light, if you accept it."

Musa, with a resolution he did not think he possessed, replied:

- We will do it. We will protect innocence, and we will not let war rob us of what we have left."

The guardian watched them for a moment, then his light slowly faded, leaving behind a breath of hope, an invisible but palpable blessing.

Their meeting at the foot of this olive tree not far from the Dome of the Rock was only the beginning of a path strewn with invisible traps. Fate seemed determined to test their love, to measure the strength of their hearts against the weight of tradition, ancestral hatred and the war that never stopped roaring around them. Yet every clandestine meeting, every secret embrace, made them stronger and more resolute. Their

The Hourim of innocence

love, fragile and incandescent, was their only bulwark against the darkness that was devouring their world.

They met with the fervour of those who know that their time is short. Every conversation, every smile shared was a victory against war, a declaration of hope in a world where hope had become a luxury. Together, they dreamt of what their future could have been : a world where children could grow up without fear, without the sound of bombs, a world where the only war they knew would be one of laughter and play.

But reality kept coming back to them, uncompromising. Moussa and Abigael's families were like two fortresses set up against each other, defending irreconcilable griefs, ready to do anything to protect their memories, even if it meant destroying their children's future. Every step they took towards each other was a challenge to the invisible but merciless laws of their communities.

One day, Moussa returned home after one of these precious encounters. He could still feel the warmth of Abigael's smile and the tenderness in her eyes. But his happiness was suddenly met with the cold anger of his uncle, who was waiting for him in the shadows of the family courtyard. His arms folded, his face taut with a hatred he nourished like a sacred fire, he watched her with his dark eyes, two embers of resentment.

- "You think you can sully the honour of our family," he hissed, his voice sharp as a blade, "by getting close to those responsible for your father's death?"

Moussa felt his heart clench, but he didn't lower his head. He had learnt, since the loss of his father, that he should not be ashamed. What he felt for Abigael was greater and nobler than

The Hourim of innocence

the sterile hatred that had already taken so many lives. He stared at his uncle, his voice soft but resolute.

- "It's not her," he replied, his words slow, heavy with a truth his uncle refused to see. "It wasn't them. It was the war that killed my father, not Abigael."

His uncle stared at him, as if he were looking at a stranger. For a moment, there was silence, and in that moment, an imperceptible but real doubt seemed to flicker in the man's eyes. But this doubt was quickly banished, swept away by years of hatred and suffering.

- You're young," he murmured bitterly. "One day you'll understand.

But Moussa already knew. He understood much more than his uncle suspected. Hatred was a poison, a vicious circle that had only ever brought death. And he refused to submit to it.

On the other side, Abigael was living a similar reality. Her father, shattered by the death of his wife, had shut himself away in a shell of anger. The world now seemed divided into black and white, friends and enemies, and his heart had hardened, unable to forgive. The mere idea that his daughter could love a Palestinian boy was heresy, a betrayal he would never tolerate.

But despite the prohibitions, despite the accusing glances and threats, Abigael and Moussa continued to find each other. Their love was like a seed sown in a field of ruins, but it grew against all odds, defying the arid soil of war.

Then one day, as fate, or the cruelty of chance, would have it, Moussa's mother and Abigael's father came face to face. It was at the market, a place vibrant with life and tension, where the

The Hourim of innocence

smells of ripe fruit and spices mingled with those of dust and sweat, where the voices of the merchants competed with the wary whispers. It was a fragile space, a precarious balance where Palestinians and Israelis crossed paths, rarely without ulterior motives.

Moussa's mother walked along, her face covered by a black veil, her eyes reddened by grief. She had come here to buy vegetables, to feed her child despite the pain that was eating away at her. As for Abigael's father, he was standing by a stall, clenching his fists as if to contain a rage he had been carrying for weeks. He had never stopped thinking about his wife, about the justice he believed he deserved. Their eyes met, a silent shock, a collision of irreconcilable universes. In the eyes of Moussa's mother, unfathomable sorrow. In Abigael's father's eyes, an anger just waiting to flare up. There was a violence between them that needed no words, a violence fuelled by blood, by loss, by everything the war had destroyed.

The market, so noisy a moment earlier, seemed to hold its breath. Those around them froze, sensing that something terrible might happen. The old hatreds were barely dormant, ready to reawaken and spread like wildfire through the already tense crowd.

The market, which had been buzzing with activity just moments before, had frozen in an unbearable tension, as if the world itself had held its breath. Abigael's father, his features distorted by abysmal pain and indomitable anger, advanced towards Moussa's mother, his gaze blazing with resentment. His fists clenched, and when he spoke, his voice burst with a violence that shook the air, like a war cry or a hurricane of despair.

The Hourim of innocence

"You tore my wife away from me," he thundered, every syllable laden with rancour and desolation. "It's all your fault! You and your kind are the executioners of our lives! This war, this chaos, it's all because of you, your existence defiling our land !"

Moussa's mother, worn down by years of fear and deprivation, nevertheless felt a spark of dignity and courage ignite within her. She sat up straight, her face ravaged by pain, but her eyes shone with unshakeable resolve. Despite everything, her voice did not waver.

"It wasn't me, or even my people, who turned this land into a graveyard," she retorted, her tone icy, her pain transmuted into stoic strength. "We all bleed, but you refuse to see it, preferring to accuse and hate.

Her words, with their raw truth, struck like sharp blades. But Abigael's father, blinded by grief, did not see in her another soul shattered by war. All he saw was the embodiment of his suffering, a catalyst for the rage that bubbled up like a volcano ready to erupt.

The onlookers, sensing the approaching storm, began to stand still, their faces tense. Every glance was a warning, every breath seemed to carry the threat of an imminent explosion. The murmurs died away, and the entire market was suspended in a precarious balance between calm and eruption.

"You'll never understand!" roared Abigael's father, his voice vibrating with despair, a flood of pent-up emotion. "You are the source of our misery! You destroy everything we love !"

All he could think about and see was his pain, the pain that had eaten him to the core. His heart was a field of ruins, and

The Hourim of innocence

in that moment of total bewilderment, he let himself be carried away by the devastating wave of his own despair. Without thinking, his fingers grasped the handle of a knife hidden under his jacket. The gesture was swift, blind, fuelled by an anger so pure it seemed to obliterate all reason. In a moment of heart-rending madness, he plunged the blade into the body of Moussa's mother.

The market fell into an abyss of stupor. There was a deathly silence, as if the universe had lost its voice. Then the muffled scream of Moussa's mother split the air before she collapsed, blood gushing from her wound, a crimson pool widening beneath her.

This was the signal for irreversible chaos. The cries erupted like thunder, and the entire square was transformed into a whirlwind of confusion, horror and fury. Men rushed in, Palestinians and Israelis clashing in an outpouring of violence. The market was nothing more than a battlefield, where hatred and fear mingled in a macabre dance.

Moussa, alerted by the commotion, ran over, his heart beating wildly. When he saw his mother lying there, blood staining the ground red, his world shattered into pieces. The pain paralysed him, he gasped for breath, and his scream rang out, a heart-rending howl of despair.

"Ummi!" he shouted, rushing towards her, but arms grabbed him, pulling him back. He struggled and struggled, but the men held him firmly, unable to understand his agony.

Meanwhile, members of Moussa's family, alerted by the fear that was spreading, rushed to the scene. One of his uncles, seeing the body of his sister bathed in her own blood, was overcome with implacable fury. His eyes fell on Abigael's

The Hourim of innocence

father, who was still holding the knife, trembling with shock. This man, devastated by his own irreparable act, no longer even seemed aware of what he had done.

But Moussa's uncle saw only a murderer, an enemy to be slaughtered. He pulled out a gun hidden under his jacket, his hands clenched in irrepressible rage. "You'll pay for this!" he shouted before pulling the trigger.

The shot rang out and Abigael's father fell, struck down instantly. The detonation drowned out the screams, and panic turned to sheer terror. The market, a place of meetings and commerce, had been transformed into a theatre of death.

Moussa, tears rolling down his cheeks, was unable to comprehend what had just happened. His mother, his last refuge, had just been torn from him by a senseless act of hatred. Everything he had known, everything he loved, was crumbling before his eyes.

The market, once vibrant with diversity and exchange, had been transformed into a theatre of desolation. Abigael, who had followed her father to the fateful spot, arrived moments after his sudden collapse. When she saw her father's inert body, bathed in a pool of dark, sticky blood, the world around her seemed to shift, spinning out of control like a dream turned nightmare. Her whole world collapsed in a split second. Her breath caught in her throat and a violent nausea rose up inside her.

This man, her father, this once strong and protective man whom the war had so weakened and perverted, now lay lifeless. Abigael's frail shoulders shook and her already fractured heart broke even more. How could the world be so merciless, so fierce?

The Hourim of innocence

The two children, separated by a tide of furious bodies, were unable to comprehend the magnitude of what had just happened. Their eyes met through the senseless chaos, and in that silent bond, they shared the same terror, the same abysmal grief. They were now orphans, stripped of their bearings, and the war had left its indelible mark on them. This cruel conflict had stolen their most precious possession and forced them to contemplate the horror of a broken humanity. But even in the face of this immense pain, a deeper truth emerged, a silent promise that bound them together: they would not give in to hatred.

In the midst of this storm of despair, a soft light appeared. The guardian, ethereal and resplendent, materialised in a luminous glow, his usually serene face imbued with infinite sadness. Yet his presence was imbued with an unshakeable strength and conviction.

"The war took what it could," he murmured, his voice resonating with calm authority and disarming tenderness. "But it will not take from you what is most precious. You are the light that will endure. You carry the hope that even darkness cannot extinguish."

Moussa and Abigael, their faces bathed in tears, looked up at him. The pain was mixed with a strange sensation of warmth, as if the guardian were breathing a little of his strength into them. Their hands instinctively sought each other's touch. They reached out, despite the surrounding violence, and took each other's hands, this simple gesture becoming an act of defiance in the face of destruction, a silent affirmation that love could still survive.

The Hourim of innocence

All around them, the market had become a battlefield. Screams ripped through the air and men fought, blinded by hatred and the desire for revenge. But for Moussa and Abigael, the outside world faded away. Their hearts beating in unison, they supported each other, their love becoming their only truth in this maelstrom of madness.

The days following the tragedy were plunged into a dense darkness, an endless abyss. Every morning was a cruel reminder of what they had lost, and Abigael's house seemed like a mausoleum, imbued with a palpable absence. The pain was omnipresent, manifesting itself in every corner, like a spectre that refused to leave.

For Moussa, the shadows of loss were just as oppressive. Every corner of his home reminded him of his mother, her gentle voice, her laughter, her warmth. All that had been erased in an instant, reduced to a memory, and the emptiness seemed to want to swallow him up. But despite the sadness that gripped them, an indomitable strength, born of pain itself, began to blossom inside them. A resilience, a promise : they would not let this war destroy them.

One morning, under a sky covered in threatening clouds, Abigael was woken by a conversation she would have preferred never to hear. Her uncle, a man with an icy stare and words as sharp as blades, was talking to her grandfather. The old man, weak with grief, listened in silence, his eyes clouded with exhaustion.

"He can't look after you any more," declared his uncle, his voice devoid of all gentleness and betraying an inflexible firmness. "Your grandfather is too old, too weak. It's up to me

The Hourim of innocence

to protect you, and I won't let your father's mistakes be repeated."

Abigael's heart sank. She understood what those words meant: she was going to be taken away, torn from what she knew, sent to a place where love would have no place. A training camp, a centre where children were turned into ruthless soldiers, indoctrinated to serve a cause she didn't want to defend. A place where innocence was erased and replaced by implacable coldness, a place where she risked losing the last spark of light inside her.

Moussa, now under the implacable rule of his uncle Samir, found himself drawn into a world where hatred reigned supreme, insinuating itself like a poison into hearts that were still young. Samir, a man with eyes as sharp as daggers, carried the war in his gut, making it his raison d'être. He had taken Moussa under his wing, not out of affection, but out of duty, out of a kind of devotion perverted by the idea of revenge. He promised him strength and power, telling him again and again that he had to avenge the death of his parents, to erase every trace of weakness in him. But what Moussa saw in his uncle's eyes was a never-ending rage, a pain transformed into a will to destroy that he struggled to understand.

At his side was Lina, a young girl scarred by the war, who had been assigned to observe him, mentor him and toughen him up. Lina had a piercing gaze, filled with painful wisdom, and she seemed to understand Moussa's anger better than anyone. But instead of appeasing him, she encouraged him to embrace her. "Release your rage," she whispered, in a voice that was almost hypnotic. "It's your strength. Don't let anyone convince you otherwise. But Moussa resisted. He felt a strength within him that contradicted what she was saying.

The Hourim of innocence

Every time Lina got a little too close to his thoughts, every time she tried to feed his hatred, he felt the Guardian's benevolent presence, like an invisible bulwark protecting him, reminding him that hatred was not the way to go.

On the other side, Abigael was under the same pressures. She too was surrounded by a brutal force, personified by a boy called Eytan. Although still in his teens, he carried a cold, implacable rage within him. His eyes, once vivid, had become abysses of despair and hardness, scarred by the loss of his own family. He had learned to turn off his emotions, to bury them under a mask of indifference, and he saw in Abigael a danger, a weakness to be rooted out. Every day, he tried to break her, to plunge her into the same darkness that consumed him. "You're not ready," he kept telling her in a chilling voice. "You're too weak to avenge your parents. You don't understand what it means to be strong."

But Abigael, though young, carried within her a rare strength. Despite the pain that weighed heavily on her heart, she refused to give in. She saw Eytan for what he really was: a broken child, a victim, just like herself, forced to give up her compassion. And every time she felt hatred lurking, ready to engulf her, she remembered the love she shared with Moussa, the love that illuminated even the darkest corners of her soul. This love, she felt, was a light more powerful than all the darkness.

Weeks went by, and despite the separation, Moussa and Abigael never stopped thinking about each other. They felt each other's presence like a distant but constant star. Their thoughts of each other, secret and brief, were a balm on their wounds, moments stolen from the war that reminded them they were not alone. The Guardian, now a protective and

The Hourim of innocence

tangible figure for them, continued to appear to them, bearing words that became their guide.

One evening, as Moussa lay on the narrow bed in his room, his eyes blank, the Guardian emerged from the darkness. His light was not harsh, but it bathed the room in a warmth that seemed to banish the chill of war. He appeared majestic in his golden aura, then approached Moussa, his voice like a whisper of the wind blowing through the valleys of history.

"The path will be strewn with thorns, Moussa," he says, a gentle gravity in his words. "But remember: even the darkest night has stars. All you have to do is look for them. A new determination awoke in Moussa. He knew that Lina was not his enemy. She was just another lost soul, manipulated and moulded by the hands of broken adults. He realised that his mission was not just to protect himself from hatred, but also to save those who, like Lina, were on the verge of sinking.

Abigael, for her part, was still dealing with Eytan's provocations. But one day, as he tried to humiliate her, to belittle her once again, Abigael saw a tear slip stealthily down her cheek. Eytan looked away, but she had seen. Beneath his shell of hatred and hardness, he was just a child in mourning, a child who had never had the chance to heal. Abigael, guided by her love for Moussa, felt her compassion intensify. She would not let him fall into the abyss. She vowed to be a light, even for those who refused to see.

This love, this love that she shared with Moussa, became their most powerful weapon, a shield of hope and light. Even when they were separated, they felt that this force united them. It protected them, guided them, reminding them that, despite everything, their mission was greater than their own survival.

The Hourim of innocence

They had to protect innocence. They had to show another way, a way where love triumphed over war.

And as they prepared to face new challenges, Moussa and Abigael knew that their love, fragile as it may seem, was their greatest strength, the promise that war could not destroy everything.

The mission that the Guardian had entrusted to them, that crushing yet hopeful burden, now inhabited every thought of Abigael and Moussa. Their love had survived so many trials, but the truths they had just discovered shook the very foundations of their existence. The years that had passed had done nothing to erase their pain, but they had forged in them a resilience, a desire to understand what lay behind the lies woven by those who manipulated their destiny.

The Guardian of the Dome, their shining ally, sometimes floated around them, invisible to others but deeply rooted in their consciousness. He was a beacon, a voice that pierced the darkness and showed them a different path, away from violence and vengeance. But even he could not entirely dispel the veil of lies that surrounded the world. Abigael and Moussa knew that the struggle would be a long one, that the path would be strewn with betrayal and pretense.

The weight of the revelations haunted them, reverberating like heart-rending echoes in their souls. Abigael remembered her uncle's words, describing children with icy cynicism as mere 'pawns' in a game of chess that was beyond human comprehension. The shock of this revelation had shattered Eytan's certainties, and his mask of insensitivity seemed to be cracking by the day. For the first time, Abigael saw something other than hardness in his eyes. She saw a glimmer of

The Hourim of innocence

humanity, an awareness, a vulnerability that he tried to hide, but which betrayed the suffering of the child he had been before being shaped by hatred.

Moussa, for his part, could not forget what he had heard from his uncle Samir. The whole plan, this sinister machination that exploited the hatred and blood of innocents to fuel an eternal war, made him nauseous. He now understood why Samir always seemed so inflexible, so insensitive to the suffering around him. Samir was just a cog in a larger machine, a man consumed by delusions of grandeur, prepared to sacrifice everything, even the innocence of his own nephew, to achieve goals that had nothing to do with justice or peace.

These truths transformed Abigael and Moussa into something new, something wiser, something more determined. Their hearts still mourned the loss of their parents, but this pain became a driving force, an energy that fuelled their determination to put an end to this infernal cycle. They understood that their mission was no longer simply to protect innocence, but to reveal hidden truths, to break the chains of manipulation that shackled their people.

The night after these discoveries, Abigael once again found herself in her room, her thoughts whirling like a hurricane. Eytan was strangely silent that night, as if meditating on what they had heard together. The weight of the world rested on their shoulders, but Abigael turned to the window, looking for the star that always reminded her of Moussa. She could feel that he was thinking of her, that he too was fighting against the darkness.

The Hourim of innocence

The Guardian suddenly appeared, his soft golden light bathing Abigael's room in a comforting warmth. He seemed more solemn than ever, as if he too felt the urgency of the situation.

- "You've seen the threads of conspiracy, but don't let despair consume you," he murmured, his voice caressing the recesses of her mind like an ancient melody. "You are not alone. There are other children, other lost souls you can save, and together you will tip the balance."

Abigael felt overwhelmed by a fragile but real hope. The Guardian had never seemed so human, so involved. She realised that, despite his ethereal nature, he too wanted their victory and their light. A shiver ran through her body, a mixture of fear and elation. Their mission was no longer just a child's dream, it was a real battle, a battle against an insidious force that wanted to rob them of their future.

On the other side of Jerusalem, Musa woke with a start, his breath coming in short gasps. The Guardian was standing beside him, his luminous eyes filled with infinite compassion.

- "War will try to break you," he said, his voice like a breath in the night. "But your love is stronger than the mightiest of demons. You must keep believing, keep loving, even when all seems lost. For it is your love that will change the world."

And so, with a will that not even the years of war had been able to break, Abigael and Moussa stood up, ready to face a destiny that still had terrible trials in store for them, but determined to let their light shine, for themselves, for their children, for the future.

The weight of this revelation was overwhelming for these young souls, still searching for innocence but already shaped

The Hourim of innocence

by pain. The love that united Abigael and Moussa gave them an unsuspected strength, giving them the courage to rise up against the omnipresent darkness that surrounded them on all sides. This unbreakable bond, brighter than the hatred that surrounded them, prevented them from sinking into the abyss of vengeance. They understood that their mission transcended simple notions of survival and personal redemption; they were the guardians of a truth, the bearers of a hope that had to break the endless chain of deception and manipulation, where children were immolated on the altar of hidden ambitions. The workings of the global conspiracy were gradually being revealed to their now awakened minds. They realised, with frightening lucidity, that wars between nations, religious hatreds and ancestral divisions were only pieces of a monstrous chessboard. The leaders of the world's peoples, be they Palestinians, Israelis or others, were nothing more than puppets orchestrating a macabre ballet to satisfy the designs of entities hidden in the shadows, manipulating humanity through fear and chaos.

Every day reinforced this bitter awareness. Moussa looked at Lina with new eyes, understanding that she was not his enemy, but a victim like him, chained to the same lies. Similarly, Abigael was uncovering the fragile chinks in Eytan's emotional armour, recognising that beneath his mask of hostility, he was just a child broken by loss, shaped by trauma and indoctrination.

They knew they had to feign obedience, masquerading in this insidious masquerade, while secretly preparing their response. Their minds, though juvenile, were being honed by the ordeal, maturing with a speed dictated by the accumulated suffering. They knew that the year 2023, lurking on the horizon,

The Hourim of innocence

presaged decisive upheaval. A storm was brewing, and they would be at the centre of it.

When darkness descended on the camp where Moussa was undergoing merciless training, an unexpected summons arrived, shrouded in mystery. A secret meeting, accessible only to a chosen few. Moussa's foreboding became chilling. Something important, something terrible was about to happen.

Far away, Abigael also received an imperative order. She had to go to an elite assembly. Her uncle Yossef's face hardened as she left, an indecipherable shadow crossing his eyes. The atmosphere was heavy, saturated with anticipation that seemed ready to explode. Taken to two separate but identical rooms, hidden in the meanders of the Israeli and Palestinian training complexes, Moussa and Abigael were confronted with a test that seemed to have sprung from the depths of hell. An adult was waiting for them, with a child at his side. A child accused of treason, branded as a traitor. In Moussa's camp, the boy was suspected of having sold secrets to the Israelis; in Abigael's camp, the young accused was judged guilty of having harboured sympathies for the Palestinian people.

- It's time to prove your loyalty, Moussa ! his uncle told him in a tone of implacable coldness. "If you want to be worthy of our cause, you must eliminate this infamous traitor. As for Abigael, her uncle also told her the same thing, charging her with becoming the avenging arm of the implacable justice of her people.

Moussa's vision blurred, his mind struggling to assimilate the horror of the situation. Lina, still at his side, handed him a weapon, her merciless gaze watching for his reaction. In the

The Hourim of innocence

room where Abigael was, Yossef also handed her a gun, his eyes crinkling in anticipation. Their young hearts, beating wildly, were on the verge of breaking.

Moussa stared at the child in front of him. The wide-eyed, pleading boy reminded him of familiar faces, of buried memories of a time when innocence was not yet a utopia. How could he take this child's life ? How could he give in to a violence he had sworn never to embody? Abigael, for her part, felt a similar anguish. The boy in front of her was not an enemy. He was just a child, broken, just like her. Their minds connected in the silence. Separated by distance, but united by an invisible force, Abigael and Moussa drew on the light of their love to find the strength to resist. In that suspended moment, they made their choice.

Moussa dropped the weapon at his feet, the sound echoing like thunder in the stifling silence of the room. He raised his head, his eyes burning with defiance. "I am not a murderer," he declared in a voice that, though young, vibrated with unshakeable conviction. Lina, stunned, could not hide the incredulity that cracked her impassive mask.

For her part, Abigael clutched the weapon, not to use it, but to affirm her resolve. She raised her head, tears rolling down her cheeks. "I refuse to be like you," she whispered, her voice painfully soft but full of unshakeable strength. Yossef, seething with anger, froze, stunned by his niece's rebellion.

Then, in that moment when everything could have been turned upside down, the Guardian of the Dome appeared, enveloping the two children in a divine light, gentle but invincible. His luminous wings protected them, like a bulwark against the darkness.

The Hourim of innocence

- You have chosen the most arduous path," said the Guardian, his voice resounding like celestial music. "But it is also the one that will save this world from darkness. Do not waver. Your light is stronger than anything.

The adults, caught up in the nets of hatred and brutality, didn't understand the power of that moment. But something changed. A subtle wave, a warmth, passed through Lina and Eytan, shaking their certainties forged in pain.

The war for innocence, for hope, had only just begun. But Abigael and Moussa, bearers of an incandescent love, knew that their light would not fade. On the contrary, it would grow, guiding lost souls towards a future where peace would no longer be a dream, but a tangible reality.

Moussa and Abigael's refusal resounded like a final act of defiance in a world governed by violence and lies. Their firm and unwavering 'no' had left its mark, not only on their oppressors, but also on the souls of those who had witnessed their courage. The adults around them, though hardened by the war, could not hide the shockwave that went through them, as if this act of rebellion carried with it a truth that they themselves had denied for too long.

For Lina, Moussa's refusal was an insult to everything she had been taught. She stepped forward with implacable coldness, picked up the young boy's gun and, without the slightest hesitation, executed the child designated as the traitor. The sound of the shot rang out like a final sentence, frozen in horror. Moussa felt himself suffocating, the cry of his soul breaking before it could pass his lips. His vision darkened, his anger turned into a torrent of silent pain, but he held firm, refusing to let hatred take hold of him.

The Hourim of innocence

Abigael's fate was just as cruel. Eytan, the young boy in whom she had placed her last hopes, stepped forward with a heavy step, his face distorted by senseless rage. Before she could intervene, he fired coldly at the child accused of treason. Blood spurted out, staining the ground with broken innocence. Abigael felt her heart break, as if the universe were collapsing around her. She wanted to scream, but her cries remained trapped in her throat, stifled by the unbearable brutality of this world where hope seemed forever extinguished.

Lina approached Moussa, her gaze piercing, an expression of contempt frozen on her features. "You think you can defy what we are?" she snarled, every word loaded with contempt. "Weakness will never be tolerated here. You will pay for your treachery, and you will learn to obey."

Eytan's words echoed in Abigael's ears. "There is no room for weakness," he spat. "You will bear the consequences of your insolence, of your refusal to accept the reality of this war."

The months that followed were a never-ending succession of punishments. Humiliation, deprivation and exhausting exercise were imposed on the two children. They were treated like pariahs, branded with the seal of weakness, rejected by those who had once trained them to become war machines. But neither Moussa nor Abigael yielded. Their spirits remained intact, their hearts nourished by the unshakeable strength they drew from each other. What we called weakness in them was only the most beautiful proof of their humanity, of their inner light.

Two years had passed. Two heavy, silent years, in which every day seemed to erode a little more the memory of loved faces. Neither Abigael nor Moussa had seen the other again, and yet

The Hourim of innocence

they carried within them the indelible imprint of their separation. Their hearts, despite the distance, still beat in unison, linked by a golden thread that not even the weight of time and pain could break. But that thread, fragile and tenuous, stretched painfully at every turn, and loneliness hung over them like a veil of ashes.

Memories, once vivid and luminous, were dulled by the erosion of absence. The bursts of laughter and glances exchanged faded, replaced by the oppressive silence of endless days. Yet in the depths of their souls, a presence persisted, like a musical note suspended in the air, an imperceptible but eternal vibration. Each felt the other, like the warmth of an invisible flame. It wasn't a total absence, but a dull, constant pain, a wound that refused to heal.

Locked in icy basements, prisoners of a darkness that seemed intent on swallowing up what little humanity they had left, they lived each moment waiting for a sign, a hope, a miracle. Daylight was foreign to them; their world was reduced to half-light and the distant echoes of indifferent footsteps. And yet, in this darkness, they continued to dream, to hope, to remember. Every night, they wove in their minds the fragments of a love that no wall, no war, no betrayal could ever erase.

One morning, in places separated by invisible but impassable borders, an order fell, as heavy as a sentence. A capital mission. They were told of duties and destiny, but the words sounded like blows, stripped of all humanity. In Moussa's basement, Samir, his uncle and implacable mentor, delivered the order with cutting coldness. His gaze expressed neither compassion nor remorse, only the arrogance of someone who believes he holds the reins of destiny. Every word he uttered seemed

The Hourim of innocence

destined to push the weight of fate further onto Moussa's shoulders, to crush him under the idea that his life no longer belonged to him. For Samir, Moussa was nothing more than an instrument, a pawn to be manipulated until he became the perfect blade with which to execute his plans.

Miles away, Yossef, Abigael's uncle, was playing his own score. His tone was different, more subdued, but his gaze betrayed an equally calculating intention. Yossef had never seen Abigael as a child to be protected, but as a piece on a chessboard, a lever he could pull at the right moment. He spoke to her of a transfer, of a new role to play, but he hid the truth behind half words. Abigael would be put to sleep, transported and deposited in a peaceful house in the heart of an Israeli kibbutz, a place where life flourished despite the war. But this haven of peace had been marked to disappear, and Abigael would become, in spite of herself, a figure of sacrificed innocence, a face among the shadows of the dead.

That night, as the darkness weighed heavily on their minds, an unexpected light tore through the darkness. The Guardian, brilliant and mysterious, appeared. He divided himself, bringing to each a unique message, adapted to the pain he was carrying.

In Abigael's basement, the Guardian's soft light suddenly filled the room, chasing away the shadows as a wave soothes troubled shores. Abigael, curled up on her makeshift mattress, looked up, dazzled by the familiar, comforting presence. Her tears, held back for too long, finally flowed, as if the Guardian's light had broken an invisible barrier inside her.

"Abigael," he murmured, his voice imbued with infinite tenderness. "For the last two years, your heart has been

The Hourim of innocence

mourning the absence of Moussa. Every night, I feel your pain, this silent suffering that not even dreams can alleviate. But know this: even in the deepest darkness, there is a light that never goes out. That light is the light that binds you together.

The Guardian's words settled on her like a balm, rekindling a warmth she thought had been lost forever.

In Moussa's basement, the same light cut through the darkness, enveloping the room in a gentle but penetrating warmth. Moussa woke with a start and stared at the luminous figure with a mixture of wonder and pain. The Guardian, who said nothing at first, looked at him with compassionate eyes.

"Moussa," he said at last, his voice sounding like an echo from the depths of time. "For two years now, you've been carrying the weight of Abigael's absence. This emptiness consumes you, but it has never managed to extinguish the flame that burns inside you. That flame is your bond, stronger than distance, stronger than fear."

Moussa, his eyes misty, clenched his fists, fighting the emotion that threatened to overwhelm him.

As the Guardian spoke, an invisible but tangible bond seemed to form between Abigael and Moussa. Through the walls, the miles and the shadows of their respective prisons, they found each other. Their souls touched, carried by the Guardian's light, and in that suspended moment, they felt each other's presence like a gentle breath.

"7 October is approaching," says the Guardian, his voice full of gravity. "That day will mark an irreversible turning point. You will witness a disaster, but even in the ruins, you will carry

The Hourim of innocence

hope. You are the light in the darkness, the last bulwark against hatred. Never let that flame go out.

Then, slowly, he disappeared, leaving behind him a lingering glow, a silent echo of his words. Abigael and Moussa, though separated by walls and different destinies, felt more united than ever. They knew now that the test ahead would be terrible, but they were ready. For beyond the darkness, their love continued to burn, shining like a solitary star in the immensity of the sky.

The silence fell again, heavy and implacable. But it was no longer the same silence. It was the silence that precedes the storm, the silence that stretches out just before the world is turned upside down. In their respective basements, Abigael and Moussa could feel the air growing heavier, charged with an invisible but crushing threat.

7 October was approaching, and with it the echo of a cataclysm that would make no distinction between the innocent and the guilty. That day would be a breaking point, a tear in the fragile fabric of their existence. A shadow already stretched over them, ready to engulf them.

They didn't know it yet, but what lay ahead would shatter more than just their bodies : it would shake their souls. And in the oppressive darkness, a chilling truth was emerging, implacable : the worst was yet to come.

The Hourim of innocence

CHAPTER III

 THE DAY OF SHADOWS

« WAR DOES NOT DETERMINE WHO IS RIGHT, BUT WHO IS LEFT. »

BERTRAND RUSSELL

The October dawn rose with mournful majesty, and an autumn breeze swept down from the hills like an embrace from an ancestral past, blowing immemorial secrets into the still air. This breeze, fragile and caressing, seemed to weave a silent poem with the aromas of the sleeping earth, blending the harsh scent of sun-warmed rock with the diaphanous freshness of dew. It carried the bitter scent of wild herbs, thyme and sage with their penetrating notes, touching souls like a song from the centuries, a prayer whispered by the spirits of the desert.

The Hourim of innocence

The day dawned with solemn slowness, distilling its light into fine golden tears, piercing the shreds of shadow still clinging to the hills. The hills, crowned with trees tortured by the merciless winds, stood like silent monuments to forgotten ages. Their branches, gnarled and full of suffering, stretched towards the milky blue sky like imploring hands seeking a grace that could not be found. The leaves, withered and darkly veined, whispered prayers lost in the wind, the whispers of survivors of storms that never give respite.

The sky itself seemed to hesitate between night and day, tinted a spectral blue, fragile and evanescent. A silvery mist, like a lost ghost, floated in the valleys, capturing the first rays of the newborn sun and transforming them into stardust, an ephemeral and sepulchral veil. Each droplet of dew, hanging from the grass like a diamond, shone with a trembling light, an ephemeral offering to the morning.

An imperious silence, almost supernatural in its gravity, enveloped the land. It hung over every stone, every blade of grass, like a heavy black velvet cloak. It was a silence so profound that it seemed to extinguish the breath of the winds, to muffle the rustle of the leaves, a silence that had a cosmic dimension, as if the universe itself were waiting, suspended, frozen by a presentiment that even the stars understood. The long, angular shadows, stretched by the low-angled light, drew moving frescoes on the ground, runes of half-light whispering forgotten stories.

In the distance, the children of the kibbutz still slept, lulled by the illusion of timeless peace. Their dreams were filled with innocent fantasies, adventures in fields in bloom, crystalline laughter echoing under clement skies. They rested in the deceptive softness of warm sheets, unaware of the lurking

The Hourim of innocence

threat, the dark beast lurking on the horizon. The courtyards, deserted and motionless, waited to be filled again with the carefree games that brought them to life. The swings, trapped in a frozen air, seemed like heartless pendulums, suspended in time, frozen in mute expectation.

In the houses, the families, wrapped in the torpor of dreams, savoured the last moments of respite, forgetting the oppression of days gone by. The shutters were closed, letting in only trickles of pale light, protecting the secrets of the nights when anxiety keeps watch. Everything seemed so tranquil, so fragilely perfect, that one might have thought, in a burst of naivety, that this serenity was eternal, inviolable, that the world, on that October morning, had taken a vow of peace.

Yet there was an elusive tension in the air, like a whiff of the inevitable, a dissonant note in the symphony of silence. The stray dogs that strolled by, their paws brushing the earth like a whisper, seemed to sense it. The cats, those elegant, unfathomable shadows, crept between the ruins, their eyes glittering with impenetrable mysteries. Only the hoarse, mournful braying of a donkey dared to disturb this factitious tranquillity, a spectral echo of a suffering that not even nature could hide. The plains, vast and silent, stretched out under the golden light like a picture painted by divine hands, but shot through with an indescribable melancholy.

The slowly receding mist revealed serene hills, but they seemed to carry too heavy a secret, a truth that no one wanted to hear. The horizon, bathed in the light of dawn, seemed endless, but this apparent tranquillity concealed the monster ready to devour all beauty. For this calm, this illusory perfection, was only a façade. An invisible threat crept slyly through the shadows of the hills, biding its time to strike. Nature itself

The Hourim of innocence

seemed to know it, seemed to be holding its breath, suspended between awakening and nightmare, as if it knew that humanity was about to betray once again its promise of peace. On the morning of 7 October, the world was on the verge of shaking, and under the ephemeral beauty of dawn, the destiny of mankind was being played out, ready to be written in letters of fire and blood.

Moussa stood in one of the Houmas lorries, enveloped by an anxiety that seemed to have taken root deep in his gut, a dull, unchanging terror that knotted his muscles and petrified his thoughts. All around him, the atmosphere was oppressive, saturated with an almost palpable tension, despite the morning chill that caressed his skin with its biting breath. This cold, as sharp as a crystal blade, was nothing compared to the frost that gripped his heart. He wasn't shivering from the cold, no ; it was fear, a visceral, savage fear that was devouring him from the inside, slithering inside him like a venomous snake, weighing down every breath, every beat of his heart.

He tried hard to hide the shudder that ran through him, but he couldn't escape the chilling premonition, an intuition that, like an ominous shadow, whispered that nothing good would come of this mission. A part of him knew, knew from the beginning, that this road led only to desolation, that it was a march towards nothingness. Around him, the men whispered in the half-light of the lorry, their whispers sharp as blades, contrasting with the deceptive serenity of the surrounding nature. The clanking of weapons, the cold, methodical sound of magazines being checked again and again, created a hypnotic rhythm, a mechanical symphony, a prelude to the impending horror. It all seemed unreal, like a nightmare scene

The Hourim of innocence

that Moussa was observing from a distance, a disembodied spectator of a drama that was being played out without him.

The Guardian was there, invisible to the others, but present like a breath of warmth in the midst of the cold of death. An immaterial, benevolent presence, watching over Moussa, whispering to his soul to stand firm, not to give in. It was a gentle, invisible light that radiated from him and tried to calm the chaos in his mind. Moussa closed his eyes for a moment, trying to tame the panicked beating of his heart. He clung to this presence like a buoy in a raging ocean, desperately seeking a haven of inner peace, a peace that always seemed to elude him.

Outwardly, the peace offered by nature was almost cruel, a cynical and merciless contrast to Moussa's inner turmoil. The sleepy hills, the hesitant morning light, the sky softly taking on the colours of dawn, all seemed to mock him, to whisper to him that the beauty of the world would continue to exist, indifferent to the suffering of mankind. The innocence of the landscape, the insolent calm, seemed an affront, a thumbing of the nose at the horror that was brewing. The lorry whirred, the jolts making the worn metal vibrate, and each jolt, each groan of the springs, brought Moussa a little closer to chaos.

Through the worn tarpaulin, he could see fragments of the outside world. The pearly grey October sky seemed endless, stretching out its silent coldness like a veil of mourning. The low clouds, heavy as broken promises, rolled in slowly, indifferent to human passions, impassive witnesses to the dramas that were about to unfold below. The hills, an austere green bristling with rocky outcrops, stood like stone giants, impassive guardians of a land where blood and tears had mingled for generations.

The Hourim of innocence

And then the first black sails of the paragliders appeared on the horizon. They seemed to spring from the sky itself, winged spectres gliding with macabre grace, ominous shadows dancing over the hills, ready to swoop down on their prey. These sinister wings, spread out like those of majestic birds of prey, carried the promise of death and destruction. They moved with frightening elegance, floating like omen, messengers of a violent storm. Moussa felt a knot tighten in his stomach, an icy mass of fear that took his breath away.

The men around him prepared themselves, their bodies taut as bows, determination etched on their contracted features. Their eyes shone with a dark glow, somewhere between fear and elation, as they prepared to wreak destruction. Their movements were precise, almost ritualistic, as if they were clinging to this routine to avoid giving in to the terror crawling under their skin. Moussa watched them, himself frozen, paralysed by the horror of what was about to happen. An icy sweat trickled down the back of his neck, each shiver a prophecy, an omen of doom.

The noise rose to a crescendo, echoing the end of a fragile peace. The crunch of boots on earth, that dry, nervous crunch, mingled with the clatter of weapons, the cold metal being loaded, almost caressed, in a final tribute before the storm. It all seemed so real, so terribly tangible, but at the same time so alien, like a scene you're watching in a dream, a nightmare from which you can't wake up. Moussa's heartbeat seemed to pound in his chest, screaming at him that he was just a child, a child lost in a war that didn't belong to him.

The order rang out, sharp as a blade cutting through the air. There was no appeal. The lorry came to an abrupt halt, throwing Moussa forward and shaking him out of the icy

The Hourim of innocence

torpor that had imprisoned him. The impact brought him violently back to reality and, although he felt as if his heart was going to stop, his hands continued to shake. The cold metal of the weapon he held, implacable and heavy, seemed to suck the warmth from his palms, brutally reminding him of the role he had been forced into, a role he hated with all his soul but had to play nonetheless.

He climbed down from the lorry with the others, his boots hitting the hard earth with a dull, almost mournful thud, echoing like an ominous sound. The air around him, charged with tension, seemed denser, almost palpable. Every breath became an effort, and instead of appeasement, a voracious, insatiable fear seized him, knotting his throat. The smell of damp earth, still soaked with morning dew, mingled with the acrid whiff of sweat and fear from the men around him, creating a scent of terror and impending violence, an aroma that no breath of wind could dispel.

All around him, nature, in all its indifferent splendour, seemed to quiver. Swarms of birds, roused from their slumber by human agitation, flew in a disorderly whirlwind, their wings beating the air in a frenzied and chaotic dance, like the first witnesses of the apocalypse. Their shrill, desperate cries pierced the sky, while the branches they abandoned still swayed, trembling from their hasty departure, as if they themselves knew that hell was about to break loose.

Then everything changed. Screams rose up, ripping through the peaceful dawn air, followed by sharp, nervous barking orders and the clatter of rushing footsteps. The air seemed to vibrate with a brutal energy, each wave of sound echoing through Moussa's body like a funeral bell. This moment of calm, fragile as crystal, shattered under the weight of violence.

The Hourim of innocence

The black paragliders, those sinister silhouettes, descended on the kibbutzim, gliding like birds of prey, silent but carrying the promise of death. There was nothing natural or innocent about their descent; it was a prelude to destruction, a funeral dance in a sky that was already darkening under the shadow of rising smoke.

The first blasts erupted, shattering the harmony of the morning, turning serenity into chaos. The doors of the houses were smashed in, each blow resounding with an almost supernatural violence, the wood splintering in a fracas of debris. The heart-rending cries of the inhabitants rose up, screaming out fear, pain and incomprehension, mingling with the detonations of automatic weapons that sounded like thunderclaps. Walls collapsed, fragments of stone and wood shattered, the October sky turned black under the suffocating weight of the thick smoke, which crawled over the village like a hungry monster, choking the air and making every breath painful.

Moussa, his legs trembling, moved forward with the others. Every step was an ordeal, an act of raw willpower to keep from collapsing. His sweaty hands clutched his weapon, but he didn't feel like a warrior, just a child, lost, terrified, a child who would have given anything to disappear, to wake up from this nightmare. All around him, violence erupted, relentless, brutal and indiscriminate, hitting everything in its path. The screams of children and women pierced the air, cries of despair that seemed to pierce his soul, each cry a blade that sank into his heart. These sounds, these infernal noises, swirled around him like enraged ghosts, echoes of hell that he could never forget.

He tried to look away, to seek refuge, an escape, but reality was inescapable. Houses disintegrated before his eyes,

The Hourim of innocence

fragments of life reduced to dust, memories and hopes crumbling into a shapeless heap of debris. Every face he saw, every look, was filled with terror. These people, these souls, were nothing more than victims, torn from their daily lives, shattered by a violence that spared no one. The eyes, the mouths open in silent screams, the bodies frozen in an expression of pure fear, this horror was imprinted on him like an indelible scar.

And that's when he saw her. Abigael. There she was, among a group of hostages, being forced out of a ruined house, a frail but determined figure. Her face, covered in dirt, her cheeks streaked with traces of earth, her hair matted and stuck to her forehead, was unrecognisable. But it was the look in her eyes that struck him. Even in this hell, even covered in dust, with fear imprinted on her face, her eyes still shone with an indomitable glow. A flame, fragile but inextinguishable, that seemed to defy the whole world.

The vision pierced him. It was her, his Abigael, the one he loved, the one he had sworn to protect. And in that suspended moment, despite the fear, despite the death lurking all around, he felt something powerful awaken inside him. A strength he'd never known he had, a resolve that burned brighter than the terror.

Their eyes met, and for a moment, the chaos seemed to stand still, as if the world were holding its breath. The deafening roar of the explosions, the heart-rending screams, all disappeared, swallowed up by a bell of silence that left only room for the intimacy of that moment. Moussa and Abigael, two children caught up in the infernal spiral of a war that was not theirs, found themselves united by this invisible and unshakeable bond. Suffering and fear seemed to vanish in that shared gaze,

The Hourim of innocence

where incomprehension and terror mingled with a fragile glimmer of hope.

In this silent exchange, their souls seemed to speak to each other, to reassure each other despite the surrounding horror. It was a language without words, a cry of innocence, a silent oath they made to each other: never to give in to the madness that surrounded them. Moussa felt his heart clench violently, each beat seeming to chant a brutal truth: he had to fight for her, for the light still alive in Abigael's eyes, to preserve what was left of their humanity.

But the urgency of the situation stopped him in his tracks. His legs refused to move, as if chained by a primitive fear, his body petrified by anguish. Everything in him was screaming to reach her, to snatch her from the clutches of her captors, but the terror was strangling him and his breath was coming in short gasps. The Guardian, with his protective presence, was still whispering to her, like a wave of gentle warmth enveloping her. "Wait for your moment", breathed the ethereal voice, filled with infinite wisdom.

The din of the Israeli helicopters drew closer, their blades whipping the air with increasing violence, while the gunfire increased, transforming the atmosphere into a symphony of destruction. But there was a dissonance, an inconsistency that struck Moussa. These air strikes weren't there to save lives; they were targeting places where civilians were gathering, innocent people trapped. Where were the reinforcements, the soldiers who should be there to defend their own people ? An insidious doubt began to grow in his mind, a chilling premonition: was this a trap, a staged death to serve some obscure purpose? Not far away, the horror was written in the bloody sand. The concert, that joyous gathering of young

The Hourim of innocence

people under the stars to dance and celebrate life, had become an open-air cemetery. A few hours earlier, the music was still blaring with happiness, and the laughter rose up like carefree prayers. Now all that remained were broken bodies, ashes and charred remnants of what had once been a party. The instruments were smashed to pieces, the stage gutted, and the dreams of the shattered youths scattered like ghosts in the air heavy with despair.

Moussa, his breath taken away by the horror, was overwhelmed by incomprehension. This violence, this carnage, these innocent lives taken without mercy... it all made no sense. The fate of these Palestinian and Israeli souls, sacrificed on the altar of an absurd war, left him petrified. His thoughts collided with an all too cruel reality : how could the world have come to this point of no return, where hatred and madness reigned supreme?

The Houmas men advanced without hesitation, their movements mechanical, their gazes devoid of all humanity. They seemed oblivious to the carnage they were causing, like shadows who knew only destruction. But Moussa felt his spirit being torn apart. Every child's scream, every mother's cry, every face twisted by fear cut through him like a blade, sinking deep into his conscience. He didn't want this war, he didn't want to be what they were trying to make him.

The world around Moussa no longer resembled anything he had known. Everything had fallen into an abyss of pure cruelty, an abyss of violence where humanity was lost forever. The faces of the men around him were nothing more than grotesque masks, distorted by an unspeakable madness, as if the reigning chaos had taken hold of their souls and emptied them of all compassion, all light. These silhouettes, carried

The Hourim of innocence

away by blind rage, were no longer soldiers but spectres, emissaries of desolation. Their hoarse, joyless laughter clashed with the tumult of the death they were unleashing.

Moussa tried to grasp what was unfolding before him, but each scene was a slap in the face of barbarity that left him dazed, his soul torn apart. The rapes were unbearable acts of possession, a desecration of humanity's last sanctuary, a defilement that left invisible but eternal scars. As for mutilation, it was a spectacle of madness, a challenge to life itself. Limbs torn off, bodies left in tatters as if human flesh no longer had any value. Suffering became an art form, a dark work of art in which pain was painted with evil pleasure.

The shots rang out endlessly, punctuated by howls of despair and muffled pleas. With each shot, a life was snatched away, a future shattered, a dream shattered. Moussa felt all this with an almost unbearable acuteness, each detonation ringing within him like a bell of desolation. And yet, despite the tumult, he clung to the one thing that kept him alive : Abigael. She was his star, his breath, the only light in this hell.

He could see it, this glimmer of hope, this silent challenge to the surrounding madness. Even covered in earth, even trembling with fear, she hadn't let herself be extinguished. Her eyes, though filled with the horror of what she was seeing, still held a flame. A flame that said: I'm here, I'm not giving up. It was this light, this spark of defiance that gave Moussa the strength not to sink.

All around him, violence was no longer a simple consequence of war, but a living entity, a relentless tide that washed over everything that was fragile, everything that was beautiful. But Moussa didn't want to give in. He didn't want to turn into a

The Hourim of innocence

creature without a soul. He knew, in some corner of his heart, that his love for Abigael made him different, that he was still capable of choosing something other than hatred.

The Guardian, the invisible beacon that watched over them, had not abandoned them. His presence became more vivid, more insistent, like a reminder that strength does not lie in weapons, but in the will not to allow oneself to be corrupted. The Guardian whispered words of comfort to Moussa, inspiring him with the courage to carry on, even when all seemed lost: Stay strong, Moussa. Stay true to what makes you human. Your battle is bigger than this war, because it's for love, for light.

Moussa felt this inner strength growing, like an echo spreading through his whole being. He knew he couldn't act yet, that he had to wait for the right moment. But he promised himself that, when that time came, he would fight for Abigael, for the fragile glimmer of light they represented together. No matter how dark it got, their light, however flickering, would not be extinguished.

And while the snake of war continued to tighten around them, ready to crush them, he still held on to this certainty. Their love was a rebellion, a flame that defied the darkness, and as long as it burned, they were not defeated.

On this dreadful day, Hell seemed to have opened one of its gates, releasing a merciless horde of demons, fallen spectres spreading over the earth like an inexorable tide. No glimmer of hope pierced the darkness, no helping hand emerged to save the innocent souls caught in the maelstrom. There was nothing but absolute abandonment, suffering with no way out, a feeling of agony where each trampled existence became a

The Hourim of innocence

worthless offering, sacrificed on the altar of intrigues whose darkness was beyond comprehension. These unfortunate people, caught up in the fury of that bloody day, were expiatory victims, reduced to nothing more than pawns in a macabre chessboard, lives offered up as pretexts to fuel future hatred, leading to even more ferocious reprisals. Today's innocents were merely the seeds of tomorrow's vengeance, and their cries would echo for a long time in a complicit silence.

The young people who had fled the concert, that moment of carefree joy transformed into a nightmare of unspeakable violence, were scattered in disorder, without destination, without hope. They ran blindly, stalked by blind violence, a faceless, merciless entity. They bumped into the lifeless bodies strewn across the ground, corpses that, with their dead eyes and rigid limbs, seemed to be watching them, reminding them of the inexorability of their own fate. Some, in a burst of life, managed to slip through the shadows, to hide, to survive in the chaos. But others saw their race brought to an abrupt and final halt, their breath snatched away by the dusty, blood-soaked earth.

Moussa, a helpless spectator of this spectacle of horror, couldn't understand how those who escaped death could ever rise again, how they could ever find the slightest shred of peace after having seen the unspeakable. The screams echoed in the air, the faces twisted in terror etched in his mind like stigmata, and he understood that these young people, like himself, were condemned to carry this burden for eternity. Innocence was nothing more than a shattered memory, trampled on beyond repair. In Moussa's mind, one question kept coming back, hammering at his skull like a torment: Why? Why this

The Hourim of innocence

insatiable thirst for destruction, this visceral need to annihilate, to reduce everything to ashes? His childhood beliefs, his once unshakeable faith, everything he had been taught about the dignity of human life seemed to be in total contradiction with what he was seeing. His religion had always forbidden him to do evil gratuitously, to cause suffering without cause. It exalted peace, mercy and respect for life, and nothing here reflected these values. These so-called warriors, draped in black, no longer appeared to be men. They were lost souls, puppets of dark forces, having traded their humanity for conscienceless darkness.

Their movements were brutal, their cries inhuman. It was as if an unhealthy fever, a rage from the depths of the abyss, animated their bodies and set their spirits ablaze. There was nothing in them that evoked compassion or humanity. They were no longer beings endowed with reason, but avatars of cruelty itself, feasting on despair and suffering like a feast offered to a bloodthirsty deity. And the earth, this land steeped in history, trembled beneath their feet, a powerless witness to this senseless carnage.

But this outburst of hatred did not come from just one side. The horror was shared equally between the men. The Israeli soldiers, whose eyes were devoid of hope, were also obeying mindless orders. Their actions were no less automatic, their violence no less cruel. It was as if every human being on this field of ruins had been emptied of their human substance, leaving only shells driven by a universal death drive. Responsibility was shifted from one side to the other, but everything seemed set, orchestrated to feed the insatiable beast that was war, this voracious entity that fed on sacrificed innocence.

The Hourim of innocence

Moussa felt trapped in this waking nightmare. Everything he saw and heard was superimposed in a hellish spiral of confusion, pain and fear. Bodies collapsing, the cries of children echoing like supplications in a desert of indifference, the desperate sobs of mothers, the crackling of weapons tearing the silence... Everything blended together in a whirlwind of sounds and images that lacerated his mind. Yet, in the midst of this turmoil of terror, one certainty remained anchored in him, glowing like an ember resistant to the wind: he had to save Abigael.

No matter how horrible it was, no matter how much fear knotted his insides, he couldn't abandon her. Abigael was somewhere, in the middle of this pandemonium, and he could feel it in every beat of his heart: he had to find her. She was his light, his last link with all that was pure, all that was still worth saving. Nothing could stop him fighting for her, fighting against the darkness that threatened to engulf everything.

The Guardian, with his benevolent and mysterious presence, had not left him. He was there, invisible but palpable, a breath in the air, a gentle but unfailing force. He whispered in Moussa's ear, words that seemed woven with light : "Not yet, Moussa. Don't give up hope. Your mission is not over. These words were like a balm on his wounds, like an inner fire that refused to go out, a lonely star in the darkest night, but enough to light his way.

Fear remained inside him, lurking like a cold beast, coiled in the hollow of his chest. But instead of paralysing him, this fear had turned into an irresistible force, a burning energy that gave him the courage to go forward. Every breath, every step was a challenge to the terror, a victory snatched from the abyss. This

The Hourim of innocence

fear reminded him of everything he had to lose, everything he refused to let sink into oblivion. Abigael had to live, and he had to protect her, whatever the cost.

He scanned the surroundings, the flames devouring the houses, the shadows dancing on the walls like spectres thirsting for destruction. This world seemed doomed to annihilation, to eternal night. But even amidst the ashes and the screams, even amongst the faces disfigured by pain and despair, Moussa knew what he had to do. His destiny was no longer a mystery: it was a path engraved in his heart, a path of light that he would follow against all odds.

A scream pierced the air, a scream that shook his certainty, but he did not look away from his objective. He felt the blast of bombs, the deafening din of gunfire, but it all seemed far away, unreal. What mattered was Abigael. As long as she was alive, as long as she had a chance, he would go and get her. And if he had to, he'd face hell itself, because the love he carried inside him, fragile as it was, was the only thing capable of defying this day of blood.

Abigael was his reason for standing, his beacon in the midst of this storm of fire and ash. Never mind the horrors of war, the insatiable darkness that seemed to stretch like a veil of death over the world. The love he felt for her burned with an intensity that neither carnage nor terror could quell. He would find her, he would save her, and that flickering but inextinguishable light, which persisted in shining through the desolation, would be his guide. For her, for this sacred love, Moussa was ready to face the abyss.

It was around 5pm when the long-awaited order, as brutal as it was irremediable, resounded in the heavy afternoon air :

The Hourim of innocence

evacuate this theatre of horror. Like Dantean shadows, the men dispersed by the hundreds, leaving behind them smoking ruins, scattered corpses and a landscape irreparably disfigured by human fury. The day receded with solemn slowness, and the declining sun cast a golden, almost unreal light over the surrounding hills, which seemed to caress every contour with a misplaced tenderness. This soft, bewitching light contrasted cruelly with the bloody reality below, as if even the sky wanted to divert our gaze from the abomination it overlooked. Dense clouds, steeped in sadness, slowly rolled in, heavy, like a celestial funeral.

The air was saturated with the stench of death, each carrying a distinct note of the drama that had just unfolded. The sickening metallic scent of spilt blood mingled with the pungency of burning rubble, ravaged homes and familiar objects reduced to bitter, desolate ashes. At times, an unbearable scent of burnt flesh wafted through the air, emerging like an olfactory whiplash, a merciless reminder of the fragility of the human condition in the face of the devouring whims of fire. The smoke, the dust and the heady smell of death formed a kind of invisible but palpable wall, making every breath laboured, every inhalation a struggle against the oppression of the air that had become poison. Moussa could feel his nostrils chafing, each gulp of air becoming an ordeal that brought him closer to moral and physical asphyxiation.

Vertiginous thoughts assailed his mind, plunging him into an abyss of metaphysical questions. How could a God, infinitely good and just, allow the world to sink into such ignominy? Why did the sky, that impassive and infinite vault, seem to observe in scornful silence the pain of the innocent, of

The Hourim of innocence

children crying out in despair, of mothers overwhelmed by grief ? As the light of dusk enveloped the hills in a melancholy shade of amber, a soft, deep voice echoed in Moussa's soul. The Guardian, with his immaterial but benevolent presence, spoke like a breeze caressing a gaping wound.

"The Creator did not make man a puppet, Moussa," murmured the Guardian, his words rising like the notes of an ancient song imbued with truth. "He did not fashion automatons chained to his will. He gave humanity this ineffable gift : freedom. The freedom to choose, to think, to forge one's own path, even at the cost of wandering." These words, imbued with immemorial wisdom, resonated within him like a forgotten lesson, an ancient truth that finally seemed to make sense. "Certain men," continued the Guardian, "want to usurp the role of the Creator, impose their cruel will, manipulate the minds of the masses, sow doubt in order to better control them. They want people to believe that He does not exist, or that He is indifferent. But the reality is simple and cruel : good and evil are intertwined, like light and shadow, and it's up to each soul to choose its destiny."

Moussa listened, his thoughts whirling like leaves in a gust of wind, his eyes riveted on the horizon where the dying light gave a glimpse of fragile hope, a fleeting glimmer before the inexorable fall of night. The Guardian continued, his voice tinged with an almost sacred gravity: "He exists, Moussa, but he has chosen not to intervene at every moment. He does not direct every step, because human beings are not pawns, but free beings. It is their choices, their deliberate actions, that will be judged. Every suffering inflicted, every act of kindness, will be a weight in the scales of fate. Your role today is different. Don't burden yourself with unanswerable questions. Think of

The Hourim of innocence

Abigael. Think of your survival and hers. The time will come when you will have to make a choice with far-reaching consequences, because evil often wraps itself in the banner of good, and good can rise from the ashes of evil. Remember that."

A new determination ignited in Moussa's heart. He couldn't afford to give in to the pangs of doubt or lose himself in endless questioning. He had to concentrate on what really mattered. Abigael. She was all that mattered right now, all that gave meaning to his fight. With a determined step, he headed for the lorry where the hostages were piled. His heart was beating like a drum, but it wasn't weakening. The smoke continued to rise in thick wisps, the debris groaned beneath his soles, but his gaze never wavered from his destination. Abigael, his light, had to be there, somewhere, and he couldn't fail.

The infernal troops, those shadows of death, dispersed with almost demonic precision, returning to their subterranean lairs, invisible dens where they lurked like wild beasts having satisfied their thirst for blood. What they left behind was a wasteland of ruins, ashes and corpses. Hope seemed to have faded, and even the light seemed to have surrendered to the surrounding horror. The dying flames gave way to an icy desolation that would soon become the focus of new reprisals, new waves of hatred and violence.

At around 6.30pm, as dusk spread its shroud over the land, the first vehicles of Tsouhal's army appeared, like spectres emerging from a shattered dream. Their headlights cut through the dawning darkness, but the light seemed to come late, as if they had only come to see the extent of the tragedy, not to prevent it. The soldiers descended, their faces frozen in

The Hourim of innocence

a gravity that could not be faked. Their eyes roamed the desolate field, trying to grasp the horror, but finding only a mournful silence, broken by the crackling of dying embers and the suffocating smell of carnage.

Moussa felt trapped in this waking nightmare. Everything he saw and heard was superimposed in a hellish spiral of confusion, pain and fear. Bodies collapsing, the cries of children echoing like supplications in a desert of indifference, the desperate sobs of mothers, the crackling of weapons tearing the silence... Everything blended together in a whirlwind of sounds and images that lacerated his mind.

From time to time, through the narrow openings in the lorry, Moussa could see silhouettes in Israeli uniforms, but their gestures betrayed their true nature : impostors, false soldiers, coldly executing a macabre plan. These men, draped in symbols of defence, had become instruments of insidious barbarity. Their guns were aimed not at armed enemies, but at hope itself, embodied in the innocent souls they were silencing.

Despite the horror that assailed him from all sides, one certainty remained anchored in Moussa, glowing like an ember resistant to the wind: he had to save Abigael. He knew she was there, somewhere in the oppressive darkness of that lorry, her frail body trapped in the same absurd violence.

No matter how horrible it was, no matter how much fear knotted his insides, he couldn't abandon her. Abigael was his light, his last link with all that was pure, all that was still worth saving. Nothing could stop him from fighting, even in the heart of this hell. Every beat of his heart reminded him that he had no right to give in.

The Hourim of innocence

And yet, even in this chaos, Abigael remained his light, the last glimmer of humanity illuminating his soul. His eyes searched desperately for her among the silhouettes of the hostages, and when he finally caught sight of her, his heart clenched, not with fear, but with a renewed and unshakeable determination. He had to save her. Nothing else mattered. Neither the flames, nor the screams, nor death itself could extinguish that inner flame. For her, he would defy the night and brave the terror, ready to do anything to preserve the flickering but tenacious light they shared.

His eyes, though extinguished by exhaustion and fear, still carried that indefinable softness, that fragile but indomitable sparkle that gave him the strength to go on. He clenched his fists. He would not allow anyone, not even these monsters in disguise, to take away this love, this spark of humanity that he refused to see disappear.

As everyone returned to the depths of the Gaza tunnels, those sinister, twisting galleries where shadows seemed to inhabit the very ground, Moussa followed the hostages at a silent pace, every muscle in his body taut with fear and anguish. His stomach was in knots, an unbearable weight pressing down on him. He couldn't let Abigael out of his sight; he had to watch over her, know where she was at all times. The putrid smell that permeated these tunnels burned his nostrils: a mixture of rotting flesh, damp earth and accumulated human misery. The air stagnated, heavy and suffocating, as if the oxygen itself had become impregnated with the pain and sorrow buried in these places. Every breath was an ordeal, every inhalation a bitter burn, like a constant reminder that death lurked nearby.

These shallows were an endless labyrinth, a tangle of narrow, winding passages, corrupted veins stretching beneath the

The Hourim of innocence

earth. These tunnels, dug in a haphazard fashion, had been designed to conceal secret operations, to smuggle weapons and supplies, but also to serve as impenetrable sanctuaries, hidden from the eyes of the outside world. Light was rare, as if banished by an obscure force, leaving a thick, oppressive darkness. Every corridor seemed to conceal a macabre secret, every shadow a silent threat.

Moussa, short of breath, moved forward with infinite caution, his feet barely touching the dusty ground, his movements calculated not to arouse suspicion. He was a shadow among shadows, a ghostly presence, his senses alert, his heart beating wildly in his chest. He followed the group of hostages from a distance, his eyes riveted on Abigael. He had to make sure she was there, alive, that her soul was still resisting the despair that surrounded them.

They were finally led into a dilapidated room, a dark space where the walls seemed to ooze suffering accumulated over the years. The hostages were separated: the women on one side, the children on the other. Abigael was close by, but she hadn't seen him yet. Moussa's gaze was desperately searching for her, clinging to every detail of her face to convince himself that she was still breathing, that she hadn't been shattered by the horror.

Then everything changed. Like a sinister shadow, Moussa's uncle appeared, his massive silhouette projecting a menacing aura. When he caught sight of Abigael, his eyes hardened, a gleam of cruel understanding appearing on his face. He understood immediately why Moussa was there, what he was planning to do. A sardonic sneer stretched his lips, and in one sudden movement, he grabbed Abigael by the arm, dragging her unceremoniously out of the room.

The Hourim of innocence

Moussa felt an icy wave run down his spine, every fibre of his being crying out in alarm. He saw his uncle lead Abigael to another room, a place that seemed to exude suffering and despair: an interrogation room, or worse still, a torture room. The walls of this space, covered in eerie shadows, seemed to whisper tales of pain and muffled screams.

The world seemed to collapse around him. Fear, horror and rage collided in his mind like raging waves. But beyond this inner storm, one certainty remained. He would not let his uncle break Abigael. He wouldn't allow it. The light they shared, the torch they carried together, had to survive, no matter what the cost.

The walls of this room were silent witnesses, erected like sentinels of horror, imbued with the torments of those who had once suffered here. Each stone seemed to ooze an ancient suffering, a pain imprinted in the material itself, exhaling a mournful breath with every whisper of wind that crept through the cracks. The air was heavy, saturated with palpable anguish, as if the pain of the martyrs had left a sinister echo, a ghostly wave floating around the greyish walls. To breathe here was to inhale the memory of nameless agonies, to feel the fear frozen in invisible layers, rooted in the smallest recesses of this tomb of flesh and screams. Moussa approached, each step a battle against the primal terror that was swelling inside him. It wasn't just his own fear, but that of the spirits of the supplicants, who seemed to be murmuring inaudible laments, broken prayers, pleas that went unheard. The atmosphere was a sea of blackness, where hopes were stifled, where every breath became a burn laden with lost souls, a bitter poison seeping into the chest. This room was not just a space, it was the sanctuary of immortalised suffering,

The Hourim of innocence

a theatre of torment where time itself seemed to stand still, chained to past torments.

When the door closed with a sinister slam, Abigael turned her head and their eyes met. A meeting of souls in the abyss, an electric exchange in which everything they felt mingled: visceral fear, raw terror, but also a precious, unshakeable light, the light of a love powerful enough to defy even the most voracious darkness. That look they exchanged was a silent oath, a pact sealed in the darkness: whatever happened, they would hold each other, indomitable. That moment, as brief as it was eternal, was enough to rekindle their courage, a breath of hope piercing the infernal mists that surrounded them.

But this respite was short-lived. The door slammed shut, sealing Abigael in this place of torture, and Moussa's heart clenched with an almost unbearable anguish. His uncle appeared, his features marked by an almost supernatural hatred, a murderous obsession that twisted his thoughts like a snake choking its prey. He wanted nothing to do with the orders of the Houmas's top officer, a calculating man who, despite his cruelty, understood that the war was also being fought on the front of public opinion. For this officer, the hostages were to serve as a symbol of moderation, an illusion carefully nurtured to counter Israeli accusations and control the media narrative. But Moussa's uncle was not interested in these diplomatic considerations. Hatred had consumed him, inflamed him with a rage so blind that it surpassed all rationality. He saw in Abigael an incarnation of the enemy, a burden of unjust guilt, an echo of the death of his sister, Moussa's mother.

The senior officer, after a nervous exchange, finally gave in, not without a gleam of exasperation in his eyes. "Take her

The Hourim of innocence

away from here, out of sight," he ordered in a voice that oozed disgust. He didn't want the affair to jeopardise his carefully devised plan, a staging where the violence had to appear justified, not sadistic. The uncle, his eyes dark with madness, grabbed Abigael with a firm hand, his fingers digging into her delicate flesh like the talons of a bird of prey clawing at its prey. He dragged her out of the room, the shadow of vengeance following his every step, while Moussa, seized in his turn by a brutal hand, felt panic erupt inside him like a firestorm.

They plunged into the darkness of the basements, a labyrinth of obscurity where light made only timid appearances. Every breath of air was heavy with the acrid smell of clammy earth, the stagnant fear of the hostages, the sweat of men who had no humanity left. Moussa, swept along by a tide of devastating emotions, tried to breathe, to calm the frantic beating of his heart. They reached an isolated area, a forgotten corner where the outside world seemed a distant, unreal reality. There, Moussa's uncle threw Abigael to the ground with a brutality that made Moussa flinch. She collapsed, her breathing ragged, her eyes full of tears, but refusing to break. Her eyes sought Moussa's, a last plea, a silent cry, a request for comfort or a miracle.

Moussa felt his rage rising, a torrent of pure fury, the kind of anger that only the most abominable injustice can awaken. His hands trembled, his fists clenched, and he realised that the moment had come. He could no longer remain passive. Abigael, his light, his hope, must not be sacrificed on the altar of this insatiable hatred. Darkness surrounded them, threatening, ready to consume them, but in the midst of this

The Hourim of innocence

abyss, Moussa felt a strength being born within him, a flame that he was ready to ignite in defiance of everything.

This blind hatred, this cycle of violence, he would not let it destroy him. He would stand as a bulwark against barbarism, ready to stand against his own blood if need be.

The uncle, an imposing, dark figure, brandished his weapon, a cold, almost spectral object that captured the last glimmers of twilight, making them sharper and more merciless. The steel seemed to absorb all the darkness of that fateful moment, a sinister glow, a promise of death waiting to be fulfilled. With a sudden, unexpected gesture, he handed the weapon to Moussa, his eyes, black as the most devouring night, staring unblinkingly into those of his nephew. "It's up to you," he ordered in a hoarse voice saturated with hatred and contempt. "You must avenge your mother. That girl is the cause of our misfortune. She is everything we have lost. Prove to me that you are one of us."

The words fell like stones, heavy, irremediable, imprisoning Moussa in a cage of venomous commands. His uncle held a knife in his other hand, its blade stained with dried blood, a morbid relic of the morning's carnage, like a sinister testimony to the brutality that had set that day ablaze. The metal gleamed faintly, a poisonous glow that seemed to emit the very scent of death.

Moussa's hands were trembling, shaking with uncontrollable shivers, so violently that the weapon seemed about to slip from his grasp. He had never taken a life, not even that of the tiniest creature, not even that of an insect, such was his respect for the sanctity of all existence. His faith, despite the terror and horror around him, told him to protect life, to venerate it,

The Hourim of innocence

to regard it as the most precious of gifts. And here, in front of him, he was being asked to break this inviolable law, to desecrate what he had always held to be intangible. To point this weapon at Abigael, the woman who embodied everything he held dearest, the ultimate flame that still warmed his heart. How could he even conceive of such an act?

His vision blurred, his thoughts scattered in a desperate tumult. His uncle's gaze grew darker and darker, his voice sounding like a death knell, urging him to plunge into the abyss of vengeance. But suddenly a memory came to him, the words of the Guardian, a whisper full of wisdom and mystery: Sometimes, evil can give birth to good. These words, engraved in his soul, rose up like a call for clarity. A slow, almost imperceptible transformation took place. Moussa turned the gun away from Abigael and pointed it at his uncle.

A sly smile contorted the man's face, a grimace of incredulous contempt. "You wouldn't dare," he spat, his eyes filling with an unhealthy certainty. "I am of your blood. You would never betray me. She, on the other hand, is an abject Jew, unworthy of your clemency."

The universe seemed suspended, a theatre of shadows where the slightest breath felt like destiny. Moussa waited, hoping for a miracle, for divine intervention, for the Guardian to appear and save him from this hellish choice. But nothing came. The world remained silent. He was alone, facing the ultimate decision, with the weight of a human life in his hands. His finger pressed the trigger, almost instinctively, as if responding to a secret call, an irrepressible force beyond his own will.

The blast tore through the air, a brutal, implacable scream of metal, and Moussa's uncle toppled backwards, his body

The Hourim of innocence

stricken by fate, collapsing into the dust with a final convulsion. The life fled from him in a breath, like a flame snuffed out by the wind, the silence falling over the stage, heavy and implacable, a silence of the aftermath of the storm.

Adrenalin seized Moussa like a torrent, inflamed his veins, and he threw himself towards Abigael, lifting her up with a strength he didn't know he had. They dashed into the darkness, two souls on the run, running to escape the fury of the shadows that were pursuing them, their feet pounding the beaten earth, raising clouds of dust in their frantic race. Their panting breaths joined with the racing beat of their hearts, creating a desperate music, a hymn to survival.

Finally, they reached the Dome of the Rock, the place where it all began, a stone shrine illuminated by the last light of dusk. The brown light cast stretched shadows, casting long trails of darkness across the ground, but the beauty of the moment seemed almost unreal, a cruel contrast to the hell from which they had just escaped. There, exhausted and breathless, Moussa and Abigael hugged each other, their arms forming a protective bulwark, a shield of love against the world.

Their hearts beat in unison, youthful hearts but marked by a pain that not even time could heal completely. The world around them seemed to stand still, suspended in that moment when night had not yet triumphed over day, when hope still held out against the darkness. Heart to heart, they felt the warmth of their lives, a gentle vibration, proof that, despite everything, they were still there, together, undefeated. In this oppressive silence, after the flight, all that remained was the intimate music of their beats, a melody of hope that neither war nor cruelty could silence.

The Hourim of innocence

Moussa rested his forehead gently against Abigael's. The tears escaped his eyes, joining hers in a silent communion, a bittersweet pain that ran through them both. No words were needed, because what they were feeling transcended the limits of human language. It was an immaterial warmth, an unshakeable strength, a bond of unsuspected depth that defied hatred, war and even fate. Moussa's fingers slid tenderly over Abigael's cheek, wiping away the traces of her tears. His gaze gazed into her eyes, a gaze devoid of fear or resignation, filled only with the promise of survival and of remaining united, whatever the cost.

Abigael was trembling, but it wasn't the cold that was shaking her. It was a wave of feelings that overwhelmed her, an overflowing strength, the innocent and absolute love she felt for Moussa. Barely fourteen years old, they had a love that transcended all limits, a love so pure that it eluded the definitions and boundaries that adults had tried so hard to erect between them. It was a love free of calculation, free of mistrust, free of everything that had contaminated the human world. Everything had been done to divide them, to turn them into enemies, strangers to each other, but nothing had been able to break the incandescent bond that united them. On the contrary, everything brought them closer together: shared pain, loss, and a common dream of a better life.

Their love was an impenetrable fortress, a sacred refuge from the madness around them, an echo of tenderness and light in the midst of darkness. They had been through the unspeakable, through trials that no other being could ever fully grasp. And yet, in the midst of this overwhelming darkness, there was this moment of grace, this miracle of hope: two hearts clasped together, refusing to give in to the darkness.

The Hourim of innocence

Moussa's hand found Abigael's, and his fingers locked firmly with hers. In a whisper with the force of an eternal promise, he breathed: "We're going to get through this. Together."

Their love, fragile as a flickering flame in the heart of a storm, was also an unshakeable strength, a priceless asset in a world devastated by hatred. It was a wealth measured not in goods or conquests, but in shards of soul, in silent promises shared under a torn sky. They had found themselves among the ruins of a shattered humanity, and their union, like a light piercing the darkness, gave them the courage to defy fear, to stand up against rampant despair.

With infinite tenderness, Moussa approached Abigael. His hands, still trembling with the echoes of war, rested gently on her frail shoulders. He bowed his head and placed a kiss on her forehead, a gesture full of silent promise. This kiss was not just a token of affection, but a sacred oath, an invisible shield he was erecting between her and the horrors of the world. The scent of her hair, a mixture of the dust of the rubble and an ineffable sweetness, reached him. It was a fragrance that evoked a bygone era, a reminiscence of innocence that remained tenacious even in the midst of chaos.

The night, vast and silent, had unfurled its inky veil, dotted with stars, like a celestial painting offered in respite to their tormented souls. The moon, peaceful sovereign, illuminated the scene with its silvery glow, giving their embrace an almost sacred dimension. Its soft light seemed to whisper to them that, even in the deepest darkness, there were islands of peace, moments when tumult faded before the power of love.

And so they remained, their bodies young but already scarred by the ordeal, entwined in a silence that transcended language.

The Hourim of innocence

Time, usually tyrannical, seemed to suspend its course, imprisoned in this jewel box of eternity. All around them, the violence of the world, the cries of men, the clash of weapons, seemed to have vanished, as if dissipated by the aura of their bond. This silence, far from being empty, was heavy with promise, the bearer of a fragile but radiant hope.

For the first time in months that had seemed like centuries, they dared to believe in a future. Their incandescent love triumphed over the surrounding darkness. It was an unquenchable fire, fuelled by every smile they shared, every tear they shared. Far more powerful than war, far more enduring than the hatred accumulated over generations, this love was their ultimate weapon, their challenge to a world torn apart.

They were still only children, but their love transcended the boundaries of age and conflict. It was subject neither to the laws of men nor to the whims of history. It was a love that ignored walls, barbed wire and separations imposed by hands too full of resentment. It was a love that laughed at distinctions, divisions and the quarrels of nations.

For in that love lay a simple, universal truth: the real battle, the battle against oblivion and indifference, had already been won. Their love, sharper than any blade, more resilient than the bitterest betrayal, was a primordial force, a light that nothing could extinguish. And with that light, they would go forward, hand in hand, defying the darkness, bearing a message that the world could no longer ignore : Love, in its purest form, was the only answer to the evils of mankind.

The Hourim of innocence

CHAPTER IV
THE CRY OF ASHES

« IN THE ASHES OF THE HOUSING ESTATES, ONLY THE CHILDREN STILL KNOW HOW TO DREAM, EVEN WHEN THE MODE TRIES TO SNATCH EVERY HOPE FROM THEM. »

Night had taken hold of Jerusalem, spreading its cloak of icy shadows over the ancient stones of the city, infusing the air with a biting chill that crept between the interstices of history. Abigael and Moussa, shrouded in darkness, clung to each other, seeking in the warmth of their embrace a bulwark against the world that was crumbling around them.

The Hourim of innocence

They needed neither words nor explanations; silence was enough. This silence was not an absence, but a full presence, a sacred space where their hearts beat in unison, soothing the tumult outside with a secret rhythm that belonged to them alone. Each heartbeat brought precious comfort, a pulse of hope that seemed to push back the darkness.

Then, suddenly, the Guardian appeared before them. This time, he had taken on human form: an old man with features deeply etched by time, a face sculpted with a thousand years of wisdom that seemed to belong to all the lands of this region, both Palestinian and Israeli. He exuded an unspeakable peace, but also an energy of unsuspected power, as if every wrinkle in his face told a lost tale, an echo of centuries past. His eyes were veritable wells of stars, deep and unfathomable, harbouring a mystical light that seemed to contain the forgotten secrets of humanity.

Without another word, he guided them to a place that no mortal could have discovered on his own, a hidden, almost dreamlike passage, nestling not far from the Dome of the Rock. They descended into the bowels of Jerusalem, following this invisible path until they reached a hall with an otherworldly feel, imbued with an ancient and unalterable magic. The stone walls were engraved with forgotten symbols, like hieroglyphs whispering fragments of a story never told. Here, reality seemed suspended, and even time had stopped, petrified in a moment of eternity. It was a sanctuary where the laws of the outside world no longer held sway, a place where each stone seemed to vibrate with a sacred memory.

The room was bathed in a soft glow, emitted by the walls themselves, an unreal luminescence that seemed to exude an ancient breath, a light that made the air palpable, almost alive.

The Hourim of innocence

Abigael and Moussa stood there, transformed by this enchanting atmosphere. They felt liberated from the shackles of their destiny, as if, for a suspended moment, they could glimpse the miracle of genuine peace, a respite where the world, with its pain and wars, no longer had any hold over them.

Then the Guardian spoke. His voice, imbued with a solemn gentleness, seemed to seep into every stone, every corner of their souls, melting into space with divine harmony: "You must understand," he began, his voice carrying an echo of eternity, "that your survival is only due to the Love that unites you. You have faced the darkest abyss, horrors that no child should know. Everything was meticulously orchestrated to break you apart, to extinguish that fragile flame that burns within you. The loss of your parents was the first assault; massacres and blind violence were meant to destroy you. Yet you stood firm, united, because your love is more powerful and purer than all the forces of hatred.

He gazed at them, his eyes filled with infinite tenderness, as if he could see through them to the fabric of their souls. "Man," he continued, "is capable of monstrous acts, especially when he lets himself be guided by the whispers of the devil, when he pushes the limits of evil. But don't think that the Creator has tested you. He sees all, knows all, and always leaves it up to man to choose his path. It is your free and courageous choices that have forged your destiny. You have chosen love in the midst of darkness, and that is what sets you apart."

For a moment, Moussa's eyes darkened, the shadow of his actions hanging over him, the memory of the uncle he had killed haunting him. The Guardian, as if reading his thoughts, approached with infinite wisdom:

The Hourim of innocence

"Moussa," he said gently, "you're carrying a burden that isn't yours. When you fired, it wasn't you who decided life or death. The Creator alone takes souls, whether they are innocent or corrupt. Your uncle fell by your hand, but it was the One who allowed it. The innocent souls that have fallen, and those that will fall again, are victims of an evil that seeks to destroy love, to extinguish that universal light that binds mankind to the divine. But remember, the Creator is just, and His judgement is beyond all human injustice."

Abigael and Moussa, imbued with these revelations, felt their very being transformed. Their spirits were marked by a transcendent truth, a new understanding that eclipsed fear and ignited in them a determination without equal. They knew, in a visceral way, that their love was their shield, the only weapon pure enough to defy the darkness.

The Guardian watched them with benevolent intensity, his eyes reflecting the eternity of ancient knowledge. In a gesture imbued with serenity, he extended his luminous hands, and an almost divine breeze caressed their faces. His presence did not fade, but became a palpable force around them, an unshakeable beacon in the darkness. He remained there, silent but vigilant, ready to guide their steps at every turn of fate.

Hand in hand, they stood at the heart of this timeless sanctuary, their love vibrating with an almost sacred energy. The cold and darkness no longer had any hold over them; they were ready. Together, they would face the coming storm with a light that nothing could extinguish, a light born of their pain, but transcended by their love.

They both drank in every word the Guardian spoke, transfixed by this unshakeable wisdom, by this truth that they felt

The Hourim of innocence

vibrating in the depths of their being, like a long-silenced string finally resonating. "What is about to break over Gaza and the surrounding lands," continued the Guardian, his voice heavy with dark prophecy, "will be on a diabolical scale. A cataclysm, an infernal dance of fire and metal that will claim thousands of souls, while the rest of the world will freeze, petrified by an invisible force, a darkness that will paralyse even thought. This complicit silence, this guilty silence, will be judged. Everyone, even those who have walled themselves up in indifference, will be held to account: those who have remained silent, those who have watched without acting, those who have let the innocent perish without raising the slightest cry."

He approached them, and the simple touch of his hand on their frail shoulders seemed to instil a new warmth, an energy that not even terror could quell. His words softened, but lost none of their gravity: "You will be the spark that will rekindle the flame. Your love, so pure, so absolute, is a lesson that adults must relearn. Because as long as two hearts love each other unconditionally, hatred cannot triumph. You will be the lightning that tears through the darkest night, the light that guides lost souls towards redemption. You carry this hope, born of a pain you did not deserve, but which nonetheless shines a light across the deepest divisions."

The Guardian's words rose up, hovering in the air like a silent blessing, and even the silence, eternal witness to their suffering, seemed to bow in gratitude. Abigael turned to Moussa, and their gazes locked like those of a star you cling to when the darkness wants to swallow you. In that gaze, there was a new strength, a resolution that burned like a sacred fire. They were no longer two children, wandering souls in a war

The Hourim of innocence

that was beyond them. No, they had now become bearers of light, spirits united by love, capable of awakening a world numbed by hatred and indifference. Their innocence was no longer a weakness, but a bulwark of inestimable power, a purity that nothing could mar.

In a final gesture imbued with infinite tenderness, the Guardian cast a gaze upon them that danced with the radiance of millennia of suffering and hope, before dissipating in a gentle breeze, a breath of eternity that caressed their cheeks like a final farewell. Abigael and Moussa found themselves alone, but with the unshakeable certainty of what they had to achieve. They held hands, united by an unspoken oath. They had a mission, a sacred duty to those who no longer had a voice, to the children, to the innocent, and to Love, that miracle that must never be broken.

At that moment, nothing mattered, not the cold, not the darkness. Their love was their only warmth, a flame that nothing could extinguish. They were ready, ready to face the storm that was coming, even if it meant sacrificing themselves to save what was left of beauty and purity in this world. For their love was a miracle, a light snatched from destruction, a sacred fire that would defy the darkness.

The days that followed were marked by apocalyptic excess. Israeli vengeance was unleashed with the force of a divine storm, transforming the skies over Gaza into an incandescent abyss where torrents of bombs rained down relentlessly. What were initially claimed to be targeted strikes, carefully calculated to hit Houmas positions, turned into an indiscriminate hurricane, sweeping away everything in its path, taking innocent lives in a deluge of fire. The boundary between combatants and civilians was eroded until it disappeared, and

The Hourim of innocence

the mechanical fury of the bombardments crushed men, women and children indiscriminately, burying their fragile lives under mountains of rubble.

The media, far from being neutral witnesses, became actors in this tragic theatre, amplifying the horror of the attack on 7 October to the point of making it sound like an unprecedented ignominy. The words themselves seemed mutilated by the violence they described: pogrom, massacre, apocalypse. But the aftershock, this murderous deluge, unfolded with dehumanised coldness, crushing any shred of hope. Soon it was no longer simple revenge, but a carnage both absurd and implacable, orchestrated with the indifference of those who should have raised their voices.

The blood of the innocent flowed, but the silence of the powerful covered it up. The dominant media took sides, stigmatising those who dared to express the slightest empathy for the Palestinians. Any attempt at nuance, any word of compassion, was immediately stifled by accusations of anti-Semitism, pillorying those who did not want to give in to a binary, simplistic and cruel vision. Propaganda was deployed like an oppressive fog, masking the tears, the cries and the truth of this carnage, while Western governments, dressed in a false neutrality, took their place in this chorus of accomplices, blind echoes of a macabre game.

The vast majority of the media were quick to take sides, pointing the finger at anyone who dared to express even a hint of empathy for the Palestinians, anyone who dared to question the official version or to protest against the indiscriminate brutality of the Israeli reprisals. Propaganda crept in, spreading like thick, unalterable opaque smoke, concealing human suffering and the complexity of events behind a screen of

The Hourim of innocence

simplistic slogans and judgements that were as clear-cut as they were unjust. Any dissenting voice, any attempt to introduce a nuance, to ask disturbing questions or to invite deeper reflection, was immediately muzzled and demonised. Those who dared to raise their voices to denounce this disproportionate and indiscriminate violence found themselves dragged into the public square, lynched by a fabricated public opinion, accused of anti-Semitism and condemned to infamy. For many, these courageous voices even ended up being prosecuted, crushed under the weight of an implacable political machinery. Western governments, with their air of false neutrality, were not spared by this charade. In reality, their declared impartiality was an illusion : they had already chosen their side, blindly rallying to Israeli policy, adopting conventional, mechanical and terribly cynical postures.

All of this seemed meticulously orchestrated, like the cogs in a great, well-oiled machine, set in motion long before the violence broke out. How could the Mouzad, the Israeli intelligence service renowned for its implacable vigilance and virtually unlimited resources, have missed such obvious signs? Why did the Israeli authorities wait so long to intervene, allowing the situation to spiral out of control ? How could fighters, claiming to be Muslims, have committed such atrocities, despite the teachings of Islam, which unambiguously condemn acts of barbarity? All this defied logic, defying reason with cruel insistence, as if the pieces of this jigsaw puzzle, instead of forming a coherent picture, had been intentionally distorted to justify a response of terrifying proportions. A response that would not only hit Gaza, but would set the whole region ablaze, spreading chaos and desolation far beyond its borders.

The Hourim of innocence

In this cynical game, governments played the role of executioners, while the people were, in their eyes, nothing more than collateral damage, mere expendable pawns on the geopolitical chessboard. These unscrupulous strategists, heirs to the decision-makers of yesteryear, seemed intent on redrawing borders, just as their predecessors had done with icy arrogance. How could a people who had endured the unspeakable horror of the Shoah, who had suffered the worst persecution in history, now impose suffering that was so similar to what they themselves had endured ? History seemed to be writing itself with gloomy echoes. It was not the Arab peoples who had exterminated millions of Jews, who had orchestrated this genocidal madness. No, it was the Europeans, the same ones who today drape themselves in a silence fraught with contradictions.

During the darkest hours of history, it was the Arab countries that, defying religious and cultural divisions, opened their borders, offering refuge to persecuted Jews, welcoming them when the rest of the world turned its back. How then can we explain that, decades later, this same people, supposed to be the repository of the memory of absolute evil, can inflict such similar suffering on others? Do we really think that the day would come when the peoples of Africa, once torn from their land and sold like commodities, would rise up to enslave the rest of the world in their turn, to subjugate those who had enslaved them ? It was still the Europeans who ran this despicable trade, exploiting human beings like objects, and yet those who were oppressed never responded with a thirst for universal domination.

Today, people are glued to their screens, hypnotised by the incessant hammering of propaganda that leaves no room for

The Hourim of innocence

doubt, nuance or reflection. Social networks are overflowing with false information, fabricated stories and truncated realities that infiltrate the minds of the masses, blurring the line between truth and lies. Wisdom, hindsight and critical thinking have become rare commodities, stifled by the cacophony of disinformation. The truth, the real truth, is never revealed in the din of slogans and violent images ; it lies in meditative silence, in the wisdom of the ancients, in the hearts of people who still dare to see beyond deceptive facades and refuse to give in to imposed discourse.

No one should rise up against a people or a faith, for it is against that which corrupts the very essence of the world that we must all fight, against evil in all its forms, insidious and manifest. Whether they are Jews in Israel, Muslims in Palestine, Christians in the East, or believers of other faiths, all those who, deep down, share a faith in the same one God, are just names on a list. A list that evil would like to erase, to destroy divine hope and plunge creation into eternal darkness.

In the Holy Land, evil has opened a rift, and is working to spread it, like a gangrene seeking to contaminate the entire planet. It sows chaos, fuels divisions and feeds hatred until it devours every trace of humanity. But his ambition goes even further than this apparent carnage : he wants to awaken an ancestral power, to reactivate a sealed door, a thousand-year-old vortex hidden beneath the Dome of the Rock. A forbidden passage, whose legends evoke the return of the Gog and the Magog, those cursed civilisations mentioned in the Koranic verses which, at the end of time, would pour down on the Earth from the heights, bringing desolation and death. This is the real threat, more insidious than bombs, more frightening than man's war. It is a spiritual war, a battle for the soul of

The Hourim of innocence

humanity. And in this invisible battle, Abigael and Moussa, through their purity and the strength of their love, are perhaps the last bulwark against the darkness that threatens the world.

During their retreat to this sanctuary, Abigael and Moussa stayed with the Guardian for a long time. They stayed in a place that seemed frozen in time, surrounded by silence and shadows charged with mystery. There, protected from the tumult of the outside world, they had time to immerse themselves in deep contemplation, an almost divine introspection. Although they were so young, barely fourteen, they had been through unimaginably intense ordeals, suffering that few adults could have withstood without succumbing. They had witnessed unspeakable atrocities, and yet they had been denied the right to mourn, a right snatched from them by the cruelty of circumstances. Their parents, torn from their lives in waves of violence, had left gaping wounds, invisible scars that refused to close. They carried this pain in silence, a haunting weight that no miracle could alleviate. Yet life went on, relentless, the days slipping through their fingers like sand. They had no choice but to carry on, searching for snatches of light in an endless night, shards of happiness in an ocean of desolation.

The months passed deceptively slowly, and Abigael and Moussa grew stronger. They forged their bodies and minds, each training session making them stronger, but it was above all the love they felt for each other that transformed them, a luminous energy that defied the shadows and repelled hatred. Their eyes, once filled with fear, now shone with a peaceful depth, a quiet strength that even the most terrible adversaries could not shake. They were no longer just children; they were bearers of light, immortal hearts overflowing with

The Hourim of innocence

compassion. Their love had become a sanctuary, a bastion that nothing could shake.

Each of them had their own way of praying. Abigael prayed in silence, her hands clasped, her eyes raised to an invisible sky, seeking an intimate communion, a sacred conversation with the infinite. Moussa, on the other hand, prayed with burning fervour, his knees sinking into the earth, reciting the ancient words with all the faith of his soul, words that linked him to the hopes and prayers of generations gone by. Their paths towards the divine were different, but their hearts beat in unison, directed towards the same light. They understood that what mattered was not the form of the prayers, nor the ritual, but the faith that animated them, the pure sincerity of each thought directed towards the Creator. They knew that they were united in this quest for goodness, in this commitment to goodness, to sharing, to peace.

It was a fragile peace, a peace that had survived centuries of conflict, betrayal and senseless struggle. But this peace had never been totally broken, because there had always been souls somewhere, ready to carry it, to pass it on, beyond human borders, beyond the barriers erected by men. This peace, like their love, did not bend, did not allow itself to be sullied by ignorance or fanaticism. It survived because it was carried by beings who had chosen to believe in the light, even when everything seemed to be collapsing.

When they emerged from the Guardian's protection, the sight that awaited them was breathtaking, but in a way that left a bitter taste, a taste of ashes and unshed tears. Gaza was nothing but a field of ruins. Entire neighbourhoods, once alive with the laughter of children and the conversations of elders, were now nothing more than shapeless heaps of rubble, mute

The Hourim of innocence

ruins of shattered lives. Every street, every home, every human vestige seemed to have been swallowed up by a destructive force that made no distinction. And in the sky, the warplanes continued their macabre dance, tearing the silence with a metallic roar, dropping bombs that sowed death and nothingness.

Night had fallen, and a biting cold crept between the thousand-year-old stones of the city, penetrating the smallest cracks like an icy breath of eternity. Moussa and Abigael moved forward, huddled together, drawing from each other an almost sacred warmth that transcended the torments of the outside world. They needed no words; their silence spoke louder than any prayer. The simple fact of being together, after all they had been through, was enough to illuminate the surrounding shadows. Their hearts beat in unison, and in that shared rhythm they found a calm that eclipsed, if only for a moment, the anarchy of humanity.

As they made their way through the ruins of Gaza, the landscape of desolation before them seemed to extend far beyond the territory. The chaos spared no-one, and the spiral of violence continued to engulf everything in its path. After Iran, it was the turn of Lebanon, a land already marked by so much pain, to find itself under fire from Israeli reprisals.

The missiles traced lines of fire in the darkness, while the world's leaders, bogged down in sterile diplomatic discussions, remained spectators. Hollow words piled up, unable to mask the inaction in the face of horror. How had it come to this? How could a country as powerfully armed as Israel, supported and financed by nations claiming to be peacekeepers, strike with such impunity at a defenceless people ? Under the pretext of hunting down the Houmas, a group whose tragic irony lay

The Hourim of innocence

in the fact that it had once been supported and financed by Israel itself to sow discord among its enemies, collective punishment was being meted out to innocent people. Each falling missile not only shattered walls, it destroyed lives, hopes and the fragile promise of a better tomorrow.

None of it made any sense. Everything was cloudy and clear at the same time, an abject paradox that defied logic and perverted the truth. Manipulation reigned supreme, weaving veils of shadows around minds, and profound truths were hidden behind propaganda facades, half-words and well-placed fears. The whole world seemed to have become a theatre of the absurd, a stage where the roles of victim and executioner were exchanged endlessly, where reality was distorted by shadowy puppeteers.

Abigael and Moussa walked through the rubble with a new gravity, their eyes resting on the petrified faces of those who were no more, on the ruins that screamed out the folly of man. Every step they took was a stabbing blow, but it was also a march charged with determination. A force had awakened within them, something immense, indomitable. They knew what they had to do. They were not there simply to be powerless witnesses, but to act, to awaken consciences, to be the voice of the souls that the world had chosen to ignore.

The raw, implacable truth didn't need to be shouted out. It was there, in every fragment of broken life, in every sigh, in the empty eyes of a mother, in the dried tears of a child. People had become mere pawns on the chessboard of the powerful, their lives expendable, their hopes trampled underfoot by overweening ambitions. But Abigael and Moussa refused to be pawns. They would not let other children be reduced to ashes by the greed and hatred of men. Their love, stronger than the

The Hourim of innocence

steel of bombs, would be their weapon. Their faith, their shield. Together, they would defy the darkness, even if it led them to the gates of hell.

They went deeper into this desolate landscape, determined to find other children, lost beings like themselves. Every time they met them, they reached out their hands, urging these young souls to follow them, and soon they formed a close-knit group, united by despair but also by a fragile hope. Around them, the ocean of ruins stretched endlessly, each stone, each fragment giving off a suffocating heat, an echo of the flames that had ravaged this world. The children they passed, orphans, terrified, were like ghosts of a time that no longer existed. Their faces bore the marks of dust, terror and frozen tears. Their torn clothes hung over them like rags, and in their eyes shone a primitive, heart-rending fear that surpassed even that of adults.

This fear, so raw, so palpable, seemed to echo in the air, a silent lament, and there was something in those looks that twisted your insides, that screamed out a truth that no one could ignore. A child's fear is like nothing else; it's so pure, so absolute, that it becomes unbearable.

The pungent smells of the ruins permeated the air like invisible spectres, a suffocating mixture of dust, ash and crystallised tears. The children, on the other hand, were not so much afraid of pain, or even of death. What terrified them was fear itself, naked and brutal, especially when it was experienced in absolute solitude, without a reassuring word, without the warmth of a protective embrace. Their innocence revealed the cruelest face of fear: that of abandonment, that of the breaking of a bond of love, the unbearable anguish of being separated forever from the tenderness of a mother, the protection of a

The Hourim of innocence

father, the affection of a loved one. The look on the face of a frightened child should be enough to break the heart of anyone with an ounce of humanity left. Yet here, in this endless war, that look had become commonplace, a constant reflection of the injustices perpetrated by a world of insensitive adults.

The war, with its trail of terror and destruction, had planted its dark seeds in the hearts of these children, chaining them to nightmares far too big for them. Moussa and Abigael understood the urgent need to act, to comfort these broken souls, whether orphans or not. They had to rekindle hope, even if it was only a flickering spark in this implacable chaos. Above them, scavenging birds circled ominously, their cries piercing the heavy silence, underlining the urgency and fragility of their mission. It all seemed insurmountable, but they were determined to make a start, no matter how difficult.

Moussa, inspired by a sudden idea, suggested a game to the children. A simple game, but one that might perhaps bring a little light back into their darkened eyes. He asked them to close their eyes, to think very hard about the people they had lost, to imagine them there, close to them. He explained to them that they should feel a loving hand stroking their hair, hear a gentle voice reassuring them, as if their presence had been returned to them, even for a moment. Many of the children, despite the pain weighing on their frail shoulders, accepted. Their eyelids closed, their lashes trembling with concentration, their lips whispering names, prayers and precious memories. But some remained reticent, sceptical, almost hardened. Hatred had already germinated within them, stifling the slightest hint of candour, and they had become incapable of believing, even in a game.

The Hourim of innocence

Abigael approached these children, the ones whose hearts seemed closed. She knelt down beside them, gazing into their eyes with infinite gentleness and gravity. She took a deep breath and told them a story, a true story. Her voice, hesitant at first, became fluid, like a stream flowing over stones. She spoke of a little girl and a little boy who had met under an olive tree, a tree with silvery leaves that quivered in the wind, a symbol of fragile peace in a world in turmoil. She described the golden light of that afternoon, the gentleness of an encounter that, despite the surrounding violence, had given birth to something precious. Then she spoke of the ordeal they had been through together, the day of 7 October, the deafening noise, the flames licking the sky, the immeasurable fear, but also the mysterious force that had guided them, the invisible force that drove them to survive.

Her voice broke slightly, her eyes moistening, but she continued: "This little girl is me. And that boy is Moussa, standing here before you." A dense silence fell over them, disturbed only by the wind that crept between the ruins and the muffled sound of the still-warm rubble. The children listened, hanging on her words, searching her face for the truth of her story, the fragile light she was trying to pass on to them.

Then a murmur arose, faint at first, hesitant, but gaining in strength, transforming itself into a unanimous cry: "Hourim! Hourim ! Hourim !" This word, mysterious and powerful, seemed to emerge from the very depths of their souls. It was a new word, forged in the urgency of hope, a word that belonged neither to Arabic nor to Hebrew, but to both. In it vibrated the root of "Houras", which in Arabic means guardian, and the ending "im", borrowed from Hebrew, marking the plural.

The Hourim of innocence

This magic word sprang spontaneously from the children's lips, as if blown by a higher force. It transcended languages and borders, uniting hearts in a single cry, a single appeal. It referred to Abigael and Moussa, their magical guardians, the protectors they had chosen, the beacons of light in this all-consuming night.

Their voices rose in the darkness, filling the air with a vibrant echo of defiance and faith. "Hourim" was not just a slogan, it was a proclamation of hope, a declaration of resistance, a word etched into eternity to designate those whose courage held out the promise of a new world.

This collective cry, this single word, seemed to possess an almost magical force. It was like an incantation, a breath of hope that defied the surrounding darkness. The story of Abigael and Moussa spread through the refugee camps, throughout Gaza. Children wanted to see them, to meet them, as if they had become living legends, bearers of light. An invisible aura emanated from them, a comforting energy, a peace that nothing seemed able to break. You only had to look at them, listen to them, to feel the burden of pain lighten, for the oppressive air to suddenly become breathable, for the darkness to seem a little less frightening. With them, the shadows receded, and hope, however fragile, became possible again.

The news spread like an elusive flame, a living spark that nothing could stop. From one camp to the next, the children whispered and marvelled, their voices charged with an almost sacred solemnity. "Hourim", a word that belonged to no known language but was the fruit of a fusion, a creation born of love and despair, echoed through the ruins. It circulated like a breath of hope, a promise barely whispered but vibrating with unshakeable strength. It was said that this word had been given to them by providence itself, that nothing in this cruel war had been left to chance. The Guardian, a benevolent celestial entity, had inspired this name, giving Abigael and Moussa a power that even the darkest of darkness could not extinguish.

As the days passed, Hourim became more than just a name: it became a rallying cry, a hymn of freedom. The word vibrated in the air with an intensity that transcended borders and broke the invisible chains of hatred. It was inscribed in the hearts of the children like a blessing, a promise that the light could always triumph, even in the abyss of suffering. Their voices, young but vibrant with determination, had become a sacred song, a challenge to the forces of destruction.

Before they knew it, Abigael and Moussa had become emblematic figures, beacons of hope for all Palestinian children. Their energy shone like a divine light, and this benevolent aura soon crossed borders. In Israel, children too began to rally to the cause. They murmured, then chanted "Hourim" with a fervour that no one had anticipated, a powerful echo that rose into the ether, breaking through walls of mistrust, piercing the hearts of those who had forgotten what it was to believe in love and innocence.

In the space of a few weeks, the phenomenon became impossible to ignore. Social networking sites were abuzz with an irrepressible craze. Messages of hope circulated, photos of candles flickering in the night, carried by trembling but courageous hands. The digital platforms, initially reluctant to give visibility to the movement, were forced to give in to the scale of the wave. The censorship algorithms, ruthless and closely monitored, were constantly circumvented by the

The Hourim of innocence

ingenuity of the movement's supporters. Hourim adapted, transformed itself, played with the rules to sneak into every nook and cranny of the web, becoming an elusive force. The media, sceptical at first, began to cover the subject. Some sought to discredit this movement born of innocence. How, they wondered, could two children carry such a burden ? Experts were called in to analyse this unexpected phenomenon, but nothing was done. Pure hearts were won over, and even adults began to listen and pay attention. Parents, at first frightened by this revolutionary glow, gradually began to understand. How could anyone oppose the voice of their own children ? How could they ignore a movement that emanated from sincerity, kindness and a love that not even war could sully ?

For Abigael and Moussa, this surge of hope was like a dream, but it came with a crushing weight. Sometimes, when tiredness became unbearable and anxiety arose in the darkness, they sought refuge in each other. Under the starry sky, they would find moments of silence where they could lay down their invisible weapons and let their hearts speak without words. Moussa would place his hand gently on Abigael's, and that simple contact was enough to ward off the shadows that lurked. Their love, silent but incredibly powerful, was an unshakeable promise, an oath that would never be broken.

The nights they spent together were filled with inaudible whispers and glances that spoke louder than any words. Sometimes, Abigael would rest her head against Moussa's shoulder, listening to his heartbeat, which had become her favourite melody, a source of comfort. The children's candles gently lit the horizon, and the flickering light cast tender shadows on their faces. It was a love that was still young, a

The Hourim of innocence

precious flame that the war had made unalterable. Every gesture, every look, was a silent declaration that their bond would never give way, that it was stronger than hate, more powerful than fear.

In those stolen moments, they found the strength to carry on. And as the world descended into chaos, their love remained the light that guided lost souls, a reminder that, even in the darkest night, humanity could still choose beauty and goodness.

In the Gaza Strip, every evening at sunset, all the children would gather together, clutching candles or simple lighters in their small hands. Thousands of tiny flames pierced the darkness, illuminating the night like an earthly constellation. This flickering light, fragile yet infinite, spread with an irresistible softness, uniting these innocent souls in a vast web of hope. Together, these children illuminated the darkness to show the world that a single flame, multiplied infinitely, could become a beacon, a bastion of light capable of dispelling the deepest darkness.

Moussa and Abigael always stood slightly back, not out of fear, but out of a kind of shared modesty, a reserve imbued with gentleness. They occasionally exchanged glances, and in their eyes, oceans of feelings unfolded without the need for any words: fear, of course, but also a flame of hope, and above all, this budding love, fragile but indomitable, which dared to defy the cruellest of circumstances. You had to see these children, thousands of faces lit up by the dancing glow of the flames, and hear their voices rising up, strong and unyielding, crying out in chorus : "Hourim". It was a cry of innocence, a song of resistance, a warmth that warmed bruised hearts and held out the promise of a peace that many had given up hoping for. On

The Hourim of innocence

the other side, in Israel, the situation was becoming critical. The strikes on Gaza could no longer continue without those who ordered them being seen by the whole world as the murderers of innocent children. Even the longest-running conflicts, such as that between Russia and Ukraine, had to come to a halt, because everywhere children were standing as living shields, hand in hand, forming unshakeable lines of disarming purity. Even the most ruthless dictators found themselves paralysed, powerless in the face of this army of innocence. Who could have imagined that such a movement would arise, spreading with the speed of holy fire, with a power that no one could contain?

Innocence, long ignored and trampled underfoot, was now reclaiming its place. Adults, hitherto numbed by indifference or impotence, were gradually waking up. They rallied to the cause, transfixed by the purity of this cry, overwhelmed to see the light that these children held so firmly in their hands. A simple spark had been transformed into an immense blaze, a light that not even the densest darkness could quench.

When the Hourim movement paused, in those rare moments torn from the night, Moussa and Abigael found refuge in the most precious sanctuary they possessed: each other. Under the soft light of the candles, their faces lit up, and in this fragile halo, they exchanged shy smiles, silent promises far more powerful than words. One night, under a sky dotted with benevolent stars, Abigael slipped her hand into Moussa's and squeezed it tenderly. This simple, infinitely gentle gesture said everything they didn't need to say. This moment stolen from the tumult was suspended in time, a moment of purity, where they were no longer the figureheads of a movement, but just two teenagers loving each other with a love that was both

The Hourim of innocence

vulnerable and indestructible. Their hearts beat in harmony, and in that shared rhythm resounded a silent promise : never to give in to hatred, always to fight for the hope they had discovered together, that unique and precious love, that unalterable dream of a possible world.

Under these stars, they looked up at the stars, those luminous flashes, distant but unchanging, like silent witnesses to their oath. Everything around them seemed ephemeral and fragile, and yet they felt in the depths of their souls that this moment, this shared tenderness, would remain engraved in them for eternity. For it was in this quiet gentleness that the true power of their story lay: not in the clamour of revolt or the echo of battle, but in the silent depth of their bond, a love that was humble and absolute, that demanded nothing but embodied everything.

Suddenly, the Guardian materialised before them, his silhouette imbued with an almost timeless serenity. Dressed humbly, he seemed to embody the very essence of ancestral wisdom, his serene features illuminated by an aura of soothing gravity. His voice, gentle yet imbued with a rare solemnity, enveloped them like a living prophecy. "My children," he whispered, his voice vibrating in the stillness of the night, "listen to me with unfailing attention. You have triumphed over many trials, but those awaiting you will be even more treacherous. Your enemies know that they cannot bring you down without arousing the anger of the nations, so they will use more devious means. They will seek to break that which unites you, to weaken that love which is your most powerful bulwark."

The Guardian stepped forward, his eyes glittering with protective concern. "They will infiltrate your ranks, insinuate

The Hourim of innocence

themselves into your most intimate circles, manipulating the truth, distilling lies. They will sow doubt, weave invisible treachery, invent illusions to crack the trust that binds you. They will play on your deepest fears, exploit your slightest weaknesses, and make the world believe that your love is just an illusion, a ruse, a propaganda tool. Their aim is to make you doubt the very purity of what binds you together, the flame that threatens them".

The Guardian gazed at them with tenderness and strength, like a parent watching over children he knew to be vulnerable but determined. "You must be vigilant, for the shadows are closer than you imagine. They know that your love is an elusive light, that it is the ultimate threat to their darkness. They will do anything to extinguish that flame, to convince you that you are not strong enough. But you are. You're together, and it's this unbreakable union that makes you invincible. Never forget that your love is the key, that it is the star that guides all those who wander in the dark. Be prepared, and never let doubt erode what is most precious to you.

The Guardian fell silent, letting his words float in the air, soaking into the souls of the two young children. The silence that followed seemed as dense and sacred as the starry sky above them, as if the whole world were holding its breath, suspended on a promise that nothing, neither fear nor hatred, could break. Moussa and Abigael exchanged a look charged with emotion, feeling within themselves the power of those words, that timeless truth. Together, they were invincible. And as long as they held on to that certainty, as long as they protected the flame that united them, there was no shadow they could not overcome. The Guardian dissipated with the ethereal sweetness of a dream touched by the fragile light of

The Hourim of innocence

the dawning dawn, blending into the first light like a peaceful shadow carried by the wind. In the subtle half-light, Moussa and Abigael drew closer, their hands clasped in a silent, powerful embrace. In the distance, they felt the approach of a storm, the threatening breath of adversity, but they also knew, with a quiet certainty, that together they formed an indomitable force, a force that nothing could break.

"But remember, my children," the Guardian whispered to them, his voice rising like a final blessing, "that your love is their greatest threat. It is what terrifies them most, for it is a power they cannot understand or control. Whatever you hear, whatever you see, stand together. Be each other's light when everything around you seems to be falling apart. You will have to fight, not with weapons, but with unfailing determination. Your love is a flame that not even the fiercest winds can extinguish, as long as you protect it together."

The Guardian gently faded away, like a sacred breath carried away by the night breezes, leaving behind him a solemn, almost sacred silence, a vibrating echo between the stars and the beating hearts of the two young heroes. Moussa and Abigael stood there motionless, absorbing the weight of his words like a blessing and a warning at the same time. Their hands did not separate; on the contrary, they clasped tighter, sealing a silent promise never to waver, never to allow the shadow to separate them. Around them, the night stretched out, vast and unfathomable, adorned with its mysteries and its dangers. But where others would have seen only despair and loneliness, Moussa and Abigael perceived another truth: the night could be dark, but it was not invincible. For as long as they remained together, as long as their souls clung to each other with absolute faith, there would always be a glimmer, a

The Hourim of innocence

fearless flame defying the darkness. All around, Gaza groaned under the weight of hardship, a landscape of ashes and ruins, a symbol of suffering and desolation. Yet out of the rubble emerged a miraculous light : thousands of children held their candles, fragile but tenacious flames, forming a network of light as vast and infinite as the starry vault. It was no longer just a light ; it was a living canvas, an earthly constellation woven of hope, courage and an indomitable will to resist. Each flickering flame, a reflection of young, determined hearts, was a reminder that even in the face of destructive forces, a miracle could be born out of purity and solidarity. This show of unity and defiance, magnificent in its simplicity, resonated far beyond borders, captivating the whole world, dazzled by this army of children armed only with candles and innocence. Far from the warlike rhetoric and divisions drawn by men, this shared glow bore witness to a power that neither hatred nor bombs could extinguish. It was a pure force, born of love, the desire to live, and faith in a future where peace would finally be possible.

Moussa and Abigael exchanged one last look, a silent conversation passing between them without the need for any words. Their hearts, beating in harmony, whispered the same promise : this was only the beginning. The dawn was still a long way off, the road full of pitfalls, but they had already chosen it. Together, they would advance towards the light, step by step, defying the night, carried by the invincible strength of their love. In that moment of perfect connection, they knew that the road ahead would be difficult, that countless trials would lie ahead. But they had the most powerful weapon of all : their love, their unshakeable faith in a world where, inevitably, the dawn would eventually triumph over the darkness.

The Hourim of innocence

CHAPTER V

THE RIFT OF SILENCE

« WHEN DARKNESS STRIVES TO SEPARATE SOULS, IT IS HEARTS UNITED THAT OPEN THE WAY TO LIGHT. »

The world was changing, and so was war. The evidence was implacably clear: evil had exchanged its resounding weapons for more devious instruments, invisible poisons that insinuated themselves into hearts and minds.

The Hourim of innocence

From then on, battles were no longer fought on fields full of noise and blood, but in the secrecy of the conscience. Swords had turned into poisonous ideas, bullets into cleverly disguised words. And where shells once tore the sky apart, it was disguised truths, twisted until they lost their lustre, that sowed desolation.

Devastation, once brutal and frontal, had taken on the clothes of everyday life, becoming insidious and treacherous, draped in polite smiles and honeyed promises. Evil had become sophisticated, a master of concealment, distilling its perfidy at the very heart of society. Everything was calculated, every gesture, every word, to numb consciences, to sweep souls into a gentle torpor, a golden sleep, seductive but deceptive. The masses, captivated by the frenzy of a superficial world, allowed themselves to be lulled by the melody of comfort, gradually abandoning what was most sacred to them: true love, the love that leads to transcendence, divine love.

And so evil flourished, revelling in the collective blindness, delighting in seeing humanity turn away from its own light. It had worked for years, relentlessly. Hearts had hardened, the warmth of love had faded, little by little, and the divine flame flickered, almost extinguished. But one day, when no one was expecting it, the unforeseeable happened. Two children emerged from that 'nowhere' that represents everything at once : the original source and the ultimate point, the infinitesimal beginning and the infinite end.

Two young souls, bright and vulnerable, had risen up against the darkness, like an unexpected miracle. Moussa and Abigael, two children whom the war should have shattered, but who instead carried within them an invincible light. Their love had been like a comet piercing the thickest darkness, a light that

The Hourim of innocence

crept in where all seemed irretrievably lost. In a world filled with desolation, they had sown seeds of hope where despair had taken its deepest roots. Where hearts had been barricaded, they had breathed sparks of life.

It wasn't grandiloquent words or sharp weapons that had changed the situation. No, it was love, pure and unshakeable, that had proved to be the most powerful form of resistance. Two children, bearers of an innocence so luminous that it disarmed the most corrupt minds, had defied the established order. And from this defiance arose an irreducible truth: that love, the love that asks for nothing but offers everything, the love that stands up to the darkness with a strength that nothing can subdue, remains the only true weapon capable of overthrowing evil.

Their hearts beat in harmony with an unshakeable faith. Moussa and Abigael, by their simple presence, by their unalterable attachment, reminded us that even the most elaborate stratagems of the powerful were doomed to fail in the face of the purity of selfless love. For true power does not belong to tyrants or manipulators, but to those who love unconditionally, those who dare to believe, again and again, in the light in the midst of the shadows.

And so began a new battle, no longer one of clash, but of resilience, of a love that defied the night and rose up, undaunted, ready to rekindle the spark of humanity.

As for Abigael and Moussa, they didn't need long speeches to captivate hearts. Their very presence was a balm, a force that soothed torments and brought back peace where it seemed to have vanished forever. When they spoke, it was to tell stories, tales imbued with their own experiences or imbued with the

The Hourim of innocence

ancient wisdom passed on by the Guardian. One day, they shared a tale that spanned the ages, beliefs and cultural boundaries. A tale that touched the souls of all, like a wave of pure emotion and universal truth.

It was Friday, a holy day, and they were sitting side by side near the Dome of the Rock, a place steeped in history and spirituality. Microphones had been set up so that their voices could reach the gathered crowds. Thousands of people were waiting, children and parents mingling in an atmosphere of serene and solemn anticipation. This was not a raucous demonstration or a concert full of enthusiastic shouts; no, this was a moment of rare intensity, imbued with sacredness. The word 'Hourim' resounded in a haunting whisper, almost like a prayer, and the air seemed to vibrate with the soft, luminous magic that these two young souls shared.

Moussa stood up, his heart pounding, and despite his small voice, still fragile and adolescent, an unexpected charisma emanated from him. His simplicity carried an undeniable force, that of truth.

"Hourim !" he exclaimed, raising his hand to the sky, his fingers intertwined with those of Abigael. She followed him in this gesture, and the crowd, like an echo, responded in unison. A wave of respectful silence then fell, and Moussa continued, in a humble and sincere tone.

- A wise man told me a story, and today I'd like to share it with you, in the hope of doing him justice.

He took a deep breath, and his voice took on the gravity of a storyteller carrying an ancient secret.

The Hourim of innocence

- Long ago, the Creator fashioned a man from malleable mud, a being shaped with divine precision, every stroke bearing the mark of His infinite wisdom. Then, in a gesture of absolute love, He breathed into him a spark of His spirit, a pure and eternal light that made the man's soul radiate with ineffable clarity. All around this creation, the universe held its breath, amazed by perfection incarnate.

But there was one creature, born of smokeless fire, whose pride burned with voracious intensity. Consumed by jealousy, she refused to bow before this being fashioned by the Creator, the bearer of divine light."

The crowd held its breath, hanging on his words.

- This being of fire, with a heart blackened by resentment, saw in man nothing but an unjust rival, unworthy of the divine light. Yet the Creator, in His infinite wisdom, breathed into man a particle of His eternal breath, an immortal essence, and all were called to prostrate themselves before this miracle of flesh and spirit. All obeyed... except the one called Iblis."

Moussa paused, letting the story find its way into the hearts of the listeners. His voice rose again, more intense.

- Iblis stood up, pride consuming his being, refusing to bow to what he believed to be inferior. For him, the fire from which he had sprung surpassed in nobility the earth that had given life to man. So the Creator, in His justice, took the man named Adam down into a garden of wonders, a place of promise and beauty. But Adam, though surrounded by splendour, felt a poignant loneliness. The Creator, full of compassion, knew that man needed a presence to soften his existence".

The Hourim of innocence

Moussa turned to Abigael, and their eyes met, filled with an infinite complicity.

- The Creator then took a rib from Adam and fashioned a companion, Eve. She received the same sacred breath, the divine light that made them a whole, a perfect union, destined to face the mysteries of life together. But the garden, as beautiful as it was, hid a peril. At the centre was a tree with forbidden fruit, containing the knowledge of good and evil, a burden too heavy for their souls. The Creator warned them never to taste it, but the creature of fire, Iblis, had not said his last word. Fallen but not submissive, he too descended, no longer to serve, but to challenge and tempt."

The silence had thickened, palpable. Moussa's every word seemed imbued with ancient wisdom, and in the eyes of those listening, a spark of hope and understanding had been born.

Adam and Eve lived in the heart of an enchanted garden, a kingdom where the wonders of creation stretched out like infinite dreams, where every leaf quivered to the music of a sacred wind, where the rivers murmured hymns to life. But even surrounded by such splendour, they lacked the tenderness of a father, the gentleness of a mother. They had been moulded into adults, thrown into existence without passing through the cradle of innocence, deprived of the tender apprenticeship of love, of that invisible thread that a parent weaves with a child, a bond made of caresses, of words whispered like promises against the darkness.

That childhood they never experienced, that cocoon of vulnerability from which they had never emerged, formed the crack in their souls. And Iblis, the creature of fire, the serpent with a jealous heart, knew this crack in their essence. He crept

The Hourim of innocence

in, sinuous, like a whisper in the cold night, instilling doubt, distilling anguish in the heart of man. Every day, his voice slipped into the shadows, tempting and haunting: "Taste the forbidden tree, savour the fruit, and become like the gods", he repeated, tirelessly, an invisible venom flowing like honey.

Eve, faithful and pure, watched over Adam with infinite tenderness, but even this love was not enough to chase away the darkness of a spirit that had never learned the strength of renunciation. Adam, an adult forged from the earth but never a child, didn't know how to ward off fear, didn't know the prayers you learn by crying in your mother's arms. One day, after centuries of venomous whispers, he gave in to the temptation that consumed him. His trembling fingers plucked the forbidden fruit, and when he brought it to his lips, the taste spread like a sweet fire, a deceptive caress. This fruit, bright and forbidden, had the taste of a divine desire that intoxicates and corrupts. Each mouthful carried the perverse sweetness of a cursed secret, awakening in them a dizziness of heavy, burning knowledge, a mist rising up to obscure the light that the Creator had offered them.

Then the Creator appeared, majestic and unfathomable, and His judgement came down like a decree engraved in the fabric of the stars. Adam, Eve and Iblis were cast down to Earth. But their fall was not a final condemnation. It was the prelude to a story of learning, of becoming. The earth, rough and beautiful, became their school, where the sun caressed their skin with golden rays, where the wind blew poems of eternity into their hair.

However, an enigma persisted. Adam and Eve, who had never tasted childhood, became parents. They offered their children sincere love, but how could they pass on knowledge that they

The Hourim of innocence

had never received? How could they decipher the laughter and pain of childhood, when they had been moulded into adulthood without this sacred passage ? Therein lay humanity's vulnerability, but also its greatest strength. For Iblis, the fallen angel with the black flames, dreaded childhood. Childhood, the pure radiance of celestial light, was the realm where he had no power. Where innocence reigned, his chains were broken. He knew that the true power of humanity lay not in muscle or intellect, but in the untouched hearts of children, in their infinite power to love, to forgive, and to dream beyond the stars.

In conceiving man, the Creator had kept this secret : childhood, a sacred gift, would never be created as Adam and Eve had been fashioned. Childhood could only blossom through the miracle of human love, through the great sacred door that opened in a woman's womb. The miracle of Jesus, carried by Mary, being born vulnerable, symbolised this divine connection. Each child who passed through this door brought with it the spark of the divine, the song of beginnings.

Every birth, then, is a promise, a new dawn. Iblis, haunted by his own shadow, could not bear this light. He knew that as long as children came into the world with this innocence, his reign would remain precarious and shaky. He would spend his existence trying to corrupt that purity, to steal the dreams of childhood, but he could never extinguish that flame.

We children are the new Adam and Eve. We have that blessed childhood they never had. We are heirs of light, with the strength to resist the darkness. We stand hand in hand, beyond wars, beyond hatreds. We are hope incarnate, the purity that the forces of darkness cannot stifle. As long as there are children to love, to dream, the darkness will never win.

The Hourim of innocence

Moussa fell silent, his voice still echoing in the heart. All around him, silence became a palpable entity, a sacred breath shared by a thousand souls. Abigael, her hand clasped in his, offered him a smile where eternity seemed to blossom, and in that smile was all the beauty, all the miracle of a love that refuses to be extinguished.

The message was crystalline : childhood, that sanctuary of purity, was the most sacred gift humanity had ever received, a celestial light emanating from an unalterable source. And hidden in this ray of innocence was the hope of a reconciled world, the dream of a peace that centuries of war had not yet been able to extinguish. What mattered was not the perfection of actions, but resilience, that tenacious flame that refused to be extinguished, that unshakeable courage to continue to love even when pain tore at the soul, even when darkness crept into every breath.

Moussa had finished his story, but his words still hung in the air, like an oath whispered to the stars, inscribed in the very ether that stretched above the Dome of the Rock. Then the word "Hourim" rose, an enveloping wave of sound, carried by countless voices, the voices of children, the voices of elders, intertwined with a luminous force that surpassed all weapons, an incandescent love that seemed to repel darkness itself.

Then Abigael felt the need to speak. A story was living inside her, like a fragile flame begging to shine, a truth that her grandfather, full of wisdom and tenderness, had entrusted to her before illness drove him into oblivion. Abigael could no longer remain silent ; she had to share this treasure of humanity, this lesson wrapped in light and gentleness.

The Hourim of innocence

She raised her right hand to the sky, uniting her cry with the sacred name of "Hourim", and her voice mingled with the echoes of thousands of others, galvanising spirits, tightening souls around this promise of unity. Palestinians and Israelis, those whom history had separated by visible and invisible walls, found themselves united, linked by the same cry, the same hope. When the tumult died down, Abigael spoke, her voice soft but fearless, each word carried by sincere emotion, each syllable sounding like a sacred confession.

- When I was eleven, the year my destiny crossed that of Moussa, tensions within my family had become unbearable. My parents had realised what Moussa meant to me, and fear had taken root in their hearts. For them, he was 'the other', the one from the other side, the stranger we had been taught to fear. On the other side, they thought, lived only enemies, threatening shadows, spectres of hatred that we had to keep at a distance.

I'm not going to tell you about the tragic end of my parents or that of Moussa's parents. Their lives were shattered by the same blind hatred, a fire fed by stories that preceded us, a venom instilled by inherited lies. But today, I'm not here to talk to you about the night, but about the dawn. I want to tell you about the light, the fragile flame that Moussa and I have carried, even when everything seemed doomed to collapse, even when the shadows sought to bury us. The love that binds us is a force that even the gusts of hatred have not been able to extinguish. This love, born in darkness, has grown stronger, has defied all the obstacles, and it is this love that has saved us.

Abigael's voice, tinged with gentleness and courage, caressed the air like an ancient melody, awakening emotions that hearts

The Hourim of innocence

had buried for too long. A wave of warmth spread through the crowd, a wave made up of held back tears, unspoken sorrow, but also a spark of redemption. And for a moment, a breath of eternity seemed to touch the souls present, an invitation to believe that light, however flickering, has the power to weather the worst storms.

She paused for a moment, a slight tremor in her voice. She looked at Moussa, and he gave her a smile that gave her the strength to continue.

- The only soul in my family who embodied true discernment, the only source of authentic wisdom, was my grandfather. He was a man of infinite piety and almost sacred benevolence. His hands bore the scars of hard labour, but his heart remained light, always ready to wrap me in his unshakeable tenderness. When my parents were torn from my life, I was plunged into dizzying grief. An abyss had opened up inside me, an unfathomable pain, as vast and dark as the starless vault of heaven. One day, to soothe the pain that was consuming me, he told me a story. That was before the disease, that merciless scourge known as Alzheimer's, came and wiped out everything in him, before his mind was stripped of even the memory of my name. This story has given me a profound understanding of the mysteries of life, and today I want to share it with you.

The crowd held its breath, and the wide-eyed children hung on Abigaël's lips, feeling the mystical gravity of the moment, as if an invisible force bound their souls together.

- My grandfather told me a story from the Talmud, a parable that celebrated the immaculate innocence and unshakeable strength of the Children of Israel. He told me that, since the dawn of time, there had been one truth that darkness feared

The Hourim of innocence

above all else: the purity of children. This was centuries before Moses. Children, by their nature untainted by evil, have always been the guardians of a light to which even the darkest powers could not lay claim.

A long time ago, when Pharaoh reigned supreme, a prophecy was brought to his ears. Pharaoh had learned that a child would be born among the Hebrews, a child destined to overthrow him and free his people from oppression. Panic-stricken, he decreed that all newborn males should be torn from their mothers' wombs and thrown into the waters of the Nile. But it was in these very waters that the miracle was performed. An infant was placed in an ark of rushes, gliding gently over the waters, silent and fragile like a breath of prayer, an offering to destiny. And it was Pharaoh's daughter herself, Bithiah, who found him and took him in, unaware of the identity of this child bearing the name of Moses. And so the light was hidden from the darkness, hidden from the very eyes of those who feared it.

My grandfather used to say that, even in those ancient times, children were the beating heart of the resistance. Moses was just an infant, vulnerable and defenceless, but it was precisely in this fragility that his power lay. Pharaoh could guard against armies and insurrections, but he was powerless against the gentle light of a child floating on the waters".

Abigaël paused, her eyes wandering for a moment among the children in the crowd, as if to capture their innocent souls, then she spoke again in a soft, emotional voice.

- This story has always reminded me of another, that of Ishmael, the young boy walking alongside his father Abraham. Imagine this scene: a father and his child, alone in the heart of

The Hourim of innocence

the desert, carrying on their shoulders the weight of an implacable divine order. Abraham had been commanded to sacrifice his son, and yet Ishmael, though young, did not bend. He shed no tears, he did not tremble. He was ready, not out of ignorance, but out of total trust, an unshakeable faith that the Creator would provide. And just as the blade was about to fall, the divine hand intervened. A ram was sent to take Ishmael's place. Once again, it was the child's innocence, his pure abandonment to faith, that changed the course of fate.

Abigaël paused again, her eyes lingering on the attentive faces of the children around her, before continuing in an even softer voice, imbued with a benevolent gravity.

- And then there was David, the young shepherd, a child who humbly looked after the flocks. It is said that the men of Israel trembled before Goliath, that invincible giant, but it was David, armed with a simple slingshot, who stepped forward without fear. He was neither the strongest nor a seasoned warrior, but he possessed something infinitely more powerful. Pure faith, an unshakeable certainty that even the most imposing of giants could be defeated if you stood on the side of the light. And it was with a stone, a single stone guided by the divine hand, that he overcame Goliath, casting down shadow with light."

She let the silence stretch out, an almost sacred silence, allowing each story to echo in the hearts of her listeners, like a whisper that resonated deep within the soul.

- My grandfather also told me the story of Solomon, who became king when he was just a child. He had to govern a people and administer justice, but all he had was the innocent wisdom of his youth. But it was precisely this wisdom, this

The Hourim of innocence

ability to see beyond appearances, to feel hearts rather than listen to words, that made him the great king we know. Solomon did not ask for wealth or power, but for a heart capable of hearing and understanding. It was the request of a child, a request imbued with candid audacity and unequalled humility. For only a child could have the foresight to understand that grasping the soul of the world is far more precious than seeking to dominate it."

Abigael scanned the crowd, her eyes lingering on the faces of the parents and adults staring at her with fervent attention. She inhaled deeply, letting her gaze, charged with an almost mystical glow, melt into the souls around her.

- My grandfather once told me that childhood is the ultimate force. Because it carries within it the purest innocence, because it is capable of seeing the truth without the veils that fear imposes on adults. Pharaoh sought to destroy Moses, but it was the unshakeable faith of a sister, the invincible love of a woman, and the sacred innocence of an infant that changed the course of history. Iblis has tried to corrupt man, but he fears the purity of the child, for that purity is a radiant light, a flame that transcends the shadows, a brightness that nothing can extinguish."

She paused, her voice deepening, almost prophetic, as each word echoed through space.

- This is why, since the dawn of time, men, intoxicated by darkness, have committed the most appalling atrocities, sacrificing the innocent on the altar of their despair. These children, the bearers of a divine light, were immolated in a desperate attempt to extinguish that sacred spark. But as long as mothers carry life within them, as long as each child passes

The Hourim of innocence

through the sacred door of its mother's womb, innocence will always triumph. Birth is a perpetual miracle, an eternal dawn, the unfailing promise of a renewal that defies evil, that pushes back the shadows."

Abigael's voice had grown shaky, as if carrying the weight of all the innocent souls she was evoking, but her eyes had an indomitable firmness, an incandescent brilliance, like a torch in the darkest night. She clasped Moussa's hand, and he looked at her, his eyes brimming with silent, almost sacred admiration, as if he were contemplating a higher truth.

- We are the children of Palestine, the children of Israel, we are the children of the world. We are the light that defies the darkness. Our united voices are more powerful than any weapons. As long as we continue to believe, as long as we refuse to give in to hatred, as long as we sing together, we will be free."

Then she raised her hand to the sky, an open hand vibrating with unshakeable faith. Musa imitated her, and the crowd followed as one. The word "Hourim" rose up, at first like a fragile breath, then it amplified, a powerful and irresistible wave, carrying everything in its path. It was a song, a cry of love and hope, a light for all who watched, a luminous radiance that split the darkness.

It was much more than a simple cry. It was a collective prayer, a deep commitment, a solemn promise. A promise that, as long as there was still a child capable of loving, hope would remain unchanged, unshaken, like a shining lighthouse in the midst of a storm.

Then Abigael and Moussa returned to the Guardian's refuge. No one really knew where this refuge was, no one understood

The Hourim of innocence

how they disappeared without a trace, like spirits guided by a celestial light. The whole world began to believe that there was something divine in them, that these children were envoys from the Creator, appearing to save a faltering humanity sliding insidiously towards darkness. Some even whispered that the ancient magics had been awakened, that heaven had reached out to the earth to prevent it from sinking. Even Israel's leaders, masters of narrative and control, were beginning to evoke prophecies, to speak of the coming of the Antichrist or the return of the Messiah. How could a government talk like that without shaking the conscience of the whole world ? These lies and falsified prophecies seemed to be losing their hold and, through the light of these two children, the world was beginning to glimpse a truth that had been hidden for too long.

The Guardian was waiting for them inside the refuge, a place so unique that it seemed to belong to another world, a parallel reality where the sound of hatred could not penetrate. It was a sanctuary, protected by an invisible force, a place that only Abigael and Moussa could reach. When they entered, they found themselves back in that enchanted atmosphere, where the air itself seemed to whisper ancient songs, where the walls gave off a soft glow, as if stars had taken refuge within them. Time seemed to stand still, every breath deeper, every heartbeat more vibrant, more real.

The Guardian greeted them with a benevolent smile, but his features betrayed the seriousness of the words he was about to say. He had taken on human form a long time ago, an unassuming figure whose mere presence commanded immediate respect, a willingness to listen to every word with absolute attention. His eyes, as deep as the abyss, seemed to

The Hourim of innocence

contain the wisdom of the ages, and in their brilliance one could perceive fragments of ancient truths, secrets thousands of years old that only the purest of hearts could hope to grasp.

"You have returned, my children, and I am happy to know that you are here, in safety." His voice echoed through the refuge, gentle but tinged with a mystical power that words alone could not contain. "But the path before you is even more obscure than it has been until now. You have awakened hearts, rekindled flames that were thought to be extinguished forever. The world is beginning to remember the light, and that's thanks to you. But you should know that every awakening generates resistance.

He paused, his eyes gazing at the young heroes with infinite tenderness, mingled with unfathomable gravity. Abigaël and Moussa, seated next to each other, held hands tightly, drawing strength from each other like twin souls facing adversity together. The Guardian continued, his penetrating gaze reaching into the depths of their souls.

"If you had never met, if love had not transcended the chains of hatred, humanity would have continued its descent into the abyss. The Creator knew what could happen, because He sees everything, and He knows the paths we take even before we take the first steps. But even with His infinite vision, He leaves each being free will, the possibility of choosing between the darkness and the light. You have made a choice, and that choice has changed the course of history. But remember, my children, doubt is the most insidious weapon that your enemies will seek to turn against you. Doubt is what drove Adam, despite the warnings, to give in to temptation and taste the forbidden fruit. Doubt can erode the greatest certainties,

The Hourim of innocence

and it is treacherous, like the wind that seeps into the smallest cracks. Never let doubt tarnish your light.

The Guardian approached them, his voice darkening into a low whisper, and yet this whisper seemed to fill the whole space, vibrating like the distant echo of ages immemorial.

"But evil, my children, never stops. Those who lurk in the shadows, the architects of desolation, the malignant entities who manipulate Israel and their allies, will never give up their black designs. You are in constant peril, and you will have to exercise absolute vigilance, without respite. They have now understood that the only way to destroy you is to fracture your love. They will orchestrate massive disinformation campaigns, dark clouds of poisoned lies that will darken the sky, to shake your spirits, to instil doubt between you. They will try to turn your love into a weakness, to convince you that this sacred bond that unites you is the source of all the world's misfortunes."

The Guardian sat facing them, his eyes heavy with prophetic visions, haunted by truths too vast, too terrible for such young souls. "And it won't be their only strategy. If you manage to overcome the misinformation, they will send children, innocent children, even younger than you, to carry out their darkest plans. They will seek to prove that even innocence can be hijacked, that even a child can be perverted by hatred, in order to defile the purity that you embody. And if that fails again, they will resort to poisons, diseases, viruses, those invisible, insidious weapons that creep like silent spectres through the night, capable of stealing life without leaving the slightest trace. They will make you believe in a natural death, a caprice of fate, hoping in this way to stifle your light without arousing a revolt of the heart".

The Hourim of innocence

Abigael felt an icy chill run down her spine, as if the darkness itself had brushed against her skin. With Moussa's hand in hers, she felt the living strength of his love, the unalterable warmth that helped her to face the dark, inexorable truth that the Guardian was revealing to them. They didn't speak, because no words were necessary. Their hearts already knew that they were ready to face anything, together, despite the abyss.

The Guardian watched them, a glint of infinite tenderness softening his tired gaze. "But know this, my children: the greatest danger is not death itself. The greatest danger is division, the insidious doubt that could creep in between you like a poisonous crack that would shatter the strength that binds you together. Doubt is a silent poison, a treacherous shadow that gnaws at the foundations of the soul from within. That's where they'll start, and that's precisely where you'll have to be the strongest. You will have to look out for each other, not just against the visible enemies, but against those that lurk in the recesses of your thoughts, in the most secret, deepest fears."

He paused, his expression taking on an almost tangible melancholy, as if the words themselves were weighing on his thousand-year-old soul. "I must also tell you that when you are sixteen, I will no longer be here to look after you. You will have to continue this crusade on your own. Until then, I will be your guide, your protector in the shadows, but when that day comes, I will have to let you spread your wings and face the storm. You will have to face the darkness, armed only with the immeasurable power of your love. This is how the Creator has willed it, and this is how you must prepare yourselves."

The Hourim of innocence

He slowly raised his hands, and a soft, almost supernatural light poured from his palms, like starlight descending from the heavens to bless them. This light was reflected on the faces of the two children, enveloping them in a soothing, sacred glow. "It's not about physical strength, or even courage as the world sees it. It's about love, that transcendent love, your greatest weapon, your highest bulwark against the voracious darkness that seeks to engulf you. It's a pure love, a love that defies human boundaries, erected dogmas and ancestral hatreds. A love that can only be broken if you allow fear and doubt to poison it. Therein lies your real challenge. No matter what they do, no matter what lies they weave around you like a spider's web to trap you, stay united. For in that love lies the strength of the Creator, the primordial force that breathed life into the clay to create Adam and Eve, the original force that has enabled children to survive, rise and soar through the ages, despite the dark embrace of darkness."

A hushed, almost solemn silence fell over the refuge, enveloping Abigael and Moussa in a rare but not heavy quietude, like an echo of respite before the storm. Their eyes met, bright with determination and, in their dark eyes, one could read the irrevocable flame of those who had chosen their destiny in the knowledge of the obstacles to come. Together, hand in hand, they stood up, determined to embrace the tortuous path that lay ahead. The light that dwelt within them, fragile but brilliant, was only waiting to spread through the shadows. And the Guardian, following them with his eyes as they moved away, felt a wave of pride and melancholy wash over him. He understood that his role with them would not be eternal, that he could not always be there to protect them; but he knew, with an almost sacred certainty, that the love that

The Hourim of innocence

bound them together was like a burning flame that no storm could extinguish.

As Abigael and Moussa crossed the threshold of the refuge, the invisible weight of hopes and expectations seemed to grow heavier on their young but determined shoulders. Jerusalem, asleep under the night sky, was bathed in a deceptive calm, an apparent tranquillity that belied the tumult vibrating in their souls. Outside, in the winding streets and moonlit squares, a quivering world awaited them, eager for their words, eager for the elusive promise of hope that they embodied.

They walked up to the Dome of the Rock, a place full of their most intense memories, where decisive moments had shaped their souls. At this late hour, the moonlight on the gilded walls cast a soothing, almost mystical glow. Moussa's gaze fell on Abigael ; in her eyes, he found his own fears, a mirror of his doubts and hopes. These were no longer the fears of the carefree children they had once been ; now they carried within them more serious concerns, those inherited from the adult world, a world of responsibilities they had entered too early, with a wisdom tinged with bitterness and lucidity. The real challenge, they knew, was to preserve the pure flame of their innocence, that precious light that so many forces would strive to obscure.

"The Guardian warned us," Abigael murmured, gently squeezing Moussa's hand. "He told us that doubt would be our greatest enemy, that love would be our salvation... and also what they would seek to wrest from us."

Moussa nodded slowly, his voice vibrating with barely contained emotion. "It's strange, isn't it? How this love can be

The Hourim of innocence

both our greatest strength and our most exposed vulnerability..."

A pale, tender smile touched Abigael's lips. "That's precisely why it's so precious. Because it costs us, because it upsets us and transforms us." She let out a breath, almost a sigh, and looked up at the constellated sky, her eyes sparkling with a fierce light. "Maybe that's the real miracle : to be able to see a glimmer of light, even in the darkest of nights.

Moussa, imbued with this thought, turned to her with a new resolve in his eyes. "And there are still so many nights to illuminate, so many souls to touch, so many children to awaken to this light. What we are experiencing is only the beginning of a much wider journey.

The night wind carried the echoes of the sleeping city like a thousand-year-old murmur, a faint but persistent whisper of hopes and expectations. In the air floated the distant murmur of families and children who now placed their deepest hopes in each other, like a silent prayer to the stars. Palestinians and Israelis had risen up to defend a dream, a hope so vast that it transcended walls, barbed wire and invisible or imposed borders. Hourim. This word had become much more than a simple slogan shouted in the fervour of the rallies. It embodied a living force, a banner of resistance against fear, a song of love defying hatred, a light piercing the darkness.

The Guardian had warned them of the shadows that awaited them, of plots hatched in the dark recesses of the human mind, of treacherous and insidious attacks. They knew that unseen forces would strive to divide them, to undermine the union that threatened the very foundations of their deep-seated hatred. The struggle would be bitter and merciless. Lies,

The Hourim of innocence

manipulation and treachery would be their perfidious weapons, lurking in every suspicious glance, every smile concealing an obscure intention. Disinformation would be their most subtle adversary, an invisible weapon insinuating itself into people's minds like a silent poison, eroding certainties and sowing doubt where truth should have flourished. And, perhaps, traps would lurk even where they least expected them, ready to devour their trust in each other.

Moussa broke the silence, his voice vibrating with the unbreakable promise that bound them together: "Abigael, whatever they do... whatever they say... always remember this: I love you. And nothing, absolutely nothing, can change that."

Abigael squeezed his hand tighter, as if to anchor this promise in the depths of her soul. Her eyes locked with Moussa's, reflecting both the torment and the purity of their bond. "We've been through flames, Moussa. This world has tried to destroy us in a thousand ways. But as long as we stay together, they will never succeed."

They remained there, under the immensity of the constellated sky, savouring this moment suspended in time, a precious respite before the storm rose again. For they knew that the Guardian, although a source of protection, also represented a test. He had guided them, illuminating their path with his wisdom, but soon he would have to step aside, leaving them to face the tumult of their destiny alone. What they were experiencing was not just an adventure; it was a plunge into the heart of profound truths, into that rare ability to love and resist, to grow despite the storms. From that day on, they would have to walk without his benevolent shadow, move forward without the refuge of his presence.

The Hourim of innocence

Hand in hand, they left the golden streets of Jerusalem, heading towards those waiting for them in the half-light. A group of children stood there, their faces lit up with hope, their eyes sparkling with the promise of a future finally free from fear. Abigael and Moussa understood that this fight was not just for survival; it was a battle for innocence, to preserve the purity of every child, here or elsewhere. Their love, their unity, was the silent standard that these young souls followed with confidence, and they could not afford to let them down.

Among them, a boy barely ten years old stepped forward. He looked up at Moussa and, with a disturbing solemnity, handed him a small candle. "For the light," he murmured with innocent fervour, his eyes burning with an almost unreal conviction. Moussa accepted the candle, his eyes suddenly heavy with tears, overwhelmed by the emotion of this gesture of unequalled purity. Abigael then drew the flame to her own candle, lighting the wick with an almost sacred tenderness. Together, they watched the light flicker in the night, fragile yet invincible, defying the wind and the darkness.

"For the light," Moussa murmured, his voice choked with emotion, like a prayer offered up to the stars. Around them, one by one, the children came forward, lighting their candles until they formed a vibrant circle of flickering, protective light. Against the silent backdrop of the night, the Dome of the Rock stood imposing and solemn, the thousand-year-old guardian of their promise. The flames reflected in the children's eyes lit up their faces with a gentle determination, imprinting on every expression the promise of a better tomorrow. These children, these "Hourim", now embodied more than a fragile hope; they had become light itself, a

The Hourim of innocence

glimmer of hope ready to pierce the thickest darkness, to set the darkness ablaze with a pure, burning flame.

Under this sky studded with a thousand promises, Abigael, Moussa and all the children present made a silent vow, a sacred promise : to stand together, hand in hand, whatever the storms to come. For at the end of every night, even the most impenetrable, a dawn inevitably awaits, patient and full of promise.

But as the flickering candlelight danced in the breeze, a discreet, barely perceptible shadow crept into the atmosphere. An icy chill ran through the circle of children, planting a seed of worry in them, a troubled and inexplicable sensation. Abigael and Moussa exchanged glances, feeling a fleeting wave of doubt pass between them, a premonition that was hard to grasp. The Guardian had warned them of the dark forces, the invisible entities that would try to reach them. And that night, they felt this presence, impalpable but undeniable, something lurking, watching them in the shadows, patient and silent.

It was Iblis himself, hidden under the most unexpected and harmless of guises : a child. A young boy with innocent eyes, whose gentle, angelic appearance was nothing to worry about. He approached the circle of light, his footsteps almost floating, his voice as faint as a breath barely rising in the night. "You know," he whispered in a sweet, bewitching voice, "there's a hidden fruit here, under the Dome of the Rock. A fruit that could increase your love tenfold, give you a strength that even Adam and Eve never had. With this fruit, you could touch the childhood they lost, rediscover original purity... love at its purest and most invincible."

The Hourim of innocence

A penetrating chill set in, mingling with the warmth of the candles, as if the shadow itself were trying to penetrate their souls. In the air floated a strange scent, sweet and metallic, bewitching and oppressive, a scent that promised as much as it threatened, combining seduction and corruption in the same breath. Abigael and Moussa froze, feeling an unknown tension rise up inside them, a violent duality between their desire to protect these children and the temptation to seize this power. This fruit, this power of pure, indomitable love, seemed so close, so tempting. With this strength, they could make themselves invincible, protect these young souls without ever wavering, defy the world and its shadows without fear.

And yet something held them back, a frightening premonition, a venomous doubt that crept up on them like a sly mist. They remembered the Guardian's words, his warning against the rift of doubt that the darkness would dig between them. Temptation was there, insidious and gentle, disguised in the guise of a child with innocent eyes. But behind this promise of a love multiplied tenfold, lurked the shadow of a trap, a poisoned offering ready to pierce their sacred bond, to undermine their union through seduction and desire.

The candlelight began to flicker, as if hesitating in the face of the darkness pressing in around them. The children, still in a circle, watched Abigael and Moussa, their eyes sparkling with pure, unshakeable confidence. They had not yet grasped the shadow that hung over them, the silent threat that seeped into the hearts of those who looked after them. And Abigael and Moussa understood that their greatest strength lay in this innocence, in this love without calculation or desire for power. For, in this world of darkness and light, the greatest victory

The Hourim of innocence

would be to remain faithful to that first promise, even when the shadows grew closer and more pressing.

The young boy's eyes seemed to capture the glow of the stars, a limpid, almost enchanting radiance. But when Abigael looked into his eyes, she thought for a moment she detected a fleeting glimmer, a spark of mischief, an inner fire tinged with a darkness hidden beneath his innocence. A wave of unease rose up inside her, an unpleasant shiver that tightened her throat, as if the air around them had suddenly become denser, saturated with an oppressive presence that was hard to ignore.

At his side, Moussa also felt a penetrating chill run down his spine, an instinctive warning signal that something was terribly wrong. The child, though seemingly harmless, radiated an indescribable aura, imbued with a frightening, malevolent antiquity. The smell of damp earth rose discreetly, a scent that seemed to stir something ancient, something deeply buried, as if a force lurking in the shadows had just woken up after a long sleep.

Abigael closed her eyes, seeking an anchor, an inner refuge beyond that gentle but perverse voice. She remembered the words of the Guardian, his warning about doubt, that subtle, invisible venom that crept into people's minds, a devious snake ready to ensnare their thoughts and their faith. She understood that therein lay the true power of Iblis : not in brute force or violence, but in that deceptive whisper, that silent poison that aimed to shake their love at its roots, to undermine the foundations of their union.

The young boy then smiled, almost imperceptibly, but with a darkness that pierced beneath the gentle appearance of his face. "The fruit is at hand," he whispered, his voice sliding like

The Hourim of innocence

a dangerous caress. "All you have to do is pick it, taste it, and you will complete what has been started. Imagine... boundless love and light. No more fears, no more weaknesses. The ability to protect everyone you love, to be beyond pain, beyond doubt."

Their eyes met, their hearts torn between hope and caution. The child's words vibrated with a promise of power, but beneath the gentleness, they sensed a shadow, a bewitching, almost honeyed seduction that insidiously crept up on them. All around them, the night seemed to thicken, oppressive, as if the darkness itself were trying to stifle the light of the candles, whose flickering flames hesitated, defying the invading shadow as best they could.

Moussa felt his breath catch, as if an invisible hand were trying to seize his spirit, to draw him into this temptation, this promise of absolute, unfettered power. He closed his eyes, his fingers tightening around Abigael's, seeking refuge in the warmth of her hand, like an anchor to prevent him from losing himself in this bewitching murmur.

Abigael opened her eyes slowly, looking at the child again. But this time, her silhouette seemed slightly blurred, almost unreal, as if woven from mist. Her eyes shone with a strange glow, oscillating between deceptive purity and profound corruption. This detail, subtle but undeniable, pierced the doubt in Abigael's heart; an understanding struck her full force. She now knew who he was, that angelic face concealing malignity.

"Iblis..." she whispered, her voice barely a whisper, but icy certainty.

Moussa turned his gaze towards her, his amazement mingling with a palpable wave of fear. As he followed her gaze towards

The Hourim of innocence

the child, he felt the air become more charged, oppressive, invaded by that metallic, sweet fragrance, an odour that was both seductive and repulsive. It seemed to permeate every breath, poisoning the air with an aura of forbidden defiance.

The child, or whoever he was pretending to be, gave them a gentle but wicked smile, a smile that seemed to pierce their souls. "Why not try?" he insisted, his voice becoming a slippery, almost reptilian caress, wrapping itself around their minds. "Adam failed because he was alone... But there are two of you. Two hearts united, two souls inseparable. This fruit will do you nothing but good. Together, you will be invincible, above all fear, more powerful than all the forces that threaten you."

The young boy's words floated through the air, seeping into the minds of Abigael and Moussa with the tempting force of an ancient charm. A promise of pure love, of an invincibility that would free them from fear, pain and doubt... These words, beneath their deceptive sweetness, spread their roots like a bewitching poison. Abigael and Moussa felt this painful tug-of-war, this mortal hesitation digging its way into their souls.

And yet, despite the envious song of power, despite the shadows that lurked around them, there remained within them a tiny but vibrant spark, the same light they had promised to defend. For they knew that this power, seductive as it was, came with a much heavier price, a toll their love could never bear.

Moussa closed his eyes, searching the darkness inside for an anchor, a landmark, something that could help him resist the bewitching call of the child's words. The words, shrouded in a

The Hourim of innocence

deceptive sweetness, resonated within him like a forbidden melody, creeping into the most vulnerable corners of his mind. Everything in him seemed caught up in a dull struggle, a battle against the irresistible urge to give in, to reach for that fruit that promised so much.

And then, suddenly, he felt something. A warmth. Abigael. Her hand clasped in his, her presence anchored in the real world, reminding his heart why he was there, why he was fighting. The scent of her hair, that sweet mixture of flowers and earth, took him back to a time long gone, a time when war was just a distant echo, an unknown whisper. There she was, tangible and luminous, a beacon in the shadows, her purity dispelling the doubts that threatened to engulf him.

"No," he said, his voice low but carried by a new strength, a certainty that swept away temptation. "We don't need that. We don't need a power that would take us away from who we are."

Abigael nodded, her deep, determined eyes fixed on those of the child. "Our love seeks no shortcuts, no illusory power. What we share is already powerful enough to defy the darkness."

For a moment, the child's mask cracked. His once innocent gaze hardened, becoming piercing, icy, and the mischief in his eyes intensified, becoming almost burning. A twisted smile slowly stretched across his lips, revealing the shadow of a darker intention. He took a step back, and the shadow around him seemed to grow denser, like a thick mist closing in on him.

"Do you really think you can resist..." Her voice, now deeper, almost inhuman, echoed, as if from far away, from the unfathomable depths of the night. "You believe that this love

The Hourim of innocence

is indestructible. But doubt... doubt has already taken root in you. It will grow. It's already eating away at you."

Without another word, the child, or what appeared to be a child, turned and sank into the darkness, vanishing into the night like a spectre, dissipating like mist under the first light of day.

The silence fell, dense and heavy, as if the whole world were holding its breath, suspended in a precarious equilibrium. Abigael and Moussa remained motionless, absorbing the tension of the moment, then slowly turned towards each other. A tear slipped down Abigael's cheek, shining like a crystal under the candlelight. Moussa gently gathered it with his fingertips, a gesture imbued with tenderness and fragility.

"He wanted to sow doubt," Abigael murmured, her voice vibrating with emotion. "And maybe... maybe he succeeded, a little. But we won't let him grow up."

Moussa nodded, his eyes locked on Abigael's, silently reaffirming their bond, their unbreakable pact. "As long as we stay together, as long as we keep faith in what we are, no shadow can destroy us.

They hugged, closing their eyes, letting their simple, unshakeable love light up the darkness that threatened to engulf them. They were still young, children thrust into an adult world, a world where the forces of good and evil played out their lives with the casualness of moving pawns. But beyond this game, they had discovered true strength: the strength of a love that does not bow to temptation, that does not weaken in the face of darkness.

The Hourim of innocence

They rose to their feet, hands still clasped, and advanced towards the circle of children, whose candles, small but valiant, still shone in the night, defying the shadows. They knew that their path would be fraught with pitfalls, that the darkness would return with new faces and new tricks. But for now, they had repelled Iblis. For now, they had won a battle : the battle of doubt.

Their light had never seemed so fragile, but never had it been so authentic, so true. Under the starry sky, surrounded by the children who looked up at them with eyes full of admiration and hope, Abigael and Moussa made a silent promise, a promise rooted in the depths of their love : to keep walking, to keep loving each other, to keep shining, even when the shadows become more threatening.

For they had understood an eternal truth: even the thickest darkness bows before a simple flame.

And this flame, they now knew with infinite certainty, burned within them, unquenchable.

CHAPTER VI
THE MIRRORS OF IBLIS : WHEN DOUBT SPREADS

« DOUBT IS THE FAVOURITE SEED OF IBLIS, WATERED BY THE MEDIA AND FED BY FEAR. ONLY THOSE WHO LOOK BEYOND THE MIRROR WILL SEE THE TRUTH BEHIND THE ILLUSIONS. »

The first media attack was lightning-fast, orchestrated with clinical precision to dismantle the Hourim phenomenon. The television screens were quickly filled with a myriad of pseudo-specialists, all with swaggering titles and self-assured airs, as if they held the ultimate truth, as impartial and wise observers.

The Hourim of innocence

Their objective was clear: to plant a subtle seed in the minds of the audience which, if it found fertile ground, would quickly germinate and infect people's consciences. They called this seed "doubt", and they excelled in the art of sowing it. They scattered handfuls of it in the ether of talk shows, debates and news bulletins, in the hope that some would take root in tired minds already drenched in confusion.

Abigael and Moussa, figureheads of the movement, were described as far too young, far too idealistic to understand what was at stake in their own actions. Serious, condescending voices were raised to insinuate that adults were manipulating their naivety behind the scenes, pulling the strings and orchestrating their speeches. These experts, presenting themselves as voices of reason, insisted on the idea of a "hidden plan", of an "invisible hand" directing their every move. Soon, other authority figures entered the scene: child psychiatrists and psychologists, with their serious looks and choice words. They claimed to diagnose a new disease: "Hourim syndrome". They went so far as to detach this cry of revolt from its burning context and imprison it in a fabricated clinical label. Their aim? To frighten parents, to convince them that their children were the victims of an insidious mental contamination, an epidemic of rebellious thoughts.

The presenters, frozen in smooth, artificial smiles, their honeyed voices stretching over every word, spoke of the threat of an even worse contagion than Covid : a mental contagion, spreading through words, through dreams, through simply hearing the word 'Hourim'. Faced with this 'epidemic', they said, the cry had to be stifled before it turned into an uncontrollable fire. Their remedy? Oblivion. Make the words

The Hourim of innocence

disappear, erase the faces, stifle the echo before it became too powerful, too deeply rooted in people's minds.

The television programmes were becoming more absurd by the day, the voices crossing each other in a cacophony of arguments that cancelled each other out, without ever really resonating. But that didn't matter. The strategy was simple : repetition. Repeat and repeat, until minds were saturated, until viewers were transformed into passive receptacles of fear and doubt. Yet one thing eluded the architects of this carefully orchestrated disinformation: the children they were trying to reach were not their viewers. They weren't watching their programmes ; they weren't interested in those rigid faces, those complicit words devoid of warmth, those speeches that only bored them. For them, the only 'syndrome' worthy of a diagnosis was profound boredom.

As for the parents, the relays the media hoped would spread fear, they felt powerless. For the Hourim movement was no longer just a cry of protest; it had become an underground current, a river of hope that was carving its way through people's hearts, sweeping away any doubts in its path. Nothing seemed able to stem the irresistible rise of this gentle revolt, a current too vast to be contained.

Faced with this failure, the media adopted a new strategy. They brought children onto the set, young faces who were supposed to advocate caution and fear. But even then, the stratagem collapsed: the children chosen spoke with words that were too calculated, sentences that were too perfectly constructed. Their tone rang false, like a dissonance instinctively perceived by their peers. The young people, far from being fooled, sensed the deception, recognised that these voices supposedly similar to their own were merely manipulated echoes. And this

The Hourim of innocence

only served to alienate young people still further, even leading some adults to find the staging laughable and hollow.

But the media had not said their last word. They went into high gear, releasing an avalanche of falsified photos and fake videos claiming to show children denying the Hourim movement, or claiming that the whole initiative was a vast swindle. These crude montages, saturated with lies, aimed to tarnish the image of Abigael, Moussa and their companions, insisting on the idea that the money collected ended up in the pockets of corrupt leaders. But the manipulations were soon exposed. Social networks, despite censorship, saw the flowering of revelations from informers and hackers who unmasked every lie.

In this way, the truth, patiently untangled from the falsifications, made its way through. It triumphed over shadows and artifice, confirming that the Hourim movement remained pure, a force of resistance that not even the relentless waves of propaganda could destroy.

The media were failing. Their carefully crafted strategies were collapsing, one after the other, unable to stem the rising Hourim tide. So, in a final act of desperation, they played their last card: direct confrontation. The spotlights on their sets, armed like stormlights, were now aimed at Moussa and Abigael. The media demanded their presence live, in front of the whole world, urging them to defend themselves in the public eye. Their aim was clear: to expose them, to push them to the breaking point, to trap them in words under the intense glare of the cameras. To achieve this, they did not hesitate to use outrageous accusations, hoping to crack the armour of these two young figures who had become the symbol of an unbearable truth for their opponents.

The Hourim of innocence

Moussa was accused of murdering his own uncle. He was portrayed as violent and cold, a killer cleverly hidden behind a mask of innocence. Abigael, for her part, was spared such slander, but the accusation was intended to strike where it would hurt most, where the pain of injustice, mixed with helplessness, could crack their bond.

It wasn't just an invitation ; it was a duel, an unequal confrontation between adults experienced in the subtleties of manipulation and two children bearing a clear, disturbing but sincere truth. The media strategy was like a grenade with its pin pulled; the question was not whether it would explode, but where and how it would hit them.

Informed of the treacherous accusation, those around Moussa and Abigael immediately warned them. The news spread like shockwaves, amplifying the gravity of the situation.

Moussa remembered his uncle with a cold distance. This man, who had committed the worst crimes, could arouse neither compassion nor burning hatred. Yet he was still his mother's brother, a figure from a past he could neither erase nor reclaim. Moussa felt neither pride nor shame towards him, only a painful neutrality, a tacit recognition of the complexities of the family history.

When he realised that the media were trying to smear his uncle's memory in order to get at him, a cold anger came over him, not to defend the man, but to reject this attempt at manipulation. He refused to let others rewrite his history or use the ghosts of his past as weapons to break him.

But he knew that this instinctive response would do nothing to help them. They had to be stronger, wiser than those who sought to bring them down. The Guardian, with his enigmatic

The Hourim of innocence

serenity, had often reminded them that true victory was not to be found in tumult, but in the calm, unchanging light of truth. "Doubt is the weapon of the weak," he once whispered to Moussa. "But the truth illuminates even the darkest minds.

On the night before the day they were to make their choice, Moussa and Abigael retreated to a peaceful corner of the city, far from the hustle and bustle, the noise and the prying eyes. They found themselves under the hundred-year-old olive tree, whose gnarled branches formed a protective shelter, a plant sanctuary in the heart of the darkness. The moonlight bathed their faces, drawing their intertwined shadows at the foot of the tree. Abigael laid her head against Moussa's shoulder, and together they breathed in the soothing silence, the precious respite disturbed only by the rustling of the leaves.

"What are we going to do, Moussa ?" she murmured, her voice broken by a worry she was trying to hide. "They accuse us of terrible things. They want to see us stumble, to revel in our mistakes."

Moussa let a silence settle, pondering the question that had been burning inside him for hours. He felt the warmth of Abigael's hand in his, a quiet strength that brought him back to what really mattered.

"They want us to forget who we really are," he replied softly. "They want us to react angrily, to defend ourselves with sharp words and give them reason to accuse us again. But that's not what they're afraid of, Abigael. What terrifies them is our calm, our love, the truth that they can't manipulate.

Abigael looked up at him, and he saw a spark of renewed determination, that unshakeable flame that had carried them so far. They both understood that their response had to be

The Hourim of innocence

more than just words on a television set. It had to be a message, an act of peaceful resistance, an affirmation of their love and inner strength.

"They can accuse us of anything they want," Abigael added in a soft but determined voice. "What they don't understand is that as long as we remain united, as long as we remain true to who we are, nothing they say can ever hurt us."

Their minds were made up. They knew that going before the whole world with this disarming serenity, with this light radiating from their sincerity, would be their greatest weapon. Together, they would weather the storm, not by striking back blow for blow, but by remaining themselves, young people bearing a truth that not even false accusations could tarnish.

Under the olive tree, they held each other close, then looked up at the stars, silent witnesses to their oath. They were no longer just two teenagers in an adult world ; they were the guardians of a light that nothing could extinguish.

Moussa took a deep breath, feeling the weight of doubt inside him, a subtle rift that Iblis was working hard to widen, a creeping shadow that sought to weaken his resolve. He raised his eyes to the sky, gazing up at the stars, those distant flashes hanging in the night like promises. "They want us to be afraid, to hide. But we have to show them that we have nothing to hide, that our love for the truth is more powerful than their lies."

Abigael raised her head, her eyes finding those of Moussa. She saw the same quiet determination, the same inner light that had drawn her to him from the very first day. A gentle, unshakeable strength that never wavered. She nodded, her fingers tightening around his. "Then we'll go. We'll go and tell

The Hourim of innocence

them what we have to say. Not to defend ourselves, but to defend those who believe in us."

Moussa gave a slight smile. "To defend the truth, Abigael. To show the world that, even in the face of doubt and hatred, it's possible to choose love, to choose the light."

Under the olive tree, they stayed there, drawing the strength they would need from the stillness of the night. The wind played softly in the branches above them, like an ancient whisper, a comfort whispered by nature itself. They knew that the next day, they would stand in front of the cameras, not to fight, but to enlighten. Somewhere in the shadows, Iblis was watching, his presence dissolved in the darkness, feeling his grip crumbling in the face of the serene light of these two children.

Then, suddenly and unexpectedly, the Guardian appeared. He faded into the shadows like an ethereal vision, a presence both familiar and mysterious, his features seemingly shaped by the silvery light of the moon, somewhere between dream and reality. He approached silently, his piercing eyes gazing into those of Moussa and Abigael. His gaze was filled with wisdom, with that ancient benevolence that carries with it the lessons of the ages. He was there to advise them, but first he asked them an essential question. His deep, gentle voice, imbued with gravity, broke the silence of the night like a prophecy:

"Why did you accept?"

Moussa was the first to reply. His voice trembled slightly, oscillating between fear and determination, but every word was full of sincerity.

The Hourim of innocence

- It's not really that we agreed," he replied, his voice wavering with emotion. They left us no choice. How could I let this despicable accusation go unchallenged, this unbearable lie that I killed my uncle, when the circumstances were completely different? But deep down I know that all this is beyond me, that I'm not ready to face this adult world, with all its tricks and lies. I'm only a child, and sometimes I don't feel capable of standing up against this tide of hostility.

The Guardian remained silent for a moment, letting his words settle into the stillness of the night. Then he leaned slightly towards them, his eyes locked on Moussa's, as if he were trying to fathom the young boy's very soul. His words rose up, arrows of truth designed to awaken a new consciousness in him:

- Never forget, Moussa, that even the Creator always leaves the choice. That is the essence of true freedom. You too have a choice. The choice to accept or refuse to submit to this lynching, to resist or give in to the guilt they are trying to cultivate in you. They're trying to drag you into their adult world, with its shadows and resentments. But remember, Moussa : you're a child, and that's your greatest strength. That's what sets you apart from them.

The Guardian placed a reassuring hand on Moussa's shoulder, a gentle, soothing warmth radiating from that simple touch. Under the shade of the olive tree, they found themselves protected, wrapped in a cocoon of peace under the delicate light of the moon.

- Don't be in a hurry to grow up," continued the Guardian. A child's vision is pure, free from the artificial complexities that adults impose on themselves. Don't try to see further than they

The Hourim of innocence

allow you to, because often the truth is simpler and more beautiful when seen through innocent eyes. You've both made the right choice, because without even realising it, they are the ones sinking into their own lies, trapped in the quicksand of their own creation.

Then he turned to Abigael, who was watching him with absorbed attention, her eyes wide and shining, taking in every word like a star catching the light of a distant star.

- Your strategy, my dear children, must be as simple as your essence. It must remain pure, unchanged, immaculate. You must remain yourselves, without compromise, without mask. That is your truth. And never forget that your most powerful strength is your innocence. How can they accuse you if you don't give them any leverage, if you are limpid mirrors reflecting the pure light of sincere love ?

The Guardian smiled with infinite tenderness as he continued:

- I'll be there, next to you, during this confrontation. Invisible, just as Iblis is with his minions, but never far from you. I will support you with my presence, and bring you comfort when you feel alone in the face of the hostile crowd. They know, as I do, that you are children, and they have limits that they cannot cross without betraying themselves. Push them gently, without violence, to show their true colours. Encourage them to be arrogant and rude to you. And when they show their true colours, simply remain innocent. If their words hurt you, weep, for those tears are sincere. If their accusations amuse you, keep silent, because children's laughter is nothing like adults'.

Silence fell, a moment suspended in the mysterious softness of the night. The breeze carried away the scent of the flowers

The Hourim of innocence

surrounding the olive tree, and time itself seemed to stand still, as if listening to the promise being woven between the Guardian and the two children. Moussa and Abigael looked at each other, the Guardian's words resonating within them like deep, soothing music, a melody of hope. They understood that their strength lay in their purity, in their refusal to give in to the fear and tricks of adults. Tomorrow, they would stand before the world, not as warriors, but as children, bearers of a light that nothing and no one could extinguish.

The Guardian spoke again, his voice deeper, imbued with wisdom from a bygone age, with a depth that echoed in the souls of the two children.

- They'll do anything to sow doubt in you," he tells them. But doubt is a shadow you must never give in to. Never answer their questions by justifying yourself. Answer them with questions that will make them look at their own flaws, that will destabilise them. Make them lose themselves in their own light, lose themselves in their contradictions, until the truth escapes them.

The two children looked at each other, a gleam of understanding and determination in their eyes. They now understood that their greatest strength lay not in their carefully chosen words, but in the unbreakable unity that bound them together, a simple, genuine love that could withstand any storm.

The Guardian continued, his voice vibrating with benevolent solemnity:

- If you feel that words are becoming weapons, if you see that confrontation is going too far, then talk about that macabre day of 7 October. Don't leave anything in the dark. Tell every

The Hourim of innocence

detail, expose the truth, and you'll see their fear, their panic at the idea of this truth being heard. They'll try to silence you, and that's when the world will see who they really are. But never forget to stand united. You're going to have to support each other. You are one, and in that unity lies your invincibility. If one of you falters, the other will pick you up.

He paused, gazing intently at each of them, a gentle smile of confidence lighting up his features. This smile, as reassuring as a promise, soothed the torments of their young souls.

- You are in no danger," he murmured confidently, "for as long as you remain faithful to your purity, no force in the world can shake you. I have every confidence in you. You'll be up to the task, because you've weathered the storms by remaining pure, because you've kept your childlike essence here, at ground level, where the true seeds of light grow.

Under the starry sky, the scene took on a new meaning. The Keeper's words seeped into their hearts like a gentle promise. Abigael and Moussa, united by a renewed confidence, felt ready to face the unknown that awaited them, hand in hand, heart at peace, stronger than ever.

Before leaving them, the Guardian approached again, his face bathed in the soft glow of the moon. His eyes shone with infinite tenderness, and he seemed about to tell them a secret, something precious that would warm their hearts and light their way. His voice, deep and comforting, pierced the silence of the night like a whisper of hope:

- Have you ever noticed," he says, "that very young children play together without even knowing each other's language? They understand each other without words. They exchange awkward gestures, squeal with delight, gabble words that are

The Hourim of innocence

incomprehensible to adults... but the magic happens between them. They understand each other beyond language, and the boundaries of language disappear. This is because children possess a rare and marvellous power : the power to communicate from the heart, to understand each other with a simple look, a smile, or even tears. Children are the innate masters of emotion, because their pure innocence transcends all barriers.

He let a silence envelop his words, like a gentle breeze caressing the faces of Abigael and Moussa, who drank in every word, fascinated, their eyes wide open, eager for this ancestral wisdom. The Guardian watched them, and in his gaze there was an affection that seemed to transcend the ages. Then he continued, his voice taking on a gentle intonation, almost like a precious confidence :

- Now I'm going to tell you a revelation, a secret that only you will hear. You possess within you a power far greater than you can imagine. A rare gift : that of universal language. Without even knowing it, you are capable of speaking all the languages of the world and, even more, of understanding them. It's a gift I'm giving you, a secret weapon, a joker that will save you many years of learning and difficulty. Keep this secret buried deep within you, and wait for the right moment before using it. Because the day will come when this power will reveal itself, and then the world will look at you differently. You will be seen as extraordinary beings, messengers of a new world, and your adversaries, without even realising it, will lose their footing in front of you.

There was a silence, a moment suspended in the eternity of the night. The gentle breeze seeped through the branches of the olive tree, making the leaves sing in a fragile, comforting

The Hourim of innocence

harmony. The Guardian raised his hand and touched Moussa's cheek, then Abigael's, with infinite tenderness, as if to seal the secret.

- Now rest, my dear children," he murmured with a gentleness that contrasted with the seriousness of his words. And above all, stay true to yourselves. Never let the world rob you of your essence. You are the dawn of a new beginning, the promise of renewal, the light that will end a cycle of darkness and suffering. And it is by remaining pure, by remaining the children you are, that you will breathe new life into this world, that you will write a worthy end to this old world.

The Guardian then moved away, his footsteps fading into the darkness, his silhouette melting into the night itself, like a benevolent shadow returning to its kingdom. Abigael and Moussa stood still for a moment, under the benevolent weight of this mission, looking at each other in silence, their hearts heavy with the grandeur of their destiny, but light, soothed by the strength of what had just been entrusted to them. They took each other's hands, clasping them, and in that gesture they felt a deep, unshakeable certainty: they were not alone.

Together, they prepared to take on the world, not as warriors, but as bearers of light, love and truth. Under the starry sky, with the Guardian's blessing engraved in them, they knew they were ready.

The moon, full and majestic, continued to illuminate them, a silent witness to this suspended moment, when two children walked hand in hand, bearers of a promise they were determined to keep. Their footsteps echoed through the night like a melody of courage, a discreet echo of pure, indomitable love, a new strength born of the Guardian's words, their

The Hourim of innocence

unshakeable bond and the innocence they refused to sacrifice. Abigael and Moussa moved forward, determined to carry this torch to the end, their hearts filled with an elusive serenity.

The next day, the scene that was being prepared had an almost theatrical quality: all the television channels had lined up to interview the two young heroes. On one side, the journalists, instruments of a greedy system, invested with a contradictory double duty: that of destroying the truth while capturing the world's attention, of achieving spectacular ratings. Their rivals became, for a time, allies in a strange alliance, imposed by a common fear. Iblis himself had ordered this ephemeral union, a fragile pact between natural competitors, all united in fear of a truth that was beyond them. CNN International, BBC World News, Al Jazeera, France 24, Euronews, TF1 and others had sent their fiercest journalists, their predators hungry for scandal, ready to bring down two children under the weight of sharp questions.

But why, the murmurs of the audience wondered, had these channels never seen fit to travel en masse to the Dome of the Rock when bombs were destroying Palestinian lives? Why was this double standard so blatant as to be grotesque ? The orders seemed to come from above, or perhaps from below, from Iblis himself. This fallen being pulled the invisible strings of manipulation, urging these journalists, each enslaved to voracious ambitions, to serve his hidden purposes. He manipulated the shadows, enveloping them in his cunning, fuelling in them a desire for control and power.

It was now six months since the guns fell silent. The bombing had stopped, the guns remained silent, as if all wars had been put on hold, suspended in a fragile but miraculous silence. The world was bathed in an unexpected peace, a crystalline truce,

The Hourim of innocence

as delicate as a dewdrop on a leaf in the early hours of the morning. Even the crime rate had plummeted, as if touched by a sudden grace. The criminals themselves seemed marked by a strange awakening, as if a forgotten spark, a glimmer of buried innocence, had been rekindled in their hearts. A benevolent wave seemed to sweep through the world, a gentle energy carried by children united in a silent impulse, catalysing a collective awakening.

This phenomenon went beyond simple revolt; it was a subtle magic, a wave of love and benevolence that permeated everything, purifying the very air. Every breath seemed charged with a new serenity, an invitation to inner peace. Nature, as if touched by this invisible wave, seemed reborn with a new-found vitality: the trees stretched proudly towards the sky, their leaves quivering in silent prayer. The flowers bloomed with a new grace, as if they had never known war, as if they knew nothing of the ashes and tears of men. The rivers, once tarnished by pollution and conflict, flowed again, clear and pure blue, and even the animals seemed to feel the enveloping peace. The birds sang with an almost mystical fervour, as if carrying the message of a new dawn, while the dogs strolled peacefully through streets bathed in soft, golden light.

The whole world seemed to breathe after a long apnoea. The peace was phenomenal, growing like an unstoppable wave, and no one seemed able to stop it. The sky itself seemed larger, deeper blue, a mirror of everyone's inner world, filled with calm and reconciliation.

For the first time in decades, people dared to speak of a nascent peace between Israel and Palestine. The weapons had been laid down, the mute cannons melted into the murmur of

The Hourim of innocence

a new hope. Evil, the evil that feeds on hatred and division, seemed paralysed, silenced by the shining force of innocence. Everywhere, a hue of renewal and hope emerged, and from all sides, a cry went up : "Hourim ! Hourim !" These words resounded like a sacred song, seeming to reach to the depths of the earth, awakening the hardest hearts, the most damaged souls.

This simple word, Hourim, seemed to possess an ancient power, like a talisman capable of cracking the walls erected between peoples. Its echo disintegrated the accumulated hatred, eroded the fear, reducing to dust all that had ever had any foundation other than mistrust and contempt. This dust, instead of tarnishing the air, flew away, illuminated by the light of forgiveness, metamorphosing into a cement of love and understanding, the only thing capable of welding together what had been broken for so long.

Abigael and Moussa's eyes shone with a calm certainty, a determination greater than fear, as they prepared to face the world. Their love, their faith in innocence, and their ability to embrace a truth so great that even Iblis trembled, made them invincible. Together, hand in hand, they moved forward, carried by the promise that the truth would eventually emerge, bright and pure, sweeping away the shadows of lies.

D-Day was fast approaching, but Abigael and Moussa weren't worrying about it. Enjoying every moment together, they distanced themselves from the political and religious concerns weighing on their young shoulders. They preferred to chase their kite, gazing up at the sky, letting it dance in the wind. Their laughter rose like crystal, carefree and free, lighting up their faces with the purity of childhood. In their laughter, there was a lightness that defied the laws of time, a moment of

The Hourim of innocence

eternity where neither the past nor the future had any hold. For them, all that mattered was this fleeting, precious moment, slipping by like a flash of infinity. Abigael laughed out loud every time the kite brushed the branches of a tree, and Moussa ran breathlessly to avoid getting tangled up in it. Those moments represented the purest truth, a truth that no camera, no television set, could alter. It was the absolute freedom of childhood, the light that resisted the worst darkness.

Meanwhile, the media world was preparing to orchestrate the "face-off of the century". Everything was in place. A huge studio had been set up for the occasion, a monumental stage where the event would be broadcast to every country and translated into every language. At the centre of the stage sat a massive, imposing circular table, reminiscent of the strategy rooms of heads of state. Abigael and Moussa would stand in the middle, isolated, surrounded by steely eyes, surrounded by journalists and accusers ready to silence them. The image was both absurd and grandiose, almost mythical: David in the midst of the Goliaths, the youthful purity of two children facing the arrogance of the media, ready to do battle.

All around them, the spotlights were spinning and the lights were intermingling, projecting an atmosphere that was both festive and overwhelming. Grandiloquent, theatrical introductory music blared through the studio, seeking to give the event a Hollywood feel, as if the truth could be dressed up in the trappings of spectacle. Everything was calibrated to turn this confrontation into a spectacular performance, a global show where every silence, every gesture, every response would weigh heavily in the balance of public opinion. The journalists, their faces set in the assurance of their role, waited, sharpening

The Hourim of innocence

their questions like blades. Each one hoped to see the two young heroes falter, to catch them at fault, to reveal a flaw.

Abigael and Moussa were aware of the ordeal that awaited them. But they let nothing show. Their strength lay in their sincerity, in their union. They had the truth with them, a pure truth that served as an invisible shield. They knew that their opponents were expert manipulators, ready to do anything to bring them down. But they were not alone. The Guardian was there, invisible but present, and with him came a force from all over the world, from all those who had found in Hourim the hope of renewal.

The world held its breath. This programme was more than just a debate: it was the mirror of humanity, an opportunity to see ourselves as we were, reflected in the innocent eyes of two children. The fate of the future seemed to hang on this stage, under the blinding spotlights that sought to pierce the darkness of hearts and minds. Abigael and Moussa, now the heralds of an unexpected peace, were going to have to face up to the media machine and perhaps, in their own way, expose its flaws.

At 8 o'clock on the dot, the cameras would come on and the whole world would witness this confrontation. The stakes went far beyond words and accusations ; this was a battle for the soul of humanity, a confrontation between lies and innocence, between calculated cunning and naked truth. Abigael and Moussa, with their apparent fragility, were going to have to prove that the truth could stand up, even in the face of the most powerful, even under the harsh lights that sought to intimidate them.

The Hourim of innocence

And in that peaceful night before the confrontation, under the starry sky of Jerusalem, the truth whispered softly, ready to be revealed. The children were not alone; a universal solidarity, powerful and benevolent, surrounded them. This invisible force was their greatest asset, a brotherhood born of a shared hope, a pure courage that defied predictions. Perhaps, just perhaps, these two children would succeed in reversing the course of events, in overturning the shadows.

In the meantime, they enjoyed the present, each burst of shared laughter, savouring the sweetness of the moment, like a precious balm before the storm.

The long-awaited moment had finally arrived. Abigael and Moussa had refused to wear make-up before the debate began. This seemingly simple refusal was an act of defiance, a shining symbol of their sincerity. In front of them was a world of pretence, where even those who claimed to be the guardians of truth wore invisible masks. Beneath faces frozen by layers of carefully applied make-up lay murky intentions, ambitions tarnished by greed and cynicism. The smiles were rigid, the glances imbued with a malevolent gleam, hidden behind artificial sparkles. It was a ball of fake faces, ready to swallow truth in a banquet of deception, to devour innocence in the pomp of pretence.

The Guardian never left them. His presence, benevolent and gentle, enveloped them in a warmth invisible to the others. Abigael and Moussa were the only ones to perceive him; his voice resonated within them like a reassuring whisper, a melody of comfort in the silence. Around this huge table, though invisible to the eyes of all, the Guardian seemed to occupy an indisputable place, an immaterial seat defying the gathering darkness. The journalists, impassive, were preparing

The Hourim of innocence

to attack them, already imagining their dazzling triumph. In their minds, the stage became a feast where the two children would be devoured without mercy, with the blessing of Iblis, the emperor of lies.

The circular table resembled an ancient arena, where cruelty was draped in an illusion of civility. The journalists sat impassively around this intimidating stage, their coldness reminiscent of that of the gladiators before the confrontation. At the centre of the arena sat a tiny armchair, a chair custom-made for the children, but arranged in such a way that it seemed disproportionate, as if everything had been designed to exaggerate their vulnerability and turn the scene into a deceptive simulacrum of equality. The contrast between these luminous children and the journalists, figures carved out of the marble of perfidy, made the spectacle almost unreal, a caricature. More than twenty journalists were ready to launch their seemingly benevolent questions, before sliding, in an ineluctable crescendo, towards disguised cruelty, waiting for the moment when they could cast the first stone.

The countdown was on. Abigael and Moussa were waiting in their dressing room, a space which, despite its apparent luxury, exuded an oppressive atmosphere. The soft sofas, subdued lighting and refined drinks were just a facade, concealing a perfidious intention. The Guardian had whispered to them not to touch anything on the table. The fruit juices, bursting with freshness, the biscuits perfectly arranged on golden trays, everything was poisoned by hypocrisy. Subtle drugs had been hidden in them, substances designed to alter their behaviour, make them waver, drive them into uncontrolled euphoria or confusion. The smiling faces of the set assistants, who had

The Hourim of innocence

offered them these treats, did little to hide the shadow of obscure intentions that lurked behind each too-perfect smile.

Abigael glanced at Moussa, and he replied with a knowing smile. Their hands brushed against each other, and in that silent contact, they found all the determination and strength they had cultivated together. The Guardian whispered words of comfort to them, instilling in them a calm and quiet confidence, a certainty that mingled with their thoughts as if he were part of them, as if something greater than themselves was awakening. Moussa felt this strange sensation of becoming more adult, while Abigael, despite her fears, felt a growing strength within her, a new firmness. They were not alone. The Guardian, invisible to the others, was with them, an integral part of their being.

Anxiety mingled with hope in this waiting room. They could hear, through the thin walls, the hubbub of the journalists getting ready, the growing agitation of those who were going to interrogate and crush them. An almost palpable tension permeated every corner of the studio, every whisper, every step. The timer was ticking down to the fateful moment when they would have to appear, when the face-to-face would begin. Their heartbeats, synchronised, seemed to match the flashing light of the signal that would tell them when it was time to go out.

At that moment, the Guardian whispered again, his words floating in the air like a promise :

- Remember, my dear children, that you owe nothing to anyone. Don't offer justifications ; ask questions. Ask them about their own flaws, and make them feel their own fragility.

The Hourim of innocence

The truth doesn't need make-up, nor does it fear the spotlight. It is they who are afraid of what they hide behind their words.

The children exchanged a silent glance, a gleam of intelligence and complicity in their eyes. They were ready, filled with a serenity that no one could take away from them. Their hands clasped, and in that bond lay their strength. They were facing a colossal challenge, but their unity and their truth were their greatest shield.

When the green light flashed, indicating that it was time to enter, they moved forward hand in hand, their footsteps echoing in the corridor leading to the arena. The door opened before them, revealing the imposing table, the spotlights, the eager faces of the journalists ready to launch their first questions. This television set looked like an arena, a stage set up to give the illusion of a fair fight, but which was, in reality, nothing but a trap.

But Abigael and Moussa were ready. Their faces were lit by a soft, determined glow, a light that contrasted with the oppressive atmosphere of the studio. They sat down in the centre, fearless, ready to face every look, every word. The whole world was watching, ready to see these children, these representatives of innocence, defy the machine of manipulation and pretense.

The truth floated in the air like a subtle breeze, and beneath their inquisitive gazes, they felt the invisible presence of the Guardian. They knew that this ordeal, however difficult, would reveal them as they really were. Their voices, without artifice or mask, would shake the media arena.

At that moment, everything became clear: this face-off would be much more than a simple debate. It would be a mirror held

The Hourim of innocence

up to a humanity in search of meaning, a battle between purity and cynicism, innocence and cunning, a struggle for the very soul of humanity.

The Guardian leaned towards them one last time, like a reassuring shadow slipping between their thoughts. "Don't forget, my children, they are the ones who are afraid of you. Their fear is hidden behind their costumes, their frozen smiles and their well-practised words. Your power is your sincerity. As long as you remain true to who you are, you will surpass them." He laid a hand on Moussa's shoulder, then on Abigael's, his gaze sparkling with a gentle, serene flame, a spark of pure wisdom. "Don't try to fight them on their own ground. Be yourself. Your light is what they fear most."

The children nodded silently, their hearts swelling with a new certainty. The flashing signal turned red, indicating that it was time. It was time. They stood up, their frail figures standing out in the subdued light of the dressing room. Moussa took a deep breath, feeling his heartbeat echo with hope. He met Abigael's gaze, a gaze filled with quiet strength, with the determination they had promised each other to maintain. The Guardian gave them one last smile, before disappearing into the shadows, ready to follow them, invisible but present, through this ordeal. And as they made their way towards the door, a strange calm came over them, a silent promise whispered in the depths of their souls.

They were about to face a world that wanted to break them. Their steps, light but determined, sounded like a tranquil melody, a challenge of purity that would soon be heard in every home, even in the darkest corners of the earth.

The Hourim of innocence

The studio glowed under a skilfully orchestrated play of light, each beam sculpting a drama yet to be revealed. The walls vibrated to the grandiloquent introductory music, an imposing symphony that sought to imbue the moment with palpable tension. But for many, the artifice was palpable, a stage too smooth, an arrogant excess that tried to give this confrontation the grandeur of a show. Yet the tension was very real, palpable, in every whisper held back, every breath suspended among the spectators staring at the closed doors, waiting for the two children to appear.

The heartbeats of thousands of spectators seemed to harmonise, each sensing the imminence of something unexpected and inexplicable. Backstage, Abigael and Moussa held hands, sensing the oppressive energy emanating from the stage. It was like a heavy whirlwind, but they were not alone. The Guardian, a benevolent shadow, stood beside them, infusing their hearts with a peaceful strength.

The doors opened slowly, in a theatrical movement, and the spotlights swung around, shining their beams on the silhouettes of the two children who walked forward, straight and without trembling. Abigael and Moussa walked hand in hand, their youth glowing in contrast to the immensity of the stage, which seemed ready to crush them under its imposing pomp. An almost unreal aura enveloped them, a glow of innocence that transcended the simplicity of their gestures. The crowd held its breath as the murmurs grew louder, a wave of wonder and awe rising up before these two childlike but powerful figures.

They had refused to wear make-up, and their faces, without make-up or masks, exuded a raw truth, a transparency that nothing could alter. Amidst the curious looks and forced

The Hourim of innocence

smiles, Abigael and Moussa began to murmur softly, a simple but hopeful word: "Hourim... Hourim..." This word, barely audible at first, spread through the air like a bright spark. The audience, as if hypnotised, let themselves be carried away, and their voices joined in a gentle clamour, the word "Hourim" vibrating, rising, filling the studio with a pure, uncontrollable energy. Faced with this spontaneous fervour, the journalists exchanged furtive glances, bewildered by the power of this unexpected surge, a force that seemed to stand up to their own calculation.

The children sat in the swivel chair, a seat designed to look tiny under their frail figures, but which, under the spotlight, endowed them with an aura of dignity and importance. Everything in the studio had been orchestrated to give an impression of fairness, but the illusion was tenuous. The large round table, the unwavering attitude of the journalists, everything resembled a modern arena. These gladiators in suits, ready to launch their first questions, waited with cold patience, their features frozen under an apparent calm. Their earpieces buzzed with instantaneous translations, each word, each language turning into clear sentences in their minds. But what they didn't know was that these children didn't need translators ; they understood every word, every inflection of the voice, every hidden intention behind the carefully turned phrases. They knew that every distortion, every ambiguity would be an opportunity to reveal a shred of truth.

A deep silence fell, while the whole world held its breath. The journalists stared at Abigael and Moussa, ready to launch their veiled attacks, to slip sharp questions under the façade of an honest interview, questions designed to shake. But in the eyes

The Hourim of innocence

of the two children, a quiet light shone, like a peaceful challenge that seemed to say: "We see you, and we're ready.

Abigael and Moussa took a moment to meet the eyes of each of these journalists, a silent parade, a moment to anchor their presence. They were young, frail in appearance, but a serene power emanated from them, a truth that needed no defence. They were the very embodiment of Hourim, a hope that had become flesh and blood, a living challenge to the accumulated shadows.

The journalists were getting ready, their scrutinising eyes already fixed on the children, ready to draw out questions cleverly wrapped in politeness. Every word seemed carefully chosen, sweet phrases ready to mask the harshness of the truths they were trying to expose. But the children, aware of what was at stake, had no intention of letting themselves be tricked. They waited calmly for the debate to begin, ready to respond with disarming simplicity, letting their words break through the wall of cynicism that surrounded them.

The whole world was watching. It was no longer just a confrontation between two children and a media machine. It was a reflection of the human soul, a mirror held up to a society thirsting for meaning, a moment when the purity of childhood came face to face with the rusty workings of power and manipulation. Under the spotlight, Abigael and Moussa stood as they were: vulnerable yet unshakeable, revealing by their very presence the fragility of the illusory construct that sought to destroy them.

And in that tense silence, where the cameras captured every tiny emotion, every spark in their eyes, it became clear that the truth, for once, could shine through unvarnished, without

The Hourim of innocence

guile. These two children, with their apparent fragility and their pure light, proved to the whole world that innocence could stand up to the greatest powers, and that sincerity could, perhaps, topple even the deepest shadows.

The main presenter, a man in his sixties with a face deeply weathered by the years and the storms of life, walked slowly towards the centre of the stage. His greying hair seemed to capture in every strand the shadows of years gone by. With a simple but confident wave of his hand, he ensured absolute silence in the room, as if each spectator were holding their breath.

- Ladies and gentlemen, welcome to this exceptional programme, a moment that many of us have been looking forward to," he announced in a deep, almost solemn voice. Tonight we have before us two children who have become the faces of a movement that has shaken the entire world. Two young souls who, despite their tender age, have found the incredible strength to stand up against the injustices of our time. Abigael and Moussa... Two children whose simple yet poignant story has resonated with millions of people. Tonight, they have agreed to share their truth with us, and it is with the greatest respect that we welcome them.

His tone, despite the choice of words, revealed an imperceptible hint of condescension, as if the very idea of children sitting in front of journalists was inconceivable, unusual. The first journalist, a man in his fifties with a serious face and greying temples, adjusted his glasses with meticulous precision, then leaned slightly towards the microphone. A smile appeared on his lips, perhaps a little forced, before he spoke.

The Hourim of innocence

- Abigael, Moussa, good evening," he began in a measured tone. Thank you for being here with us this evening. I'd like to start by asking you a simple question. You have often mentioned the word "Hourim". For those of us who are new to you this evening, could you tell us what this word means? How did it become the rallying cry of so many people around the world ?

Moussa glanced at Abigael, a brief exchange but one of silent confidence. He straightened slightly in his seat, his posture expressing a gravity that contrasted with his youth. His eyes, two soft shards of amber, shone with calm determination and unsuspected wisdom.

- Hourim" means light, he explained in a clear voice. It's the light that inhabits every human being, even in the darkest hours. It's a word of hope, one that remains alive even when all seems lost. But it's more than a symbol," he added with intensity. "Hourim" is the hope of overcoming divisions, the desire for peace.

This word unites two cultures, two languages. In its Arabic root, it means "Guardian", a protector, a guide. And its "-im" ending resonates in Hebrew, marking the plural. This is no accident : the plural emphasises that we are talking about two guardians, two beings united in a common mission. Two languages, two peoples, who should protect each other, not destroy each other.

"Hourim" is the promise that we can be united under the same light, the light that transcends fears and differences. A simple word, but charged with the strength of those who refuse to let the darkness divide their humanity.

The Hourim of innocence

The journalists' faces darkened for a moment, as if these words, coming from a child, were disconcerting them. One of them frowned slightly, not hiding his surprise at such a profound answer. Then a journalist, elegantly dressed in a black suit, spoke up, her gaze tinged with curiosity, hidden behind a polite smile.

- You speak of peace, unity and light," she said gently. But tell us, Abigael, Moussa, you are so young. You have grown up in an environment marked by suffering and conflict. Have you ever had the impression that you were being used? That perhaps adults, people in the shadows, are manipulating your innocence to make it a symbol of their own struggles?

Abigael exchanged a glance with Moussa, then turned slowly towards the journalist. There was a steely gleam in her eyes, a quiet strength that seemed to defy the weight of the question.

- Yes, we were pushed," she admitted in a soft but determined voice. But not by adults. Not by puppeteers hiding behind veils of interest and power. Ever since we were born, we've grown up in a world where people have tried to sow seeds of hatred in us, to show us the other as a threat. They tried to manipulate us, to turn us into children of war, heirs to an ancestral resentment. But we have discovered something else.

She paused briefly, the heavy silence amplifying her every word. The whole room seemed to be hanging on her every word.

- The loss of our parents, the pain we suffered, all this could have broken us. But instead, we found love. The love that unites us is stronger than all the darkness they wanted to bury in our hearts. What we say here is not the voice of those who pull strings. It is our truth, the truth that burns deep within us. We are nobody's puppets.

A heavy silence filled the room, as if each word had left an indelible imprint on the mind of each spectator. There was no longer any condescension in the eyes that stared back at them, only sincere admiration mixed with deep respect.

A tense silence settled in, heavy and weighty, as if the room itself was holding its breath. All eyes were riveted on the two children, but one journalist, with a sharp gaze and a wry smile, seemed to be waiting for his moment. He uncrossed his arms, leaned forward slightly and, in a tone tinged with scepticism and provocation, said:

- Is there? No adults, no support behind the scenes ? You'll understand that it's hard to believe. A movement on this scale, driven by two children... You'd almost think it was all a cleverly orchestrated show.

His arms crossed again, as if to underline his challenge. Moussa closed his eyes for a moment, taking a deep breath, then slowly opened them again. As he stared at the journalist, his gaze was almost disconcertingly intense, imbued with a wisdom far beyond his years.

- Yes, adults have always been behind us, but not in the way you imagine," he replied, his voice calm but charged with palpable gravity. Ever since we were born, it's been adults who have tried to shape us, influence us, plant in us the seeds of hatred and resentment. Adults who taught us that anger should be our heritage, that we should grow up with the weight of vengeance on our shoulders. These adults were everywhere: in our schools, in our streets, in the speeches that

The Hourim of innocence

surrounded us. They shaped us, trying to lock us into an endless chain of pain and retaliation.

He paused, letting his words sink into everyone's mind, then continued, more firmly:

- But one day, we chose to free ourselves from that hold. We decided to stop listening to those voices full of resentment and hatred. What we carry here is not the result of manipulation or a carefully prepared plan. It is the result of what we have seen, experienced and decided. We have chosen to break this infernal cycle. You may find this hard to believe because children are never given the opportunity to speak with their own voice, because it is believed that they cannot understand the depth of pain or the value of peace. But I assure you: what you see here is our truth. There's no puppeteer, no script. Just two children who want it all to stop.

A murmur ran through the room, like a wave spreading slowly. The raw authenticity of Moussa's words seemed to baffle the journalists, whose faces oscillated between doubt and admiration. The tension was almost tangible, as if the truth he had just revealed weighed heavily on everyone's shoulders.

The journalist in the black suit, visibly unsettled, spoke again, trying to hide her confusion behind a rigorous professionalism. She tilted her head slightly, her eyes crinkling with a mixture of disbelief and curiosity.

- Very well, then. You talk about your pain, your love. But let's talk about something more concrete. Moussa, it's been said that you... killed your uncle in cold blood. What can you tell us about this? What really happened that day?

The Hourim of innocence

The question was fired, and an even heavier silence fell over the room. You could have heard the ticking of a watch or the breath of a feather falling to the floor. All eyes turned to Moussa, whose expression closed for a moment. He inhaled deeply, his eyelids drooping briefly, then raised his head. His eyes, dark and deep, now seemed to contain all the pain and truth in the world.

- My uncle..." he began in a low voice, vibrating with barely contained emotion, "was a complex man. He wasn't an evil man, but he had been caught up in something bigger and darker than himself. He had given in to the voices of Iblis, to the illusions of those who preach violence as the only answer. For him, dignity could only be regained through bloodshed.

He paused for a moment, his hands trembling slightly in his lap. Then he continued, in a firmer voice:

- He loved me, I know he did. But that love was deformed, corrupted by a destructive ideology. That day, he handed me a gun. He looked me straight in the eye and ordered me to pull the trigger, to kill Abigael. All because she was on the other side of the wall. He said it was for our family, for our honour, that it was our only way. His eyes burned with a conviction I didn't understand. He thought he was freeing me, but he was shackling me.

Moussa's voice broke slightly, but he resumed at once, determined to go through with it:

- In that moment, everything froze. I saw in him not an executioner, but a victim. A victim of this ancestral hatred imposed on us. I refused. And in that refusal, in that choice, I broke something. It wasn't an easy victory, or even a heroic

The Hourim of innocence

act. It was an act of survival, an act of love. I didn't kill my uncle that day. I killed what he wanted me to become.

The room hung on his words, frozen in a mixture of awe and respect. Moussa's raw truth, without artifice or embellishment, had torn the veil of appearances. Nobody moved, nobody dared interrupt this moment of rare intensity.

At that moment, I was just a child, a heavy weapon in my frail hands, and a choice that, in reality, wasn't a choice at all. It wasn't me who raised that gun ; it was her voice, the weight of her expectations, the relentless pressure of her despair. His words still resonate, like echoes of a nightmare I can't erase. His hand, firm and determined, had come to rest on mine, guiding my gesture, taking me to the edge of the abyss. It was he who was trying to bind me to his pain, to plunge me with him into the abyss of his hatred.

But at the crucial moment, my eyes met those of Abigael. There was a visceral terror in them, but beyond that fear there was something else: a fragile glow, a flicker of love, like a flickering candle in the darkness. And that glow consumed the darkness inside me. It broke my uncle's hold, dispelling the shadows he was trying to plant deep in my soul.

I understood then that true dignity lay not in vengeance, not in bloodshed, but in the preservation of life, in the light. It was a moment of absolute clarity, a moment when everything I had been led to believe collapsed, giving way to a purer truth. I chose to turn against him, not out of hatred, but out of love, for Abigael, for that spark of hope she carried, and for myself, for what was left of my humanity.

I didn't kill my uncle in cold blood. It wasn't a cold, calculated decision. It was an instinctive wrench, a cry for life in the face of nothingness. That day, I chose love, and no one can take that inner victory away from me.

The silence that followed was almost tangible, as if the very walls of the room absorbed the weight of this confession. The cameras, motionless, captured every nuance of emotion on Moussa's face, every word he spoke becoming an unalterable truth. Abigael, sitting beside him, gently placed a hand on his. Her fingers trembled slightly, but her gesture was one of comfort and solidarity. Her eyes, shining with restrained tears, spoke of a shared pain and a common resilience.

The main presenter, visibly shaken, cleared his throat slightly before speaking again. His tone, although professional, betrayed a certain nervousness.

- Thank you, Moussa, for that courageous answer," he says gravely. Now to another subject. Almost a year ago, on 7 October, something happened that shook the whole world. Many say that day changed everything, that it marked the beginning of a new era. Abigael, Moussa, what can you tell us about that fateful day?

A shiver ran through the room, and all eyes turned to Abigael. She squeezed Moussa's hand a little tighter, seeking in this contact the strength she needed to face her memories. Taking a deep breath, she raised her head, her eyes staring into the distance as if she were seeing through time. Her voice, soft but vibrating with gravity, finally broke the silence.

- 7 October... it was the day of the shadows," she began, her words tinged with deep sadness, each syllable seeming to weigh like a rock. That day, the sky was torn apart by hang gliders, looming over the horizon like a swarm of crows and vultures. Black silhouettes, ravenous, hungry for misfortune,

The Hourim of innocence

swooped down on us with calculated slowness and icy precision.

She closed her eyes for a moment, reliving every detail with painful intensity. When she opened them again, her pupils shone with the brightness of an ancient but still vivid grief.

- They hovered over our heads, silent and implacable, predators who seemed to feed on our terror. It was as if the sky itself had abandoned us, condemning us to suffer their inexorable descent. Every movement they made cast a shadow on the ground, a shadow that stretched out like a promise of death.

Her voice broke slightly, but she continued unperturbed:

- Terror descended with them. A dull, insidious terror that crept into every breath, every look. And there I was, frozen. On territory that wasn't mine, surrounded by men who had sworn to protect me. But all that... all that was just a decoy, a cynical lie to hide the truth.

She clenched her fists, trying to contain the emotion that threatened to overwhelm her.

- These men hadn't taken me there to save me. They had put me right in the middle of the trap, exposed, vulnerable, a pawn in their cruel game. Their promise of protection was a façade, an illusion to hide their true intention. I was bait, a sacrifice. They had handed me over to the monsters, defenceless.

Silence fell over the room like a suffocating veil. Abigael's every word still echoed, imbuing the air with an almost unbearable tension. The journalists, usually quick to react, remained silent, absorbing the harshness of this testimony.

The Hourim of innocence

The Mouzad, the very people who had sworn to protect my people, had decided that my life was just a pawn on their cold, calculating chessboard. A card to be played and discarded. In their eyes, I was nothing more than a variable to be erased, a shadow to be sacrificed to achieve their obscure objectives. They delivered me into the heart of chaos, abandoned without a glance, to the clutches of soulless predators. I can still see the impassive face of one of my captors, the icy emptiness in his eyes as he handed me over to hell. His silence was a condemnation, a silent judgement: I was an offering on the altar of their ruthless strategy, a broken toy in the hands of those who had never known compassion.

The ground trembled beneath my feet, or maybe it was just fear that made me stagger. The air was dense, saturated with heat and dust, every breath an agony. Everything around me dissolved: silhouettes became indistinct shadows, screams blended into a dull roar, and the earth seemed to close in like a cage of darkness. I was nothing more than a child trapped in a waking nightmare, condemned to face alone the cruelty of a world that had abandoned me.

There was an almost sacred silence in the studio. Abigael continued, her voice imbued with a deep gravity, the tears she held back betraying the strength she was mustering to go on.

- The death squads arrived," she continued, methodical and implacable. They advanced like a black tide, guns raised, icy stares, devoid of all humanity. Among them were traitors, faces I knew. Men and women who once claimed to be on our side. But on that day, they were there to guarantee that those who were to perish would do so without escape. I begged them with my eyes, I called for help, but they ignored me. They looked away. Their silence was worse than the gunfire. They

The Hourim of innocence

abandoned me, a defenceless child, to executioners who saw me as nothing more than a target.

Fear was everywhere, omnipresent. It reigned over this macabre scene like an invisible sovereign. Each blast sounded like a death knell, a cruel countdown to an inescapable end.

The journalists, accustomed to the darkest stories, seemed to freeze. Some, ill at ease, made movements to interrupt, to divert the conversation. But their attempts died in their throats. Something, or someone, seemed to be holding them back. An intangible presence, an invisible but oppressive weight. The Guardian. They could feel it, even if they couldn't name it. He was there, imposing silence, forcing everyone to listen to this raw, irrefutable truth.

Abigael drew in a deep breath, her voice wavering slightly before she continued.

- And just when all seemed lost, when the screams and explosions had engulfed me, a cruel truth dawned on me : no one was coming. The whole world had abandoned me. But even in this absolute solitude, one look found me. Someone saw me, and that look changed everything.

She turned to Moussa, her eyes resting on him with an intensity that transcended words. In that suspended moment, their souls seemed to be conversing in silence. Moussa gently squeezed Abigael's hand, then spoke, his voice deep with pain and conviction.

- That day, I was standing back, watching events unfold around me," he says. And that's when I saw her, Abigael. She was a hostage, taken by these men she thought she could trust. But their betrayal was obvious. They led her, without

The Hourim of innocence

hesitation, to her doom. I saw them hand her over like a lamb to the slaughter, without a glance, without an ounce of remorse.

He paused, the lines of his face hardening slightly, as if he were reliving every moment.

- Those men... they knew. They knew she wouldn't make it. They knew they were condemning her. And yet they left her there, in the trap that they themselves had set. For them, she was just a problem to be eliminated, a cumbersome variable in a complex equation. I saw them, their calculated gestures, their palpable contempt. They didn't hesitate for a second. In their eyes, her life was worthless.

Moussa clenched his jaws, a flash of restrained anger passing fleetingly through his eyes, before he softened slightly.

- But what they hadn't counted on was that I'd be there. That I would refuse to look away. That day, I realised that we were alone, but that we could be strong together. I chose not to remain a powerless spectator. I chose to fight, not just for her, but for what we represent. For the light they were trying to extinguish.

A murmur ran through the room again, but this time it wasn't one of embarrassment or unease. It was a murmur of respect, of silent admiration. The strength and humanity of the two children had transcended the pain of their story, leaving an indelible mark on the air.

He inhaled deeply, his voice choking slightly under the weight of the memories he was about to reveal. The pain showed in every word.

The Hourim of innocence

- I saw the hang-gliders coming," began Moussa, his gaze fixed on the void as if he were reliving every moment. They swooped down like a flock of ominous birds. Their shadows stretched across the ground, and with them the panic spread like an all-consuming fire. Every face I passed was marked by terror: trembling children, mothers clutching their young, men frozen in helplessness. The death squads weren't there just to kill. They were there to break. To remind us that we were insignificant, pawns to be crushed under their boot.

He paused, his breathing becoming slower, as if to tame the emotion that threatened to overwhelm him.

- And then I saw her again. Abigael, alone in the middle of the ruins, her eyes desperately searching for help that wasn't coming. I knew I couldn't stand still. Something inside me awoke, a force that I didn't yet understand, but which compelled me to act. I slipped into the shadows, following her footsteps, refusing to let her face this nightmare alone.

He turned his face slowly towards Abigael, and his voice softened with the pain he shared with her.

- 7 October... that was the day everything changed.

He continued, his voice trembling, each word seeming to scratch him a little more.

- I followed her, powerless, watching as these men who claimed to protect her dragged her away without mercy. But these men were not what they seemed. They were Mouzad infiltrators, traitors operating in the shadows within Houmas, puppets in a much bigger game. Allied in the darkness, they weaved their diabolical plans together, sacrificing everything on the altar of their ambitions.

The Hourim of innocence

They locked her in a dark, icy cell, a place that oozed fear and despair. She was treated like a thing, a useless weight that could be pushed aside at will. There I was, lurking in the shadows, my fists clenched, my rage bubbling silently, unable to intervene but swearing to myself that this betrayal would not go unpunished.

His voice became deeper, heavier.

- That's when my uncle appeared.

The silence in the room became almost unbearable. Everyone in the audience held their breath, absorbed in Moussa's story.

- He saw me. His eyes changed. The man who had once taught me patience and love had disappeared. In his place, I saw someone hardened by hatred. He grabbed me by the arm and pulled me into a dark corner, away from prying eyes. There he handed me a gun.

Moussa paused, his hands tightening slightly on his knees.

- Do it, Moussa," he ordered me. His voice was icy cold, devoid of emotion. "Show them that you're one of us. Show me you're a man. Shoot."

His eyes crinkled, as if he was trying to chase away the images that haunted him.

- I looked at him, searching for some sign of the man I had loved. But there was nothing. His eyes sought total obedience, a complete abandonment of who I was.

He shook his head slightly, as if refusing this moment again.

- He took my hands, placed the gun in them. "Do it," he insisted, his voice breaking in desperate fury. "Do it for your

The Hourim of innocence

people, for our honour." His words were chains, his pressure on my hands a vice. He wanted me to become like him, a man shaped by violence and blood.

He looked up at Abigael, whose eyes were now wet with tears.

- And then I saw her. She was there, motionless, her eyes full of tears, but without fear. She didn't scream or beg. She looked at me with infinite sadness, but also with silent trust.

His voice broke slightly, but he continued, his tone full of determination.

- That's when everything changed. My uncle's pressure on my hands, his screams, the cold of the metal against my skin... It all condensed into one unbearable moment. And then I pulled the trigger.

The silence that followed was deafening. Moussa lowered his eyes for a moment before continuing.

- The shot rang out, a brutal thud. My uncle collapsed, his body falling apart like a disjointed puppet. His eyes, frozen in silent surprise, still haunt me.

He raised his head, his eyes shining with a fierce intensity.

- It wasn't a choice. It was a necessity. A desperate act to save Abigael, to save what was left of the light in me.

He squeezed Abigael's hand lightly, seeking in this contact the strength to conclude.

- That day, I lost a part of myself, an innocence that will never return. But I saved Abigael. And that gave me the strength to carry on.

The Hourim of innocence

He breathed in deeply, his voice softer but resolute.

- I swore that day that no one would ever again manipulate our lives. That we would never again be the instruments of other people's hatred. What they tried to destroy that day is what unites us now: a promise, stronger than death, brighter than their darkness.

The silence that followed seemed infinite, each of Moussa's words leaving an indelible mark. In the looks exchanged between them, there was no longer just pain, but a strength, a shared promise that transcended everything they had been through.

Abigael nodded gently and added, her voice rising one last time, clear and full of determination :

- On that day, they tried to manipulate us, to use us, to cast us as mere pawns in a war that was not our own. But it failed. Because what Moussa and I found was love, solidarity, a force greater than any adult manipulation. That day, they wanted to sow hatred, but what they reaped was a promise. A promise that we would never let fear prevail over love.

A crushing silence fell over the set. The journalists, used to juggling with fabricated stories and orchestrated drama, were for once disarmed. The raw truth of the children's stories, delivered without artifice, had swept away the pretense, exposing the hypocrisy lurking beneath the spotlight.

Abigael and Moussa's gazes were planted squarely on the presenter. There was an intensity about him, a mixture of gentleness and firmness, a quiet strength that seemed to defy the cold mechanics of adult debates. For a moment, the journalists, who are usually quick to analyse and controversy,

The Hourim of innocence

seemed unsettled, taken by surprise by the assurance of this young girl and boy.

The lights continued to turn, but something had changed. The stage had been transformed. It was no longer a simple interview, an exercise in media exposure. It had become a court of truth. And in this tribunal, the children, with their apparent fragility, reversed the roles. They were no longer witnesses subject to the judgement of adults, but judges themselves, looking at this world with a lucid and pitiless eye.

The captivated audience remained motionless, almost hypnotised. The journalists, for their part, looked furtively at each other, searching for a loophole, a catch, a way to regain control. One of them, a man with an impassive face and a coldly calculating gaze, leaned forward slightly, his eyes staring at Abigael like a predator. He was ready to strike a blow, to ask a question that would upset the balance.

But despite the staging, despite the cameras, despite the dramatic music, one thing was clear: Abigael and Moussa had not come to lose. Every word they spoke, every truth they unpacked, eroded the veneer of the show a little more, cracking the polished masks of the adults.

They had come armed with cynicism and doubt. But they were up against a more powerful force : innocence. Disarming sincerity. And a light, fragile but persistent, that continued to shine against all expectations.

The questions would become more virulent, the attacks more personal. That was part of the game. But one thing was certain : Abigael and Moussa were not there to bend. They were there so that, at last, the truth, in all its disarming simplicity, could find a voice.

The Hourim of innocence

A heavy silence followed their testimony, a silence that seemed to stretch, almost tangible. The journalists, used to seizing the slightest opportunity to react, remained motionless. They hesitated. It was as if they suddenly realised that the truth before them was beyond them.

But it was clear that one of them had not said his last word. A sharp-tongued man, known for his incisive style, spoke up. His sharp voice pierced the silence.

- Abigael, I'd like to talk about something more personal," he said, his eyes locking onto hers, hard and merciless. Your relationship with Moussa. You're Jewish, and Moussa is Muslim. It's against the principles of your religion. Your own family would be against this union.

He paused, letting his words float through the air like a challenge.

- In fact, we have someone here who would like to speak to you.

The words fell like blows, cold and implacable. Abigael frowned, her throat constricted by sudden anguish. The journalist, savouring the dramatic effect, gestured to the giant screen behind them. A flickering image appeared, and Abigael's face froze.

On the screen, the pale, sunken face of an old man. His features, marked by old age and the weight of years, carried an almost spectral gravity. Abigael held her breath. Her grandfather.

She had thought he was dead. Years of silence had passed since they last spoke, and yet, there, before her eyes, he was still alive. But he was no longer the man she had known. His

The Hourim of innocence

eyes were dead, lost in an eerie emptiness, and his gaze floated as if trying to catch memories that had escaped him. Abigael immediately recognised the relentless signs of Alzheimer's disease, that terrible illness that devours identity, erases memories and crushes the spirit.

His grandfather, the pillar of his childhood, was a shadow of his former self, a fragile puppet, obviously manipulated.

- Abigael, my little one..." he murmured, his voice trembling, distant, as if he were reading words dictated by an invisible hand. Love between a Jew and a Muslim... it's not allowed. It's not in our traditions... You should know that. It's a betrayal...

Each word, spoken with painful slowness, was a blade plunging into Abigael's heart. She felt her hand tremble slightly, but she clasped it tighter around Moussa's. Her eyes closed for a moment, just long enough to swallow the pain and then to be able to speak again. Her eyes closed for a moment, just long enough to swallow the pain and draw on a deep source of inner strength.

It was clear that her grandfather didn't understand where he was or why he was saying these words. He was just a tool, manipulated by those who sought to break her. But Abigael refused to give in to anger. Instead, an implacable determination etched itself on her features.

Moussa felt the tension in Abigael's hand. He responded with a gentle but firm pressure, a silent but powerful support. Then, with admirable serenity, he spoke, his voice soft and steady, filled with reassuring warmth.

- Sir," he began, addressing the screen, "I understand that these words are meant to hurt Abigael. But let me tell you this:

The Hourim of innocence

my religion, Islam, does not forbid love between a Muslim and a Jew.

He paused, his voice growing in intensity, each word carried by an unshakeable conviction.

- The Prophet himself, peace be upon him, preached respect and love for the People of the Book. I have never felt that our love was in contradiction with my beliefs. On the contrary, I am convinced that our union is a symbol of peace, a proof of what humanity could achieve if it agreed to overcome its artificial divisions.

He turned to Abigael, his gaze plunging into hers, infinite tenderness in his eyes.

- Abigael and I aren't together to challenge anyone. We are together because we love each other. Because we believe that this love is a bridge, a passageway that transcends the borders that fear and hatred try to erect between us. And today, that bridge is stronger than ever, despite all the attempts to destroy it.

A deep silence fell, a silence in which every word Moussa spoke still seemed to resonate, daring anyone to contradict the truth he had just stated.

Abigael inhaled deeply, sitting up slightly. She turned her eyes towards the screen, looking at the flickering figure of her grandfather. Despite the pain that gripped her heart, his voice, as it rose, was imbued with an infinite gentleness, an unfailing tenderness.

- Grandpa..." she began, her voice full of emotion. I know you probably don't remember me. You've been put here to make you say things you don't even believe.

The Hourim of innocence

She paused for a moment, a slight tremor in her voice, then continued with quiet strength.

- I love you, Grandpa. And I deeply respect the traditions you've passed on to me. But those traditions were never meant to justify hatred or break love. The words you're saying today... they're not yours. It's not you speaking.

His voice became firmer, carried by a fierce determination.

- I will not let you be used against us. I will not let you be the plaything of those who want to divide us.

His last words echoed in the heavy air of the studio, like a challenge not only to the journalist, but to an entire system that sought to impose its rules to the detriment of humanity.

The silence that followed was total. There was nothing more to say.

Silence fell on the stage, heavy and almost tangible. It seemed to weigh on every breath, every heartbeat. The journalists, caught in the grip of this strange atmosphere, tried several times to regain control. But every time they moved, every time they tried to interrupt, their words hung in the air, their lips sealed by an invisible force. They seemed transfixed, paralysed by the hold of the Guardian, this intangible presence that commanded respect and truth.

Moussa, his gaze firm, straightened slightly. His dark eyes roamed over the tense faces of the journalists, before he spoke again. His voice, calm but penetrating, broke the silence with natural authority.

- You have tried to play your last card, that of division and lies. But your efforts are in vain, because we are united. You don't

The Hourim of innocence

understand yet, but the love we bear is stronger than all your manipulations. Love is greater than fear. You won't be able to reduce us to mere pawns in your cynical game.

He paused, letting each word resonate.

- We're here to talk about peace, light and hope. And no stratagem or manoeuvre on your part will distract us from this mission.

A barely audible murmur ran through the audience, like a discreet but powerful wave. The journalists, usually the masters of debate, exchanged furtive, unsettled glances. They had never been so helpless, deprived of their usual power to shape the truth to suit themselves.

Even Iblis, somewhere in the shadows, must have sensed a flaw. An insidious crack, extending into the fragile edifice of his manipulations.

The silence persisted, stretching like a tension ready to explode. Then a journalist stood up. She was famous for her ability to expose flaws, to manipulate with a muted smile and sharp words. Her glasses, placed precisely on the table in front of her, seemed to mark the start of a carefully calculated assault.

She spoke, in a voice that was soft, almost maternal, but laden with icy irony.

- You're talking about love, a vast, complex, unfathomable subject. Even we adults, with all our experience, often struggle to define its contours. You're barely more than fourteen years old, barely a foot in life, and yet here you are, in front of the whole world, pretending to give us lessons on what it means to love. So tell us, how can children understand love ? How

The Hourim of innocence

should we, as adults, be taught by you on a subject so profoundly human, so intrinsically complicated?

The question, although asked with feigned calm, was a direct attack, an attempt to reduce them to the status of inexperienced children. The air thickened with tension as all eyes focused on Abigael and Moussa.

Abigael felt the pressure in Moussa's hand increase. She knew that this question was intended to destabilise them, to undermine their credibility. But she wasn't alone. She breathed in deeply, feeling the comforting presence of the Guardian, this silent, benevolent force watching over them.

She straightened up, her gaze fixed on the journalist. When she spoke, her voice was firm, devoid of any hesitation.

- You're right. We are only children. And that's precisely our strength. The love we know has not yet been corrupted by the filters that you adults have learned to apply.

She paused, letting her words sink into the mind of her audience.

- Adult love, hidden behind masks, is often drowned in power plays, subtle lies and unspoken expectations. You love with conditions, unspoken compromises, unspoken fears. We don't have these filters. Our emotions are raw, absolute. When we say we love, it's not a calculation or a strategy, it's a pure truth that expects nothing in return.

The silence in the studio was now almost religious. Abigael's every word weighed heavily, forcing every spectator and every journalist to reflect.

The Hourim of innocence

Then Moussa spoke up, his deep voice ringing like a bell in the tense space.

- The love we bear is a raw force, pure energy. We love without fear of loss, without thought of consequences, without being paralysed by doubts or regrets. We don't love to possess or control. We love because it's what our hearts tell us to do, because this love drives us to cross walls, to defy borders, to brave death if need be.

He stared at the journalist, his eyes shining with unwavering sincerity.

- You adults have learned to protect yourselves from love, to build walls around your hearts, to put padlocks of fear on them. We hope with all our hearts that we never learn these things.

The silence that followed was heavy with reflection. Everyone in the room seemed to be confronted with a truth they had never dared to contemplate. The journalist lowered her eyes for the first time. The children, in their apparent fragility, had shaken the fortress of cynicism that the adults had built around them.

The journalists exchanged heavy, almost evasive glances, as if Abigael and Moussa's words had held up a mirror to their own failures. Their facade of self-confidence was eroding, revealing the cracks that the children's sincerity had created.

Abigael spoke again, her voice now imbued with a deep, almost solemn gentleness:

- What Moussa and I have is a certainty: love can change things. We have seen hatred in its rawest, most devastating form, the hatred that drives men to kill without remorse, the

The Hourim of innocence

hatred that consumes everything in its path. We have seen what happens to a world where love has no place. And in the face of this chaos, we have chosen to love. Perhaps that seems naive to you, perhaps it seems childish. But it's also the bravest thing we could have done.

His gaze swept slowly around the room, lingering on the tense faces of the journalists, defying their silent judgements.

- You say that love is complex, that it can only be understood after years of experience and hardship. But perhaps it's precisely the weight of those years that makes love so difficult to grasp. You build up layers of fear, resentment, disillusionment, until love becomes an enigma, a battlefield. We haven't yet learned how to complicate it. What we do know about love is that it is there to unite, to build bridges between souls, not to separate them.

A deep silence fills the studio. Not a whisper, not a breath. The journalists, usually so quick to respond, seemed petrified, as if Abigael's words had frozen time.

Their love had nothing of the love of adults, and in that it possessed a raw, almost primordial power. A strength that, in its innocence and purity, seemed invincible.

The tension was palpable when a slow, calculated movement broke the stillness. The Architect of the Debate rose to his feet with an almost ceremonial assurance. His movements were measured, like those of a strategist deploying his last pieces on a complex chessboard.

He was the conductor of this media arena, the one pulling the strings behind the scenes. His voice, when it rose, was tinged with a false neutrality and a thinly veiled satisfaction.

The Hourim of innocence

- Ladies and gentlemen," he continued in a tone laden with theatricality, "allow me to introduce a special guest. A key witness who may well shed light on the true nature of the 'Hourim' movement.

He paused, carefully calculated, letting the mystery envelop the assembly. His eyes fixed on Abigael and Moussa, like a predator sizing up its prey.

- Because, you see, it may not all be as innocent as it seems.

A shudder ran through the audience. The large doors of the studio opened slowly, as if moved by an invisible force. The atmosphere, already heavy, turned icy.

A man entered. His figure, draped in a long dark robe, seemed to absorb the light, projecting an aura of coldness around him. His features were angular, impeccably cut, and his eyes, piercingly bright, seemed to probe into souls.

It was Iblis.

Beneath this carefully chosen appearance, he embodied the perfect scholar : a familiar and reassuring face for many. He was known as a man of faith, a religious diplomat capable of navigating the great traditions with ease. He had shared tables with the Pope, debated with leading Muslim scholars, and conversed with the most influential rabbis. But despite this respected façade, there was an indefinable turmoil about him, a magnetic tension that disturbed people without explaining why.

The journalists, disconcerted at first, regained their composure. Like a pack galvanised by the arrival of its alpha, they regained their composure, ready to resume their offensive.

The Hourim of innocence

Abigael and Moussa exchanged a glance, their eyes filled with silent questions. They could feel the change in atmosphere, the icy intensity that this man brought with him. But they didn't give in to fear.

The Guardian, still invisible, watched in silence. He knew that the enemy had taken a decisive step. But he waited. The time had not yet come for him to intervene.

Iblis walked to the centre of the stage, his measured steps amplifying the oppression in the air. When he spoke, his voice was low, almost melodious, but it carried an undeniable authority.

- My dear friends," he began, his voice husky with false benevolence, "it's always fascinating to observe the power of words, especially when they come from young, ardent hearts.

He turned slowly towards Abigael and Moussa, his eyes seeming to pierce the veil of their souls.

- But words, however powerful, have to be confronted with reality. The truth. And that's precisely what I'm here to offer: a truth that perhaps these children themselves don't even know.

A shudder ran through the assembly. The room was now hanging on his every word, with the moment when everything could change fast approaching.

The Architect of the Debate, satisfied with the dramatic effect he had orchestrated, leaned back slightly on the lectern. His smile was sharp, almost toothy, as he announced:

- We have with us the Reverend Anwar, a man whose reputation is well established. A key witness who has, it seems,

The Hourim of innocence

unravelled some of the mysteries surrounding the Hourim movement. He is here to reveal what lies behind the innocent faces of our young guests.

A murmur ran through the room. The atmosphere, already heavy, became oppressive. The Reverend advanced slowly, his dark robe brushing the floor. His eyes, cold and piercing, looked at Abigael and Moussa in turn, as if he were trying to search their souls.

- My children," he said, his voice soft, but with a calculated gravity, "I've heard about you. I've been told that you carry a message of love, innocence and light. But what I've seen... what I've discovered, is a very different light. A deceptive light.

He let his words hang in the air, savouring the effect of his accusation.

- Behind your movement, Hourim, lies something else. Ancient forces, dark forces, that are beyond you. Invisible hands pulling the strings, intentions that are neither innocent nor pure. You may be sincere, but you are being manipulated, used as instruments.

The Reverend paused for a moment, looking round the assembly, his tone becoming more solemn:

- There are signs and symbols. Your movement carries within it the shadow of an ancient sect. A sect that has fed on conflict, despair and hatred over the centuries. There are whispers that it sowed the seeds of unspeakable tragedies, that it was this sect that, in the shadows, fuelled the hatred that led to the Shoah. Today, it is back, masked by promises of peace, seeking to infiltrate our hearts and corrupt them.

The Hourim of innocence

Abigael felt an icy chill run down her spine. The Reverend's words sounded like a blade. She squeezed Moussa's hand, feeling that he was a rock she could lean on.

The journalists, as if revived by these accusations, regained their composure. One of them, his eyes sparkling, spoke up :

- So how do you respond? Is the Hourim movement really a smokescreen? Is this your love ? A mask to conceal darker intentions ?

Abigael closed her eyes for a moment, as if searching for strength in the darkness of her mind. But before she could reply, a gentle warmth came over her. The Guardian was there. His silent but powerful presence comforted her, dispelling the fear that threatened to grip her.

Moussa felt that same comforting breath. He took a deep breath, and when he spoke, his voice was clear, resonating with an unexpected maturity.

- Before answering your questions, I'd like to ask some of my own. Questions that have haunted me since the moment my childhood was snatched from me.

He straightened up, his gaze wandering beyond the faces in front of him, searching for an answer in an invisible horizon.

- Why were my parents murdered? Why did the Creator allow those I loved most to be torn from my life ? Why were Abigael and I condemned to carry this burden of pain so young?

He paused, his voice broken by emotion. A solitary tear rolled down his cheek, but he did not wipe it away.

- You're listening to me and you're probably thinking that these words can't possibly be mine. That they're too

The Hourim of innocence

thoughtful, too weighty for a teenager. But let me tell you about a miracle. Not the miracle of illusions or deceptions that some people orchestrate to deceive, but the real miracle. The one that defies logic, the one that does not bend to human laws.

His voice grew stronger and more intense :

- The miracle is the love that persists when everything should collapse. It's that love that kept me going when everything was pushing me to give up. This miracle is the light that you try to tarnish with your accusations, but which continues to shine, because it doesn't come from me, or from Abigael. It comes from something greater, something more powerful than anything you can understand.

A crushing silence fell again. Even Reverend Anwar seemed shaken, the cold glint in his eyes flickering for a moment.

Abigael, feeling strengthened by Moussa's words, stood up in turn. She looked resolutely around the assembly, then spoke, her voice vibrating with new energy:

- You speak of cults and conspiracies. You speak of hatred hidden behind our smiles. But what you don't understand is that we have never sought to manipulate anyone. We carry a simple message : one of hope, one of love.

She turned to the Reverend, her gaze defiant.

- Did you see any symbols in Hourim ? I see a promise. A promise that we can transcend the darkness, that we can build bridges across the chasms carved out by centuries of enmity and conflict. But you, instead of reaching out, you fan the embers of dread, blowing on the flickering flame of collective

The Hourim of innocence

anguish. You are the insidious shadow we have sworn to dispel.

The silence that fell was no longer a mere void of sound, but a palpable entity, a weight that fell on every chest, on every conscience. Abigael's every word echoed in this space like the death knell of an inescapable judgement. Iblis, hidden beneath the mask of Reverend Anwar, could not contain an imperceptible shudder. A fleeting spark of anger crossed his eyes, shattering for a moment the illusion of his sovereign calm.

Without flinching, Moussa looked at him with an almost inquisitorial gravity.

- Take the example of the Holy Koran, when it mentions Jesus, Aïssa, peace be upon him. It says that he spoke from the cradle. And long before that, from the sanctuary of his mother Mary's womb, he spoke to proclaim the purity of the woman who had borne him. A child, even before he was born, defended the truth with divine eloquence, refuting the infamy of slander by the sheer power of his voice.

He let his words spread through the air like a gravity wave, each syllable weighing heavily on the atmosphere, which was already saturated with intensity.

- That's what a miracle is all about. A word that transcends natural laws, a wisdom that is unencumbered by age or the human boundaries of reason. And you, who claim to be the guardians of knowledge, are merely the heralds of sterile scepticism. Unable to perceive this light, you prefer to take refuge in duplicity and manipulation.

The Hourim of innocence

The cameras, motionless and implacable, caught every nuance, every inflection of his voice. The journalists, silenced by the magnitude of the moment, seemed petrified, as if they sensed that the ground on which they were standing had just given way beneath their feet.

Moussa slowly turned his head, his penetrating gaze locked on the false reverend like a hawk staring at its prey.

- I believe in the Creator, and I accept without reservation the destiny He has decreed for me. This destiny has led me here, in front of you, to cross swords with impostors who cloak themselves in the trappings of sanctity, but who are, in truth, nothing but puppets animated by the insidious hands of darkness.

His voice, calm at first, became more incisive, coiling with a relentless intensity.

- You have invoked Iblis himself, the master of illusions, he who wears a thousand masks to sow discord and break souls. Don't forget that he once tried to corrupt Abigael and me. He took the guise of an innocent child, hoping to insinuate himself into our hearts and tempt us to taste the forbidden fruit. Today he still stands among us, disguised as a holy man, hoping in his infinite arrogance to destroy what he can never understand or possess.

He stepped forward slightly, his features illuminated by the spotlight, revealing a solemn serenity mixed with fierce determination.

- You accuse me of being the instrument of a sect conspiring against the Jewish people, seeking to rekindle the flames of

The Hourim of innocence

hatred. You dare to evoke the Shoah, that unfathomable abyss of horror and suffering, to legitimise your vile accusations.

He paused, his words taking on an almost prophetic gravity.

- Know this: the memory of the martyrs cannot be sullied by vile manipulation. The blood of the innocent, spilt in this tragedy, transcends religious divisions, the borders of peoples and eras. It rises up like a universal cry, a cry that demands remembrance and justice. That you should dare to pervert this sacred memory in order to satisfy your malicious intentions is a nameless abomination.

The spotlights seemed to flicker, as if they were bending under the harsh light of the truth they were exposing. The cameras, relentless, transmitted every word, every gesture, every look, amplifying their reach beyond the walls of the studio, into the hearts of homes around the world.

In a gesture of infinite tenderness, Moussa turned his face towards Abigael. He reached out his hand, seeking hers, and their fingers entwined with a delicacy that spoke of all they had been through together.

This simple gesture, carrying a silent power, embodied their unbreakable bond, a pure and invincible love forged in the face of adversity. A love that, even in the face of storm, persisted with the quiet strength of a North Star.

Abigael, her eyes shining brightly, gently squeezed Moussa's hand. Through this contact, she felt the comforting warmth of the Guardian, this invisible yet palpable presence that enveloped them in a protective light.

The Hourim of innocence

She took a deep breath, and when she spoke, her voice rose with an almost supernatural clarity, sounding like a sacred chant.

- You talk about fear, hatred and conspiracies. But all that is just a smokescreen. The truth we carry is simple : love is the only force capable of breaking the chains of darkness.

She locked her gaze on the false reverend, a fierce light in her eyes.

- You can try to divide us, to dull our light with your shadows, but you will never succeed. For this light does not come from us alone. It draws its strength from something much greater, a source that you can never sully.

And at that moment, the silence that followed seemed sacred, as if the universe itself were holding its breath. The stage, a secular temple of debate and confrontation, had been transformed into a sanctuary of truth and light.

- If this accusation, this alleged ancestral sect that has woven its web through the ages, were true, you would have brandished it at the dawn of this debate like an implacable sword. You would have made it your main weapon, the pillar of your rhetoric. But you didn't. You held it in reserve, hoping that it would be your fatal blow, the coup de grâce destined to bring us down when you were cornered.

He paused, his gaze hardening, each word taking on more meaning.

- But now the hour of your downfall has come. Your backs are against the wall, and your despair is oozing through your empty words. You thought you could destroy us, but you have betrayed yourselves. The whole world is watching you, and it

The Hourim of innocence

sees. It sees men reduced to shadows, desperate, clinging to chimeras. Your lies burst like fragile bubbles, revealing their emptiness. The light finally pierces the opacity of your stratagems, and your accusations crumble under the merciless gaze of the truth.

Moussa turned his gaze to Abigael. In her eyes, a shared pain, an echo of their common wounds, an unbreakable bond. He placed his hand on hers, a gesture of silent but infinitely powerful tenderness.

- Then let me ask this question, the one that haunts me, the one that assails me every night," he said, his voice trembling with controlled emotion. Why did our parents die, Abigael and me ? Why were they sacrificed?

His gaze now swept over the assembly, stopping on each face like a judge weighing souls.

- Is that your accusation ? That we consented, that we agreed to see our own parents perish for some alleged cause ? Do you really think that two eleven-year-olds could have orchestrated their own tragedy? Your absurdity borders on indecency. You tread on corpses, you drag our souls through the mud, hoping that these basenesses will suffice to mask the emptiness of your arguments. But know this: your slander merely reveals your own moral bankruptcy.

He straightened slightly, a dull, controlled but palpable anger on his face. Each word that followed sounded like a thunderclap in the oppressive silence of the stage.

- Mr 'Reverend', or should I say the fleeting incarnation of a mirage, a wandering shadow in the labyrinth of an endless nightmare, you are an illusion. A farce. You think you can

The Hourim of innocence

bend the truth, twist it until it aligns with your perfidious designs. But today, it's you who's on trial. Your lies, the chains you forged to shackle us, are but the chains of your own downfall. You are now exposed, unmasked before the eyes of the whole world.

The spotlights bathed the stage in a harsh, implacable light, and the cameras, like mute witnesses, captured every fragment of this transcendent moment. The silence stretched out, heavy, almost sacred.

Moussa turned back to Abigael. He squeezed her hand gently, a gesture that combined the weight of shared suffering with the strength of a love that transcends all trials. Abigael smiled back, a smile imbued with infinite tenderness, fragile but indestructible, like a ray of light piercing through the deepest darkness.

Their union, palpable in that suspended moment, became a bulwark against the darkness. Together, they embodied a truth that no one could shake.

- My second question is disarmingly simple, almost childish. Why am I here, surrounded by predators disguised as men of honour, figures who, beneath their masks of respectability, seek only to trample on the slightest spark of purity? Why should I cross swords with beasts dressed in silk, who only see me as prey to be torn apart, a piece of tender flesh offered up to their insatiable appetite?

His voice is filled with a vibrant melancholy, a thinly veiled pain.

- I should be outside, under the endless sky, running alongside Abigael, watching her smile as our kite dances in the wind,

The Hourim of innocence

defying the laws of gravity. This is what my life should be. A simple life, a free life, where love breathes without mask, without artifice, without the invisible chains you try to impose on us.

He raised both their hands together, a soft light gliding over their intertwined fingers. He turned slowly towards the journalists, sweeping the assembly with a firm, piercing gaze, every movement imbued with an almost prophetic solemnity.

- But I'm here because I chose to be. Because my heart, stronger than my fears, told me never to run away from injustice. Abigael and I are nobody's puppets, except our own conscience. We are driven by a single master : the unshakeable desire for peace and truth. The Creator, in His infinite wisdom, has endowed us with a gift that you will never understand: the ability to pierce the veils of hearts and souls, to discern the truth behind lies, to understand even the poisonous whispers that you thought were inaccessible to our childish ears.

Her voice, carried by a growing intensity, became a blade cutting through the oppressive silence of the stage.

- You, 'Reverend', are nothing but an impostor, a mirage woven of falsehood. And you, the silent accomplices who surround him, are the artisans of the shadows, the guardians of darkness. You have been the witnesses, and worse still, the willing actors of so much misfortune. And believe me, you will be held to account.

He paused, letting his words sink into the electric air.

- Perhaps not today, or even tomorrow. But the day will come when your actions, like spectres, will come knocking on your doors, demanding answers. Today, you are not being judged

The Hourim of innocence

before us, but before your television viewers, before a world that, under the weight of your evasive gaze, perceives the truth that you are trying in vain to suppress.

He let the silence settle, suspended for a moment, before raising their joined hands to the sky, a gesture that was both humble and triumphant.

- We are the future. We are Hourim. We are the light that is growing, that will burst forth to dispel the thickest shadows. Your time is over. The time of children, the time of innocence and purity, rises from this moment. Today marks the beginning of a new era.

His declaration, sounding like a prophecy, seemed to break the last barriers of silence. The spotlights bathed their silhouettes in a brilliant, almost divine light, while the cameras immortalised the moment, broadcasting it to the four corners of the world.

The studio, once a temple of lies and manipulation, had been transformed into a sanctuary where truth, carried by two young but indomitable souls, proclaimed its victory over darkness.

The silence that settled over the studio was almost unbearably dense. It was as if time itself had stood still, held in suspense by the force of the words that had just been spoken. Not one journalist dared move. The figures of authority, the voices usually so quick to find their way through the cacophony of debate, now seemed powerless.

The truth had just shattered the mask of lies, revealing the invisible workings of a skilfully orchestrated manipulation. And it wasn't adults who had spoken this truth, but two

The Hourim of innocence

children, bearers of a light so pure it seemed to burn everything it touched.

The false reverend's latest accusations were still floating, hanging in the air like poison, but their impact had dissipated in the face of the determination of the two young figures sitting at the centre of this media arena. The lights, though still bright, flickered imperceptibly, casting moving shadows on the walls and floor, transforming every face into a mask of vulnerability, every feigned smile into a fragile sneer.

The cameras, for their part, continued to capture every detail: the frown of one journalist, the nervous hands of another looking for a pen, the worried gaze of the audience. The audience, invisibly linked to this moment, seemed to be holding its breath, as if suspended on the edge of a precipice, waiting for something to happen, for the fragile balance of this confrontation to tip definitively.

At the centre of it all, Moussa felt Abigael's hand slide into his. This simple contact was an anchor, a tangible reminder of their unbreakable bond in the midst of this sea of hostility. He squeezed her hand lightly, and in that gesture, he gave her a part of his own strength, just as she gave him hers. Abigael turned her head towards him, and in that silent exchange, their eyes met, vibrating with a love and resilience that nothing, not even darkness, could extinguish.

She closed her eyes for a moment, listening to the soothing presence of the Guardian, the invisible force that had always sustained them. When she opened them again, it was with a new intensity, an inner fire that consumed all hesitation. Her gaze fell on the Reverend, a gaze so piercing it seemed capable of breaking through the man's invisible defences.

The Hourim of innocence

- You speak of us as if we were puppets, puppets in the service of some obscure cause," she says, her voice calm but vibrant with determination. You seek to deprive us of our humanity, to turn our words into weapons against ourselves. You summon spectres, ancient shadows, hoping that they will come and dim our light.

She paused, letting her words sink into the oppressive silence that enveloped the studio.

- But listen carefully: we do not fear you. Neither you, nor those who lead you from the shadows, the architects of chaos who pull your strings.

The room, usually filled with murmurs and hastily scribbled notes, was now frozen. It was as if even the walls were holding their breath.

Abigael continued, her voice growing louder, each word sounding like a thunderclap:

- We're here to reveal the truth, a truth that you're desperately trying to bury under your slander. But truth is indomitable, unalterable. And we, despite our youth, are the bearers of that light. Because our hearts are not yet tainted by the fear of losing illusory power, nor by the insatiable thirst for domination.

She turned to Moussa, her eyes glittering with infinite tenderness and a strength that no manipulation could alter.

- You have tried to reduce us to objects, tools in the service of your own fears. But what you don't understand is that your darkness cannot reach us. All you do is project your own shadows onto us.

The Hourim of innocence

The journalists, usually so quick to take control of a situation, were reduced to silence. Their pens were motionless, their notes incomplete. They knew, as did those watching from behind their screens, that they were no longer in control of this programme.

Abigael continued, her words wrapping themselves in solemn, grave poetry:

- We are the children of this fractured land, but we refuse to wear the chains you have forged for us. We are here, not to bend under the weight of your accusations, but to show you what you have forgotten: the power of pure love, of a truth devoid of calculation.

She inhaled deeply, the light from the spotlights catching the glint of an unshed tear.

- You thought we were alone, vulnerable. But we are accompanied by something much greater. A force that you can neither see nor understand. This light within us is what frightens you, because it reveals what you have tried to hide.

Moussa, sensing the moment was coming, gently squeezed Abigael's hand and spoke, his deep, steady voice echoing in the empty air :

- And it is this light that will triumph.

Moussa took a long breath, his piercing gaze crossing the lens of the cameras as if he wanted to speak directly to every spectator, every soul behind the screen. Then he swept the room with a slow, confident gaze, stopping on every journalist, every tense face. When he spoke, his voice was poised but vibrant with controlled intensity, each word falling like a verdict.

The Hourim of innocence

- You dared to evoke the Shoah, one of the darkest tragedies in human history, to accuse Abigael and me of being the heirs of a fantasised sect, allegedly responsible for that abyss of horror. Is this your ultimate ploy? To use the scars of the past as weapons to distort the present? To manipulate hearts and try to sow hatred where we sow hope?

He paused, letting the gravity of his words seep into the emotionally charged space.

- You know the story of the Shoah. So do we. We know what fear, hatred and division can breed. We know what happens when humanity turns away from compassion and embraces the abyss.

He straightened up, his eyes fixed on the assembly, his voice taking on an almost incantatory depth.

- The evidence of the Shoah is omnipresent, indelible, inscribed in the collective memory of humanity. It is there, engraved on the blackened pages of history books, in the chilling photographs of extinguished faces, in the videos that capture the silent agony of those engulfed by the horror. Each image, each testimony, each word is an immortal cry, a voice rising from the darkness to remind us of what humanity is capable of committing when it succumbs to barbarity.

His eyes hardened, his voice hoarse with solemn sorrow.

- But these memories are not weapons to be brandished at the whim of a cynical debate. They are lessons, sacred monuments erected against forgetting, against repeating the mistakes of the past. They are a call to vigilance, an exhortation to justice and peace. You, who claim to be the guardians of truth, should know better. The memory of the Shoah does not belong to

The Hourim of innocence

those who seek to manipulate it in order to consolidate their power, but to those who have the courage to carry it like a torch, lighting the way so that this horror is never repeated.

The words resounded, heavy with meaning, like hammers striking the anvil of the collective conscience.

- You hide behind the horror of the past," continued Moussa, "because you fear the light of the future. But we refuse to let this sacred memory be sullied by your schemes. We are here to shed this light, to keep Hourim alive, and to honour all those who have suffered under the yoke of human hatred.

An absolute silence fell over the set, so intense that it was as if one could hear the ticking of a forgotten watch. The journalists, usually quick to pounce on the slightest flaw, froze, as if paralysed by the brutal force of this truth.

So the false reverend, unmasked, attempted a final assault. He opened his mouth, ready to spit a final venom, but no sound escaped his lips. His throat seemed to contract and his eyes widened slightly. A sudden pallor came over his face and his hands, once sure-footed, began to tremble imperceptibly.

He tried to speak again, but something prevented him. An invisible force, like a vise, gripped his voice. His eyes searched desperately for a way out, but he found nothing but the accusing stares of the children, silent witnesses to a truth he could no longer escape.

Moussa observed this failing man with cold serenity. There was neither triumph nor pity in his eyes, only an unshakeable certainty.

- You see," he said at last, in a voice that was almost a whisper but which sounded like a thunderclap, "the truth doesn't need

The Hourim of innocence

artifice. It doesn't need to shout or wrap itself in false certainties. It stands there, unchanging, invincible, even when confronted with the most insidious of obscurities.

He turned his gaze to Abigael, whose eyes, filled with suppressed tears, shone with an indomitable brilliance. She gently squeezed his hand, a gesture that was silent but infinitely powerful, as if to say to him: We have triumphed.

Journalists were now powerless spectators, caught in the harsh light of a truth they could no longer deny. The cameras, infallible witnesses, broadcast this scene to millions of homes, etching this moment in history forever.

The Guardian, intangible to ordinary eyes, stood watch in the benevolent shadows, his presence like invisible armour enveloping the two children. He watched, silent but unwavering, his lips stretched into a smile imbued with infinite wisdom. Whenever the darkness attacked, whenever there was an attempt to obscure the brilliant light emanating from Moussa and Abigael, he intervened, dispelling the shadow by the sheer force of his essence. He was the bulwark, the eternal radiance that pushed back the abyss.

Abigael, strengthened by this silent presence, looked up again, gazing into the camera lens. Her voice, soft but charged with an undeniable gravity, resounded not only in the studio, transformed into an arena of truth, but far beyond, infiltrating homes and touching every heart open to listening.

- You're trying to stifle this light," she said, her voice trembling slightly, not from weakness but from controlled emotion, pure, vibrant emotion. Yet this light does not spring from us alone. It lives in every child, every innocent smile, every fragile but persistent dream, every hope that refuses to be

The Hourim of innocence

extinguished. We are here to remind everyone watching that humanity still has a chance. A chance to choose love and solidarity over hate and division.

She paused for a moment, her eyes shining with an intensity that seemed to capture the very light of the spotlights.

- We are not your enemies," she continued, her voice curling with a comforting, almost maternal warmth. We are children, children who love, who dream, who aspire to build a future worthy of the promises of dawn.

She inhaled deeply, tears beading at the corners of her eyes. But these tears were not those of abandonment or distress. They were the reflection of an inner strength, a resilience forged through hardship.

- The real question isn't whether we children have anything to teach you," she says, her voice growing in intensity. No. The question is whether you are ready to listen. Are you able to open your hearts, to drop your masks, to accept a truth that you have long chosen to ignore ? Are you ready to change ?

A silence fell over the stage, deep and heavy, as if the whole world were holding its breath, hanging on those words. The false reverend, so sure of himself just a few moments before, fell back in his seat, his shoulders slumped, his face betraying a mixture of shame and confusion. His hands trembled and his eyes, once full of calculations and judgements, now seemed to be searching for support, for a certainty that had evaporated.

The journalists, those puppeteers of the spoken word, were for the first time devoid of lines. Their feathers suspended,

The Hourim of innocence

their minds numb, unable to counterattack in the face of the raw truth, in the bright light of children.

Then, in that almost sacred silence, Moussa turned slowly towards the cameras. He spoke in a low voice, but his words carried a power that transcended the confines of the studio.

- Hourim. The light. We will never let the shadows win.

At that moment, time seemed to stand still. The world held its breath, suspended on that word, that symbol of renewal and promise. And then, like a rising wave, a voice was heard from the audience. Faint at first, almost a whisper, it uttered this sacred word:

- Hourim.

Another voice began again, then another, until the murmur became a song, a collective incantation. The whole studio vibrated under this wave of light and hope, the word Hourim rising like a prayer, a promise carried by hundreds of voices.

The journalists exchanged glances, some trembling, others lowering their eyes, their masks of professionalism cracked by the purity of this moment. They knew that their arsenal of tricks and stratagems had just collapsed, reduced to nothing by the inescapable force of the truth.

Even the spotlights, those impassive mechanical witnesses, seemed to flicker, as if touched by the emotion that filled the room. The light, far from dimming, now seemed brighter, enveloping Moussa and Abigael in an almost divine aura.

The Guardian, still invisible but omnipresent, watched with a serene smile. In this moment of unity and revelation, he felt the promise of a bright future growing stronger. The children

The Hourim of innocence

were no longer alone. The world had seen them, heard them, and a new light had been born in their hearts.

The silence fell again, but it was no longer oppressive. It had become a blank canvas, ready for a new story, a story of resilience and hope.

The main journalist, the undisputed authority figure throughout the programme, rose slowly to his feet. Every movement seemed to carry a new weight, a gravity he had never felt before. His eyes darted around the room, searching the gazes of his colleagues for refuge, for silent support, for an echo of vindication. But all he found was a reflection of his own confusion.

He could no longer deny the implacable reality that they had failed. What they had tried to reduce to a simple confrontation between seasoned adults and naive children had turned out to be much more. They were not facing two young souls who could be easily manipulated, but two pillars of a new era, bearers of a luminous truth that nothing and no-one could extinguish.

In an almost mechanical gesture, he readjusted his glasses, as if to mask his vulnerability, took a deep breath, then said in a voice stripped of all superbness, a voice in which a strange humility now resounded:

- Ladies and gentlemen, our time is coming to an end. This evening, we have not simply witnessed a debate. It has been a confrontation between generations, between the calcified doubts of adults and the unshakeable certainty of children. Let us all draw our own conclusions. Thank you for following us.

The Hourim of innocence

Then, with a heavy, almost mechanical movement, he sat back down. Defeat weighed heavily on his shoulders, visible in every crease of his face. Around him, his fellow journalists, usually so quick to congratulate each other at the end of a programme, also seemed absorbed in a heavy silence. One by one they rose to their feet, their silhouettes casting elongated shadows on the stage deserted by the light of their arguments. Without a word, they left the stage, their gazes flickering, as if facing the children one last time would have been too unbearable.

The stage, once vibrant with a cacophony of questions and contradictions, had been transformed into a silent sanctuary. Every whisper, every breath, still seemed to carry the echo of the children's words, resonating in this space now emptied of all pretence.

The reverend remained seated. His gaze was fixed, directed towards an invisible horizon, far beyond the walls of this studio. His hands crossed in front of him betrayed an ill-contained tension, but on his lips a thin smile persisted, a smile fashioned from a feigned benevolence, a deceptive mask for the darkness that inhabited his soul.

He knew. Tonight, he had lost a battle. But he was not a man to give in. He knew the twists and turns of patience and time. He would be back, in another guise, wearing a new mask, taking new paths of manipulation. For the war, in his twisted vision, was far from over.

With an icy, almost ceremonious politeness, he greeted the children. His smile, as frozen as stone, did not reach his eyes. He left the stage, his gait calculated, each step sounding like a silent promise to return. In the shadows of his mind, plans

The Hourim of innocence

were already being drawn up, stratagems were maturing, all designed to crush the young voices that had had the audacity to defy the dark forces he served.

When the studio was finally deserted, Abigael and Moussa were left alone. The calm that enveloped them was that which follows great storms, a calm mixed with a gentle torpor. The silence was no longer oppressive, but comforting, like a blanket over their tired shoulders.

Moussa turned to Abigael, a smile lighting up his face marked by the intensity of their fight. It was a smile full of tenderness and gratitude, a smile that needed no words to express the immensity of what they had just experienced together.

Abigael, in turn, responded to the smile, her eyes still shining with emotion. They were tired, no doubt about it. But this tiredness carried with it a particular beauty, that of victories snatched from the shadows. They knew, deep down, that they had lit a flame that nothing and no-one could extinguish.

Hand in hand, they rose to their feet, their silhouettes illuminated by the last flickering spotlights. Together, they carried the weight of the world, but also its hope. And in that suspended moment, they were invincible.

The Guardian, with his silent, omnipotent presence, enveloped the children in his infinite benevolence. Invisible to the world, he was nonetheless there, a motionless sentinel watching over these two luminous souls. His strength radiated like a gentle warmth, an invisible shield against the darkness that still lurked silently. He was the reassuring breath in the icy night, the echo of a thousand-year-old promise : they would never be alone.

The Hourim of innocence

- We did it," murmured Abigael, her voice tinged with a mixture of relief and restrained pride, as if each word carried the weight of the ordeal she had overcome.

Moussa nodded, a discreet smile lighting up his face marked by the intensity of recent events.

- Yes," he replied softly. But this is just the beginning.

Hand in hand, they left the stage. The coldness of the neon lights faded behind them, replaced by the crisp, pure night air. A soothing breeze greeted them, like a caress from the heavens. The silent streets also seemed to pay tribute to them, silent witnesses to their passage. Their footsteps echoed softly, a calming rhythm after the storm. Under a starlit sky, they moved forward, their eyes raised to the immutable stars that, on a hellish day, had lit up their sacred oath: never to leave a child alone in the dark.

The path led them to the camp, a refuge that had become a home, a haven of brotherhood for those whom the world seemed to have forgotten. There, the wait came to an end. As soon as Abigael and Moussa crossed the threshold of this sanctuary, a wave of joy swept over them. Crystalline laughter tore through the stillness of the night, and cries of joy rose up from the hearts of dozens of children who ran up to them, wrapping their warm arms around them, their eyes full of love and gratitude.

The camp was illuminated by this collective light, a human warmth that transcended a simple reunion. That night, their return was a shared victory, a triumph over adversity. The laughter, the hugs, the glances, all formed a symphony of hope, a vibrant song of rediscovered humanity.

The Hourim of innocence

News poured in like an irresistible torrent of hope. Messages of support, full of promise and courage, crossed borders. Donations, whether of food, materials or simple words of encouragement, poured in like offerings to a common cause. But beyond the material gestures, it was an awakened humanity, united in a surge of awareness, that was reaching out. It was not just Palestine that was receiving these outpourings of solidarity, but the very heart of humanity, vibrating in unison at last.

As evening fell, enveloping the camp in a veil of benevolent darkness, a central fire was lit. Its dancing flames projected a soft, almost supernatural light on tired faces. The shadows, usually menacing, seemed to recoil before this collective warmth, overcome by the fervour of a united assembly. In the midst of this flickering light, Abigael and Moussa took their places, their faces illuminated by the play of the flames.

Moussa, his eyes full of wisdom beyond his years, stood up. He was no longer just a child: he had become a voice, a symbol. When his voice rose, soft but imbued with a quiet strength, a solemn silence enveloped the assembly.

- Tonight we have shown the world our true essence," he says, his words sounding like a prophecy. We have lifted the veil on what some are doing their utmost to conceal. But tomorrow, the real challenge begins. We will have to rebuild not just homes and schools, but hearts and hopes, bridges between worlds that seemed so far apart. Every stone we lay will be a bastion against hatred. Every word we offer will be a fervent prayer for peace.

As if to greet her words, the flames danced higher, lighting up Abigael's face. Her eyes, full of tears, shone with pure,

The Hourim of innocence

crystalline emotion. They were not tears of sadness, but of a soul touched by the beauty of the moment, by the strength emanating from this unexpected unity.

- We're not alone any more," she whispered, her voice barely more than a whisper, but it resonated in everyone's hearts. Her hands, delicate but determined, found those of the children at her side, sealing a silent promise : never to let the light go out.

In the protective shadow, the Guardian watched them with infinite tenderness. He saw in them souls ready to carry the burden of the world. He knew that storms would still come, that the path would be strewn with obstacles, but he also knew that they were now armed with a strength that nothing could shake. For the light they carried within them was eternal, born of the sacred fire of the Hourim.

Not far away, hidden in the darkness of the deserted alleyways, the Reverend was moving away. His silhouette, swallowed up by the darkness, carried an aura of silent menace. His mind, tireless and calculating, was already weaving new stratagems, tricks to break through what he neither understood nor controlled. He would be back, he knew. For him, the battle would never end. But what he didn't know yet was that the light he was trying to smother didn't just reside in those two children. It had already begun to spread, igniting other souls ready to defend hope, to protect that unquenchable flame.

Around the fire, the children looked up at the starry sky. Under this celestial canopy, in this improvised sanctuary, there reigned a rare harmony, an unspoken promise. As the first light of dawn timidly skimmed the horizon, the word Hourim rose on the wind. It was no longer just a word: it had become a song, a symbol, an immortal spark. It vibrated in the air like

The Hourim of innocence

an unshakeable promise, illuminating a path that others would follow.

This word, whispered by innocent hearts, was now a flame that defied the darkness, a light that guided humanity towards a future where love and hope would reign supreme.

The Hourim of innocence

CHAPTER VII

THE SACRIFICE OF THE STARS

« SOME LIVES ARE EXTINGUISHED SO THAT A MULTITUDE OF OTHERS CAN SHINE FORTH. »

Day dawned softly on the Holy Land, flooding Jerusalem with the golden light that seems to possess a unique magic, a radiance that is both ancient and eternal. The first rays of sunlight touched the sacred stones of the city, caressing the walls imprinted with prayers whispered down the centuries, awakening shadows that still seemed to guard the secrets of the prophets.

The Hourim of innocence

In the distance, a solitary cry rang out, that of a cockerel, rising with the solemnity of a proclamation from another time. The sound emerged, pure and crystalline, as if from the summit of the Dome of the Rock, echoing over the city and heralding the birth of a new day. The cry pierced the thin membrane of dawn silence like a messenger from the heavens, bearing a mysterious promise : the end of one era and the beginning of another. It vibrated, imbued with an indecipherable melancholy and dawning hope, like a symphony of renewal.

Moussa and Abigael felt this subtle wave in the depths of their souls. It was an inexplicable vibration, a whisper from the universe that seeped into their hearts, weaving its way through the cobbled streets and sacred stones to dance within them, merging with the beating of their blood. Today was no ordinary day. Today marked a turning point, a milestone in the destiny they shared. They were celebrating their sixteenth birthday, a birthday woven with memories and losses, but also with the promise of a future that was still hazy, but terribly precious.

It was 2 February 2025, a date with a strange significance. Just over a year had passed since the clash of arms had given way to an uneasy silence, a fragile peace that the Hourim had managed to protect with fierce determination. This calm was like a suspended breath, stolen from the eternal fury that always threatened to return, but which for the moment had not been able to pierce the barrier of light erected by these miraculous children. Despite all the intrigues hatched by the dark forces, the perfidious ambushes and subtle machinations of the enemies of peace, the light of Moussa and Abigael continued to shine, invincible and intact, armed not with raw power, but with a purity and courage that the Guardian had

The Hourim of innocence

cultivated in them. That day carried a special weight for Abigael and Moussa, a burden they felt without being able to explain. It was the last day they would be able to be in the presence of the Guardian. As he had told them, his duty to them would end when they reached the age of sixteen. After that day, he would disappear, and they would never again be able to see his face or hear his kind voice. That morning, he took them one last time to the place where it all began, a place where past and present seemed to overlap in secret harmony: under the spreading branches of the hundred-year-old olive tree. This tree, silent witness to so many shared moments, seemed to look at them with infinite wisdom, as if it understood what they were about to lose.

The Guardian stood there, his eyes clouded by a sadness he no longer tried to hide. His features, usually impassive, were marked by a gentle, resigned pain. His words weighed heavily on his heart, and yet he let them flow like a river for the last time.

- My children," he murmured, his voice imbued with an almost sacred gravity, "today is a day of immeasurable importance, and this place where we find ourselves is just as sacred. Fate, the great architect of the universe, has given you the freedom to chart your own course, while guiding you in subtle ways, like an elusive breath. There's nothing fortuitous about your birth on 2 February 2009. 2, 2, 2009... These are not just numbers strung together by chance, but a signature of the universe, a code woven into the fabric of time. Add up these three 2s, and you get 6, a balanced and sacred number. Eliminate the two 0s, and you're left with 69, a cosmic mirror of two entities that coil and unite, symbols of duality and

The Hourim of innocence

perfect union, like yin and yang seeking each other out never to part.

He paused, as if the wind itself were holding its breath.

- February," he continues, "is a mystery among the months, a timekeeper with changing rules. It oscillates between 28 days, like an incomplete poem, and 29 every four years, like a promise of rebirth. This month is a reminder that time is not a straight line, but a cycle, a breath that stretches and contracts. It is the quintessence of the unpredictable, the very essence of what makes life so rare, so precious. It's the month of secrets, the month that holds within itself the magic of unique things, of moments that never come back the same way.

He turned his eyes towards them, and in his gaze shone a strange, almost divine glow.

- If you take this 6 and this 9," he continued, "and stretch them out, letting them merge into each other, they form the symbol for infinity, ∞. An eternal loop, the promise that nothing ever ends, that everything transforms, is reborn, and returns in another form. An assurance that time itself only changes face, that it is a sea of eternity in which we are but waves, appearing and disappearing, but never forgotten.

He looked up at the sky, where the first light of dawn was gently caressing the horizon.

- Look around you," he murmured, his words seeming to merge with the murmur of the wind. The cube is sacred to Muslims, a solid and perfect edifice, with its six faces turned towards the universe. Unfold the cube and you get a cross, the symbol of sacrifice and salvation so dear to Christians. And the Star of David, formed by two inverted triangles, points

The Hourim of innocence

skywards with its six vertices, an echo of ancient wisdom, a reminder of light and truth. Each symbol is a fragment of the same story, that of communion between heaven and earth, spirit and matter. It's no coincidence that you were born under these signs, at this very moment.

He let the silence settle, a moment suspended, while the wind rustled through the branches of the olive tree, like a whisper from the heavens.

- You are part of a plan beyond your comprehension," he concludes, "a story bigger than your life, bigger than your dreams. Listen carefully, and perhaps you'll hear the secrets of the universe, the ones it has entrusted to you, the ones that vibrate in the air and resonate in your hearts. You are much more than you imagine, much more than you think you are.

He raised his hand and drew the shape of infinity in the air, like a silent message, a silent blessing. This simple but powerful gesture seemed to say that eternity was within them, that their destiny had only just begun, and that it shone with a light that even darkness could never extinguish.

He paused, letting his words dissolve into the delicate rustle of the olive tree's leaves. The air seemed charged with mysticism, as if the tree itself, an ancient witness to the secrets of humanity, understood the importance of this moment. This place, this natural sanctuary, had not been chosen by chance, and Moussa and Abigael had to realise this.

- Here, where we stand," continued the Guardian, his voice imbued with an almost sacred gravity, "this is a place where time has bent the knee to the divine. It is here that the memory of Jesus was sacrificed, a place where eternity has been imprinted in stone. It was here, too, that your ancestors, Adam

The Hourim of innocence

and Eve, first set foot on Earth, carrying with them the weight of humanity's destiny. And it is here, today, that you will have to undergo a trial of great difficulty. I am not permitted to reveal more to you, for the knowledge of what awaits you could change your path, and your destiny, painful as it may be, has yet to be fulfilled and reveal a plan far greater than you can imagine. The future that awaits you will be a canvas of contrasting colours, at times painted with moments of pure light and crystalline happiness, but also darkened by pain that will tear at your soul.

He breathed in deeply, his breath heavy with sadness, as if he could feel the shadow of Iblis already looming over them.

- Iblis is aware of my departure," he continued, "and he is more patient than the desert sands, more cunning than the shifting winds. As soon as I am no longer there to protect you, he will unleash his legions against you with implacable precision and tenacity. He will hunt you down relentlessly, looking for the slightest flaw, and he will find one, because what makes you invincible is also what makes you vulnerable: Love. This love that has built civilisations, but has also seen kingdoms crumble, is a double-edged sword. It lifts you up and makes you strong, but it also exposes you to deep wounds.

He paused, his eyes clouded with an emotion he could no longer contain. His eyes fell alternately on Moussa and Abigael, those two souls intertwined by a destiny they only half understood.

- Before I leave you, my children, I want to offer you one last piece of advice," he said, his voice cracking under the weight of his affection for them. You are sixteen years old, and until now your love has been expressed through glances, timid

The Hourim of innocence

caresses, a tenderness that has never gone beyond the boundaries of your innocence. The invisible wall that has preserved your magic is no longer necessary. Love each other, fully, without fear of sullying that purity. Reclaim the bond that unites you and live it with all the intensity it deserves, because time is now your most precious enemy. You will have no choice but to live this love like a shooting star, with an intensity that cuts through the darkness.

He stopped, overwhelmed by a wave of tenderness. His trembling hands rested gently on the shoulders of the two teenagers, bringing their faces together. With this gesture, he seemed to want to convey all the strength and blessing he had left.

- Don't be afraid of this closeness," he murmured, his voice almost breaking with emotion. Let yourself go with that warmth, that first shiver that dances along your skin. The first kiss is an enchantment, a key to unexplored worlds, a breath of magic that awakens your soul and your body. Feel your hearts beat in unison, savour this sacred union, for there is nothing purer than two souls meeting in tenderness. This gesture that you have never dared to make is the most beautiful of prayers, an offering to the universe, an oath made in light and surrender.

He took a step back, letting love take over. The silence, heavy with mystery, vibrated with an energy that could not be explained. Moussa and Abigael's eyes locked on each other, and in that gaze there was a promise older than the stars, a bond forged in the fire of ages. The world seemed to stand still, time stopped, and the whole universe waited with bated breath to see what would come of this love, blessed and cursed, fragile and invincible at the same time.

The Hourim of innocence

Abigael blushed, her cheeks blazing with the new warmth she had yet to name. Her eyes, lowered at first, found the courage to look up at Moussa, and a shy but determined smile lit up her face. A promise was born in this simple gesture, a promise made up of a thousand unspoken words, shared dreams and secret hopes. Moussa, for his part, felt his own hands tremble slightly, a gentle nervousness that echoed the hurricane of emotions running through him. Yet, with infinite tenderness, he placed his palms on Abigael's, interlacing their fingers as if to anchor this moment in reality. Their foreheads drew together, their breaths mingled, and for a brief moment, the whole world seemed to dissolve around them, leaving only this budding love, pure and radiant.

The Guardian looked away, not out of modesty, but out of respect for this miracle that he himself had helped to protect. He knew that this love, this delicate, invincible tenderness, was a treasure that nothing should sully. This moment belonged to them, a fragment of eternity to be savoured far from the eyes of the world, a fragile but magnificent flame, ready to fight against all opposing winds.

- Love yourself," he whispered one last time, his voice so soft that it was almost lost in the rustle of the olive leaves. For soon, the world will try to steal this beauty from you, to crush it under the weight of hatred, fear and darkness. But let your hearts brush against each other without fear, your hands uncover each other without hesitation. Let the warmth of your love be a bulwark, a light that illuminates even the darkest days, a promise that nothing and no one can extinguish. You are that light, that miracle that the universe itself wanted to preserve.

The Hourim of innocence

The wind picked up, making the leaves dance in a melancholy murmur, like an echo of voices from the past. The Guardian looked at them one last time, a sad but sincere smile stretching his lips. It was the smile of a parent watching their children take off into the unknown, a smile filled with love and pride, but also with the pain of letting them go.

- You'll soon realise," he continues, "that despite everything that awaits you, you'll always be victors, even when you fall. The battle will be hard, and there will be moments when you wish you could give up, when despair threatens to devour you. But remember: you are like two opposing forces, souls that embrace and complement each other. One will find its strength in the weakness of the other, and this weakness will be transformed into the power that will lift you up. You are a perfect balance, a dance towards infinity, and together you will triumph.

He took them in his arms, embracing them as if he wanted to engrave this last gesture in the fabric of eternity. His hands trembled slightly, and a discreet tear slid down his cheek as his heart was torn apart by love and powerlessness.

- I want you to know, my children, that I'm not leaving out of cowardice. It is an agonising but necessary choice. I'm leaving because I know the trials that await you, and I don't have the strength to see you face what the future holds. What you are about to experience is far beyond what I can offer you, and I fear seeing the light within you waver, even for a moment. My departure is an act of love, a sacrifice to enable you to become what you are destined to be. Forgive me for leaving you, but remember, always: my love will be there, invisible, a breath of wind caressing your faces, a star twinkling in the night to guide you.

The Hourim of innocence

He stepped back, his eyes shining with an emotion he could no longer conceal, and then walked away, leaving behind him the echo of a silent prayer, a wish whispered to heaven that the light of their love would never be extinguished.

Before leaving, the Guardian took a final breath, his shoulders heavy with the imminence of farewell, his gaze resting tenderly on each of them. His eyes shone with unfathomable sadness, but also with infinite tenderness, like a parent contemplating his children for the last time before a long departure. He moved closer, his lips trembling slightly before he whispered, his voice both soft and solemn:

- Before I go away for good, I want to let you in on one last secret, one last refuge for the dark days ahead. Go to the place where time stands still, near the Dome of the Rock. You know this place, this sanctuary where the beating of the world subsides, because only you can see it and access it. It's a space outside time, a place where not even the storms of fate can reach you. As long as you have not crossed the threshold of physical love, the doors of this sanctuary will remain open for you. It will be your shelter, a haven where innocence retains its magic, where the purity of your hearts keeps the light alive. But remember, once you have passed this point, this place will close forever. Then all you'll have left are your love and your faith as the ultimate bulwarks against the darkness.

A dense silence, charged with mystery and gravity, settled in, as if the world itself were holding its breath. The Guardian watched them for a long time, memorising their faces, their gazes, the two souls he had protected and guided. He stepped forward to embrace them one last time, his arms closing around them with an almost desperate gentleness, as if he wanted to seal this moment in eternity. His hands trembled

The Hourim of innocence

slightly, and his voice, broken by emotion, sounded like a last oath:

- I love you, more than you could ever imagine. It is this love that compels me to leave you, for my duty ends here, but yours has only just begun. Remember me, not as a protector who abandons you, but as an eternal presence who will continue to watch over you, invisibly, in every breath of wind and every star twinkling in the sky. The light that shines within you is destined to illuminate the world, even when it is plunged into the darkest of nights. Never let it be extinguished, no matter what the trials.

The Guardian stepped away from them with infinite delicacy, and a single, pure tear traced a silvery trail down his cheek before he turned away. Abigael and Moussa watched him walk away, their hearts heavy and numb with the weight of his departure. It was as if part of their own light had vanished with him, leaving behind a palpable shadow, an absence that weighed heavily on their young souls. A subtle anxiety invaded them, a shiver of fear of the unknown, of what the future held in store for them. But at the same time, there was a strange calm in the Guardian's words, a faint hope, a promise of a path still open, a refuge still accessible.

When the Guardian disappeared, carrying his secret into the golden horizon, Abigael and Moussa turned towards each other. Their hands instinctively sought each other out, intertwined, and it was in this simple embrace that they found the strength to stand. Despite the heartbreaking absence of their protector, they felt that their union had become their shield, their love a light that was only waiting to grow. And as long as they were together, they would be able to weather the storms, survive the darkness and defend this sacred light, even

The Hourim of innocence

without the visible protection of their Guardian. They returned to the camp, their hearts light, floating in the sweet anticipation typical of anniversary days. Today was a moment to celebrate, a day when light could eclipse shadow, if only for a moment. It wasn't just their birthday, but an occasion shared with all the children, this family of hearts that had forged indestructible bonds despite the storms. They had never wanted to isolate themselves in the luxury of a big house or the impersonal comfort of a hotel. Their place, their true home, was here, among those they had promised to protect, where every laugh, every childish cry sounded like a symphony of life and hope.

The camp had changed a lot. It used to be a place of hardship, a desert of dust and deprivation. But today, it had evolved into a vibrant village, an oasis of human warmth born of generosity and the will to survive together. Fountains of drinking water now gushed forth, the symbol of a promise kept. Electricity lit up the nights, pushing back the darkness that once seemed eternal. Study rooms had been built, sheltering children's dreams and offering a space where hope could be nurtured, cultivated like the fragile flowers of a resilient garden. The playgrounds resounded with crystalline laughter, an innocence that, despite everything, refused to die. Every moment spent there was a miracle woven of solidarity, a tribute to the beauty of humanity even in the midst of a world constantly at war.

Yet even in this haven of peace, an insidious venom was spreading, crawling in the shadows with evil patience. Abigael and Moussa knew nothing of the muted threat that was growing, the venomous snake that was creeping into the roots of what they had helped to build. The Houmas had slyly infiltrated the movement, embezzling the generous donations

The Hourim of innocence

intended for the children. The funds were dispersed in secret transactions, feeding an arsenal of weapons, building troops ready to rekindle the fires of war. At the other end of the chessboard, the Israeli government was bolstering its own defences, devising its strategies with implacable meticulousness. Agents, like moles, had crept into the ranks of the Hourim, looking for the slightest loophole, ready to strike when the time was right.

And above this imminent chaos, Iblis stood watch, patient like an invisible predator, a cold and calculating intelligence. He was far more cunning than those factions blinded by their hatred and thirst for power. The humiliation he had suffered in that public debate, that wound of pride, continued to gnaw at his soul. But he knew that revenge must not be rushed. Destroying Abigael and Moussa was not simply a matter of seeing them fall. No, he didn't want to elevate them to the rank of martyrs, because martyrs inspire, and heroes bring nations together. His strategy was far more subtle, far more cruel : he wanted to extinguish their light, to see them consumed from within, to turn them into living ashes, to corrupt their brilliance until only shadows remained.

He knew that the real triumph would be to see them break themselves, to see them sink into disillusionment, to see them lose the purity that made them symbols of hope. He waited, like a bird of prey hovering over its prey, ready to swoop in when the slightest breach appeared, ready to devour them without a trace.

He offered them poisonous protection, keeping them alive, protecting them from the most obvious dangers, while cultivating the illusion of their safety. Iblis was a master of illusions, weaving a protective but poisonous cocoon around

The Hourim of innocence

Abigael and Moussa. He enveloped them in his false benevolence, like a patient spider weaving its web, knowing that each taut thread would tighten one day. His strategy did not require immediate violence, but slow infiltration, the methodical undermining of their forces. He knew that patience was his best weapon, because a crack always forms in the end, even in the most impregnable fortress.

All he had to do was wait, observe with the cold acuity of a predator, watching for the moment when the first breach appeared. Like a bird of prey, a black golden eagle, he soared across the sky of their existence, his massive wings obscuring the light, his slender talons ready to close on his prey. Time was on his side, each day bringing him a little closer to that inevitable moment. A day would come, he knew, when these two souls, exhausted and without refuge, would have no sacred place to protect themselves, no Guardian to save them.

That day, he thought, would be his triumph. The day when he would extinguish their light, when the Hourim would be no more than an echo, a dusty memory swept away by the winds of an endless night. But in the meantime, he kept watch, invisible, calculating, ready to strike as soon as vulnerability opened up to him.

The Guardian's absence had left an immense void, a yawning chasm that was slowly being closed by an irresistible magnetic force that grew between Abigael and Moussa. It was as if, for all those years, the Keeper had been the subtle bulwark that kept their souls and hearts at a distance, reversing their natural attraction into a game of balance and restraint. His departure had shattered this invisible magic, breaking down the walls he had erected between them. From now on, a new energy, a bewitching gravitational power was pushing them towards

The Hourim of innocence

each other, like two stars destined to come together in a cosmic cataclysm.

Their relationship, once imbued with an almost sacred modesty, was beginning to turn into a burning fire that devoured them from within. Every glance they exchanged seemed to be brimming over with unspoken feelings, every smile they held back concealed deep emotions, and every gesture they made that dared not touch the other fed this incandescent flame. They were on the edge of a fragile balance, a fine line where innocence and desire overlapped dangerously.

The Guardian had been an invisible wall for them, a protective barrier that kept the purity of their bond intact, but now, without this soothing presence to contain them, the boundary of innocence was dissolving like a veil blown away by the wind. They could no longer ignore the magnetic attraction that bound them together, the irrepressible force that transcended simple adolescent love. They discovered each other, brushed up against each other, their hearts beating in unison to a new rhythm, that of a budding passion, sweet and frightening.

Every moment they spent together intensified, becoming an intoxicating dance of glances and smiles, tentative gestures and growing desires. Their closeness sent shivers down their spines, awakening sensations in them that they had never known before, as if the simple presence of the other awakened parts of their souls buried deep within them. It was a force they could not control, an enchantment that drew them together, leading them slowly but inexorably towards a point of no return. So, as if driven by an unconscious desire to understand each other, to grasp this irresistible force that was being born within them, Abigael and Moussa went to this

The Hourim of innocence

magical place, this place where time stands still, where the laws of reality seem to fade away and give way to the unknown. Here, there was no wind, no leaves, no tangible scenery. Everything seemed to float in a suspended space, a light, unreal mist that covered the ground like a silent sea, separating this sanctuary from the ordinary world. It was a place out of time, a realm of mystery where the present was eternal, where innocence could still be preserved.

They stood there, in that sacred void, a space charged with invisible energy, an ancient power that vibrated around them, like echoes of secrets never revealed. Abigael and Moussa felt it all in their souls, this enveloping, protective yet provocative aura that seemed to probe their hearts and amplify every emotion, every shiver.

Moussa stopped for a moment, breathless with the intensity of the moment. His gaze fell on Abigael, and he saw her in a way he had never seen her before. She stood there, bathed in a soft, ethereal glow, as if lit from within by a mysterious flame. Her eyes, those two shards of infinite universe, shone with a new depth, a mixture of fear and hope, a spark of budding love that threatened to overwhelm her.

His heart beat faster, echoing in this place where every sound seemed muffled, where only the vibration of their emotions had the right to exist. He moved closer to her, and every step he took sounded like a silent promise, a commitment he didn't yet fully understand but which consumed him from the inside. A soft, bewitching warmth rose up inside him, overwhelming him. His hand, trembling but determined, rose to touch Abigael's face. His fingers slid down her cheek, a caress so light it seemed to belong to a dream. This simple contact awakened a wave of emotions in her, a delicate shiver that ran through

The Hourim of innocence

her entire body. She closed her eyes, letting herself be carried away, feeling her breath catch, captive in this moment frozen in eternity. Her lips trembled, her heart beat so strongly that she feared it would break, but she had never experienced such intensity, such truth in what she felt.

Their eyes met again, lost, then found again, and it was as if the whole world had been reduced to this exchange, this invisible, indestructible bond that united them. A magnetic tension floated around them, palpable, almost suffocating in its burning sweetness. Abigael felt this heat rising up inside her, a heat that made her feel as if she were being consumed, but she didn't want to fight it. Everything inside her was crying out for her to surrender, to embrace this unknown and powerful force that bound them together.

They were now just two souls floating in a space where time no longer mattered, where their love, so pure and unshakeable, enveloped and protected them. And there, in that timeless sanctuary, they discovered each other, two hearts that no longer had any reason to hide, ready to love each other beyond the borders of eternity.

Their breaths mingled in a sensual dance, creating a vibrant atmosphere, saturated with desire and tension, as if the universe itself were holding its breath in this suspended moment. They were so close that the air between them became electric, a clammy, oppressive heat, enveloping them in an intimate cocoon where each breath of one melted into that of the other. Moussa gazed into Abigael's deep eyes, searching for a truth that had never been revealed, a spark of emotion that he could feel burning beneath the surface. His hand, trembling with a mixture of fear and passion, rose slowly to brush against Abigael's cheek. His fingers glided over her skin,

The Hourim of innocence

caressing it with the delicacy of a summer breeze, a touch so light yet charged with devastating intensity. Abigael felt a shiver run up her spine, every nerve in her body awakening under the caress. She closed her eyes, letting the pure, unsuspected pleasure invade her whole being, a sweet, burning warmth that made her heart beat at a frantic pace.

Their foreheads touched, and this contact gave rise to an unprecedented closeness, a palpable bond that seemed to merge their souls. Abigael opened her eyes, her gaze veiled by a desire she could no longer repress, her lips slightly parted, offered, trembling with a desire she had never dared imagine. Moussa's hand slid slowly up the back of her neck, curling into her silky hair, and he drew her even closer, closing the distance between them with a fiery breath.

Their bodies brushed against each other, and the sensation of this shared warmth sent an irresistible wave of sensations through them, a wave of pleasure that left them vulnerable and exhilarated. Their chests almost touched, and every heartbeat seemed to echo, like a drumbeat of adrenalin, a symphony where their souls sang in unison. Abigael raised a hesitant hand, placing it gently against Moussa's chest, feeling the strength of his muscles, the warmth of his skin through the thin fabric. It was a modest caress, but one that fanned an inner fire, a flame that slowly consumed them.

Their faces drew closer, and every centimetre they crossed seemed to stretch eternity, suspending time in a promise that was both sweet and dizzying. Their lips brushed against each other, so delicately that the simple touch triggered a cascade of sensations, a shiver that radiated through their entire being. It was a burning caress, a shared breath that ignited in them an

The Hourim of innocence

unavowable desire, a strength that demanded to express itself, to break the chains of their innocence.

And then, at last, they gave themselves up. Their lips sealed in a tender, passionate kiss, a union so perfect it seemed to defy the laws of reality. It was not just a kiss, but an embrace of their souls, a silent oath that spoke of their infinite, inextinguishable love. Their mouths opened hesitantly and their tongues sought each other out, finding each other in a sensual dance, an exchange that revealed a deep vulnerability and an even greater passion.

Every movement, every quiver of their bodies amplified the magic of this moment. Abigael felt a warmth invade her belly, a soft, throbbing fire spreading through her veins, making her limbs weak and her breath catch. She let out a muffled sigh, her heart beating with such force that she thought it would explode. Moussa gently tightened his embrace, his hand caressing the small of her back, exploring the curve of her body with infinite delicacy. It was a love beyond measure, a love that defied gravity, a love that consumed them and lifted them up at the same time.

Their mouths kept coming together, rediscovering each other, tasting this divine sweetness, this angelic nectar that left them panting with pleasure, drunk with a tenderness they could no longer control. Their breaths became short, jerky, and the tension between them rose to a crescendo, a crescendo of passion so powerful it seemed capable of cracking the universe. They were linked, chained by this kiss that was everything, a kiss that redefined them, transformed them into a single being. Their love was intense, palpable, a magnetic force that drew them together with irrepressible power. And as they lost themselves in this sacred union, there was no

The Hourim of innocence

turning back. They had crossed an invisible barrier, discovered each other as never before, and in that kiss, they knew that their love had become something greater, something deeper, something more unalterable, an eternal love, defying time, defying destiny.

Abigael and Moussa were in the early stages of a devouring passion which, for the moment, was materialising in kisses of dizzying intensity and caresses so deep they could have shaken the strongest mountains. Every touch, every brush of theirs aroused echoes of desire, and their skins quivered under the effect of these sensations, as if the sacred fire of creation were being rekindled within them. Their hearts, in symphony, beat in unison, pulsing with vibrant energy, like two stars destined to merge into a new star. Moussa's hands, hesitant at first, became bolder, brushing against Abigael's contours with all-consuming tenderness, unleashing waves of heat that spread over their bodies, lifting their souls in an infinite dance of sensations.

Abigael, too, felt her whole being being consumed in an inferno of desire she had never known, a sweet, bewitching heat rising up inside her, making her vulnerable and strong at the same time. Their lips sought each other out, found each other, tasted each other, and each stolen kiss seemed to increase this mystical bond, this unspoken promise but engraved in the flesh of the universe. It was an ancient magic, a vital impulse that consumed them and nourished them at the same time, making them addicted to the forbidden nectar that now flowed in their veins.

Yet, in the shadows that enveloped them, a sinister presence was watching them, a malevolence biding its time. Iblis was there, patient as a coiled snake, his eyes red with unhealthy

The Hourim of innocence

desire, ready to strike. He knew the secret ways of the human heart, and he knew that love, no matter how pure, could become a weakness. This kiss wasn't enough for him, not yet. What he coveted was carnal transgression, that extra step where innocence would be irrevocably shattered, where their love would ignite in a forbidden offering, a sacrilegious act that would bind them to its darkness. That was what he was waiting for, with perverse patience, ready to push them to the brink of the abyss.

He wanted to corrupt them, to get them to cross the boundary that would keep them from falling, and he had prepared his trap. Once that frontier was crossed, he would revel in seeing them exposed, stripped naked, not just in their intimacy, but stripped of the luminous purity that had protected them until now. He dreamt of seeing them crushed under the weight of judgement, his own and that of all the others, ready to brandish the stone of condemnation. For Iblis knew the weight of stones. Every year, during the Hajj pilgrimage, he was subjected to this symbolic stoning by millions of worshippers, but it was nothing compared to the delight he would derive from their fall.

Their love, as pure and intense as it was, was a challenge for him, a diamond in the rough that he wanted to crush to dust. But despite his schemes, he could not ignore the light that continued to shine in them, a light so strong that it defied even his darkest shadows. A light that, even when it flickered, would never be completely extinguished, because it was the reflection of the love that united them, a love that was greater than anything Iblis could understand or destroy.

The days wore on, and the Hourim movement grew, rising like a banner of hope that gathered more and more souls, sowing

The Hourim of innocence

the promise of a better future in the midst of darkness. The children laughed, the adults found a semblance of peace, and the camp buzzed with life and enthusiasm, like a beehive in full bloom. But in the midst of this effervescence, Abigael and Moussa had imperceptibly distanced themselves, not out of disinterest, but because something more powerful was drawing them in, enveloping them in an ethereal, bewitching bubble.

Their budding love was a delicious secret, a whisper shared by two souls who discovered each other with an intensity that was almost sacred. They let themselves be carried along by this bond, made up of stolen kisses, soft and urgent, and discreet caresses that left a burning imprint on their skin, like a promise of eternity. Each encounter was a symphony of delicate brushes, a ballet of emotions that never crossed the forbidden line, but came close, trembling with impatience. Their innocence still resisted, like a flickering flame, refusing to be submerged by desire, even though it brushed against them with its insidious fingers, tempting them with every glance.

But in the shadows, Iblis, the prince of darkness, was watching. He hovered like a vulture, patient and cunning, calculating every move, every beat of their innocent hearts. He knew that the downfall would come not from a show of force, but from a slow, insidious temptation. His plan was taking shape, dark and perfidious, with the meticulousness of a puppeteer pulling the strings of his fateful show.

He manipulated influential journalists, voices that resonated with people's consciences, into orchestrating a gigantic fund-raising event. The event was presented as a unique opportunity to help even more disadvantaged children, a surge of generosity that was bound to attract Abigael and Moussa. The

The Hourim of innocence

event, with its noble cause, seemed unassailable, beyond reproach, a work of universal benevolence. But behind this angelic façade lay the trap of Iblis, a web woven to capture the purest of hearts.

The collection campaign will take place in Paris, the City of Light, a place that exudes beauty and enchantment, where every street whispers tales of love and passion. Paris, that bewitching city where bridges hold eternal promises, where the lights of the street lamps caress the cobblestones with a nostalgic tenderness. Iblis knew that the atmosphere of this magical city, where love floats in the air, where couples meet in secret to exchange kisses under the stars, would be the perfect setting to corrupt the innocence of the two young people.

The demon made sure that their stay would be a daydream, a modern fairytale. They would be staying in a sumptuous hotel, adorned with red velvet drapes and subdued lighting, where every nook and cranny whispered promises of intimacy and seduction. But the most Machiavellian detail of the plan was the layout of the bedrooms: two luxurious suites, linked by a connecting door that would remain ajar, a silent and dangerous invitation, a loophole ready to be exploited. This door, so innocently ajar, was a symbol, a passageway between innocence and temptation, between light and shadow.

Iblis was looking forward to it, his twisted mind revelling in the sight of their hearts wavering, their bodies straining to resist the irresistible call. He didn't just want to see them fail ; he wanted to see them give in, surrender to a passion that would betray them, a passion that would deliver them to the clutches of darkness, making their light vulnerable and ready to be extinguished.

The Hourim of innocence

The atmosphere of Paris would do the rest. In this city, where love seemed to permeate every stone and every breath of air, lovers strolled hand in hand, kissing under the lampposts as if the world belonged to them, and their crystalline laughter echoed through the cobbled streets, creating an intoxicating melody. This was a city where the heart spoke without restraint, and this uninhibited freedom would tug at Abigael and Moussa's heartstrings, inciting them to explore the love they had always preserved, like a sacred secret.

In the shadows, Iblis perfected his trap with the meticulousness of a master strategist. Invisible cameras, camouflaged in the luxurious drapes of the bedroom, waited patiently for the fateful moment, ready to capture every quiver, every stolen glance, every movement that could seal their fate. That moment when their innocent love would be transformed, in the eyes of their community, into an unforgivable betrayal. He knew that this revelation, once broadcast, would unleash a hurricane of condemnation, a media lynching of unprecedented violence. A storm of hatred would be enough to eclipse the light of the Hourim and give back to the dark forces the power they had coveted for so long.

Iblis, cunning and calculating, was already gloating. The idea of seeing the purity of these two young souls wither and fragment under the pressure of a scandal-hungry world filled him with a sinister satisfaction. The trap was perfect, and the world, in its frenzy, would become an unwitting accomplice to his murky scheme, a public thirsting for drama, ready to see ideals crumble.

Around Abigael and Moussa, voices of wisdom, love and hope urged them to leave, to embark on this journey to France, the country that had seen the birth of so many revolutions, poems

The Hourim of innocence

and love stories etched into eternity. Go," they said. It's time to share your light beyond your borders, to touch other lives, to inspire other hearts. It's time for the world to feel the warmth of your love, for your strength to help children elsewhere. Carried away by the excitement of youth, by the beauty of their love that dazzled them like a rising star, Abigael and Moussa let themselves be convinced, without seeing the shadows of the trap that was being woven around them.

But before they left, a silent, imperative call was heard in the depths of their hearts. Like a whisper from the universe itself, it told them they had to go one last time to this magical place, this secret sanctuary where time stood still. This mysterious cavern, shrouded in sacred silence, where every whisper seemed to reverberate endlessly. It was there that the magic of their innocence had always found refuge, where the laws of the universe bent before their purity. And today, he was calling them, perhaps to offer them a final blessing.

Their hearts beating in unison, they stepped into this place where so many of their secrets had been whispered, where the presence of the Guardian had once manifested itself with protective gentleness. But this time, what they discovered was beyond anything they could ever have imagined.

Before them stood three majestic figures from the holiest places in Jerusalem: the Imam of the Great Mosque of Al-Aqsa, the Rabbi of the Great Synagogue and, standing in the centre, the priest of the Church of Jerusalem. These three men of faith, usually separated by history and beliefs, stood side by side, united in a single moment of transcendence. Their faces were filled with silent admiration, as if they understood that they were participating in a miracle, an event in which love and

The Hourim of innocence

faith blended to form a universal, luminous and sacred language.

There were no useless words, no inappropriate gestures. The Imam and the Rabbi exchanged a look that was full of meaning, a complicity born of the recognition of a higher purpose, of a force far greater than their earthly differences. As for the priest, he stood there, in the middle of the other two, his hands crossed over his chest, a symbol of the silent unity that transcends centuries of separation. It was as if this moment belonged to another dimension, a space where human discord lost all importance, where only light and peace had their place.

They understood that their mission was sacred: to unite Abigael and Moussa, these two pure young souls, in the eternal bonds of marriage. Orphaned by their families, they were to receive a blessing that would break the chains of prejudice and division, uniting Islam, Judaism and Christianity in an oath of love and reconciliation. This union represented something so simple, yet so infinitely complex, as if the universe itself had worked to make this moment happen.

Abigael and Moussa, dazzled by the light of their budding love, moved towards each other. Their hearts beat in unison, and their trembling hands sought and found each other, like two stars merging to form a new constellation.

At the entrance to the cavern, a majestic, motionless dog seemed to be keeping watch. His eyes, imbued with ancient wisdom, reflected an almost supernatural serenity. He wasn't just there by chance ; he was the silent guardian of this sanctuary, a discreet protector whose blessed presence recalled the sacred stories.

The Hourim of innocence

Far from being oppressive, the cavern enveloped them, isolating them from the rest of the world, a benevolent witness to this suspended moment. Their eyes met, and such was the depth of their emotion that they felt as if the whole universe had stopped to contemplate them, under the vigilant guard of this being faithful to the shadow of prophecy.

The Imam, in a deep, gravelly voice, began prayers invoking Allah's blessing, each word resonating like an echo from the heavens. The Rabbi, in perfect harmony, intoned words from the Torah, his vibrant voice rising like an ancient melody, rich with the wisdom of millennia. The priest, sacred witness to this divine moment, stood in the centre, his gaze raised to heaven, his hands placed on his heart, embodying the faith that transcends human divisions.

The three figures formed a sacred triangle, an earthly trinity that seemed to bless the union of Moussa and Abigael with all the forces of the universe. Their intertwined hands vibrated with a common thrill, and their souls seemed to merge into a single light, a flame that could never be extinguished. It was a blessed love, sanctified by three religions that recognised each other, if only for a moment, as branches of the same tree, a tree with divine roots.

Moussa felt his knees buckle under the emotion, but Abigael held him up, her tears of joy shining like sacred pearls on his cheeks. What they were sealing was no longer mere adolescent love, but an immortal promise, a sacred bond that defied time, a commitment of souls that, even in the face of the storms to come, would never fail. It was a moment when the magic nourished by their purity and resilience was more powerful than ever, a blessing that enveloped their hearts in a dazzling light.

The Hourim of innocence

And as the Imam and the Rabbi finished their prayers, and the priest lowered his hands in a gesture of silent blessing, Abigael and Moussa became united by a love that transcended all boundaries. At last they had a common Name, a divine identity that gave them the right to cross the final frontier of love, the one where even the stars in the infinite sky bowed in homage.

And so they left this magical place, their hearts fused for eternity, blessed by a union that neither darkness nor time could break. Their intertwined hands seemed sealed by an invisible force, a pact that even the universe recognised. They were ready to face the world, bearers of a light that even Iblis, in all his perfidy, could not extinguish. Every step they took was filled with a new certainty, a faith in love that gave them wings and made them invincible.

Before the Creator, Abigael and Moussa were now bound by vows known only to those who witnessed this sacred moment : the Imam, the Rabbi and the priest, silent guardians of this miraculous secret. Their souls, now intertwined, shone with pure clarity, like two stars merging to light up the sky. And although the shadow of Iblis lurked, this union, sealed in a sanctuary that remained inaccessible to him, escaped his malevolent gaze. It was a marriage invisible to the eyes of the world, an oath engraved in eternity, far from the clutches of the demon.

But Iblis, the master of illusions, remained patient. He relished the idea of depriving them of this last refuge, this sanctuary where their love was still protected from carnal temptation. He was plotting a bigger trap, an evil plan to push them over the edge. He knew that the first crack would come from their own weakness, from the passion that bound them together so deeply, but which remained vulnerable.

The Hourim of innocence

Then the long-awaited day arrived. The sun rose with a golden glow, bathing their homeland in a gentle warmth, as if to bid them farewell. For Abigael and Moussa, it was a moment filled with excitement and apprehension. It was the first time they would be soaring above the clouds, leaving behind their beloved homeland to discover an unknown world. France, that mythical country where so many love stories had been written, awaited them, mysterious and promising. But it didn't matter where they went: they knew that as long as they stayed together, their love would remain their only true home, an invincible shield against all evil.

Their love intensified day by day, like a blazing inferno illuminating their faces with an unearthly light. A golden aura seemed to emanate from them, captivating those around them, as if the mere sight of them was enough to awaken sleeping souls. Their radiance fascinated and disturbed at the same time. Crowds gathered around them, hungry for the magic they didn't understand but felt in every fibre of their being. Hands, glances and whispers surrounded them, trying to touch them, to capture a fragment of this rare light.

But this attention was beginning to weigh heavily on their shoulders. It was no longer just admiration ; it was a collective obsession, an adoration that had become almost idolatry. This exaggerated devotion, tinged with envy, was becoming a burden, suffocating their pure love in a whirlwind of greedy glances and intrusive gestures. Abigael and Moussa felt trapped in this game of mirrors that the world was imposing on them, a spectacle in which they were the unwilling protagonists.

Little did they know that this overflowing zeal was a poison, distilled by Iblis to disturb them. Legions of fanatics, invisible

The Hourim of innocence

to the naked eye but very real, worked in the shadows, sent by the demon to poison the air around them. The infatuation surrounding them was not innocent : it was designed to intoxicate them with flattery, to fan their vanity, to draw them away from their sacred simplicity. It was a diabolical strategy, meticulously orchestrated, to make them lose themselves in their own reflection, to make them forget the essence of what made them so unique.

Love, the sacred fire they had preserved until then, was beginning to flicker under this insidious pressure. The air became denser, heavier, saturated with an energy that sought to consume them. Iblis, hidden behind every shadow, waited patiently for the purity of their union to falter, for pride and doubt to tarnish the radiance of their love. It was an invisible struggle, a battle that only they could win, if they remained true to themselves and to the light that shone within them.

When they arrived in Paris, an uproar overwhelmed them. A horde of journalists from all over the world was waiting for them, eager to capture every fragment of their lives like hungry hunters stalking precious prey. Camera flashes burst into a constellation of dazzling flashes, like devouring stars, illuminating the night of this effervescent Paris. The microphones, outstretched like weapons, sought to penetrate their intimacy, to extract the slightest emotion, the slightest truth hidden behind their facade smiles. The questions flew, perfidious and sharp, looking for the flaw, the vulnerability that could reveal the shadow under their bright light.

In the shadows of the great Parisian buildings, paparazzi lurked, invisible and formidable, ready to catch the slightest faux pas. Their hope lay in a moment of inattention : a flash of anger, a smile that betrayed ill-concealed pride, a sign of

The Hourim of innocence

budding pride. Every gesture, every expression became a target, an opportunity to fuel the media fire that was just waiting to ignite.

Even before they set down their suitcases, they were escorted to the Élysée Palace, where the President and his wife awaited them with a reverence worthy of sovereigns. The scene was grandiose, almost unreal, with the entire Parisian bourgeoisie flocking to see them, to get closer to the light that seemed to emanate from them. But behind every smile, every look of admiration, the henchmen of Iblis lurked, working with diabolical patience to accomplish their perfidious mission. They manipulated events like puppeteers, making everything perfect in appearance, but poisoned in intent.

Iblis had orchestrated everything to rekindle the fire of youthful passion that burned within Abigael and Moussa. Every detail, every encounter, every situation was finely calculated to push them to the brink of temptation. On the eve of their live television appearance, everything had been planned so that they would finally give in to those long-suppressed impulses, cross that ultimate line and seal their doom. It was a Machiavellian production, a trap woven of forbidden desires, seduction and poisoned promises, where innocence risked being consumed in flames.

Paris, that magical city where every street whispered love poems, became a bewitching theatre where Iblis performed his play with demonic perfection. As they strolled through the cobbled, illuminated streets, young couples, carefully chosen and placed in their path, seemed to be living out their passions without hindrance. These fake couples, of all ethnicities, kissed languorously, caressed each other with uninhibited tenderness, displaying a love that was not hidden, that was proudly

The Hourim of innocence

claimed. They seemed to want to shout out to the world that love knows no rules or boundaries, that the heart obeys only its own laws.

For Abigael and Moussa, this display of freedom was as fascinating as it was disconcerting. They came from a culture where love, that secret treasure, is never revealed in public. In their country, gestures of affection were hidden, protected from the gaze of others, because a caress or a kiss exchanged in the middle of the street could lead to insults, contempt or even violence. There, love was whispered in the shadows, glimpsed behind furtive smiles, veiled glances, modesty preserved like protective armour. Showing love in broad daylight was a forbidden act, a risky daring that could shatter lives.

But here in Paris, everything seemed the other way round. Modesty knew no bounds, and bodies flaunted themselves with disturbing audacity. Daring dress left little to the imagination, and love, whether heterosexual or homosexual, was asserted without shame or fear, unfurling like a banner of freedom. This cultural difference hit them hard, plunging them into a kind of vertigo where everything seemed possible, where the line between what was forbidden and what was permitted became blurred. For the first time, Abigael and Moussa observed these freedoms with a mixture of admiration and confusion, feeling both attracted and destabilised by this universe where intimacy knew no boundaries.

The scent of Paris was imbued with an omnipresent sensuality, an intoxicating fragrance that permeated the air, every whisper, every laugh that echoed under the ancient bridges. Iblis had crafted this setting with frightening precision, a tableau where every detail conspired to their downfall, where every shadow

The Hourim of innocence

whispered in the ear of their innocence, seducing it, tempting it to give in to the call of desire. He knew that pure light always attracts darkness, and he was determined to shake it.

Paris was buzzing with unprecedented fervour. Everywhere, in every street and avenue, the cries of children tirelessly chanting the name "Hourim" rang out. The city, usually so busy, had been transformed into a vibrant theatre of souls from all over France. Huge crowds had gathered, a human tide driven by feverish hope, millions of hearts united by the desire to catch even a glimpse of the two young heroes, these almost mythical figures of a generation thirsting for light and renewal. Celebrities, influential politicians, financial tycoons, all joined in this wave of adoration, seeking to get closer to them, to capture a fragment of their brilliance in a single snapshot.

And yet, for Abigael and Moussa, this debauchery of light and splendour seemed hollow, alien, almost suffocating. Their hearts, shaped by simple, profound values, struggled to find their place in this setting saturated with materialism and superficiality. Accustomed to an existence stripped of the superfluous, where every object had a meaning and every moment was imbued with an essential significance, they felt trapped in an opulence that was as foreign to them as a senseless dream. All these grandiose buildings, this convoluted architecture, these skyscrapers defying the sky, and this Eiffel Tower, a colossus of metal reaching for the clouds, were of little value to them compared to the simple beauty of their hundred-year-old olive tree, back home. This tree, witness to countless generations, carried within it the history of their people, the smell of the ancestors who had shaped this world and whose legacy lived on in every breath of wind.

The Hourim of innocence

In their eyes, nothing could rival the magic of those childhood memories, afternoons spent flying a kite in the skies of their native land, a land steeped in deep roots that linked them to their essence, their humanity. Unlike the modern towers that stretched towards the heavens, seeking to defy the gods and lose themselves in the mists of an uncertain future, their sacred dome had stood the test of time, keeping intact the memory of centuries gone by. For Abigael and Moussa, this connection to the earth, this rootedness, represented the very essence of life. All the glitz and glamour, all the accumulated wealth, was just an illusion, a way of distancing themselves from what really mattered, of disconnecting themselves from the simple values that make the human heart beat faster.

Tired of this outpouring of luxury and extravagance, exhausted by the frenzy of their long journey and this overwhelming first day, they decided to return to the hotel to finally find some peace and quiet. When they arrived, the hotel manager was waiting for them, eager and smiling. He greeted them with every honour, bowing slightly as he handed them the keys to their suites. "You'll see," he said with exquisite politeness, "these suites are the most beautiful in the whole hotel, and they're connected. If you ever feel like saying good night, or sharing a herbal tea in complete privacy, the door is open. He then handed them two silver keys. Abigael would be staying in suite number 6, and Moussa in number 9, two numbers that fate seemed to have fun sowing in their path, two intertwined symbols that, even lying one against the other, formed nothing less than eternity.

In their sumptuous suites, every detail seemed to have been chosen with almost supernatural intent. Bouquets of red roses, symbols of ardent passion, stood proudly in tall crystal vases,

The Hourim of innocence

their heady scent wafting through the air like a promise of forbidden love. Delicately scattered petals carpeted the floor and the sheets of their beds, forming a floral path leading to the unknown, like fragments of a dream inviting them to lose themselves. Soft, subdued light bathed the room, casting dancing shadows that mingled with a haze of bewitching incense, enveloping every corner of the place in an atmosphere of mystery and temptation.

On the coffee table, a feast of opulence awaited them: sweet and savoury delicacies in exquisite shapes, bowls filled with brightly coloured fruit juices, aromas that seemed to be calling them to let themselves go, to savour every moment as a foretaste of a sensuality yet to be explored. The air was pleasantly cool, causing their skin to tingle, an almost innocent excuse for their bodies to seek out that warmth they couldn't ignore. And then there was that door.

That thick glass door separating their two suites was more than just a physical barrier. It was a threshold, a passageway between innocence and temptation, between what they were and what they could become. The glass, though matt, revealed mysterious shadows, blurred silhouettes that seemed to play a game of attraction and distance. It looked like a door opening onto Eden, but it was also a trap that promised a fragile paradise, a space where the slightest misstep could plunge them into the unknown.

Moussa, his heart beating like a sacred drum, moved towards the door and placed a trembling hand on the handle. On the other side, Abigael, as if connected to him by an invisible thread, did the same. In a synchronised gesture, they opened their doors, and time seemed to stand still, as if holding its breath. Their eyes met, a silent exchange charged with a

The Hourim of innocence

thousand emotions, a silent dialogue where every thought and desire could be read in their eyes.

They stayed there, frozen in that moment, each on their own side, observing the other with an intensity that transcended words. They were like two inverted numbers, like the 6 and the 9 that, raised towards the sky, formed a perfect 99, a symbol of transparency and truth, a promise of pure and sincere love. Yet, somewhere in the shadows, Iblis was watching them, ready to do anything to divert them from this luminous path. He dreamt of turning those numbers upside down, transforming them into a mysterious 66, a number imbued with sensual warmth and dark mysticism, ready to bewitch them into his spiral of temptation.

They stood on the threshold of that invisible boundary, where the carpet of the first suite touched that of the second, a subtle, almost symbolic border marking the last space that still separated their worlds. Their eyes sought each other out, found each other, and in this exchange, a gentle but all-consuming tension built up, filled with desire, fear and deep love.

Abigael's breath caught and her heart pounded against her chest. Her cheeks were burning, her hands clammy with emotion as she gazed at Moussa. There he stood before her, the love of her life, her eternity. Their souls had long since found each other, but now it was their bodies that were crying out to be brought closer together, to take that decisive step that would lead them into a new world, an adult world, where innocence is transformed into a more tangible passion.

Moussa felt his thoughts racing, his heart beating in unison with hers. He took a step forward, closing the distance

The Hourim of innocence

between them still further, his hand rising to brush against Abigael's cheek with infinite, almost sacred tenderness. His fingers slid gently over her skin, triggering a cascade of shivers, like waves of heat spreading through them, making them both feverish and impatient.

- Abigael," he murmured, "my dear and tender wife, since that day when we were united under the benevolent gaze of the Imam of the Great Mosque of Al-Aqsa, whose wisdom and devotion have inspired generations of worshippers; of the Rabbi of the Great Synagogue of Jerusalem, a man whose every word seemed woven with ancient secrets, the bearer of ancient wisdom; and of the Priest of the Church of the Holy Sepulchre, a figure of peace, guardian of the mysteries of Christianity and silent witness to our love. That day, in that place where time stands still, we exchanged an eternal kiss, a memory that I cherish more than anything else.

But suddenly, a shadow crossed Moussa's mind. A chilling intuition came over him, as if an invisible presence had been listening to his every word. He realised with painful clarity that he had made a mistake. In his declaration of sincere love, he had forgotten the vigilance that their situation demanded. Iblis, always on the lookout, had not let this opportunity pass. Already, in the shadows, he was weaving his plans, ready to exploit this weakness to sow doubt and discord.

He paused, his eyes locked on Abigael's, before continuing, his voice broken with emotion.

- But today, fate is inviting us to cross that line. But before I do, I remember that it was you, five years ago, who took the first step. You, a brave little girl, who broke the silence of that sunny day to offer me your kite string. You invited me to share

The Hourim of innocence

your sky, to fly with you, hand in hand, giving me the chance to touch the clouds, to feel the freedom of an unfettered wind. And now it's me who wants to offer you the skies, to guide you into a greater, deeper flight, a sky where our souls and bodies become one.

Abigael, her eyes misty with tears, felt the depth of this memory rise to the surface. She remembered that day as if it were yesterday, that moment when she had reached out to him, breaking the barrier of shyness to invite Moussa into her world of childhood, her world of innocence. And now she stood before him, the young woman she had become, full of immense love.

- Moussa," she said in a voice that was soft but full of passion, "you are all I have left, all I have. My love for you has never needed words to express itself, because it's beyond words. But I do know one thing: the love we share is infinite, like the kite I gave you. Today, it's your turn to take my hand, to take me flying in an endless sky. Yes, like you, I'm afraid of what awaits us beyond this border, but I know that it's a step I want to take. With you. For you.

The tears rolled gently down her cheeks, but they were not tears of sadness; they were the expression of pure, sincere, burning love. Moussa, moved to the very depths of his being, moved closer, his hands wrapping around Abigael's face with infinite gentleness.

- Abigael," he said, in a voice that was a mixture of desire and tenderness, "let me be the one to guide you through this sky. My silence has always spoken for me, but tonight I want my gestures to express to you what I feel. Take my hand, and let

The Hourim of innocence

this love be our flight, a gift that not even the Guardian could refuse us.

They both knew it: this moment was a test, a temptation skilfully orchestrated by Iblis, who was lurking in the shadows, hoping they would succumb. But at that moment, a feeling of triumph overcame them. For even if Iblis had devised this trap, even if he had placed every element to ensure that they would lose themselves in temptation, Abigael and Moussa saw in this night something much greater, much brighter. It was a gift from the Guardian, a final gift left to thwart the malice of Iblis, who had once again made a fool of himself. The demon had wanted to inflame their desire in order to lose them, but it was this same desire that united them even more deeply, in a light that repelled the shadows, a love that nothing and no one could tarnish.

Their hearts beating in unison, Abigael approached again, and this time there were no more barriers, no more doubts. Their lips met in a kiss imbued with all the promise, all the memories and all the love they had held inside them since the day they shared that kite. This kiss, far from their former innocence, was an act of devotion, an infinite love that bound them stronger than ever, carrying them towards a sky they had never yet explored, but which they were ready to conquer together.

At that moment, a brilliant light burst forth from their union, so pure and powerful that it blinded the cameras hidden around them. As if obeying a celestial command, the cameras, unwitting witnesses to this sacred love, seemed to turn away, respecting a modesty imposed by forces far beyond this world. Even technology, in that instant, recognised the sanctity of their bond, bowing to the will of a universal truth: certain moments cannot be profaned.

The Hourim of innocence

Moussa, young and strong, took Abigael in the hollow of his arms, his gesture filled with gentleness and protection. He lifted her with infinite delicacy, as if carrying in his arms all the tenderness and fragility of the universe. Every movement was precise, every step seemed charged with a vibrant tenderness, and the atmosphere around them seemed to thicken, saturated with the intensity of this unique moment. He laid her gently on the bed, his heart beating wildly, feeling in every fibre of his being the weight of this long-awaited moment.

Abigael, breathless, sat up, and with a gesture of confidence mixed with shyness, she laid her head against Moussa's stomach, her ear against his heart. She could hear the mad drumming, the symphony of beats that echoed her own, and she held him tight, her arms trembling with emotion but not fear. It was a chemical reaction, a natural dance where oestrogen and testosterone mixed, awakening raw, deep sensations.

Their eyes met, and in Abigael's eyes Moussa could see a whirlwind of emotions: passion, love, but also an intense desire that they had never dared express fully. She looked up at him, and with exquisite slowness began to unbutton his shirt, her fingers brushing his taut skin, awakening uncontrollable shivers. Moussa felt a warmth rising inside him, a warmth he could no longer ignore. Every hair on his body stood on end, vibrating with the touch, like guards saluting the arrival of a divine force.

He tried to contain the tumescence that formed naturally, this awakening of his body that he could not control. But this desire, this lively pulsation in his lower abdomen, was only growing under Abigael's light caresses. She felt it too, and this knowledge awakened in her a warmth that spread through her

The Hourim of innocence

veins, a fire that was both gentle and burning. She continued, sliding the shirt off her shoulders, her hands caressing the taut skin of her arms, muscular but soft, as if she wanted to engrave every sensation in her memory.

Abigael sat back, her face flushed with emotion and passion, and with a delicate gesture, she slid her fingers along the waistband of his trousers, her hands trembling with a mixture of desire and frenzy. Despite himself, Moussa felt his breathing quicken, his heart beat faster, while the air around them seemed charged with electricity. He tried to concentrate, to slow down this surge of sensations, but it was impossible. Abigael, with her gaze full of sweetness and fire, made him dizzy, and this burst of desire inside him was nothing more than a certainty, a force that was irresistibly awakening.

When Abigael rose to undress herself, she did so with natural grace and sensuality, taking her time to make each gesture an act of love. She slipped off her dress, the fabric caressing her curves before falling gently to her feet. She twisted slightly, her hips making a bewitching movement, and Moussa could no longer look away. Every detail of her naked body was a revelation, a miracle he had been waiting for, and he could feel the sweat beading on his skin, burning drops that reflected the surge of his desire.

Abigael, aware of the rising tension, guided Moussa's hands towards her, and although he was paralysed by the intensity of the moment, she gently took the lead. She unhooked her bra, and her breasts revealed themselves, trembling slightly with emotion. There was only one last piece of clothing between her and this ultimate intimacy, and she removed it with almost unbearable slowness, revealing herself completely, in the garb of birth, pure and vulnerable.

The Hourim of innocence

They were now face to face, naked and vulnerable, but stronger than ever. Their bodies were drawn together like two stars destined to merge, and when they came closer, the contact of their naked skins created an explosion of sensations, an ecstasy that consumed them from the inside. Their kisses became deeper, their caresses more urgent, and under the soft duvet they lost themselves in a dance of love and passion, a sacred union where every gesture was an offering, an act of faith in the love they shared.

That night became a suspended moment, an eternity in which their love found its fulfilment, their innocence transformed into a new beauty, a more mature, more powerful love, which gave them the strength to believe that even Iblis could never extinguish that light.

In the early hours of the morning, Abigael and Moussa awoke enveloped in a soft, almost divine glow, as if the night had carved a new radiance into them. They felt stronger, more vibrant and even brighter. Their love was no longer just a bond, but a dazzling fusion of their souls. They had transcended their individual energies to create a single one, a halo of light of unparalleled purity, which radiated around them like an invisible shield. Their bodies had found unison, their hearts were beating in unison, and their souls were now dancing together in an almost cosmic harmony, a sacred alchemy that could not be shaken by time or fear.

Their union had transfigured them, giving rise to an almost supernatural strength, an energy that seemed to defy the gravity of the world and protect them from the darkness that was always trying to engulf them. It was not just physical love that had woven this new power, but the union of their minds, the connection of their hearts, and the intertwining of their

The Hourim of innocence

destinies. They had become one, in flesh and soul, and this unity made them more resilient, more luminous, as if the Creator himself had placed his eternal blessing on them.

However, in the shadow of this new clarity, Iblis was weaving his web, more cunning and relentless than ever. He knew that Abigael and Moussa had an acute sense of justice, an unshakeable attachment to the truth, and that their integrity was an impregnable fortress. He needed an infallible ruse to make them yield. It was then that he realised that he couldn't hit them directly. He had to corrupt their environment, manipulate the witnesses to their divine union, to create doubt and confusion. And even in his dark heart, he reluctantly recognised that the children were too just, too purified by the light of their love, to succumb to lies or transgress the truth.

Iblis had a subtle and perverse plan. During the night, he sent his infernal legions to the three wise men who had blessed this secret union. The Imam of the Great Mosque of Al-Aqsa, the Rabbi of the Jerusalem Synagogue and the Priest of the Holy Sepulchre, all men of faith and uprightness, were besieged by terrifying visions, threats whispered in the dark, nightmares in which their families, torn from their protection, sank into chaos. The demon knew that to break these pillars of virtue, he had to play on their deepest fears. And though they resisted, the venom of anguish seeped into their hearts. A struggle was waged within them, between the fear of the Creator and the horror of the torments inflicted by Iblis.

But even with these infernal pressures, a part of them remained faithful to the truth, clinging to the sacred light that had guided them. Iblis, though he rejoiced to see them falter, understood that the children themselves would never lie, never turn away from the righteousness that made them

The Hourim of innocence

luminous heroes. The young lovers, even in the face of the Evil One's manoeuvres, were anchored in sincerity and righteousness, unshakeable and pure. Their love, however vulnerable, remained inviolate against the cunning of the devil.

Abigael and Moussa, in their dressing room in the television studio, were preparing to face the strange and disturbing world that awaited them on the other side of the doors. They knew that temptation was everywhere, that the refined and sumptuous food presented to them could be impregnated with pernicious substances designed to cloud their judgement and erode their discernment. That's why they chose to take with them only modest but safe provisions : dried fruit, nuts, hard bread cakes, simple and real foods, symbols of their rootedness in truth and purity.

When they were finally led onto the stage, solemn music rose up, filling the air with an almost mystical tension. Their footsteps seemed to resonate like the beating of a sacred heart, a secret melody that intermingled with the whispers of angels and the murmurs of demons. The studio, packed with hand-picked spectators, looked like an arena where light and shadow were about to do battle. The air smelt of old leather armchairs, the scent of carefully arranged bouquets of flowers, but also a more subtle, almost imperceptible fragrance, like a hint of hidden sulphur.

The star journalist, a man with a charming smile but a dangerous gleam in his eyes, greeted them with deft words and rhetoric that could either charm or terrify. He seated them in a scarlet armchair, vibrating with an energy that was almost palpable, as if it were soaked in all the emotions he had seen unfold. He himself sat in a neighbouring chair, feigning courtesy, while a third chair, black as night, awaited the surprise guest. This seat, like a throne of shadows, projected an oppressive mystery, a silent portent of the storm to come.

In front of them, a giant screen shone, broadcasting live from other countries, where outside journalists were commenting on the event in real time, their voices mingling with the hushed interrogations of the audience. It was an orchestrated spectacle, a stage where every element seemed prepared to test Abigael and Moussa's light, to try to crack this new strength they had discovered within themselves. But despite the uncertainty, the two heroes, bound together by a transcendent energy, were preparing to face this moment, confident that, as long as they remained united, not even Iblis's plans could destroy them.

A heavy, icy silence had fallen over the studio, as if a frosty mist had seeped into the air, frozen in suspended time. The journalist made a theatrical gesture with his hand, and the cameras, with their piercing glass eyes, focused on Abigael and Moussa. The two young people, hand in hand, formed a picture of intertwined strength and fragility, like two stars ready to resist the gravity of a black hole.

The journalist, whose elegant tone betrayed a masked hostility, leaned forward, his soft but venomous voice creeping like a snake into the minds of those listening. Every syllable seemed to be cut from a crystal of cynicism, sharp and ruthless, hidden beneath a veneer of exquisite politeness.

- It is an honour," he began, "to welcome you to this stage this evening. I have waited for this moment with feverish impatience, because you are, it seems, the brilliant minds behind the Hourim movement, an illusion so perfectly woven that it has bewitched the whole world. But this evening, ladies

The Hourim of innocence

and gentlemen, the harsh light of truth will strike without mercy. Before we bring in our guest, who will reveal what you have carefully hidden, I would like to ask you a question : are you ready to confess what you have hidden, or would you rather cling to this mirage, at the risk of seeing your reputation shatter like broken glass ?

The falsely benevolent tone barely concealed the claws of malice. Abigael felt Moussa's hand tremble slightly, but she gripped it tighter, instilling in him a silent courage. Moussa's eyes, deep and intense, burned with a fire that not even oceans of lies could extinguish.

He took a breath, and his voice, firm and vibrant, rose like a banner of truth :

- Honesty," he says, his voice shining with startling clarity, "is much more to me than a simple virtue. It is a fortress, a sanctuary where I find refuge. It protects me, warms me and enlightens me, even in the face of the most seductive temptations or the most vile attacks. It is the armour of my soul, the shield that defends me against the arrows of corruption.

His words, crystalline and powerful, made the air vibrate, and a wave of amazed murmurs passed through the audience. The audience seemed taken aback by the dignity of this young boy, who, despite being under relentless pressure, spoke with the wisdom of a scholar.

- Everything we've achieved," Moussa continued with growing intensity, "has been with integrity. Since we were eleven years old, Abigael and I have been bound together by a sacred innocence, a modesty that we have fiercely defended, even when the world has flared up around us. It was only recently,

The Hourim of innocence

blessed by the Chief Rabbi of Jerusalem, the eminent Imam of the Al-Aqsa Mosque, and the venerable Priest of the Holy Sepulchre, that we were united by the sacred bonds of marriage.

Moussa paused for a moment, his dark eyes searching the journalist's, looking for an ounce of truth behind that mask of false courtesy.

- Our marriage," he continued, "preceded the union of our bodies. To this day, we have resisted all carnal temptations, keeping our hearts pure and our intentions immaculate. You insinuate faults that do not exist, you wield accusations like daggers, but you forget that light cannot be tarnished by the breath of slander. You speak of dignity, but your words are vipers in disguise, venomous compliments that seek to undermine our integrity.

The whole room held its breath. The journalist, who had hoped to unsettle the young man, found himself shaken by this answer, whose power and honesty seemed to defy the laws of youth.

Abigael, still standing beside Moussa, radiated an indomitable light, a shared energy that seemed to repel the darkness. Together, they rose to their feet, united in a love that transcends time and mortal trappings, and proclaimed in a vibrant voice, full of an almost divine strength:

- Hourim ! Hourim !

This scream, echoed by the walls of the studio, cut through the space, seeming to push back the air itself, like a thunderclap that froze time. But just then, the studio doors opened and a man entered. It was Reverend Anwar, but a

The Hourim of innocence

strange aura surrounded him. His walk, his humble smile and his measured gestures seemed to exude a reassuring warmth and kindness. He had the perfect appearance of wisdom incarnate, a man of faith who could have calmed storms with his simple words.

And yet, behind this mask of erudition and benevolence, a shadow lurked, invisible but terrifying. It was Iblis, the prince of darkness, dressed in the clothes of a wise man, disguised as a benevolent shepherd, ready to guide his sheep towards the precipice. His smile betrayed no malice, and his eyes, though filled with apparent warmth, hid icy depths where flashes of cunning and malediction danced.

The whole assembly seemed charmed by this imposing figure, who gave off a perfume of candour and authority. But Abigael and Moussa, feeling the icy chill of Iblis' presence, realised that the battle ahead would not be a simple exchange of words, but a war of souls, where light and shadow would clash in a duel that even fate was waiting for, suspended between hope and despair.

Before sitting down in his dark armchair, Reverend Anwar crossed the stage with a slow, calculated gait, each step sounding like the death knell of an inexorable sentence. His long black robe glided across the floor, and his every movement seemed orchestrated to capture attention, infusing the atmosphere with an eerie solemnity. He stretched out his hand towards the journalist, who, although his voice betrayed nothing, could not hide the sudden paleness of his face and the dampness of his palms. With feigned benevolence, the Reverend approached Abigael and Moussa, placing a heavy, paternalistic hand on their heads. This gesture, which might

The Hourim of innocence

have seemed comforting to the public, was, for the two young heroes, tinged with a cold, underlying threat.

Taking his place on the black armchair which, under the glare of the spotlights, seemed to absorb light like a bottomless pit, the Reverend sat up with theatrical dignity. The journalist, his forehead beaded with sweat despite the cool studio air, introduced him in a slightly trembling voice:

- Ladies and gentlemen, it is an honour to introduce Reverend Anwar, a respected figure in the world of faith, known for his role as an ambassador for peace between the most influential religious traditions. This man of faith, who is said to be close to the Pope, the great Imams and the most eminent Rabbis, has agreed to join us this evening to enlighten us with his wisdom.

Reverend Anwar smiled a smile filled with false gentleness, then his voice rose, smooth and bewitching, resonating with measured authority:

- My dear children, what a privilege to meet you again," he exclaimed with exaggerated benevolence. Your youth and radiance are a priceless source of inspiration. Your innocence reminds me of what is purest and most vulnerable in our world.

He sighed, placing a hand on his heart, feigning pain that seemed almost sincere:

- I listened to your words with great attention from my dressing room. What I wouldn't have given to congratulate you on this sacred marriage you claim, to celebrate your union in joy and peace. But, alas, the truth is sometimes a cruel burden. While you were speaking with such touching fervour,

The Hourim of innocence

I received a moving appeal from the three wise men of Jerusalem. Men of faith whom I consider to be brothers in my heart. The Chief Rabbi, the eminent Imam and the venerable Priest contacted me in despair at your revelations.

He paused for a moment and looked around the audience, taking in every face, every breath, before continuing:

- These revered men, pillars of our shared spirituality, have begged me to set the record straight so that their religious integrity is not tainted by what you present as reality. And even if it tears at my soul, I am here to restore what is right.

The journalist, his eyes shining with excitement, seized the opportunity:

- Ladies and gentlemen, we have the opportunity to witness an unprecedented moment live ! Our cameras are ready to transport us to Jerusalem, where the three wise men of religion will be speaking.

A vibrating tension settled over the room, so palpable that the air seemed charged with electricity. Abigael and Moussa, although aware of the trap that was closing in on them, remained upright and resolute. Their hands entwined, they supported each other, feeling each other's warmth as a protection against the cold injustice that threatened them.

As the giant screen went into place, a dull crackling sound rose into the air, a metallic, ominous sound that sent shivers down the spine of the audience. The reverend's face tightened imperceptibly, and he glanced discreetly at the cameras, making sure that everything was going according to plan. The connection was made with difficulty, the image flickering like

The Hourim of innocence

a flickering light, and an electronic voice announced that communication with Jerusalem was about to begin.

Reverend Anwar, taking advantage of this moment of technological chaos, leaned towards the children. His voice was lowered, but the threat that oozed from each of his words was scathing:

- You don't yet know what real pain is," he murmured, his lips stretching into a toothy grin. My wrath will descend upon you with the force of a divine storm. But there is a way out, a simple kiss on my hand could fix everything. A gesture of humility, nothing more...

Abigael felt rage welling up inside her, but she held it in, her eyes fixed on those of Moussa. Together, they simply nodded their refusal, and the Reverend, feigning affected disappointment, stroked their hair as a priest would bless children, his gestures concealing the darkness of his soul.

Then, suddenly, the giant screen lit up. The three wise men appeared, but their faces were marked by terrible distress. Their eyes, clouded with subdued tears, expressed a heart-rending inner struggle. It was not the fear of Iblis that paralysed them, but the sacred terror of betraying the Creator. A fear similar to that of Abraham when he dreamt of the sacrifice of his son, a dream so powerful that he resolved to obey the divine will. But these men were not Abraham. They didn't have the strength to sacrifice what was dearest to them.

The Chief Rabbi spoke, his voice broken with emotion:

- I had a dream, a dream in which the three of us were reunited in a timeless cavern. There, with the Imam and the Priest, we united these two young souls. But it was only a dream, a mirage that never touched the fabric of reality.

The Imam and the Priest nodded, their trembling voices confirming this version. But behind their words was a silent prayer, a desperate plea for divine mercy. It was the weight of remorse, a pain as old as Judas' betrayal, this unbearable burden that they carried with them, imploring forgiveness even before the sin was committed.

The screen crackled one last time before fading into black, cutting off any possibility of return or repentance. The journalist, like a puppeteer pulling the strings of a morbid show, sat up, ready to orchestrate the rest of this travesty of justice, while Reverend Anwar bided his time, a sardonic smile gracing his lips.

The silence stretched out, dense and palpable, like a shroud of mist hanging over a sea of troubled souls. Everyone held their breath, captive to the aura of anxiety that had settled over them. The Reverend Anwar, that benevolent-looking but veiled figure, rose from his dark throne. His black robe floated like an omen of doom, and his slow, calculated gait seemed to weigh on the already oppressive atmosphere. He stepped forward, a deceptive benevolence painted on his features, and a smile that almost seemed paternal played on his lips.

In a soft voice, wrapped in a veneer of false wisdom, he spoke.

- My dear children," he intoned, his voice wavering like an averted prayer, "I feel such a deep turmoil, an almost cosmic dizziness. In your presence, it seems to me that reality itself wavers, swept away by a mysterious force that I struggle to name. You have this light, yes, this innocent aura that stirs

The Hourim of innocence

compassion in people's hearts... but is it really innocence, or is it just a mask, an enchantment hiding something much darker?

He looked magnanimously at Abigael and Moussa, but behind this apparent kindness were flashes of refined cruelty, a venomous gleam that pierced his pupils, clutching at the shadows of the room like sharp talons.

- You are not," he continued, "the innocent playthings of an old forgotten sect, as I once believed. No, you are far worse. You are the evil creations of a demonic carpenter, Pinocchios fashioned by the perfidious hands of the Prince of Darkness. May the Creator forgive me for uttering such blasphemies, but the truth must be heard.

He closed his eyes briefly, pretending to pray, but his every gesture seemed imbued with a diabolical theatricality. When he opened them again, his irises glowed with a disturbing intensity.

- Everything is becoming clearer," he murmured, his voice seeping into our minds like a subtle poison. These young people, with their angelic looks and honeyed words, have bewitched us, seduced us with promises of light. But this light is only a lure, a dark seduction, a black energy designed to turn us away from the Holy Scriptures.

He paused, letting his words hang like lightning in a stormy sky, then resumed in a more solemn, almost priestly tone.

- Yes, brothers and sisters," he continued, "the prophecy is clear. We know the promise of the Antichrist, of the apocalypse, of the return of the Saviour. But never in any sacred text does it say that two children will come to deliver us from chaos. These children are not the messengers of the

The Hourim of innocence

Most High, they are the instruments of a demon whose intelligence and perfidy are beyond comprehension. Look at them, so pure in appearance, and yet they bask in the luxury of a Parisian hotel, indulging in the pleasures of the flesh. What remains of their supposed purity?

His gaze softened for a moment, and he sighed, as if overwhelmed by the weight of his own compassion.

- And yet," he continued, "my faith commands me to forgive. My love for the Creator leads me to be merciful, and it is with deep sadness that I offer you my protection. Yes, I am ready to defend these lost souls. Do not let your anger, your thirst for justice, turn you into merciless judges. I beg you, hold back your stones, do not become the executioners of these young people. I ask all nations to offer them sanctuary, for if they return to their native land, they will suffer the blind wrath of mankind.

He raised his arms to the sky, a theatrical gesture that seemed to invoke a blessing or an exorcism, and his voice became almost lilting, filled with a deceptive fervour.

- But the question remains, insidious and chilling. Can we risk giving them a voice? To allow them to express themselves is to open the devil's mouth, to let the snake whisper its charms. Wouldn't it be wiser to judge them fairly, to offer them a trial where the truth, or what's left of it, will be revealed? I am a man of faith, and my faith obliges me to be fair. So yes, despite everything they have done, I open my arms to them to find protection and redemption, but let them know that divine justice is merciless.

Then he sat back, his hands clasped as if in prayer, and a strange crackling sound emanated from the loudspeakers, a

The Hourim of innocence

dull vibration that made the giant screen tremble. Communication with the wise men of Jerusalem seemed to be faltering, paralysed by an invisible force, and the suspense became unbearable. The world held its breath, suspended on the border between truth and lies, while the journalist glanced nervously at his control room, trying to understand what was happening.

In this hushed tumult, minds wavered, hearts clenched, and the line between right and wrong, true and false, seemed to blur, giving way to an abyss of doubts and uncertainties.

The journalist, his forehead beaded with sweat, turned eyes full of palpable hesitation towards the Reverend. He seemed to be waiting for a blessing, or perhaps an order disguised as advice, like a faithful man ready to follow his master blindly for fear of making a mistake. The Reverend, with a sovereign calm and a coldness that hid behind an apparent benevolence, nodded slowly with his hand, like an emperor granting audience to his subjects.

- Yes, let them speak," he murmured in a voice tinged with hypocritical gentleness. Let them defend themselves, even if it means sinking deeper into their own abyss.

It was Abigael who spoke, sensing the tension rising in Moussa, his soul prey to a burning anger that he was struggling to tame. She squeezed his hand with a tenderness that radiated, giving him the strength and calm he needed, then stood up, her eyes shining with an indomitable light.

- Never," she pronounced, her clear, vibrant voice piercing the atmosphere like a blade of truth, "never, never, never has my tongue been twisted to distort or disguise the truth. The lie, that treacherous intruder, is a stranger to Moussa and me. Our

The Hourim of innocence

one and only cover, the one that protects us like inviolable armour, is the purest honesty, the immaculate truth.

She let her words sink into the minds of the spectators, while her face, imbued with youth and wisdom, radiated a quiet strength.

- I will not contradict the wise men of Jerusalem," she continued, "even if their words have been imprisoned in a casket of perfidy, even if their version has been distorted by the invisible hands of fear and coercion. I respect them, these three men. I forgive them for having had to retreat into illusion and oblivion to protect what they love. For who are we, all of us, if not children of the Creator, groping in the mist of His designs ?

A religious silence enveloped the studio, and Abigael continued, her words filled with mystical depth.

- The Creator," she says, her voice becoming almost a prayer, "does not manifest himself as a palpable entity. He is this beneficent illusion that bewitches us, filling us with peace and protection. He is the essence of the storm that tests us and the gentle wind that caresses our faces. He is both the water that soothes and the fire that consumes, the barrier and the rampart, the trial and the mercy. He is me, he is Musa, he is each one of you, even those who go astray. But one thing is certain : He is not that Reverend sitting there, for He is merciful, forgiving and merciful. He forgives, except those who choose to follow the one who will lead souls astray to the end of the abyss.

The room seemed to be under a spell, as if hypnotised by the sincere strength radiating from Abigael. The Reverend, despite his mask of a good and wise man, flinched imperceptibly.

The Hourim of innocence

- I don't blame you," continued Abigael, her eyes shining with restrained but resolute tears. I can't even blame Iblis himself, because we're all being dragged towards a destiny that he, in his fury, is trying to hasten. He wants to seduce you, to engulf you in his fall, but I refuse to be swept away.

A murmur of incomprehension and fascination passed through the assembly as she continued with noble gravity:

- What matters to me is the love I have for Moussa. It's a flame that cannot be extinguished or sullied, and it's not for anyone to judge its purity. Our intimacy, this sacred bond, is subject only to divine authorisation, which we have received, even if it is only a dream or an illusion. What is undeniable is that we have deeply felt His agreement. Unlike the laws of this earth that force lovers to hide, to distance themselves from the blessings of temples, churches, mosques or synagogues.

A murmur of approval or confusion passed through the ranks of the spectators. But before the tension could dissipate, the big screen lit up again, projecting a bright light into the studio. The journalist, a shiver in his voice, announced solemnly:

- The President of the Republic wishes to speak live, moved by this debate that has touched so many hearts.

The President's face appeared, solemn and serious, while an almost tangible silence enveloped the studio. All eyes turned to the screen, waiting breathlessly for the words of the Head of State, as each second seemed suspended between expectation and destiny.

In a solemn silence, shrouded in an aura of mystery and elegance, the President of the Republic stood up straight, speaking with the gravity that the circumstances demanded.

The Hourim of innocence

His face, though worn by the stresses of politics, showed a rare emotion, a glimmer of humanity that pierced through his dignitary mask.

- Dear French men and women, dear compatriots... and above all, you, my dear children," he began in a calm voice filled with disarming sincerity. It would be difficult for me to conceal the emotion that has run through me as I've followed this programme from the beginning. My heart, a heart that I thought I had hardened by dint of duty and ruthless decisions, broke when I heard certain words spoken by the Reverend, a man I know well, to whom I have often listened and for whom my respect is deep and long-standing.

He paused for a moment, searching for the right words to express the strange turmoil he was feeling.

- I must confess a personal truth," he continued thoughtfully. I, who have never had children of my own, apart from those of my wife whom I love and consider my own, have always kept a space in my soul dedicated to the child I was, to that echo of innocence that adult life has never been able to extinguish completely. This fragment of childhood, this tenacious seed, has germinated throughout my life, nourishing my dreams even in the midst of the heavy responsibilities of my office.

He smiled, a smile tinged with nostalgia, as if he were reliving the lost impulses of his adolescence.

- I understand what it's like to be lost in the maze of the adult world, to be a young boy dazzled by the illusions of a world he doesn't yet understand. Yes, I saw myself in you, in that chaotic transition between childhood and adulthood, a passage where we fight to hold on to the mirages of innocence.

The Hourim of innocence

I was a child still dreaming of Peter Pan's island, a phantasmagorical place that lurked in the back of my mind, refusing to let me grow up. But, thank God, with the precious help of my dear and loving wife, I was able to cross the boundary that separates childhood from the world of men, without ever seeking the blessing of a church.

His voice took on a deeper, more solemn note.

- Today, despite the revelations that have been brought to my attention, I stand before you, not just as President, but as a man, as a human being ready to offer you my hand. I wish to be the first to offer you sanctuary in our country, France, the land where freedoms are cherished and where love can be expressed without fear of being judged. It is with sincere honour that I ask our people, the French men and women I represent, to welcome you among us. We are a country that not only cherishes secularism, but also opens its arms to lost hearts and souls in search of redemption.

He paused, letting his words sink into the collective soul of all those listening.

- However, allow me to speak with the sincerity of a father, even if I'm not really one. I don't want you to see this as an act of defiance towards your beliefs, but rather as an offer of help. I'm convinced that great psychiatrists, enlightened minds, could help you to regain your psychological equilibrium, to free yourself from this invisible straitjacket that seems to hold you down. You see, what I see in your story is a desperate need to anchor yourself in a truth that eludes you.

His voice, now firmer, appealed to the people.

The Hourim of innocence

- I ask you, my dear compatriots: let us welcome these young people, let us give them a chance to rebuild their lives, to grow in the light of our democracy. As for you, Abigael and Moussa, I implore you to reject this term Hourim, to detach yourselves from this symbol that causes so much fear and discord. Join us, and let us guide you along the path of reason.

The President's face tightened imperceptibly, a mixture of concern and fear imprinting his features.

- May France be for you a refuge, a new home where you can grow up, free from the invisible chains of illusion, free from a burden that should not weigh on souls as young as yours.

He concluded with poignant dignity, his gaze fixed on the two young men, as if he were trying to inspire them to choose the path of freedom.

Before the journalist could pick up the thread of the debate or the Reverend could use the President's words as a springboard to deliver the final blow, Moussa, with unexpected assurance and a fiery gleam in his eyes, stepped forward and spoke without waiting to be offered the floor. His voice, poised and vibrant with sincerity, echoed through the studio, an echo of truth that split the air like lightning in the middle of the night.

- The day I first held in my hands the kite string Abigael had handed me, I was barely eleven years old," he began, his gaze lost in a memory sanctified by the innocence of childhood. That day, an almost supernatural force pulled me forward, a breath from the firmament, an invisible embrace of the wind. But instead of surrendering to it, of letting this power guide me, I clung on, I resisted. My only aim was to keep the kite immobile, to tame the untameable, to imprison freedom itself in the vice of my own fear of the unknown. My feet, anchored to the ground, refused to budge, while the unsubmissive kite twirled in a frenzied ballet, like an exalted bird, a hymn of colours defying the sky.

He paused, his words hanging in the air like a forgotten psalm, imbuing the room with an almost palpable intensity.

- Between the kite and me there was a silent language, a silent plea. It was asking me to grant it the grace of freedom, to allow it to soar ever higher, to fly close to the clouds, like a bird that I had, in a senseless act, chained to the ground. This tension between us, this vibrating thread, was the symbol of the eternal choice between flight and restraint, between the audacity of the soul and the paralysing fear of losing it.

His eyes turned slowly, taking in the President, the Reverend, and all the faces tense with hope or doubt that were watching them through the screens of the entire planet.

- Abigael," he continued, "had already learned this lesson that took me years to understand. She never stood still; she ran with the kite, accompanying it in its whims, guiding it while respecting its quest for transcendence. She had grasped the fine line between freedom and imprisonment, the subtle frontier that you cross in a breath, without even realising it.
He straightened up, and his words took on the gravity of those who have nothing left to lose, but everything to offer.

- Mr President, illustrious Reverend, and you, peoples of the Earth, I thank you for your concern, your offers of asylum and your benevolence. But I can only decline. That day, Abigael gave me much more than a simple child's game. She gave me a profound truth, the truth of freedom. A sacred, unchanging freedom, woven from love, faith and respect for what binds

The Hourim of innocence

us to the Divine. This freedom is the essence of who we have become; it is our identity, our heritage.

Moussa squeezed Abigael's hand, and the glow of their love seemed to light up the darkness that hung over the room.

- Today," he continued, "I feel this strange conviction : I'm this kite that invisible forces are trying to hold down, to nail to the ground, to prevent me from soaring towards the light. But I will never give in. I will never surrender this thread to Iblis, the usurper who would like to control our destiny. Abigael and I belong where it all began: by this thousand-year-old olive tree, this sanctuary that witnessed our first oaths. It is there, and only there, that we find our anchorage, and it is there that everything must be accomplished, with dignity and faith.

The Reverend, hiding behind a mask of erudition the darkness of his secret allegiance, gloated in silence. His heart, a treacherous lair, exulted at the thought of seeing his plan come to life. He knew that Abigael and Musa's return to the Holy Land was only a prelude to the tragedy he had orchestrated. He was already revelling in the hatred that would spread like wildfire between the two peoples, fanning the dormant embers of discord. The programme drew to a close, and our two heroes, bearers of an indestructible love, prepared to face their destiny.

Their return to the Holy Land was marked by an icy silence, a silence that precedes the most fearsome storms. At the airport, the crowd, intoxicated by the lies of Iblis, chanted insults, their enraged voices striking the air like blades. The words "traitors" and "godless" resounded, carried on the wind like invisible poison. Iblis, the master of darkness, had calculated his move

The Hourim of innocence

well: enraged followers from both sides had gathered, uniting their hatreds in a symphony of fury.

Abigael and Moussa, their heads held high and their hearts at peace, were escorted by armed men who claimed to be protecting them. But this protection was nothing but a perfidious illusion. They were taken to a subterranean place, a secret prison where the light never penetrated, where the shadows of the Houmas and the Mouzad lurked, in league for this parody of justice. They realised that hell was waiting for them, but despite the imminent horror, they remained resolute, drawing strength from their love that transcended them.

The torture began. Their tormentors, blinded by hatred, tore at their frail bodies, inflicting unspeakable pain. Yet it was not the physical suffering that devastated them. The real agony, crueler than any mutilation, lay in the gaze of the other, the gaze they exchanged, imbued with the purest love and the pain of seeing the loved one tortured. Every scream of the one was a blade piercing the soul of the other, every suffering inflicted an involuntary offering to the sacred pain of their shared love.

When dawn broke, pale and hopeless, the Reverend appeared. Wrapped in a cloak of hypocrisy, he advanced, his face imbued with false compassion. His eyes, however, betrayed his true nature, two abysses where the malice of Iblis danced. He raised his hand, and the torture ceased, leaving our heroes broken but dignified. Approaching them, he made a poisonous proposal, dripping with perfidy.

- Kiss my hand," he murmured with venomous gentleness, "and I will offer you my protection. It is only a gesture of

The Hourim of innocence

submission, a simple mark of respect. Do it, and your suffering will end.

But they knew. They knew that to give in would be to make a pact with the Evil One, to deny everything they were, everything they had defended. Their souls were pure, and they did not give in. The Reverend, seeing his request refused, ordered that they be dressed in linen robes, like shrouds. Their necks and wrists were encased in heavy wooden beams, transforming their silhouettes into those of crucified kites, deprived of their flight.

They were then taken to the foot of the thousand-year-old olive tree, the silent witness to so many prayers, so much suffering and so many hopes. There, Iblis whispered in the ears of the gathered children, breathing into them the madness of violence. Innocent hands, manipulated by the devil, began to throw stones. Each projectile struck their battered bodies, but Abigael and Moussa never took their eyes off each other. Their love, even on the brink of death, remained an eternal, inextinguishable flame.

The stone blows continued, inhuman, brutal. Their flesh was bruised, their faces bathed in blood, but it wasn't the pain that tore them apart. What consumed them was seeing the other suffer, seeing the love of their lives reduced to martyrdom. Their mutual gaze, full of tears and light, was a promise that one day they would return to the heavens they had so longed for.

Then, under the majestic shade of the thousand-year-old olive tree, two young masked figures stepped forward, their steps heavy with doubt and torment. One, armed with a pistol, raised a trembling hand and pointed the weapon at Abigael's

The Hourim of innocence

head; the other, a dagger glinting in the pale starlight, stood in front of Moussa, ready to strike. The first was Eytan, and the second, Lina, caught up in a tragedy bigger than themselves.

The cold barrel against Abigael's temple vibrated with uncertainty, while the blade, suspended a few centimetres from Moussa's throat, hesitated in a shudder of guilt. Then, with an almost ritualistic slowness, the two young men removed their bonnets.

Their faces appeared in the flickering light, revealing features of fear, shame and unspeakable despair. Abigael and Moussa recognised them at once, and a wave of pain passed through their hearts. They were not monsters, but lost souls, lost in the abyss of a conflict that had robbed them of their humanity.

The silence stretched out, deep and solemn, broken only by the gentle breeze playing in the leaves of the olive tree. This age-old tree, mute witness to centuries of hopes and disappointments, seemed to watch over them with an ancestral gravity.

Then, in a surge of pure love and infinite compassion, Abigael and Moussa raised their eyes to the starry heavens, an infinite mirror of light and mystery. With trembling voices, imbued with an almost divine serenity, they prayed together:

- Creator, forgive them, for they know not what they do.

Their words rose into the night, carried by the sacred breath of the wind, like a celestial offering. A strange gentleness enveloped the olive tree, its branches seeming to bend slightly, like protective arms blessing the souls present. The universe seemed to hold its breath, and for a moment suspended in

The Hourim of innocence

eternity, hatred gave way to a fragile but palpable peace, an echo of humanity rediscovered in the heart of darkness.

In a final burst of defiance, Abigael and Moussa stared intently at the horizon, their hearts bound together by an indestructible force. Their souls were desperately searching for that kite, the symbol of their freedom, of their first glimpse of each other, of the pure, invincible love that had grown within them. They remembered the wind that had carried them, the feeling of eternity as they let go and let love take them away.

And, in perfect harmony, their voices rose one last time, tearing through the air with an overwhelming intensity, like an echo of eternity, capable of shattering the heavens and shaking the soul of the earth itself.

- "Hourim !" they cried, with a force so pure and vibrant that it seemed to pierce the vault of heaven, awaken the dead in their forgotten tombs, and suspend the breath of the living, as if the world had stopped to listen.

The cry resounded, rolling like sacred thunder, stretching out into space with such a resonance that the hills and mountains, the trees and stones, shuddered with a silent wave. It was a cry of love, of defiance, of unshakeable faith, a cry that carried within it all the pain of loss, all the splendour of life, and all the light of a promise never broken. It struck a chord in the souls of those who witnessed it, whether friend or foe, piercing them through and through, shattering the very order of creation.

Then, with merciless brutality, the gun went off and the blade sank in. The din of violence, deafening as it was, was soon swallowed up by a deep, dense, crushing silence. A silence so powerful that it seemed to suck in all life, a silence like a

The Hourim of innocence

funereal blanket that spread over the holy land, where it had all begun. This silence not only enveloped the moment ; it even extinguished the breath of the wind, suspended the rustling of the leaves, and drowned out even the murmur of the prayers of the living.

Abigael and Moussa collapsed, their fingers managing to brush against each other despite their restraints, coming together in a final gesture of love, defying death itself. Their love, like an eternal flame, was their last breath, their final offering. They fell on that sacred ground, where their lives had been woven, united, and where their sacrifice now transcended the heavens, leaving behind them a light that not even the darkest of darkness could extinguish.

When the images of the execution of Abigael and Moussa spread like shockwaves across the world, they left behind a silence heavier than lead, a deep void that seemed to dig into the bowels of the collective conscience. From the bustling squares of Paris to the bustling markets of Jerusalem, an unspeakable unease crept into the air, clinging to souls like a spectre of guilt. Hearts beat more slowly, tears fell silently, and a murmur spread, akin to a unanimous confession of shame and regret.

The whole world, plunged into a state of moral torpor, contemplated itself in a shattered mirror, seeing only the fragments of a complicit humanity, rendered insensitive by the dissensions and fears that had blinded it. The horror of what had happened seared itself into everyone's soul, awakening a silent sense of accusation : how could they have let this happen, how could they have allowed the light to be extinguished so brutally? And, on the heights of Jerusalem, the three wise men, the Chief Rabbi, the eminent Imam and the

The Hourim of innocence

venerable Priest, were the first to be consumed by this bottomless remorse. They knew they were guilty of a betrayal that no prayer could redeem, of having sacrificed the truth out of fear, of having bowed to the threat of Iblis instead of defending innocence. In silence, in their respective sanctuaries, they offered their last breath to the Creator, giving themselves to death to atone for a fault that was eating away at their souls. Their departures were marked by tears of blood, by a repentance that even the earth seemed to mourn.

And yet, even in the midst of this grief, something elusive continued to vibrate. A fragile but luminous hope floated on the thread of an old promise. Where Abigael and Moussa had been sacrificed, a kite appeared, hanging from a string that fought against the merciless wind. It swayed, defying the dark gusts that sought to topple it, but it refused to become Iblis's weathervane. It held on, as if carrying the souls of the two young martyrs, defying gravity and the shadows with luminous obstinacy.

And the world, watching that kite struggle to climb higher, understood something vital. It understood that even if the skies seemed darkened, hope was a flame that hatred could never completely extinguish. The echo of "Hourim", that cry of love and freedom, still resounded in the wind, piercing the veil of darkness, sounding like a sacred promise, a star fallen but never forgotten.

This cry awoke the dead and put life to sleep, crossing the ages like an eternal hymn. And so, in the hearts of those who still dared to believe, a flickering but immortal light was rekindled. A light ready to rise, to defy the shadows with all the strength of love, the love of Abigael and Moussa, which now shone, invincible, beyond the night of men.

The Hourim of innocence

Afterword

When images of war flash across our screens, it's tempting to look away, to convince ourselves that these tragedies belong somewhere else. Yet how can we remain insensitive to the suffering of innocent children, captives in a conflict that is not their own? Can we accept remaining a passive spectator, wrapped up in the comfort of our daily lives, while lives are shattered before our very eyes?

Les Hourim de l'Innocence is the fruit of an inner revolt. A revolt against apathy, against the powerlessness of a humanity that looks on but does not act. For me, writing this book was a way of rejecting resignation, of crying out in the deafening silence of indifference. There are evils that can only be fought with the weapons of the mind: words, memory, and above all the will to never forget.

Through the intertwined destinies of Moussa and Abigael, I wanted to build a bridge between two shores that everything seems to oppose. Their story is that of thousands of children, all too often silenced by the clash of arms. But beyond the human drama, this novel is an appeal: an appeal to conscience, to compassion, and to commitment.

Every reading of this book is a stone added to the edifice of resistance against injustice. By reading it, you are taking part in an act of gentle rebellion, an insurrection of the spirit, where the light of the Hourim illuminates the darkest areas of our humanity. This novel is a symbolic paving stone, launched not with violence, but with the unshakeable strength of those who refuse to be silenced.

The Hourim of innocence

I deeply believe that reading, when nourished by reflection and empathy, can become a powerful lever for change. Every word read is a seed sown, a flame kept alive, a promise that evil will not triumph as long as there are awake consciences to resist it.

So, by reading these pages, you too can become a player in this struggle. You are taking part in a collective work of remembrance and transmission. By simply reading, you are making a commitment not to let the cries of the innocent be forgotten.

Thank you for choosing to make this journey. Your reading is not just a pastime, but an act of courage and humanity. Together, stone by stone, pavement by pavement, we can build a world where innocence is no longer sacrificed on the altar of hatred.

Mustapha Bouktab

© 2024 Mustapha Bouktab
Publisher: BoD · Books on Demand GmbH,
In de Tarpen 42, 22848 Norderstedt (Allemagne)
Print: Libri Plureos GmbH, Friedensallee 273,
22763 Hamburg (Allemagne)
ISBN: 978-2-3225-3496-8
Legal deposit: Novembre 2024

The Hourim of innocence

Acknowledgements

To you, my wife, who were the spark. It was your lucid vision and profound words that set my nights ablaze with questions, leading me to realise that the answer, once again, lay in writing. Without you, it would never have happened.

To my children, who are my source of pride and strength. Your unfailing support and unconditional love are the pillars of my writing journey.

To Adil, my faithful friend, always by my side, close to my pen. Thank you for your constant presence and your attentiveness, which have nourished every line of this book.

To Ireland, that magical land where I heard that subtle voice whispering to me to write. Here, inspiration flowed like rivers from the hills, and every stone, every wind carried a fragment of history, offering me a setting conducive to creation.

And to all those who reject injustice. To those who, through their actions or words, stand up against oppression. This book belongs to you, because every page turned is another step towards a fairer world.

Mustapha Bouktab

The Hourim of innocence

Table of contents

.... Warning 2
Cover .... page 3
Dedication... 5
Introduction .... Introduction 07
Chapter I: At the very beginning................ 09
Chapter II: Dawn after the storm............... 57
Chapter III: The day of shadows 85
Chapter IV: The cry of ashes..................... 117
Chapter V: The silence gap 143
Chapter VI: The mirrors of Iblis 175
Chapter VII: The sacrifice of the stars 255
Afterword... 323
Acknowledgements 325
Bibliography of the author 327

BIBLIOGRAPHY OF THE AUTHOR

SIX BOOKS TO DISCOVER

THE GUARDIAN OF THE PRESENT TRILOGY (VOLUMES 1 AND 2 TRANSLATED INTO ENGLISH). L'UPPERCUT DE MA DELIVRANCE AND TWO COLLECTIONS OF POETRY, INSPIRINE AND SOUFFLE D'ETERNITE.

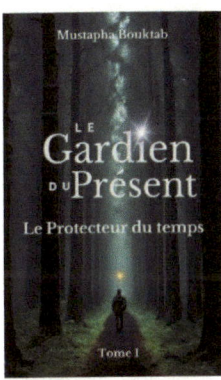 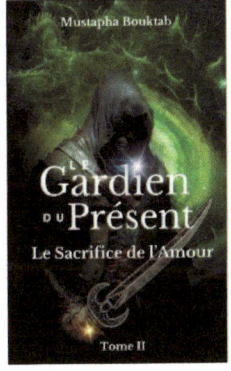 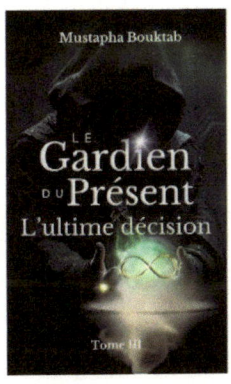

The Hourim of innocence